THE ECHOES BENEATH

METROPOLITAN
SYNDICATE
PRESS

THE ECHOES BENEATH

J. M. AMMOUN

Library and Archives Canada Legal Deposit data available.

ISBN 978-1-7382104-3-5

Printed in Canada and the U.S.A.

First edition, February 2024

AUTHOR'S FOREWORD

I've always been fascinated with how connected we are as people. How, even in the smallest way, the choices we make in our lives ripple across time and space, impacting one another. How we simply move on, oblivious to the infinite echoes of our actions. Unaware of the endless reach of a simple wave, an angered word. The generational implications that could result. This is what I attempted to capture in this story, interplayed with an examination of our primal motivations as human beings.

It has been a labor of love. A five-year journey of plotting and writing and revising. A sacrifice of countless hours to the chagrin of my wife and young children—of whom I am eternally grateful.

PROLOGUE

THE CHAIRMAN'S DEED

Idiots.

Chairman Lutz rose from his seat to the sounds of celebration filling the room. He pulled his oversized blazer closed and painted on a smile.

"Thank you, everyone," he said, hamming up the appreciative tone. "I must say, I couldn't have gotten to this point without you all." Utter nonsense but what was expected under the circumstances.

His team continued their part of the charade with a smattering of applause, an evening of phony congratulations and well-wishes that would continue until he left his office for the final time. And they'd clap joyously as he waddled out the door, waiting until he hobbled past the threshold before retrieving their knives from his back.

Lutz had always known their disdain. He could see questions about his competence dance in their eyes when he spoke, each masking their snarls beneath the simpering of their bloated egos. A bunch of clever little jerks eager to imprint their cheeks in his soon-to-be empty seat. The board hadn't yet named his replacement, but Lutz knew that would come as soon as the pavement outside scratched beneath his loafers.

There were several candidates currently under consideration: Selma Stotts, Head of Infrastructure—*great ass*; Jacob Turnby, Director of Finance—*kiss-ass*; and Reginald Ottotop, Head of Corporate Strategy—*jackass.* But of his likely successors, Astrid Shoehorn from Citizen Affairs was the odds-on favorite.

As a large, older woman, always presenting professionally in a muted-toned pantsuit and flats, Astrid caused quite the stir that evening, arriving at the party with pink streaks in her short blond hair. Lutz had overheard her trying to sell it as a means to connect with the changing demographics of Midian. But everyone knew what it truly was: a half-hearted attempt at reinventing herself after her husband ran off with that trench girl. Unfortunately, a simple makeover wouldn't be enough to retread those tires. She'd need all the king's horses and all the king's men to put Humpty Dumpty back together again. It might bode well for her chances as chairwoman, however. Too old and unattractive to be preoccupied with another man, she'd have plenty of time to focus on city business.

Lutz raised a glass of hour-warm champagne. "The honor has been all mine these last few decades. And I know Midian is in good hands with you all here to carry her forward for years to come. Please enjoy the celebration."

Beyond the sea of strained smiles and raised flutes, next

to a well-stocked table of desserts, a large easel held an old *Metro Gazette* cover blown up for the occasion. Beneath the masthead concealing his receding hairline, Lutz's monstrous, clean-shaven face spilled over the cover's margins. Emblazoned over his chin, atop the accentuated pox marks and age spots, were the words "Most Powerful Man in Midian." The honor had swelled his ego when the issue was first released, but now the joke was as obvious as his assistant's derisive huffs when he requested anything beyond a simple cup of coffee following the news of his departure.

Most powerful man in Midian, my ass. The board had all the power, as evidenced by the forced retirement soirée. The board members sat lavishly atop their crystal thrones, each plucked from the leadership of the Syndicate corporations. Thinking up ways to make a tenth of a cent more off some useless piece of plastic or moccasins from the ass hair of a goat. While he ran the entire city with his team of incompetent pissants. Listening to the peasants and their incessant complaints. Architectural preservation. Green spaces. And whatever else bored mothers used to preoccupy their attention to avoid caring for their kids. *The fucking board.* He was the chairman—both mayor of Midian and head of the Syndicate. But after forty years, he was now the cuck in the corner, watching as the presidents of each Syndicate corporation had their way with his city.

Lutz's stomach churned, likely from the anxiety of it all, but he convinced himself the off-gassing latex balloons were to blame. He reached for a thick cigar from a decorative wooden box and pulled a lighter from the breast pocket of his jacket. Sucking in the flames, Lutz pushed through a thick cloud of smoke and doddered over to the boardroom window overlooking Upper Midian. He gazed out across the miles of pristine luxury condos, shops, and lush green parks stretching deep toward the Mantle's edge. A serene urban tapestry. A success Lutz had toiled over for years. His grand symphony. Creating the perception of natural unity with the medleys of the metropolis. Leading each melody to an embrace of the other. Snuffing out dissent and rebellion to ensure total Syndicate control. Four decades, ferociously swaying his baton. Guiding the players to a heart-swelling crescendo, all while the board members huddled behind the curtain, struggling to push out the pitchy squeaks of a kazoo.

The board had no idea how precarious the balance was in reality—the implications of each move and countermove. How the splosh of a single gob of spit hitting the street in Bottoms Edge could ripple into a wave of consequences across the Undercity. The board might have a firm grip above the Mantle. An inexperienced maestro could even get away with an off-note here or there when managing Uppercity affairs. But the slovenly gestures of an untrained hand in the trench would no doubt transform the melodic tones of appeasement into a cacophony of horrors.

The fucking board.

Lutz pressed out his cigar against the flawless glass pane, tumbling hot ash and embers to the golden threaded carpet beneath his feet. It was time to leave. But not before his last act as chairman. One final wave of his baton. His final encore before leaving the harmonies of the city without a masterful hand to guide them.

CHAPTER 1

ATLAS'S NEED

It was only appropriate that the harbinger of Atlas's new fate was the scent of urine, a thought that crossed his mind as he watched the Undercity rush past his tram window. It had been a while since he'd noticed the scent so clearly out in the open. Probably not since his last shift at the gates. A time in his life he had mostly forgotten amid the pain of his earlier memories. Just a blur of *yessirs* and repellent encounters with junkies and street patrons. It wasn't until he arrived underside a few days ago that it all seemed to surge back—the good and the bad. Too bad the good didn't account for much more than a few fleeting minutes.

It hadn't been much better on the Mantle. Not since his childhood, at least. The beds too soft. The expectations too rigid. Everyone posing as someone they thought they should be rather than being the person they were. Growing up among children whose families were dead or estranged, Atlas quickly learned to distinguish the truth from fantasy. Orphans were notorious liars; most had something deep inside that made them believe they were special. Cut from a pedigree of royalty or some other fantastical lineage. Perhaps it was the mystery of their parentage toying with their imagination. But for one reason or another, most orphans were convinced of their exceptional bloodline. Atlas used to wonder if the exaggerations and fantasies were unique to orphans. But after years with the self-important braggarts of Upper Midian, he figured it was more likely a consequence of living on the Mantle. A consequence he no longer had to worry about.

The tramcar still looked almost new—new for Lower Midian, that is. The seats were showing light wear, faded pink splotches and stained silhouettes of unknown origin. The chrome handrail kept most of its shine but was dulling in spots, and the dark red paint on the hull was showing a slight peel at the seams. Atlas watched as the cold wind urged the curling paint to dance with each gust passing through a gaping window. Likely left ajar to disperse the scent of ammonia, but now the *clack-clack* of the tram wheels on the aging rails was without a barrier to smother the sound. It was loud and bothersome, but Atlas was too consumed with the consequence of the evening to let it detract from his thoughts.

It was an odd feeling being unleashed. There was something about the freedom that made him feel lighter, as if he was no longer weighed down with the wants of others. Atlas had spent his entire life under one rule or another, taking orders from his housemasters, teachers, and commanding officers. A revolving door of people controlling his every move, shaping a future in which he had no say. And now he was completely free, bound by only his whims and desires. It was a freedom he could never have imagined, even a few weeks ago. And if things went right tonight, a freedom he'd never feel again.

"I'd rather deal with the rank than that racket." Bass's grizzly voice echoed through the tram before the window clapped shut. "Gotta be clear-headed tonight. Wouldn't you agree?" He looked at Atlas with a grin, his jutted jaw emphasizing his underbite.

Atlas would have been convinced of the man's sincerity only hours ago. But now the sinister glint in his eye was as obvious as the pungent scent of human relief. Atlas had seen that look a thousand times before, mostly in his commanding officers, but the occasional teacher at the Home would also wear it as well. It was the recognition that Atlas was beneath him. A topsider only in name, with a pedigree to match the strays rummaging the trash heaps in the Bottoms.

When Atlas had first approached Basson Tate at the Citizenry Hall a couple of days ago, there was nothing more than a cordial smile and welcoming platitudes on his lips. Atlas had thought at the time it was an odd welcome for a topside stranger, especially spilling from the Citizenry's second-in-command and head of the Patrol. The Undercity caretakers were not known for their hospitality when it came to anyone from Upper Midian. And Bass, with the rugged look of a retired cage fighter, cauliflower ears and scarred pale arms, hardly appeared the welcoming sort. But there he was, as pleasant as some upscale concierge at a Mantleside resort, offering Atlas a drink and an invite to tour the Citizenry

Hall. It wasn't until they were about to leave for the tram station that cracks in Bass's pleasant demeanor began tearing through the façade, his words shifting from cordial to cutting. Atlas had almost dismissed the first barb of the night as a bad joke—something about the thick underside air suffocating his brain dim. But when he noticed the darkening of Bass's beady eyes, the tell around the fringes, he realized the kindness had all been for show.

"Cut it out," a soft voice carried over the muffled clacking. "He'll be great."

Atlas shifted his sights across the sticky tram floor to the second of his evening escorts. Seated patiently with her hands resting in her lap, Sami Salem had the same warm glow on her caramel cheeks as when they first met. Atlas had also found her oddly welcoming, making sure he was fed and scratching together a care package for his motel. But unlike Bass, her kindness appeared no more for show than the compassion she offered the dozens of Undercity residents Atlas had seen flow from her office. Sami was a liaison between the people and the Citizenry, a person in the upper ranks that could help move the peoples' matters along the churn of the bureaucratic machine. A voice for the voiceless. And when she had heard of Bass's planned excursion for the evening, she insisted she come along as well. Atlas had overheard a raucous encounter between her and Bass moments before they left for the station, Bass refusing her presence and Sami refusing the refusal. It wasn't until Sami threatened to go on ahead and meet them at their destination that Bass relented, but the tension between them remained.

The high-pitched squeal of the tram brakes pierced the cloud of murmurs from beyond the glass pane. Atlas stumbled to his feet and followed his escorts beyond the *whoosh* of the opening tram doors. Even with the Marketplace station hanging hundreds of feet below the Mantle, the station platform sat elevated above most buildings, offering a sprawling view of the Undercity beyond its steel railing. With the Mantle lamps dimmed for the evening, the streetlights were visible for miles, stretching deep into the vast Undercity neighborhoods. The monstrous support pillars restraining the Mantle above, towering over large apartment buildings and factories, pegged each neighborhood as far as the eye could see.

Stepping from a small lift that had carried them to the bustling street below, the trio pushed their way into the crowd. Shoulders in the throng bounced off Atlas's chest, and feet danced on his toes as he worked to keep up with his escorts. The scent of fried foods permeated the air, growing more pungent as they reached deeper into the chaos. The street was awash with neon lights from the flashing storefronts, and the near-endless flow of vehicles stained the air with a muted haze. Video billboards cycling through advertisements capped most low-rise buildings: an upcoming film entitled *The Witch's Keeper*, an air purifier with scent-masking technology, and the chance to turn your pocket change into millions at the Allied Citizenry Casino.

Sitting among several small shops along the busy street, a

large gothic building repurposed as a rehab center caught Atlas's eye. With its tall pinnacles and arching buttresses clashing with the plain brick structures on the market walk, the building was impossible to ignore. Even more so with the monstrous screen sitting atop its entrance. Atlas paused amid the chaos of the crowd to glimpse the video playing above a horde of addicts huddled by the doorway. Set to a soft piano ballad, saintly scenes flashed across the screen: a child cleaning up a filthy street, a teenager caring for an old woman in a hoarded room. But when the image of a man rallying a sea of thousands joined a chorus of cheers and triumphant music, Atlas's interest waned. The reenactment of the life of Jericho Sands was not worth the elbows and scorn of stalled passersby. He'd heard enough about the head of the Allied Citizenry over the years to fill volumes of books. Stories were as plentiful as addicts in the Undercity Midriff. Some were utterly rotten, like the rumors of Jericho forcing addiction on his people and evicting many from their homes. Others spoke of his saviorship, a messenger sent from God Almighty for the downtrodden of the Undercity—inspiring scrawls of messianic messages on buildings and underside landmarks. But neither seemed to ring true to Atlas. No one was ever that saintly, or that evil. Either way, he would get a sense of the man tonight. He just hoped for the sake of his plans that Jericho was more saint than savage.

Near the end of the market, they turned down an alley, and the busy sounds of the street faded. Dull moans overtook the fading bustle, and the corridor came alive with the shadows of addicts tucked away from society's judging eyes. Atlas felt a trickle of sweat run down his side as a thump in his chest swelled in his ears. It wasn't something he hadn't seen before, having spent time in the Guard rounding up junkies from the Midriff. But without the weighty reassurance of a rifle on his arm, it might as well have been his first brush with the underside plague.

Approaching the alley's end, Bass's long stride carried him over a young woman strewn across their path. Sami's gasp of horror snuffed the moans from the darkness, and she rushed toward the young woman, who lay shivering in a pool of sewer overflow. Atlas reached for the woman's other arm and helped Sami float her against the alley wall, her frail bones light as a sack of laundry. Dark rings encircled the woman's small black eyes, and a brownish tinge coated her few remaining teeth. Her smell punctured the fried aroma of the Undercity, overtaking the air with a rotten blow. But the stench did nothing to Sami's resolve as she replaced the woman's tattered and soaked clothes with the long, thick trench coat she had worn for the cold evening. When the woman cupped Sami's hand, Atlas couldn't help but shudder at the black filth stitched into her palm. It brought back the salty memory of a junkie's hand slipping into his mouth during a tussle. He hadn't been able to shake the taste of the sour fingers for months, every meal tainted with the question of where the man's hands had been. It wasn't until one of the other Guardians concocted a mouthwash to banish the memory from his tastebuds—a mix of whiskey, mouthwash, and garlic—that his mouth felt clean again. But now his tongue dried up at the thought, and he could feel his throat struggle to hold back a gag.

"What the fuck are you two doin'?" Bass's booming voice echoed down the corridor, shaking the disgust from Atlas's thoughts.

Standing at the roadway with the streetlight at his back, Bass's hulking frame blotted out the little light illuminating the end of the alley. Sami smiled warmly at the woman before slipping her hand free and pushing past Bass to the roadway without a word.

"I don't give a fuck if you're Jericho's little pet," he grumbled. "When you're with me, you don't do shit without my say-so."

Atlas couldn't believe he'd ever fallen for Bass's phony kindness. The man was as savage as a Barrens hermit spewing anger at the birds soaring over his hut. Atlas knew it wasn't his place, but he couldn't help the itch to jump to Sami's defense.

"It was just that the woman back there—" Atlas started, stepping to the large wall hanging from Bass's shoulders.

The brute turned with a glare that stalled Atlas's tongue. The sweat from Bass's brow glistened in the streetlight, trickling through a maze of days-old stubble along his bulging clenched jaw.

"Was I speaking to you?" he said, reaching for Atlas's neck.

Atlas struggled to pry the swollen arm away, but the thick

paw only tightened, driving his Adam's apple deep into his throat. He could feel his airway constrict, his trapped breath burning in his lungs.

"Then you're not to speak."

Raising Atlas off the ground with his firm grip, Bass tossed him back into a street sign with a crash that rattled out over the roadway. The impact stole the breath that had set his lungs aflame only seconds earlier. Pain radiated down his spine, dispersing tingles through his legs, and he gasped with panic to reinflate his flattened chest, wriggling on the ground, until catching his breath.

As the air returned, and Atlas's panic eased, his gaze fell to the small, smooth rocks lying scattered atop the pavement. Against the darkness of the tarry road, the stones washed in streetlight reminded him of stars in the night sky. He hadn't missed much from his time on the Mantle; it was mostly a reminder of his inadequacy. But the nights beyond the lamps were something special.

As a child, he would often sneak out after curfew with the other kids from his orphanage, slipping by the housemaster's open door while she sat distracted with her nose in a book. They'd lie out on the driftball pitch and gaze out above. Stars riddled the open sky like shiny rivets affixing the blankness to the universe. And when conditions were just right, ribbons of light would dance across the sky's edge, lighting the ground below for miles. With the cool grass beneath and night sky above, their childish ramblings would keep them busy for the early part of the night: who had been the all-time best driftball forward, what the lasagna in the commissary was made of (Jason thought it was other kids), or whether the famed Franky Filth had actually chopped up the Faith sisters of his shelter and fed their organs to a stray. The debates usually ended in a back-and-forth of insults before a spirited match played out on the pitch to settle the score. Atlas wondered how the kids underside spent their evenings with only a metal ceiling to entertain their imaginations. It seemed a sad childhood, walled in from either side with only the distant eastern sky proving an outside world. But then again, there were worse misfortunes a child could face. He knew that first-hand.

Atlas forced himself to his feet, nearly smacking his head on the sign that had broken his fall. *Stand with Us! Support Your Local Citizenry.* He would have laughed at the irony, but the pain encircling his neck and coursing along his backside sapped most of his energy.

Looking down the roadway, he could see Bass and Sami's silhouettes in the illuminated steam pouring out from the sewers. After a steady speed limp and several jolts of agony, he soon made up the distance, but neither of them acknowledged his renewed company.

They continued to ride the tension silently until arriving at a large brick apartment building. Bass gave a subtle nod to a man standing guard at the entranceway and pushed into the open lobby. The opulence inside reminded Atlas of many lavish Uppercity residences. Crystal chandeliers adorned the corridor toward the elevators, scattering trinkets of light across the dark marble floor. And the walls were lined with large ivory tiles, each hand-etched with golden depictions of Undercity history.

After thirty stories of growing quiet, the lift chime cut through the silence as the elevator doors opened into the main penthouse suite. The vaulted ceiling carried the sound until an unfamiliar voice called out from an adjoining room, "Give me a second!"

Atlas followed closely as the others stepped into the suite. The oversized flat was scant with furnishings, and the stacked moving boxes holding up the walls gave the appearance of a recent move. Bass slipped away briefly, searching through the closets and side rooms before returning to the entryway.

"Fuck, Jericho, why haven't you furnished this shit hole yet?" he called out.

Tying his wet hair back in a bun, Jericho Sands entered the room. "It *is* furnished. I've got everything I need. A table, chairs, my desk—" His lips stalled after he noticed Atlas, half-concealed by Bass's considerable bulk.

The tall tales of the great Jericho Sands had Atlas convinced the man stood seven feet with arms of solid steel. Who else could command the allegiance of someone as feral as Bass? But standing only steps away from Atlas, seemingly frozen with confusion, was a rather unremarkable man. He was of average height but much scrawnier than most underside men of his age, drowning in a worn, oversized bathrobe. His shoulder-length blond hair, tied in the back, accentuated the significant recession beyond his brow. And his thick beard, peppered with gray throughout, concealed the deep grooves in his tired and weathered face. He had no visible scars. No tattoos. Nothing to set himself apart from the crowd.

Jericho shot Sami a puzzled glance before extending his hand. "Hello, there."

"I'm…Atlas Ramsay."

"It's a pleasure. Please come sit."

Jericho retrieved three collapsible chairs from a nearby closet and placed them by a large window overlooking the Undercity. Atlas caught a few muted glances between Jericho and Sami before the old man eased into a shabby armchair across from them.

"The kid here wants to join our little band of do-gooders," said Bass.

Jericho nodded. "Interesting that you brought him here and not to the Locals."

"Oh, I don't know. Figured you'd like to meet him," Bass said with a coy smirk.

Jericho gritted his teeth before turning to Atlas. "Tell me…Atlas, was it? What about us has caught your interest?"

A slow burn rose in his chest. Bass hadn't even questioned his interest when they first met, as if joining the Citizenry was the dream of all Midianites. But Atlas always knew they wouldn't accept him without question, and he'd spent years putting together his story. *Righting the wrongs of topsiders. Searching for a purpose beyond the selfish interests up top.* But despite the years of rehearsal—the precise wording, the refined inflections—Atlas's confidence buckled. The question was too weighty, his answer too perfect. He knew it would be as transparent as the murky underside tap water—and as noxious as the smell.

"I just…want to help," he said plainly.

Jericho squinted as if tuning his eyes. "You're no undersider. So, you were a SyndiCares child, I assume?"

Atlas could now taste the burn sitting at the back of his throat. He'd done his best to blend in as a local, ditching the topside hair trend of a side part in favor of the underside bedhead. He even put together his outfit from a second-hand thrift in Bottoms Edge—a true act of blasphemy for any self-respecting topsider. Apparently, he had missed some other tell. Jericho could pin him for an outsider with a momentary glance. But what troubled him more was the mention of SyndiCares—a part of Atlas's life he had yet to share with either Bass or Sami. The Syndicate-run orphanage housed many of the unwanted children of the city, many of those born to the mistresses of Midian's elite. Information extortionists and rival city-states would find useful, making it as secure as military intel. Jericho could not have known by a simple glance or his name.

"Relax, boy," said Jericho. "I don't have a crystal ball. But I can read people. Your face is supple and suntanned as if raised under the open sky. And you possess the mannerisms and accent of someone educated on the Mantle. But your lack of confidence and snootiness—not to mention your desire to work with us—is telling of your prospects. You have nowhere to go and no one to help you on your way. Just another child raised in that corporate orphanage program. Forced into the Guard at sixteen and eventually cut loose when you failed to prove you could make it beyond a Private—"

"Sir," Sami interrupted, red-faced, confusion dancing in her eyes.

"Mind yourself, Sami," Jericho snapped back.

It was as if the old man had written Atlas's story. Listing off his chapters, one at a time. He even seemed to know why Atlas was discharged from the Guard, a mystery he hadn't yet figured out for himself.

"I didn't choose how I was raised," said Atlas. "I didn't choose to go into the Guard. It's a requirement…where I come from."

"And what? You don't want me to hold it against you? I should just ignore the years of reprogramming and make you a part of our happy family?" Jericho let out a breath. "Don't get me wrong, boy. I'm not against SyndiCares per se. Other than the brainwashing, they do some good work. And I wholly support that, but—"

"Nothin' the Syndicate does should have our support," said Bass in a deep grumble.

Jericho turned to him with wide eyes of amazement. “Really? So, we should have them cast out the orphaned and abandoned to fend for themselves?”

“We can take ’em in. They’d be better served by us, anyway.”

“With what resources? You, of all people, know we’re already stretched thin. What would you cut? Social assistance? Medical care? Patrol?” Jericho shook his head, a resigned exhaustion melting his expression. “Your idealism is blinding. We have to be pragmatic for our people. For the Undercity.”

Bass grimaced. “The way I see it, there should be no fuckin’ Undercity. We should be focusing on restorin’ Midian to the city it once was.”

Jericho leaned back in his chair with a slight curl of his lips. “And what *was* that?”

“A place where the rich weren’t perched above us, like gods on Mount Olympus. Pissin’ on our crops off the side of a metal platform. Where feelin’ the sun on your bare ass under the open air wasn’t reserved for those lucky enough to be born into money.”

“That’s some dream,” said Jericho. “And what of the hundreds of thousands living on the Mantle? The women. The children. Those whose only crime was being born into privilege.”

“They can join us or leave. Frankly, I don’t give a shit.”

“You expect them just to accept their way of life being left in shambles?” Jericho laughed.

"They'll comply in the end."

Jericho appeared to consider Bass's words before sliding forward to the edge of his seat. "Do you really believe that? Because if you do…you've learned nothing from our history. People are not as predictable as they appear. They adapt. They rebel. I've seen the strongest men taken down by the meekest of the timid after being pushed too far. True David and Goliath stories. But in these tales, there were no slingshots. No stones. Only an insatiable will to rip out their oppressor's throat. Enough to damn them to hell when their conceit blinded them to the danger." Jericho fell back into his seat. "The demons you'd unleash would only harm our people even more. You have to see that."

Bass's eyes darkened. He leaned forward as if to share a secret. "Do you wanna know what I *do* see? I see a broken city, full of broken people, too afraid to do shit to change their situation. I see people reachin' past their guns for a needle just to feel a moment of peace in their shitty lives. I see young boys, barely old enough to drive, enlisting in the same military oppressing their people because they've lost faith in our leadership. And I see an old man who fought his last fight years ago. Suckin' and blowin' everything and everyone to hang on to the little power he has left. Even if that means sellin' out his people to a fuckin' corporate oligarchy."

Jericho's eyes widened. "*Oligarchy?* You've been reading again, haven't you?"

Bass shot up from his seat, his chair crashing against the marble floor. Clenching his fists, he towered over the armchair.

Sami rushed to get between them but was shoved aside by Bass's outstretched arm. He glared down at the old man, still calmly seated, smirking with satisfaction.

After a moment of relishing Bass's anger, Jericho rose gently from his armchair. Despite the wall of a man huffing inches from his seat, he climbed to his feet with the calm of a retiree leaving a park bench after feeding the birds. Then he turned and stared out over the Undercity through the large glass pane. "We've accomplished a lot over the years, haven't we, Bass?"

Bass stood silent, a flush of red darkening his pale skin.

"Everything I've done, every sacrifice I've made, was all for the betterment of my people. I can't say I regret much, except perhaps that I couldn't do more. The problem is that everything has a cost. And often that cost pushes us to the limits of what we can afford. Sometimes, it amounts to a few dollars and cents. But most times, it requires something far greater." He turned briefly to Atlas before shifting his gaze to Bass. "I know the conditions we face are anything but perfect. But tearing down our current system will only lead to anarchy. Please understand that."

Through his clenched teeth, Bass struggled with his response. "What do you wanna do with the kid?"

Jericho let out a loud sigh. "We have no use for him."

Atlas's heart sank. He turned to the only person who seemed to care. Her face was rife with confusion.

"I assumed as much," said Bass, a simper now where the snarl had been.

"Sami, dear." Jericho cupped her hands. "We still have a lot to discuss. But do you mind if it waits until the morning? I'm terribly tired at the moment."

"Of course, sir. But Atlas—"

"Let me walk you out."

Jericho approached the doors and pushed the button to call the lift.

"Atlas, it was nice to meet you. I'm sure you're a good chap...but just not right for us. I'll put in a word for you with some of our associates in the Uppercity. We'll find you something."

Atlas had no plans to return to the Mantle. His fate lay beneath. In what form, he wasn't sure anymore. Dead, perhaps. But in the end, at least he could go out saying he tried.

The lift chime rang through the flat, and the elevator doors opened to darkness. Bass grabbed Jericho by the slender neck and pushed him out over the empty shaft, his legs flailing over the cavernous void. Before Atlas could make sense of what was happening, Sami cried out and reached for Jericho's arm. She struggled to pull him back in, leaning back with all her weight.

"Atlas! Grab her before she gets hurt," Bass yelled.

Atlas clutched her from behind and pulled her back from the open doors, slipping Jericho's arm from her grasp.

"You're a fuckin' traitor." Bass's tone was calm, menacing. "Our people looked up to you. They followed you. They died for you. And for what? So you could shit on them?"

Holding Sami firmly to his chest, Atlas could hear Jericho

choking for air through Sami's cries. Large beads of sweat formed at the nape of Bass's neck as his arm shook with exhaustion.

"This is what happens to traitors. No one will ever find your body. No martyr's cry. No pilgrimage to your grave. You'll just disappear. Hell, I might tell everyone you ran off with some Filth child to the Barrens."

A large bruise grew on Jericho's face, blotting out his pale skin. His tight grip on Bass's wrists softened until the weight of his arms dropped his hands to his sides. His legs continued to sway but were no longer animated. Sami's cries melted to sobs, and Atlas loosened his grip to an embrace.

Bass tossed the lifeless body down the shaft, peering downward after it as if to watch it evaporate into the darkness. Then, turning to Atlas as casually as someone who had just taken out the trash, he said, "We're takin' the stairs."

CHAPTER 2

SAMI LEAVES

Lenora lay on the worn wooden floorboards of the dimly lit back porch, watching as the rats gnawed holes in the trash left by the back alley fence. She seemed happy. But Sami knew if it wasn't for the cancer, she would have chased those rats right back through the drainage pipes to the Bottoms.

When she was younger, Lenora would tear through Plainsview with a youthful energy Sami had only ever seen in small pups and new addicts. She'd escape through the doggy door each evening, returning triumphantly by lamps-on, dragging the torn carcass of some poor animal through the small door flap. Sami would wake to scattered tufts of fur leading from the kitchen to Lenora's makeshift trophy pile in the corner of the main room. Her morning routine became a recurring cycle of waking up, brushing her teeth, and scraping decaying animal flesh from the tile floor. Although it pained her to see Lenora hamstrung with the corruption spreading through her body, Sami hadn't missed the extra chore of disinfecting and disposing the special trinkets. It was tiresome—and gross. But still, a tiny pit of hope would sprout each morning, and she found herself almost wishing to find another dead animal with her little furball curled up next to it.

Sami swayed on her porch swing, doing her best to avoid disturbing the night silence with the shriek of rusted metal. It was a boring pastime, but with Lenora needing a nap after as much as a tail wag, there was little else they could do together than explore the Undercity view from the discomfort of her back porch. On a few occasions, Sami tried loading Lenora up in her old half-broken-down wagon—complete with rust holes and fading red paint—and pulling her for a walk along the Undercity Wall. Lenora appeared to enjoy the slight breeze for the short while, but the loose wheels made it difficult for Sami to pull beyond a couple of blocks. By the end of the walk, her hand would crimp like an old monkey's paw, taking days to return to normal. So, sitting and swaying it was.

The view from Sami's back porch was as familiar to her as the creaks and smells of her small two-room home. The only home she'd ever known. The scenery hadn't been much to commit to memory over the years, just a few beaten-down houses and the large gray blankness of the Undercity boundary wall. Stretching from ground to Mantle, the Wall surrounded most of Lower Midian, sealing out the daylight and fresh air, leaving the stale air to be chased by only the ocean breeze through a small gap beyond the Under Eastside. It was supposed to have been temporary. At least, that's what was sold—some excuse about improving the acoustics above. But after a while, it became as much of a city fixture as the Mantle itself.

The Wall may have been intended to seal the Undercity away from the rest of the world, but as a child, Sami would use the emptiness of the towering concrete slab to be swept away from her little slice of *hole*. She'd watch grand, adventurous tales bloom from her mind and play out over the rugged gray canvas. Transporting her from the quiet Plainsview neighborhood of Lower Midian to the thunderous ranges of the Chemical Hills, ducking and dodging the Barrens scavengers that animated the rocky terrain. And on days when she felt an amorous itch, the canvas would come alive with the austere beauty of a seaside landscape, far from the chaos of the city. She would live in a sprawling palatial estate as the daughter of a wealthy mistress with servants catering to her every need. The boys of the local aristocracy would all do their best to win her heart, showering her with presents and attention. But in the fantasy, her heart belonged to the poor stable hand, a boy, a couple of years older, who was the spot-on image of Seth Finnes from her homeroom. Seth had made his way into many of her fantasies throughout her teens, often rescuing her from one danger or another—including the banal existence of underside life.

It wasn't until around her sixteenth birthday that Sami's embarrassment with the cheese of her fantasies began overshadowing the good parts. But she still found herself revisiting them well into her late teens. Cheese or not, the visions stirred her blossoming emotions, and there wasn't much else for her to do after school. By then, her mother had stopped working, her bone disease advancing too far along to hold down a job. And with Sami's father having left soon after her birth, in search of a better life—or at least a life that didn't involve her or her mother—she had few pennies to trade for a book or even those God-awful comics the other kids would spend countless hours gushing through.

On occasion, their neighbor, Mrs. Shields, would stop by with books at the end of their life from the school where she worked as a teacher. Most had been old textbooks and build manuals. But now and again, Mrs. Shields would come through with a fantastical novel of swashbuckling sailors or journeying odd couples. Sami would watch from the safety of the book's portal doors as the protagonist overcame death-defying odds, skirting and foiling the evil plans of their rival. And often, the stories would find their way into a refreshed telling on the Wall's large gray film screen, just a few blocks from her back door. With a few minor additions, of course. An official Samantha Salem rewrite. Mainly, it would include replacing the hero with herself and villains with whomever had earned her hormone-induced ire at the time. But she'd also find a way to work in Seth—even if the story didn't call for a love interest.

As she grew older, the stories dimmed, and now the blankness was a mere canvas for her thoughts. A placemat to hold her hopes and dreams. And more recently, her fears. Lately, she'd been overrun by the images of Jericho's last moments, wisping across the Wall like a haunting. Even when she smothered the visions with happy memories, the sounds refused to be muted. The gasping for air. The rumble of Bass's voice, like the dying engine of a car that had run through too much grease.

Sami had worked with Bass for years and always dismissed his outbursts as a consequence of some childhood trauma, never imagining he was capable of murder. The murder of the underside's greatest hero, no less. A man who had devoted his life to helping the less fortunate. Who had changed the lives of millions for the better. Who had given her purpose. And who trusted her with his darkest secrets. Tears welled in Sami's eyes. Jericho had trusted her, and she abandoned him when he needed her the most. She could still feel Atlas's firm embrace. He wouldn't let her go. The thought that Atlas could have known what was coming had only added to her guilt. Another possible means to have stopped Bass…if only she had told him the truth.

Lenora's ears perked up from a rattling at the front door. Sami turned to the window behind the swing and wiped away a thin layer of grime with the sleeve of her afghan. She squinted through the smudge-covered pane to the screen door on the other side of the house. Standing on the front step, Jasper peered inside, his small frame hidden behind the overflowing grocery bags clutched to his chest. Sami waved him in, and he maneuvered an elbow to open the screen door.

Sami ushered Lenora inside, holding the back door open as she doddered in. Lenora's tail inched beyond the threshold into the kitchen when she plopped herself on the cold floor from exhaustion.

"How's she doing?" asked Jasper, setting the groceries on the kitchen countertop.

Sami glanced at Lenora, now flattened on the floor, barely able to hold open her eyes. "She's okay." She wasn't. But if Sami had said as much, Jasper would spend hours going through all her symptoms, suggesting remedies, different exercises to help get her moving. And Sami wasn't in the mood.

"That's good news, right? At least she's not getting any worse?" He pulled a rubber mouse from one of the bags and knelt beside Lenora. After a scratch behind the ears, he placed the chew toy on the floor next to her. "She'll be back to normal soon. You'll see."

Sami sat at the kitchen table, watching as Lenora sniffed at the overturned mouse, too weak to play. She had long questioned whether the treatments the vet had recommended only prolonged the suffering. If the cancer wasn't to be stopped, would it have been better to let it run its course? Jasper didn't think so. "The chance of life is always better than the alternative," he would say. Sami wasn't so sure.

"How are *you*? Have you...decided yet?" asked Jasper, returning to the groceries.

Sami heard a nervous tremble ring in Jasper's throat as the words fell flat on the air. He knew she hated the question yet asked every time they were together.

"No, Jasper," she said, unwilling to mask the disdain in her voice.

His shoulders fell with a loud sigh. He placed the large tin of coffee grounds he had just pulled from one of the bags onto the counter before turning to face her. The concern in Jasper's soft brown eyes only annoyed her more. It was the look someone would give a burn victim after a house fire—sympathy in its purest form.

"Just stop," she said, rolling her eyes.

He stepped toward the kitchen table and swung a chair beside her. "Why don't you come back? Bass still wants you around."

She laughed. "Yeah. I know. I'm the only one the people trust. He needs me."

"Then come back."

"It's not that simple."

Jasper leaned back in his chair, rubbing his face with frustration. Between his long, thin fingers, she could see a large vein bubble to the surface of his forehead, his face shifting cardinal red.

"Why is this so hard for you?" His voice was raised, but not so loud as a yell, the sympathy now choked away by his anger. "You always told me your work came before everything else. It was the most important thing. Helping the addicts get clean. Or single mothers with nowhere else to turn. Or the hundreds of others that just need someone not to write them off. It gave you purpose—your words! What purpose do you get from staring at the Wall all day? Swimming in your despair. Even if Bass is a piece of shit, you can still do your work. He won't bother you. And at least you can make up for whatever craziness he starts."

Sami sat quietly as Jasper's frustration drowned under the rumble of the passing garbage truck. She looked down at her folded hands on the table, fighting back the emotions bubbling to the surface. She wanted to go back. But not with Bass. Not after what he'd done. It would be as if she had tossed Jericho down that shaft herself.

The truck soon rolled on, and the din whimpered into a distant thrum. Silence crowded the room, and Jasper sat with the somber emotion of a boy at the funeral of his pet goldfish. It almost seemed as if he'd given up the fight. But Sami knew he'd never quit. He was too persistent. Too optimistic. Traits that had won her over when they first met but now annoyed her to no end.

"A little boy came into the Hall the other day," Jasper said softly. "A Filth child."

Filth. She cringed at the word. A title given to the illegitimate children of the Faith clergy. Born into a world where strays are treated better. And why? Because their fathers couldn't keep their dicks in their pants.

Sami's mother had turned wholly to the Faith in her final years, finding peace and hope in the teachings. Often lecturing Sami on the path of Light, urging her to submit to the will of God. It made Sami happy to see her not fully resigned to fear. Her mother had held a hopeful glow right until her last breath. But the thought that any child could be forced to suffer as a matter of dogma for the sins of their parents was a hill too far.

"The boy wanted help," Jasper continued. "His adopted brother is in the Guard. He wants him to come home."

Sami stared blankly at the tabletop's unvarnished wood, counting the knots in her mind, as she had at least a dozen times since Jericho's death. *Twelve.* Although she swore she had once counted as many as fifteen. Out of the corner of her eye, she could see Jasper shifting in his seat to get her attention. An almost eager excitement, like a driftballer about to score an open goal.

"They sent him to talk to Stixx because you weren't there."

She could sense him searching her face and knew exactly what he was looking for. He was waiting for the anger to sprout. An involuntary show of disgust when her mind put the pieces of his story together.

Jasper shot up from his seat, animated with the spirit of a street preacher spewing warnings from scripture. "Stixx! That son of a bitch will have that kid run shit into the Under Eastside. He promised the kid we'd help. Do you know what will happen if he gets caught? What will happen to his brother?"

Sami's tongue stalled before coming to her defense. There was no point. It would simply fuel him with more arguments to repel. Jasper was often carried away by anger, tossing reason and civility out the window until his rage eventually calmed. It was never so much that she'd be frightened; he wasn't a violent person. But still, she'd rather await the simmer before seasoning the stew.

The vein on his forehead throbbed pale through his blood-steeped face. "So, what now? Watch the collapse from the sidelines? Let the Citizenry become a low-rent operation like Asher Punsch? Oh, and speaking of Asher—"

The view of the table Sami had been nursing quickly shifted to a probing glare of Jasper's face.

"What about Asher?" she asked.

He froze at the question, the immediate discomfort in his eyes as obvious as the plumage of a tropical bird. The vein on his forehead retreated beneath his now parchment-pale skin.

"Well…nothing, really. I mean…maybe. But…who knows. It's just a rumor, is all."

"You can't drop *his* name and expect me to ignore it," she said. "What about Asher?"

Jasper's awkwardness melted to nervousness. "Okay. But look… We don't know if this is actually going to happen. But if it is, you could probably stop it if you return. You, above all others, would be able to sway—"

"Jasper! What is it?"

He stood behind his chair, clutching the backrest, his fingernails white from his tight grip. "Bass has never been shy about what he wants. We all know that. But, thankfully, he never had the means—especially with Jericho in his way. But now…he's doing it. He's going after the Syndicate. And to do it…"

Sami's spine shuddered a nervous chill. She knew what was coming before Jasper could finish. At that moment, it took everything for her to remain composed. *Lest we look like a crazy bitch*, her mother's words rang in her ears.

Jasper's lips moved again, but Sami couldn't hear anything beyond the cries of pain. He soon melted away, and she saw instead the countless faces she'd lost over the years. Neighbors. Friends. Family. Her mother. Sami closed her eyes, hoping to darken the despair. She was falling. She reached for the table's edge as an anchor, only to find Jasper's warm hand. She felt his embrace and could no longer hold back.

"How could I ever…" she muttered, tears now rushing down her face. "Jasper. How could I go back now?" She opened her eyes, eager for a look, a glimmer, something to show her he understood.

He pressed his forehead to hers. "I know…I know."

CHAPTER 3
ATLAS RECEDES

"…but they hate us. Why are we doing this again?"

Atlas ignored his bunkmate, sliding on the pants of his uniform. He wasn't sure either why they were asked to attend. Regardless, he was excited to take part. He hadn't worn his full-dress Guardian threads since graduation a few months earlier and was eager to don it once more. The pomp of it made him feel as if he'd made something of himself. A nobody from SyndiCares Home #3 was now representing the SyndiGuard in the Independence Day parade. If only Housemaster Hesper could see him now.

The crisp pleats and ironed creases of the deep blue pants paired well with the French-cuffed white silk dress shirt, and the golden shoulder tassels that ornamented the blue woolen jacket were complemented by a hand-stitched Guardian crest on the breast. Then there was the beret. It was the *pièce de résistance*, tying it all together and giving Atlas a look of royalty.

"Atty, check this out." His bunkmate stood at attention with his rifle at his side. He then mimicked marching alongside the large parade float parked in the hangar where they'd been dressing.

"What are you doing? We can't take our guns…or can we?" said Atlas.

"They never said we couldn't. And what? We're just going to leave them here in the hangar? What if they got stolen? Besides, they would have told us to leave them back at the gates if we weren't expected to carry them."

Made sense. Atlas took one last look at himself in the full-length mirror affixed to the hangar wall before sliding on an oversized pair of reflective shades.

"How do I look?" he asked.

"Grab your gun."

He reached for his rifle resting against the float and clutched it with both hands across his body.

"Nice."

"Let me lead the float. You ride in the back," said Atlas.

"We're gonna look so badass."

As the large metal doors slid open, a flare of light in the distant sky flashed ferociously into the hangar, the tint of Atlas's glasses unable to tame its glare. Shielding his eyes, he tried looking out to the roadway through his fingers but was blinded by the golden sheen masking all beyond the opening doors. He could hear murmurs from his bunkmate, but the squeal of the doors sliding along their wheels began drowning out all other sounds around them, slowly transforming into the same wrenching cry that had haunted him these last several years.

The scream woke him. It always woke him. After so long, he had hoped the shriek's resonance would have dulled by now. It hadn't. It pierced as sharply as it had that first time, all those years ago.

Atlas used to cherish mornings. A new day, full of new possibilities. But now, waking each morning to that haunting cry made him curse the rising sun. Curse his existence, for that matter.

He rose from his bed and pushed the shaggy flower-patterned drapes to the side. Light rushed into the room, and he felt the subtle hum of the Mantle lamps chugging. *I guess that's what I get for cursing the sun.* He'd be cursing the lamps soon enough.

The street outside his window lay empty, only a stray dog in the distance bringing the scenery to life. Sleeping away the day was typical for most undersiders, an act of rebellion that started long ago after the erection of the Undercity Wall. A long-standing protest to show the Syndicate that they'd never control the day, even if they controlled the Mantle lamps.

The quiet day was when Atlas left his room to restock on food and drink at a twenty-four-hour grocer a few blocks away. Finding solace in the empty streets, he imagined himself as one of only a handful of people still alive, surviving alone in an evacuated world. Using the drink to set the stage of an altered reality and drown out the truth the best he could. Taking the drink as a companion had started as a means to escape the sting of his failure at Jericho's flat a couple of weeks ago. But with little else on the horizon, it quickly settled into a lasting partnership.

The first couple of days had been fine, mindless inebriation followed by long stretches of sleep, interrupted by a retch or two and his morning wake-up call of shrieks. But soon, the images of lifelessness returned, tearing through his drunken thoughts without regard for the damage they'd leave in their wake. For years, he'd gotten away with only the searing guilt, tucking the images of death beneath his long-standing dream of underside redemption. But with the hope he'd clung to for so long now dead and gone, there was nothing left to keep the images buried beneath. The visions were resurfacing like the carcass of a drowned rat in a filthy pond. And the drink was now making the remains more buoyant.

Atlas glanced over to a capped syringe balancing on the edge of his nightstand, still swollen with its milky suspension. It was a little token the store clerk had offered up after counting the bottles he'd run through. A gift Atlas wasn't about to turn away—not with the drink unable to drown his past any longer. Though he almost wished the clerk had offered it up in its solid form, a rigid nugget of white to be placed in water and boiled before being injected. It would have been a much easier gift to refuse.

In the fancy skeet dens on the Mantle, it was a regular occurrence. A broken rock. Microscopic particles in the air. And everyone in the room dead from asphyxiation. One fleck of dry skeet inhaled could bring down a man twice Bass's size. But once doused in water and prepared under a flame, the risk of death was ushered away. And the gift was tame enough to accept—at least enough to keep around while he decided whether to take the plunge. A decision he found growing easier with each passing day.

Atlas pulled the drapes closed and flopped back on his bed, watching the specks of dust dance in the slivered rays escaping the curtain's grasp. The smell of mothballs from the sheets enveloped the air, and the gleam of the Mantle lamps bathing the drawn curtains filled the room with a muted glow. He could feel a weight on his chest as the images of death flashed again in his mind. He tried closing his eyes to shake it away, but it only grew more vivid, as if tattooed beneath his lids and forcing his eyes to witness the eerie stillness once again. It was a stillness he'd only ever seen in *things* before that night. Things like a mug or book. Of course, he'd known dead people didn't move, but it wasn't until seeing his first corpse that he truly understood the finality of death. And the burning guilt of being its cause.

Letting go of mistakes and embarrassments had never been easy. Every flub of a word. Every mistaken gesture. Every misstep added to his inventory of failures. Each one affixed to a long rope knotted at his ankle, clanging loudly as he stepped forward through life, like tin cans chiming against a concrete walk, singing a song of his shame. But it wasn't until he'd killed a man that the rope became too unwieldy. His hope for his time in the Undercity had distracted him for a while, even lightening the load when the invasive thoughts surged forth. But with that dream as dead as the bodies from all those years ago, he was now pinned beneath the monstrous rope, struggling for breath.

Atlas's eyes sought the syringe, his veins now throbbing an invitation. The sight of his escape balancing on his nightstand excited him, like the vision of a naked woman awaiting his touch. He so wanted to reach out. Succumb to her warm embrace. Lose himself in her comfort. But as he stretched out his hand, her clutches inches from his fingertips, the smell of the rotting woman from the alley flooded his senses. The overbearing rank of shit and rot. His stomach turned over, urging him to his feet. And just as he reached the toilet, only steps from his bed, his body lurched forth in a fit, expelling the remaining drink from his stomach.

The vomiting fits worked his insides like body shots from his Guard training commander during hand-to-hand combat, the soreness seeping through his skin. After a marathon of vomit and retching, Atlas lay sprawled out on the linoleum with one thought left in his head: he needed a drink. But with the violent expulsion of his insides came a clarity of mind he knew he had to trust. Languishing in his room would only offer the seductress at his bedside table more of an opportunity to entice. He needed to escape, if only for tonight.

Atlas rose to his feet and rinsed his mouth in the sink before heading for the door.

The Mantle lamps darkened as he stepped from his motel room into the street. The frigid wind burned through his thin clothes, prickling atop his skin like a thousand thorns. He pushed through the pain down the empty sidewalk, anticipating the warmth of the heated streetlights only moments away from igniting.

Soon, the Undercity came alive in a flash of lights and symphony of sounds: the howl of the eastern wind mixing with the sounds of voices filling the air. Vehicles rumbling through the streets, chased by the marked aroma of fried foods. And the light from the Mantle's Shade Pub buzzing a welcoming glow.

Atlas climbed the stairs to the pub and pushed through the glass-paned doors into the main. He could hear the rattle of steel buckets being topped off as the bartender passed between the empty tables with a sack of peanuts, preparing for the early-evening rush. Atlas sauntered to the corner of the room and took a seat at a table half-concealed by the bar. This would be his evening's perch, far from the whispers. Far from the torment.

Atlas was on his third drink when Alanna Thistle walked through the door. He nearly choked when he spied her chocolate-brown hair amid a group of men donning Citizenry armbands. At first, he questioned his eyes. He could have sworn he'd seen her at least a hundred times during his first days in the trench. Only when he looked closer did her face dissolve beneath the stranger's true image. But as he gazed across the pub at the woman laughing among her Citizenry friends, he could make out the striking features imprinted in his mind. The large green eyes. Thick, pursy lips. Fair satin skin. It was her, without any doubt.

Atlas could feel his breathing deepen, his legs itching to run. He moved to escape his seat, but the weight of his past had turned his feet to lead. Here she was, the girl of his dreams. His sole reason for being underside and his last chance to claim everything he'd wanted. If he were to leave now, it would have to be for no other reason than to scout a spot next to the rotting woman in the alleyway. He had planned for this, after all, choosing his motel deliberately a couple of blocks from a known Citizenry bar. A quiet hope for a chance run-in if things didn't play out with his Citizenry membership the way he'd wanted. It was the first idea he'd put into motion that was actually bearing fruit. Only his past self never considered the likely degeneracy of his future. Not only had his plans for redemption been teetering like the syringe on his nightstand, but he'd also hardly impress, unbathed and reeking of drink and vomit.

Atlas sat quietly, watching Alanna flirt her way through each guy in her entourage, hanging playfully from each of their arms, pouting her lips and flipping her dark hair, as if doing her very best to draw them in. It wasn't until his fifth drink that he finally caught her eye. Her glance toward him lingered, and all he could do was smile—a large, foolish smile. She turned away, and he could feel the embarrassment on his cheeks. He must've looked crazy. A creep hiding in a darkened corner, grinning from ear-to-ear from across the bar. Atlas laid his forehead on the table, convinced he'd ruined his chances, when he heard a sweet voice in his ear.

"You're new."

He shot up in his seat. She was even more stunning up

close. There was a softness to her skin that he hadn't seen on most undersiders. And her sweet scent rose above that of the stale beer and peanuts. Her simple lavender summer dress pressed snugly against her waist, and her matching open-toed shoes revealed her brightly painted nails that stood out like petals on the floor of crushed shells.

Atlas choked back a sip of his drink, moistening his cotton tongue. "You know everyone in the trench?" he said with as much confidence as he could muster.

She smirked, slipping into the seat next to him. "No. But I do know everyone that comes to this bar." She reached for his drink. "I'm Alanna."

His blood warmed his cheeks as he introduced himself.

"So…you're from up top, aren't you?" she said before taking a sip.

Atlas stammered through a web of ums and half-words. It was as if everyone could read him.

Alanna pulled the drink from her lips and leaned in, whispering loud enough to be heard over the TVs behind the bar. "A word of advice…" The tickle of her warm breath cascaded goose pimples across his skin. "Only topsiders call the Undercity the *trench*."

Atlas shifted awkwardly in his seat, his voice sticking in his throat. His mind raced to find the right words, but his embarrassment was crowding the way. He had run through this moment a hundred times in his head. It was supposed to be his grand introduction. Step one on his path to redemption. But now he could see her smile fading as his words continued to catch on his tongue.

"I was from up top," he forced out. "A SyndiCares kid. But I live down here now." A blatant act of desperation, admitting his upbringing to drown his awkwardness in sympathy. Atlas had learned over the years that most people offered a wide berth of forgiveness to abandoned children. And he'd taken advantage of it countless times when his social awkwardness was on full display. A regular occurrence—especially with women.

Atlas watched her face, hoping to see the glow return to her smile. The dim lights on her supple skin made reading her expression nearly impossible, catching him unprepared by her sympathy when she finally spoke.

"I'm sorry to hear that. I couldn't imagine being raised so…impersonally."

She couldn't imagine.

"Oh, it wasn't all bad. Some of my fondest memories were from the Home." *Some? All.*

"Is that so? Well, what brings you down here now?" she asked, resuming her doe-like sips from his glass.

Atlas wasn't going to lie. She didn't deserve it. But this wasn't the time to release his demons—or even hint at their existence. Not when he was so close.

"I dunno," he said. "I guess…I was hoping I could find something down here. A purpose, perhaps."

"A purpose is hard to come by," she said, questions dancing in her eyes. "And it's a lot to give up—a cushy life up top—for what we have down here. The air is thick. The life is hard. Most make it their purpose to find a way topside. Doesn't really happen the other way around."

"I guess. But next to working in some corporate job or the Guard, there isn't much to make someone feel like they're making a difference."

Alanna stared through him as if working to disassemble him with her eyes. Then, with one final gulp, she finished the rest of his drink and jumped to her feet.

"I'm at the Citizenry Hall most days this week. Come find me…when you're ready," she said.

He had no time to consider her words before she started back toward her party.

"Wait! Find you for what?"

She didn't turn back. She just continued her stride and shouted over the clamor of the bar, "Your purpose!"

His purpose. The bane of his existence.

CHAPTER 4

SOLOMON'S STEED

Solomon snapped open his handkerchief with a flick of his wrist, wiping himself off with one hand as he unlatched the top of an ornate donation chest with the other. He grabbed at the loose bills lining the interior and tossed the fistful of cash on the tousled silk sheets. It was certainly more than what was expected. But then again, it had to be. It always had to be.

"Same time tomorrow?" the woman said, folding the bills neatly.

So cavalier, speaking such sin in the house of God. "Get out," he ordered.

She tucked the cash into her garter and slipped on the stained evening dress she had arrived in. Passing him slowly, she rubbed her hand across his chest and whispered, "Tomorrow it is."

Tomorrow it is.

Solomon stepped to the window and peered through the parted blinds to the street below. The crowded sounds of the nearby Marketplace resounded off the platformed sky, but only a few passersby could be seen. He watched his evening's entertainment creep out the main church doors and scurry across the roadway. The coming and going of whores in the church was not particularly noteworthy, but he still preferred to avoid any added attention.

Solomon had grown fond of whores over the years, sampling a variety over his time in the clergy. As a man of the cloth, his options were limited. And whores offered a service no ordinary woman could rival. Despite their unscrupulousness in matters of the flesh, the whorish code of secrecy tended to hold up under the harshest circumstances, a lesson he learned years ago while still at the seminary. The adamance of that poor girl accusing him of fathering a Filth was striking. She truly seemed to believe it. As if God would allow such shame to befall a believer of his stature. Thankfully, she chose not to press the matter beyond their brief discussion. The rumor alone would have forced his expulsion from the Church. But it was from that encounter that he learned of a whore's true worth—beyond their obvious charms.

Stepping from the window, Solomon glimpsed his tall, lean figure in the mirror. He rarely dressed after his entanglements. Rather, he'd allow the air to wash over his naked body, pacing the small room above the nave, preparing for his nightly sermon, as if feeling the dry church air on his bare skin cleansed him of the stink and sin. It was also when he felt the most inspired, penning his best sermons in his original form.

Watching his reflection, Solomon's eyes stalled on the birthmark just above his navel, a gift passed down from his mother, and likely her parents before her. The fringed edges of the mousy brown halo had darkened in recent years. And the center had faded a paler beige than the surrounding skin. Solomon could still remember asking his mother about the stain as a child, noticing hers as she dressed. She had told him that the eclipsed sun orbiting her umbilicus represented God's eye watching over her children. There to always guide them. A lesson he'd taken to heart in his darkest times.

Growing up in Bottoms Edge, Solomon would ride the bus each day to Plainsview Faith Elementary, a school of horrors for children bussed in from the poorest neighborhoods. The torrent of abuses pursued by some of the very same kids who now kiss his ring as adults pushed many of his peers to the streets, like moths to a flame, searching for the warmth of acceptance. Unfortunately, the warmth many found first needed to be heated atop a crooked spoon. If it hadn't been for the divine hand of God, Solomon easily could have suffered a similar fate—God and his brother Jericho.

Jericho would stop into Plainsview Faith following nights when Solomon's blackened eyes grew too swollen to be quieted by a bag of frozen peas. The spectacle of ass-whoopings for the little shits who had unloaded their torment of butt slides, snot stickers, and wet wallops was almost worth the suffering. He would watch with the amusement of an arsonist mesmerized by an air-bending flame as Jericho would unleash the full power of his fifteen-year-old might on an army of children five years his junior. Those were good days. But the respite was always short-lived.

After the welts of Jericho's beatings had faded, the torture and persecution would start again. Like the blossoming of tulips in the spring—or deadening of greenery in the fall. But God was ever watchful, intervening as the torment neared its crescendo. Not through some accident, or a divine message striking fear into the hearts of his abusers—they were not the sorts worthy of such a message. But through the revelation of one man's shame and depravity.

It turned out that Mr. Pritchard of apartment 7A had quite the collection of *Bouncing Blonde Bimbos Monthly*, a fact that had eluded Mrs. Pritchard until several minutes before Solomon and his friend Punchy happened upon the skin rags strewn about the alleyway next to their building. They approached a steady stream of flapping breasts and fluttering asses raining down over the alleyway to the chorus of Mrs. Pritchard berating her husband. The high-gloss sheen of the magazine covers glistened in the sun's setting rays. Back before the Wall, when a glow would engulf the Undercity in the late evenings as the sun eased behind the Chemical Hills on the horizon.

When stacked up, the entire collection sat just below the faint cleft of Solomon's chin. It was quite the find. But neither he nor Punchy knew what to do with them. They were interesting to look at, but in the sort of way a mantis consuming the head of their mate was interesting to watch. Punchy figured they could earn some money on the streets selling them to the other miserable married men of the neighborhood. Solomon had initially agreed, thinking it would be nice for once to have a new pair of shoes—or at least ones in which all ten of his toes were shielded from the nightly chill. But standing patiently inside his cramped locker the next day at school, waiting for the footsteps of his bullies to fade, Solomon saw the Light of God inspiring him with other plans.

Having spent countless hours huddled away with the musty stench of old gym clothes, he'd learned a trick or two in how the lockers were built. A trick that came in handy for his final act of retribution.

Solomon and Punchy stepped onto the bus the next day, lugging two large duffle bags full of vengeance. They made the necessary arrangements and headed to the school office, ensnaring the administrators with their horror-filled tale of how they'd been accosted with the blinding images of sin.

Although he never witnessed them being hauled out of class to face their expulsion, Solomon had heard that most had broken down in hysterics after the smut spilled out of their lockers at their parents' feet. He often fantasized of that moment when seeing their faces in the pews. His moment of victory. But he was also thankful for the lesson. Patience in the face of adversity. Patience for God's intercession. Even now, he practiced its teachings.

With the world having embraced the doctrine of personal gratification, allowing individuals to define their own truths and morals, madness had crowded out the Faith. The natural law of God was now seen as barbaric by many. Even the Faith's place with the Syndicate had been reduced to an afterthought. Solomon could hardly recall the last meeting he'd been invited to. The last briefing he received was nearly a year ago, announcing the demolition of the final Faith church in Upper Midian. No longer was the Faith to have a presence above the lamps, forcing God and his believers to the darkness beneath. A move that would not sit well with the Almighty. But Solomon remained patient for His guiding hand. It would certainly come.

The growing chatter of attendees below his feet grew louder, and he placed the finishing touches on the evening's message. Solomon wrapped himself in the ceremonial white silk robes, edged with broad golden trim. He glanced in the mirror and smoothed out the frizz from his long silver hair, then applied a generous dousing of oil to his thick black beard. He descended the stairs into the sacristy and peaked past the cloth curtains separating him from the seated crowd. It was the usual smattering of elders and devotees, accompanied by a few stragglers from out of town. It had been years since the pews were bursting with believers. In better times, parishioners would overflow the nave, forcing people alongside the walls, shading the light of the stained-glass compositions. That was back when people would dress in their church best. Suit and tie. Dresses below the knee. Headscarves and fedoras. Now, it was nothing but jeans and athletic wear. Skirts barely long enough to conceal ass cheeks. Sunglasses and ball caps. Dignity now came second to comfort.

Throwing back the curtains, he approached the pulpit

with his arms raised, palms to the sky, showing that he came with nothing but the word of God. The crowd responded in kind, lowering their hands as he settled in behind the darkly varnished wooden lectern.

"In the name of our Lord, our protector, our savior. We ask for his mercy and love. Mercy for those of us caught in a life of sin, and mercy for the Filth. Let us pray they receive their place in Paradise, and let us pray He delivers us from their fate in this world. We ask for His love…"

Solomon rounded out the opening prayer with a silence of personal reflection. That was when he'd note the regulars. He understood that most people reclaim their faith in times of crisis, but it was the devout under a prosperous glow that were truly the Lord's beloved.

Looking out over the half-empty pews, Solomon watched as the heads among the crowd bowed in unison—except for one. Off to the side, next to the stained-glass portrait of the Savior's Awakening, a woman cloaked in a black hooded jacket sat motionless. Despite the distance between them, he spied the glazed eyes and dead stare of a woman in mourning. She was a woman he had known at one time. A woman of clout and authority in the Undercity.

Solomon kept his focus locked on the woman and continued the evening sermon with the usual dramatics his followers had come to expect. "Brothers and sisters, I stand before you a sinner. Not a born sinner, but a sinner nonetheless. As babes, we come into the world with such a sweetness. A sweetness that wafts off us like the natural must of a flower. We are pure. Unadulterated. Heavenly beings. But as we age, and the world breaks us down, we become vile, despicable creatures. Fornicating. Defecating. Perspiring. Breathing out the foulness emanating from within. We fill our bellies with the food of our desires and strive to satiate our lowest, most abhorrent impulses. Rotting our bodies and minds to quell the anxiety of this life. But is it ever enough?"

The sparse crowd murmured a collective "no."

"No…" he mimicked softly. "Nothing will ever be enough. We will keep searching for that fix. Reaching for that which is evil while turning our backs on what is righteous. Blinded by the shiny trinkets. Unable to see the truth before us. And do you know when we will come to know the truth?" He swiped his eyes over the crowd. "When it's too late. Always when it is too late. And we cry out, 'MY GOD! WHY HAVE YOU CURSED ME!?' But in truth, it is our desires that are the curse of this world…"

Solomon preached on, hamming up the theatrics like a trained beggar roaming the Bottoms, all the while keeping the hooded woman in his periphery.

He finished the service with a welcome to all new attendees, extending an invite to any who wished to discuss their path to salvation. But he was careful enough in his words to avoid an influx of regulars; he was only interested in one from the crowd.

He stood in wait by the pulpit, nodding a gentle acknowledgment to his guests as they slowly left following their personal prayers. The woman sat alone, now with her head bowed. Although it would have been easy to approach her with most of the church having emptied, it would be unbecoming of Midian's Grand Magus to force an audience. He watched the woman rise to her feet before he started for the sacristy. Slow enough to allow her time to reach him—if she so wished.

"Your Worship?" said a soft voice from behind.

Solomon wore a muted smirk under his beard as he turned and watched the woman approach. Encircling her large hazel eyes was an obvious sorrow, further darkened by the dim church lighting that shaded her butter-brown complexion.

Excitement washed over him. "Yes, my child."

"I know it's been some time, but I hope you remember me."

How could he ever let slip the memory of a beauty such as Samantha Salem?

Solomon had known Sami's mother well. As a child, having grown up on the same block in Bottoms Edge and as a regular at his sermons before her passing. She was a strong and spirited woman, well respected among those with any authority beneath the Mantle. Not a Citizenry member in any official capacity, but a fervent supporter nonetheless. Watching a woman of her vibrancy slowly decay from her diseased bones and acquired taste for skeet was a shame. He had done his best to counsel her off the drugs, but she was adamant that the skeet was keeping her alive. "The pain is merciless, and only the needle can tame it," she would say.

As for Sami, Solomon had encountered her several times during her mother's visits to the church after-hours. But her work with his brother had given her a face. He recalled thinking that if anyone was to turn Jericho back to the path of righteousness, a young beauty such as Sami would be the one. Unfortunately, their relationship had proved platonic, and Jericho continued the path to damnation.

Solomon feigned a search of his memories before responding. "Ah, yes. Samantha Salem. How are you, dear?"

"Do you have a moment for me?"

He nodded with a warm smile and led Sami into the sacristy.

A hint of the whore's unwashed body peppered the air. Solomon rubbed his beard in hopes of releasing the oil's musk to mask the rank of sin. He had never really noticed how intimate the sacristy had been until that moment, only large enough to hold a small table, wardrobe, and kitchenette. He would have killed for a window—or rather, he'd pray vigorously for one.

He extended his hand, directing Sami to a seat at the table before reaching for a tray of figs on the counter. "You must try these, my dear," he said, sliding the figs toward her.

"Thank you, Your Worship. But I'm not here for a social call."

"What's wrong, child?" He eased into the seat across the table.

Sami took a deep breath before speaking. "Your Worship. Jericho…has passed."

Silence overcame the tiny room before Solomon realized she was done speaking.

"Oh…my dear. My dear, my dear. This is such sad news." He lowered his head and paused a moment for silent reflection. Those not of the Church had an expectation of visible grief; he risked being branded a sociopath otherwise. But Solomon neither felt aggrieved nor considered himself mentally ill. Death was just a part of the game of life. And when the player died, their score was totaled and rank assigned. Not much different from any childhood board game. Except here, it was played for keeps.

After a few moments, he looked at Sami. Her face was heavy. "As you know, my child, Jericho did lead a life of sin…"

Sami's emotions appeared to shift. First, a look of disbelief, waiting for him to finish, but quickly burning to anger when she understood his meaning. She glared through him, and Solomon paused.

"But no matter," he continued. Now was not the time for judgments. "He was my brother, and I loved him dearly." The fire in her eyes was extinguished. "So, even though the Faith cannot accept his body, I will pray for his soul." And those prayers would not do Jericho an ounce of good. The natural law offered room for repentance. But Solomon doubted his brother had tamed his ego enough to accept God's mercy.

"My child, I know you two were quite close. How are you

doing?" he said, hoping to avoid any talk of their brotherly relationship.

"Your Worship…I'm lost."

They accused him of sociopathy for his muted emotions while the masses drowned in their ignorance and selfish sorrows.

"The Citizenry is where I belong," she said. "Or rather, where I belonged. With Jericho gone, it's not the place of hope it once was."

The words pricked Solomon like static dancing atop his skin, describing the Citizenry with words that should be reserved only for the Faith. *The plotting and planning of mortals.* How they wrap themselves in their gratuitous self-congratulations with no regard for the Creator. "Look what we've done!" they cry out, not knowing that nothing was possible without God's will.

"…I just can't continue my work there. I'll only be feeding the image of what the Citizenry was. Not what it is now. It would be a betrayal to the people."

Solomon stroked his beard to mask his unease and feign the appearance of solemn reflection. He knew the solution to her problems when he first spotted her in the pews. But through his years in the Church, he'd learned people's emotions were like a battlefield after the bloodshed. Some were rocky and ominous, others serene and inviting. But buried just beneath the surface of each was an assortment of trip mines, able to maim and lay waste to those who traveled the land with a heavy foot. He would need to be as graceful and precise as a ballerino if he was to navigate his way through her blood-soaked lands.

"My child, often, when we face hardships, what ails us the most is not the challenge before us; it is the thought of what we've lost—our inability to return to once was."

Solomon rose from his seat and retrieved an old book from his wardrobe. He thumbed his way to a dog-eared page near the middle. "This, my child, is a copy of the Testaments written in the tongue of the Far Easterners. It was commissioned by Prime Faith Missionary, Aldus Hawthorn, nearly one hundred years ago." He pushed the figs to the side and spread the book out on the table, pointing to a highlighted symbol at the top of the page. "This is the Testament of Tribulation by the Apostle Kinan." He then flipped to another dog-eared page near the back of the book. "And this is the Testament of Opportunity by the Apostle Roland. Do you notice something similar between the two?"

Solomon watched Sami carefully study the symbols as he flipped back and forth between the pages.

"The symbol for tribulation is also the symbol for opportunity," he said. "Despite their lack of spiritual knowledge, the Far Easterners possess immense wisdom in matters of life. The point is, my child, you need to change your perspective."

Sami's face held an expression of bored earnestness. His little lesson had never done much in the way of persuasion with parishioners of her generation, anyway. He wasn't sure whether that nugget of ancient wisdom had been shared by one too many hipsters to resonate any longer, or if the smug self-importance of her generation had blinded them to any lesson beyond one that smacked them upside the head. But what he was sure of was that back in his day, such a revelation would have coated the hearts of followers with a renewed purpose, inspiring them to push past the pain and look to a new day. *These damned kids.*

"I've tried, Your Worship."

"You may have. But it seems not hard enough."

Solomon despised dancing around the wooden idol. He knew if he suggested she come work for the Faith outright, he risked losing her confidence as an impartial advisor. No. She needed to come to the conclusion herself.

"The Citizenry is where you have always performed your civil service. But is it the only place such services could be performed?"

That was it. He needed only to hold up a mirror to the city for Sami to see the opportunities lying in wait. He could now see the wheels turning in her eyes. He'd seen that very expression on the faces of sinners right before they accepted the Light of the Faith. One final nudge should do it.

"You see, my child, the Filth reside with us. We shelter them. Clothe them. Feed them. And they act as our runners, transporting goods between churches and Faith Centers beneath the Mantle. It's their life's work. A tradition that goes back to the early Faith foundations that gives them purpose on this Earth. Occasionally, well-intentioned families choose to open their homes and take in a Filth child as their own. But even outside the

Church, they can still perform their good works, still able to fulfill their duty in this world. My child, your purpose in life is not tied to a single group or affiliation. Your purpose is a gift bestowed upon you by God. And that gift knows no boundaries. All you need is another avenue." Solomon stretched out his hand as if offering her the church. It may have been a tad heavy-handed, but he needed to be certain the message was received.

A calm appeared to wash over Sami, and Solomon placed his hand atop hers. "I notice a peace befall you, my child."

She smirked and slipped her hands off the table to her lap. "Yes. Thank you, sir."

Solomon rose to his feet, barely able to conceal his excitement, eager to welcome his new ambassador. With someone of her youthfulness and clout as a surrogate for his message, he could reestablish the Faith as the power player it once was across the city.

"Praise be! I'm pleased to hear that," he said. But after surveying her eyes, he realized he might have been premature in celebration.

When people were touched by the Light of God, a glow would shine through them like a lampshade atop a blazing bulb. And although he could see a fortified spirit through her forced smile, the radiance was not there. The Light had not penetrated her heart.

"Thank you for your counsel," she said, turning to leave.

"God be with you, my child." Solomon pushed a smile

through his cheeks. It would be no use to speak further. And he wasn't going to give her the satisfaction of formally turning him down. He had said his piece, and God's plan would be done.

Sami stepped toward the curtain separating the sacristy from the nave, her shapely seat pressing through her tight jeans, bouncing slightly as she moved. *She should be more modest in dress,* he thought. It was for the best she didn't join.

Before parting the curtains, Sami turned back around, a snarl replacing her strained smile. "He was your brother. But you don't even care that he's gone," she said. "You didn't even ask how he died."

Solomon's skin flushed warm. "We don't choose our kin, my child. But we do choose our own paths."

"He cared a lot about you, protecting you at great cost to himself. Wouldn't it be *godly* to display a little more compassion?"

He winced at her words, anger clawing to the surface. Perhaps it was discharge from the fresh wound of rejection, or the years of history between him and Jericho reduced to a simpleton's understanding of what brotherly love should resemble. Either way, his rage was too much to hold back.

"My child, from the pain you're harboring, I can see that he meant a lot to you. I can also see from the work you commit yourself to that you are an honorable person. But in spiritual matters, you know not what you speak of. Siding with sodomites and addicts while scoffing at the path of righteousness. Damnation will befall all who dare challenge the laws of the Creator. You ask why I don't care that he's gone. His physical death means nothing. I grieved his death years ago. I prayed for him each night with such vigor, my knees would bleed from the countless splinters. Don't dare presume what I do or do not care for. All things come from God. That which we love and that which we despise. Once you accept that and understand that everything is part of a grander plan, perhaps then, maybe, you will stop pestering others with these silly little questions."

His tongue had always been his greatest source of power, inspiring people to come to the Light. But it also had the power to ruin.

Solomon watched Sami leave the sacristy. The revival of the Faith was coming. It just wouldn't be through her.

CHAPTER 5

ATLAS'S DISEASE

The Citizenry Hall was unassuming, resembling several of the old factories lining the industrial sector of Bottoms Edge: a gray brick exterior with a handful of windows. The live bushes edging the entranceway were the only hint it housed something outside the ordinary. Most greenery underside was made of plastic or silk—or anything else that could keep its color without sunlight and regular rain. Live plants were typically reserved for landmarks of importance; too much effort to keep them alive for the likes of the ordinary.

The building opened to a large foyer with reception on one side and dozens of waiting room chairs on the other. On Atlas's first visit before Jericho's death, the Hall had been teeming with undersiders. Laid-off workers searching for their next gig. Single mothers nearing the brink, their children darting up and down the row of seats. And a never-ending stream of phone calls echoing throughout the foyer. But now the Hall was as barren as the abandoned factories the building had been modeled after.

The squeak of Atlas's shoes cut the eerie stillness as he walked past the empty reception desk and down the corridor.

Unsure where to find Alanna, he took the path to Sami's office as a starting point, with a quiet hope he might even see Sami again. When he'd last left her after the night at Jericho's, she was despondent, mumbling something he couldn't make out. She'd been the only one who seemed to care since his arrival underside, and it would be nice to know that she was doing better than when he'd last seen her.

"You finally came," a voice beckoned from behind.

Atlas turned to see Alanna standing in the opposite wing of the long hallway.

It had been days since her invitation. Days of celebration Atlas had spent locked away in his motel room, feeble from the drink and his thoughts. She'd left him an opening to come by when he was ready. And it wasn't until he'd finished the last drops of his reserves that he felt he was.

Atlas couldn't remember much since that night at the Mantle's Shade, just a whirlwind of drunken images and thoughts of Alanna stitched together by the thread of his half-conscious mind. The only thing more visible than a blur was the silhouette of a motel worker sifting through the mess of his room. It wasn't until he awoke the next morning that he considered it might not have been someone from the motel. But beyond the few dollars he had left after buying out his room for another month, the syringe was the only thing of any worth. And that was emptied soon after his encounter with Alanna. He watched its insides sink like solid steel to the bottom of his toilet, twirling like a worm as he flushed it away. Imagining the stream of congealed fluid navigating his insides made him queasy. He'd more likely thicken the needle to a nail before considering that swill again.

Alanna led him a few steps down the hall to a small room. Furnishings crowded the space, and various pictures of Undercity landmarks adorned the walls. The aroma of daffodils and candy canes hung in the air, and the whispering sounds of the air purifier massaged the utter silence. Tucked in the corner was a small green couch, threadbare, with faded seats and ripped seams. Alanna took a seat on one side and gestured to Atlas to the other. Their knees touched as he worked to maneuver some distance between them. The closeness sent a flutter through his chest, and he could feel beads sprout on his brow. Alanna sat calmly until he settled in, then she cut him.

"I know who you are…"

The words snatched the air from the room. Atlas felt his stomach sink to his feet. The flutter in his chest hastened to a hammering. His entire body recoiled before his mind could put together a single coherent thought.

"What are you playing at?" Her words were soft but still cutting.

Atlas's vision tunneled, and nausea climbed his throat. Sweat trickled down his cheek, the beads on his brow now breaking. He considered coming clean before she could say any more. The words formed on his tongue, about to slip free, when his gut pulled on him to wait a second longer.

"Bass told me everything. That you were in the Guard. That Jericho turned you away before he disappeared…"

The air instantly returned, soft and fresh, as if the ceiling had opened up, dousing him with a wash of fresh Mantle air. Was that all? *She knows nothing.*

Atlas leaned back into the couch, his muscles loosening with relief. "You approached me at the bar," he said. "I wasn't selling anything. I wasn't asking for anything. Why embarrass myself sharing the rejection? I didn't even know you were Citizenry until you told me to meet you here." He had known, of course. He knew everything about her. "And by then, you were already halfway back to your friends."

The suspicion in Alanna's eyes melted away, and she smiled. "Fair enough. Then tell me… Why did you leave up top? Truthfully. There must be a story there."

There was. It involved death. Guilt. Despair.

"You ever been beyond the lamps?" he asked.

"No."

"It's nice, with the open air. Sun on your face. Stars in the sky. But expectations come with it. You have to act a certain way. Speak a certain way. Behave a certain way. And if you don't, you're made to feel…small. Like you don't belong. I never felt I belonged. Something about it never seemed right to me. But when I got down here…it just felt right. I wasn't tied to any expectations. It's liberating."

Alanna went quiet, looking at her shoes as if her response

lay beneath her soles. "I get it. I know what it's like to feel you don't belong. Feeling alone and abandoned. The need for acceptance…somewhere. But there must be something, if Jericho didn't want you around. He was always good at seeing through people. Maybe…you don't belong here as well."

The words fell on his ears like razor blades.

"I don't know," she continued. "But there's something that tells me I can trust you. It's just a feeling I have. I was like you once. The Citizenry gave me a home—a real family. It's not the life I imagined as a child, but it's the best I could ask for under the circumstances."

"What was the life you wanted?" he asked, hoping to shift the focus away from his confession.

Alanna smirked, her eyes lost in thought as if recounting a funny story from her youth. "I did want to be a dancer for a fleeting minute."

"What changed?" He knew the answer to the question and hated pulling it from her lips. But it was the natural next question, and he couldn't let on that he knew.

The hum of the air purifier swelled. Alanna sat for a moment in the silence, looking at Atlas curiously, as if struggling to decide how to respond.

"Justice," she said. Alanna jumped to her feet. The playfulness returned to her eyes, and she reached for his hand. "Come. Let me show you."

The tram stop was a few blocks from the Hall, but

Alanna's prodding, picking at Atlas's story bit by bit, made it feel miles away. Which SyndiCares home he'd grown up in. How old he was when he started in the Guard. What he had eaten last night. Although it was more like forced small talk than an interrogation, Atlas was nervous to reveal something he wasn't ready to share. She needed to trust him before he told her the truth.

They stepped onto the tram just as the Mantle lamps dimmed, triggering the lights inside the tramcar and illuminating the homeless man lying atop several seats at the back. Alanna's face scrunched from the man's odor, and she pulled Atlas to the front of the car, where they took their seats. Sitting across from him with her hands folded in her lap, she stared out at the passing Undercity. Atlas couldn't help but watch her eyes grow at the sights hurrying past. It was as if it was her first time in Lower Midian, taking in the scenery beneath the lamps. Nothing else seemed to exist. He wondered whether it was a quiet confidence or utter madness that could force a barrage of questions one moment and peaceful calm the next. Perhaps a bit of both.

As if feeling Atlas's gaze, Alanna turned to him with wide eyes and a spirited smile. Her skin shone under the white fluorescent lights, her dark green eyes drawing him in. A tickle stirred in his stomach until his sinking heart smothered it still. He needed to focus. Atlas flashed the dead bodies in his mind to ground himself. To prevent his feelings from escaping unleashed. But forcing darkness in a valley of sunshine was no easy feat, especially when he'd been starved of the warmth for so long.

They exited the tram at Bottoms Edge station. Atlas had seen parts of the neighborhood before but had never explored this deep into the ghetto. Unlike most of the Undercity, the streetlights were sparing, blanketing the area in shadows. Apartment buildings and walk-ups lined the roadway, with large cracks in their exteriors providing shelter for the rodents that scurried along the streets.

Across from the station, Atlas watched a Faith preacher scream promises of damnation to all who turned a deaf ear to his calls. The man's long, dark overcoat reached for the ground, settling around his ankles. And his broad-brimmed, high-crowned headpiece shielded his face from the gobs of spit plummeting from the open balconies above.

Alanna pulled on Atlas's hand, leading him through the filthy streets toward a darkened opening at the end of the road, beyond where the cracked pavement devolved into pulverized rocks and concrete, a sunken hollow stretching miles into the darkness. Soft flickers of light fluttered on and off, flashing momentary glimpses of rundown buildings and abandoned vehicles.

"We're going down there?" Atlas asked.

"You're not afraid, are you?"

"No, of course not. It's just… I'm not wearing the right shoes for spelunking."

Alanna's laugh echoed across the chasm. "You'll be fine. Go on," she said, nudging him toward the slope.

Atlas stepped slowly down the darkened hill, sliding the steep portions and dancing around the scattered rock debris. He could feel Alanna on his heels. The firm crunch beneath her feet resounded with a confidence he was unable to match. It wasn't until he was sure of his footing a few steps from the bottom that he turned back to check on her. Alanna walked the slope as if strolling along an even path, smirking at Atlas's caution.

"See. It isn't that—" Her foot slipped a rock free from the hard dirt, and she stumbled forward. Atlas was able to maneuver quickly and grabbed her before she tumbled. The force of her fall pushed him backward down the slope. He clutched her tightly as his back crashed against a stone pile built up at the bottom of the hill. His eyes clenched at the dull, crushing pain radiating along his backside until he felt her warm breath on his face. He opened his eyes. Alanna's face was now inches from his. He could feel her breasts against his body, and the pain faded beneath the realization.

She lingered for a moment before rolling off him, pressing all her weight down further. A sharp stone tore at his back, snapping him from his emotions. Atlas buried a dull groan and climbed to his feet, doing his best to mask the pain. Without a word or a glance, she continued to the street, only stopping to look back once she reached the dimmed streetlight.

"You coming?" she called out.

"You're welcome," he said under his breath.

Atlas sucked back the pain and stepped gingerly toward the street.

The streetscape of the Bottoms was far different from anywhere else in the Undercity. The scent of rotting eggs replaced the signature aroma of fried foods, and the moist and shifting ground made it difficult for roadways to lie flat and buildings to stand erect. Most homes were supported by makeshift walls replacing the crumbling original structures, and tarps were draped over many of the buildings to conceal gaping holes in their roofs. Beggars and junkies were strewn openly along the sparsely lit streets, as the alleyways remained reserved for large piles of trash and debris.

Walking along the cracked and uneven sidewalk, Atlas was struck by the undeniable scent of death. He blocked his nose with the rough part of his hand and searched for the source.

"Don't bother," said Alanna. "It's one dead animal or another. It's like they come down here to die. You'll eventually get used to the smell."

"I don't know if I'd want to."

She glanced at him briefly before returning her gaze to the street. "Must have been nice growing up with all that fresh air, huh?"

A wave of regret ushered away his disgust. "I'm sorry. I didn't mean—"

"It's fine," she interrupted. "I can't expect you to ignore how you lived, can I?"

Atlas refused a response, his tongue proving unreliable under the circumstances.

"It's not pretty down here, I know that. It used to be the city's landfill way back when. So, what can you expect? But it's home to thousands. The only home they'll ever know. I was lucky enough to get out. But most won't. Children growing up down here know nothing but drugs and famine. They're primed to repeat the cycle. So, when I speak about justice...this is why. These people need someone to be on their side. And who, if not one of their own?"

Atlas was taken with her sense of duty. Taken with her commitment. Despite everything she'd been through, she was still driven to help others. Still willing to sacrifice for some higher purpose.

"That's...pretty great," he said, admiration overwhelming his sheepishness. "Taking care of those who can't help themselves. I couldn't think of a better purpose in life."

Alanna let out a soft breath. "Not many people have the luxury of choosing their life's purpose, Atlas Ramsay. Most have it handed to them. And it's usually one hell of a motivator."

They came up on an old, neglected home at the end of the way. Except for the boards over the front windows, the house was showing no signs of repair. Most of the siding had bowed from moisture, and the sagging roof was on the verge of collapse under the weight of a mossy growth. The planks of the front steps had snapped in two from rot, and the wooden porch was riddled with holes from vermin living beneath.

"It looks abandoned," said Atlas.

Alanna climbed the sides of the broken planks up the porch and navigated the holes on top before pushing her way inside. Atlas mimicked her footing and followed right behind. The tiny home was lined with faded floral wallpaper and adorned with various knickknacks and photographs, all coated with a thick layer of dust and grime. Alanna disappeared into one of the side rooms, closing the door behind her. Atlas took the hint and pressed on into the main room.

A cramped kitchen was off to the side, bleeding into the living room with a filthy shag rug marking its border. The room housed a tired red couch, dusty armchair, and a small wooden coffee table, defiled with ringed water stains. There was a framed photograph sitting on a pile of old magazines used as a makeshift end table. Atlas wiped the glass clear with his hand and examined it closely. The image of Alanna in the arms of her mother as a child sapped the strength from Atlas's knees. He collapsed into the armchair, and a plume of dust enveloped the room. Choking on the filthy air, he leaped from the chair into the kitchen. He reached for an overturned glass on the counter and filled it to the rim with the discolored water pouring out of the tap. Before the glass reached his lips, a hand shot into focus and slapped it to the floor, shattering it against the filthy floorboards.

"Are you nuts?" said Alanna, pulling a pitcher of water from the refrigerator. She poured Atlas a fresh glass of cold water and handed it to him. "You can't drink from the tap down here without boiling it. It could kill you."

He finished the tall drink and thanked her.

"I guess we're even now," she said.

Alanna stepped over to the sofa a few steps from the kitchen and sat down, clutching a throw pillow to her chest.

"This was your home?"

"It's my nana's home. It's where I grew up."

At that moment, a small, frail old woman sauntered in from one of the side rooms, wearing a blue housecoat and plush slippers. Her tight curls clung to the rollers trapped in her silver hair, and her eyes were almost unrecognizable through the thick panes of her glasses.

"Lana, dear?"

"Yes, Nana?"

"When will your mother be by? She hasn't picked up that dish I borrowed from her last week."

"She'll be by later, Nana."

"Oh, good! Please wake me when she gets here."

"I will."

Atlas's breathing deepened, his pounding heart reverberating through his feet.

"She's gotten worse," said Alanna, staring blankly. "When I was little, she could go a month or two without forgetting. I could almost live normally for that short while. But under it all…under any joy or excitement…there was always a fear. Was today the day she'd forget?" She clenched the pillow tighter. "No child should ever have to see the death of their parents. But what's worse is a child having to relive that grief over and over. Reminding their grandmother of the horror and watching her suffer through the pain…every few weeks…again and again. No child should have to live through that…" Her voice trailed off into a whisper.

Atlas could feel the panic ignite, climbing his chest. He leaned back against the countertop to stabilize his footing and hauled a deep breath.

"You're not looking so good," said Alanna.

Atlas tried to force a smile to show he was okay, but it was as if he had forgotten how.

"You're probably gonna need an inhaler if you're gonna stay underside," she said. "Doesn't look like your lungs can handle the thick air."

He wished it was his lungs. At least then there would be a remedy. A solution to his anguish. But what cure was there for him? What treatment existed for a guilty conscience? Only a bullet to the head, he figured.

CHAPTER 6

SAMI'S CREED

Sami was surprised to hear the light crunch of peanut shells beneath the servers' feet, zigging and zagging their way through the pub. She hadn't noticed the sound before. But then again, she'd never been in the Mantle's Shade without the television blaring a match or the monotone anchor from the news. She glanced about the crowd, scanning the faces of the Local Citizenry leaders. She knew these men but was unsure how they'd react to what she had planned. As a child, she would listen to her mother spend countless hours trying to persuade these very same men for far less than what she was about to ask of them. Some of her mother's battles had even led to the bedroom, where the sounds of convincing took on other forms. She always seemed to get her way in the end—even if it meant a trip or two to the doctor for a shot of the cleanse. But still, their stubbornness was legendary.

The musty stench of spilled drinks and cigarette smoke displaced the clean air in the room, and the sound of beer glasses clanking added to the chorus of murmurs. Sami had erected a small stage in front of the bar, only about a foot off the ground but enough to make sure everyone could see her while she spoke. She surveyed the room while standing on the floor next to it, waiting for one more to arrive. The jewel in her crown, if she could get him. But she knew it wouldn't be easy. If the others had been legendary in their mulishness, Marcus Bertram was nearly mythical.

Marcus was of the old guard in the Citizenry's top ranks. Responsible for most of Midian's food supply, he oversaw the farms and processing plants beyond the Wall. Although principled at his core, he didn't care for facts, instead relying on his gut to steer the ship. The problem was his gut was often at odds with the right decision. *The gut is where shit is made*, her mother would say when speaking of Marcus. But despite his hard head, he was well liked among the Locals, having been with the Citizenry since he was a child. He was even considered for central leadership at one time but chose to step aside for Jericho. It was Marcus's approval that pushed Jericho to the top—a kingmaker. And Sami knew if she was going to convince many of the men in the room, she would need Marcus on board.

The doors swung open with a weight that seemed to lift most from their seats, and Marcus trotted in with two of his ginger-kissed sons at his side. He was a stocky man with a full beard and thick red hair, making him easy to spot despite settling in at the back of the crowd.

Sami took a final sip of her drink before climbing the stage. "Welcome, everyone." Her attempt to quiet the clamor went unnoticed. "Everyone! Can I get your attention, please?"

The noise instead grew, and she looked to Jasper, standing next to the stage. He shrugged.

Sami grabbed the large pub ledger on the bar and brought it down hard against the varnished wood surface like a gavel. Most ignored the thud, and the rumble of the crowd continued.

"QUIET!" a deep voice boomed from the corner of the pub.

The room instantly hushed. Sami knew that voice. She peered beyond the now silent crowd to a pair of sharp green eyes buried beneath a thick, shaggy mane of white hair. *Uncle Rupert.*

Rupert Umber was the underboss of her Local and had been a regular visitor in the Salem household when she was growing up. Most mornings, Sami would wake to Rupert's hearty laugh, paired with the sound of fried eggs and blood sausage sizzling on a hot skillet. As a child, she cherished every moment with him, hanging on to each word of his tall tales of Local happenings. But over time she found him more a nuisance than a novelty. The breaking point was when he'd chased off her first date, the crush of her teenage years, answering the door bare-chested with a sledgehammer slung over his shoulder. Rupert was always working one odd job or another around their home. And at that time, he was tearing down a portion of the back porch, fixing the rot that had set in. But he didn't share that with poor Seth Finnes—who had arrived for their date with flowers, fleeing with nothing but soil. A vicious argument followed. Doors slammed. Screams and yells carried through the small two-room house. Her mother was just arriving home when Sami spoke the words that pushed Rupert from their lives forever: *"You are not my father!"* She could still see the pain on his face. The words struck him harder than the sledgehammer resting on his shoulder ever could.

Sami had lived with regret since that day. Her porch still unfinished. Her home sapped of warmth. And her mother's final days sipping her coffee alone to the static-imbued sounds of the radio.

Rupert grimaced under his thick beard and climbed his large walking stick to his feet. "I have very few moments left in my pathetic life, and I'm not going to waste one listening to you all natter among yourselves!" He eased back into his chair and directed his cane toward the stage. All eyes were now on her.

Sami took a moment to drink in the silence before speaking. She could almost feel the stares, like a thousand little fingers pressed gently to her skin. She had wanted their attention, but now that she had it, she wished they'd look away. It was uncomfortable. Distressing. And she wondered how Jericho had seemed to manage. *Jericho.*

"Jericho is dead!" she said. Her heart leaped as the words left her tongue. "He didn't disappear. He was killed by one of our own." Her palms moistened. "And now that person heads the Allied Citizenry and is working to end our way of life."

Whispers broke out, and she braced for an eruption of outrage. But all that fell on the bar was a soft mutter that soon faded, the crowd resuming their stoic stares. Sami's head darted from face to face in disbelief, her breathing deepening to a struggle. She turned to Rupert, but his eyes were as still as the room. Her panic swelled with the growing silence until Jon Denton rose to his feet. An old Black man with short hair and wide-set eyes, Jon was a giant in the history of the Undercity. Always standing up for what was right. Defending the people mistreated beneath the lamps. Knowing he was by her side instantly extinguished Sami's frenzy. But when he motioned to the others at his table to leave, the undeniable truth could no longer be ignored. *They don't care.*

Several followed Jon's lead and started for the exit: Fredrick Wallace, Bartholomew Minsk, Jonah Turret.

Sami had sat with these people over the years, watching them shower Jericho with praise. Hanging on to each word that left his lips like children raptured by some adventurous story. She watched as they celebrated his achievements, claiming to aspire to his bravery. But now they simply whispered and walked out at the news of his death. His murder.

More from across the bar slipped from their seats and began filing out: Randolph Stintz, Derick Lowder, Abraham Bresden.

Sami smelled sulfur in the cloud now enveloping her sight. Red. Everything was red.

"WHAT'S WRONG WITH YOU ALL?" she screamed.

The pub stilled.

"Jericho was murdered! And you all act as if I just told you we're out of beer!"

Jon Denton stood in the doorway, arms folded, a look of pity on his face. "What would you have us do?" The words fell from his tongue as if spoken in charity, humoring her emotions.

Another voice followed. "Are you gonna lead us in revolt?" It was Marcus, of course.

The crowd chortled, and the weight of what she was trying to incite struck her, stealing her breath as the anger melted. She remembered the old stories her mother had told her as a child. The stories of the Undercity Wars. The stories of Jon and Marcus.

Jon Denton had not only fought side-by-side with the early Citizenry leaders, but he also fought them from within, rebelling against the Faith racial exegesis pervasive at the time. He single-handedly changed the lives of hundreds of thousands beneath the Mantle after splintering off and forming a competing faction of Black leadership. With the Locals throwing their support behind him, the Syndicate soon followed. He could have torn down everything. Started fresh. But he only fixed what was broken, sacking the entire cast of central Citizenry officials before combining the two factions into one: the Allied Citizenry. Even though he could have led for years with the full support of the people, he wanted to make sure the past was washed away and stepped down to clear the way for Jericho.

And then there was Marcus. Despite all his bluster and hot wind that could float a balloon to the stars, he had stopped the annexation of the underside-owned farms, preventing the

Syndicate's AgriCorp from monopolizing the food supply. Going toe-to-toe against the full weight of the SyndiGuard, Marcus had risked everything after they ordered a full-on incursion into the crop fields surrounding the city. He set the fields ablaze, forcing them into submission; the thick black smoke enveloped the Uppercity streets, smothering out any topside support for their plans.

These men had all done great things. *Who am I?*

From the corner of the room, another voice rumbled, "SIT DOWN! EVERYONE!" Rupert struggled to his feet. "In case you all have forgotten, Samantha here is Serena Salem's little girl. Which of you don't owe loyalty to that fact?"

The pub went silent.

"Anyone?" His eyes bulged. "Okay, then! Sit down and shut up!"

Sami's eyes moistened as everyone returned to their seats. She appreciated Rupert's help but wasn't sure what more she could say. Her entire pitch was to stand on the anger of Jericho's death. Without that anger, it would be impossible to convince them.

Rupert shot Sami a reassuring nod, and she hauled a deep breath, purging any thoughts of inadequacy before continuing her pitch. "We've worked so hard over the years fighting the scourges wreaking havoc in our communities. We've earned our independence from the Syndicate and rarely have them involved in our daily lives. We've enjoyed peace and prosperity. A complete Guard-free Undercity. We've won so much. But it isn't enough for

Bass. He wants more. And he wants to take the fight up top to get it. But if he does, we will lose everything. Our freedom. Our independence. Our lives."

Marcus stood and cleared his throat loudly to gain the crowd's attention, making sure everyone was blessed by his pearls of wisdom. "I hate to break it to you, honey, but not all of us here were fans of Jericho's pacifism. Sure, we made gains. That can't be denied. But even with our 'independence,' we're still livin' under the thumb of corporate slave masters. And I, for one, would rather die fightin' for something than live beggin' for nothin'."

Many in the crowd cheered. But with Rupert propping up her confidence with continued nods of encouragement, Sami was emboldened.

"So, you're choosing to fight with him?" she asked bluntly. Her mother had always said that forcing a man to decide on his feet was never a good idea. *The only brains men use when challenged are the ones in the coin purse between their legs,* she'd say.

"Maybe," said Marcus.

Sami let out an exasperated sigh. "Look, if we do that, the Syndicate will retaliate. They'll send in the Guard to dismantle the entire Citizenry structure. Cave in our tunnels and claim our Local offices as their own. We'll be branded as terrorists, and our people won't even be able to sneeze without a consent missive."

"Honey, if I made every decision guided by fear, we'd all be wearing diapers and sucking down bismuth from the AgriCorp *fresh* foods we'd be forced to buy," Marcus retorted. Cheers and laughter echoed throughout the bar.

Sami did her best to remain composed, but their stubbornness was eating away at her patience.

"Okay. Then fight," she said frankly. "Join the row of bodies. And when we lose, and a power vacuum is opened, let Asher pick up the pieces and crown himself king of the Undercity."

The ruckus quickly died to a murmur, and she knew she had struck a nerve.

"Then we can't lose, can we?" said Marcus. "In fact, when we win, we can finally put all Asher's rich friends up top out to pasture. And without them, he'd be all alone. The way I see it, tearin' this shit down is a win on two fronts. Bye-bye, Syndicate. So long, Asher Punsch. Honey, you've done gone and convinced me."

Sami hated to say what was on her tongue but needed to bludgeon her way through his hard head. "I see you have your two sons with you, Marcus. Where's your third?"

The red on Marcus's face now matched his hair and beard. "DON'T YOU TALK ABOUT MY SON!" he bellowed.

"I know your anger," said Sami. "I feel it too. We all know someone ruined by Asher and his venom. So, it's curious that you'd be on his side?"

Marcus's skin softened pink. "You're not listening, dear. That's not—"

"Oh, I'm listening. But you have it wrong. In his little

venture to destroy the city, Bass has called in Asher for funding. They're teaming up. A dynamic duo. And do you think Asher is supporting Bass because he thinks Bass will win? No. He sees what he can gain from it. He knows Bass needs to borrow a gun if he's going to shoot himself in the foot."

The bar hushed. Not even Marcus stirred to speak. Asher was hated unanimously throughout Lower Midian. If they couldn't be moved to action from Jericho's death, their hatred of Asher was the next best thing.

Jon rose again from his seat. "But if Bass does win—"

"He cannot win," she said solemnly. "Even if the Syndicate loses, he doesn't win. Their corporate members will flee the city with everything in their coffers, and we won't have a penny to keep the lights on."

"We could replace the Syndicate with Citizenry operations," said Jon, more with curiosity than as a matter of fact.

Sami tried to avoid it but knew it would eventually come out. It had to if they were to understand the stakes involved. But being aware of the possible fallout, she felt a pervading sense of dread seep in.

"That might work if we had something in the bank that we could use to rebuild. But Jon…we're broke."

Sami scanned the confused faces in the room, her heart in her throat. The worst was yet to come. The next words from her mouth would leave Jericho's legacy in tatters. But the consequences of not revealing the Citizenry's closest-held secret was far greater than a tainted legacy.

She continued. "Our casino. Our businesses. Our exports to the other states…none of it's enough to keep us going as we are. It's never been enough. The Syndicate has been funding the Citizenry for years—"

Bedlam erupted. Sami watched as their confusion devolved into pure rage, all directed at her, the last holdout of Jericho's loyal few. They had all proven their fleeting allegiances while she stood firm. Defending him, even after his death. She felt the soft patter of shelled peanuts shower over her. And despite the cries of *traitor* and *whore* cutting through the ruckus, all she could think was how thankful she was the Mantle's Shade had switched out their complimentary walnuts for their softer cousins.

Rupert again took to the floor. "QUIET!" He looked to the stage with cautious disbelief. "Sami. My patience is wearing thin. I won't be able to defend you if this is some sorta ruse."

"No ruse, Uncle. Just the truth." She looked over the crowd, now seething in their seats. "Years ago, after the fighting over the Wall, the Syndicate decided that funding the Citizenry would be easier—and cheaper—to maintain control of Lower Midian. Jericho used that money to build up our infrastructure, social programs, and everything else we have. As far as I know, they haven't cut the payments yet. But they will soon enough. Once they learn about Bass's intentions, there will be no incentive to continue their funding. We will be left unable to support our people, fighting a war we don't have the resources to win. Setting Asher up to take control of the entire Undercity when it all falls."

The rage in the room was deafening, and Sami wondered if they'd heard anything beyond the truth of the Syndicate's funding.

"Then let me ask you again." Jon's voice cut through the silence. "What are you proposing?"

"Many people underside are loyal to Bass. As head of the Citizenry Patrol, he's worked for years building up his support. The protection he's given the communities. Keeping the street gangs at bay. I bet that even some of *you* would never turn against him. And now, with Asher on his side, I'm not naive enough to think we could ever convince him to stand down. So…I'm asking that you join me and leave the Citizenry." The clamor swelled once again, but she wouldn't be deterred. She continued her pitch, shouting over the groans. "We will start something new. A new faction. We'll make arrangements with the Syndicate ourselves in exchange for the peace and freedom we have now."

Sami stared silently out across the room before looking to the back. Marcus sat defeated, eyes on the floor, before her pause shook him from his thoughts. He looked to the stage, and she implored, "Please."

The room fell quiet until a voice rang out from the depths of the crowd: "FUCK OFF, CUNT!!!"

Many started for the exit. Panic set in, and she looked to Rupert, hunched over with his head pressed to his cane. Two. Six. Ten. Eighteen people and counting. All exiting with the urgency of a losing fandom, trying to beat the rush out of the parking lot before the match let out. *It's over.* Bass would hear about the meeting before the end of the night. And without the Locals' support, she'd soon find herself surfing the topside of an elevator, struggling a dying breath.

But when the chaos of the exodus settled, more than half of the Local leadership remained, including Jon and Marcus. Yet, from the morose stares, she could tell those still in their seats were teetering on the edge. She hadn't yet sold them. All she had done was clear the noise.

Marcus stood calmly until her eyes made their way to the back of the pub. "You must know, Samantha, we would have never stood for what Jericho agreed to." His somber tone was a marked shift from the boisterous arrogance Sami had come to expect. "But now you ask us to leave our posts for their blood money. You're askin' us to put aside who we are as a people and submit to their will."

"No. I'm not asking that at all. I'm asking that we reclaim our posts. Choosing what's best for the people over what's best for our egos. Like it or not, the Syndicate controls this city. But because they do, they also have an obligation to its success. Asher's obligations end at his mirror.

"We need to get the people on our side now. The Syndicate will only bend to strength. And once we take back control, we won't have to continue with Jericho's agreement. We can make our own agreement. Bury the history. Start fresh." Sami turned to Jon, looking past the fear in his eyes. "It's been done before. We can do it again."

Jon wore a tamed exasperation. "Yes. It was done before. Many years ago. But under very different circumstances." He winced from the pain of the memory. "This is not that, Samantha. We fought for our rights. Rights everyone should have. That's how we won the support. Anyone with two eyes could see the truth of it. This…this is different. This is a grab for power for the sake of power. Is Bass an asshole? Yeah. He is. Even his fervent supporters would admit it. But his heart is still with the people. That will always resonate with some."

"Then we'll resonate with the rest," she said. "If we can't convince the diehards, then we'll be the opposition. Show them how wrong they are. Shine a light on Asher's plan. Maybe we can convince enough people to have Bass reconsider. I don't see him making such a bold move without the people behind him. Without *you* behind him."

Marcus slipped a quiet laugh. "I think you give him too much credit, Samantha," he said. "I don't think that son of a bitch will ever stop. Even if it was just down to him and Stixx. Regardless… I'm with you, honey."

"So am I."

"We are too."

Discussions went on through the night. Jon was tasked with putting together Local assets before Bass could order their seizure. And Marcus and the others agreed to rally support among undersiders. Sami was certain Bass would hijack the screens in the Marketplace, and they needed to reach as many people as possible before the punch was spiked.

After everyone had left and the high of the evening waned, the emotions Sami had choked back all evening broke free, and she sobbed.

"You're stubborn, like your mother." Rupert pushed through the door leading from the kitchen, waving a drumstick in the air. Grease trickled down his thick, furry hand and splattered onto the freshly swept floor.

Sami wiped her eyes and tried to mask the emotion cutting her voice. "You're still here?"

"I always enjoy a snack after a little snooze. Sorry I missed the last part of your plannin', but I'm gettin' old, darlin'. I could barely keep my eyes open during all that excitement." He ripped off a piece of the leg with his teeth and eased into the seat next to her with a groan. "Don't mean to interrupt, but I gotta sit a little before I head out."

"Interrupt? You're not interrupt—"

"Cut the bullshit tough talk, Samantha."

She felt herself blush. "You can tell?"

He laughed with the deepness of his belly. It hadn't changed in the years it last echoed through her home. "I can't tell shit! All I know is how hard I was pissin' myself when I took over my Local. You're going after the entire pitch! You'd have to be dumb or crazy not to be afraid of fuckin' up. And I've known you since you were shittin' in your trousers. You ain't either." He took another bite of chicken, and a speck of grease dabbed Sami's chin. "But you have to know…it ain't gonna get any easier. Bass isn't gonna take this lyin' down. I've known that piece of shit for years. He doesn't fuck around when someone stands in his way. Hell, with Jericho missin', everyone just assumed Bass killed him. The man doesn't stop."

Sami tried to pull together a confident reply, something to show Rupert she was ready to handle whatever came. But her response drowned under the image of Jericho fighting for breath. She hadn't been able to stop Bass then. She wasn't sure she could stop him now.

"Thank you," she said. "For everything."

Rupert's eyes glistened before he raised a thick hand in the air, pointing to his palm with the half-eaten chicken leg. "You see this? You've had me since you placed your precious little hand right here. I'm with you, darlin'. I'll always be with you."

She leaped from her seat and hugged him tightly. Over a decade of bottled-up emotion released in her grasp. She wanted to apologize. She wanted to let him know she didn't mean what she'd said all those years ago. But the words wouldn't come out.

"Okay, now. That's enough. I'm gonna get chicken grease all over you. Not to mention, Mrs. Umber might get jealous. She hasn't gotten so much as a handshake from me in years."

"Sami," said Jasper, peeking through the front double doors. "I'll be out here when you're ready to go." He nodded to

Rupert before closing the door behind him.

"You chose that little twerp to knock boots with?"

She was taken back to the night Rupert had chased off Seth. But without the hormone-induced hysteria of adolescence, she now felt warm with the thought of his concern. She had driven him out of their lives by claiming he wasn't her father. But she'd been wrong. Rupert was the only person who ever deserved that title.

"He's sweet," she said.

"That may be so, but there's a reason vermin enjoy sugar. It's easier to digest. Why don't you find yourself a real man? Someone who can protect you?"

"I can protect myself, Uncle. I did learn a thing or two from you."

Rupert let out a hearty howl that filled the empty pub. "After how you handled yourself with old Marcus and Jon, I guess you have." Pride glinted in his eyes. "Your mother would be proud."

CHAPTER 7
ATLAS RETRIEVES

The empty streets flashed by Atlas's passenger window as the engine hummed through Uptown Grove. The Grove's residential roadways were lined by detached housing, turf-laid parks, and long stretches of shops and eateries that exploded at night with families. According to Alanna, it was also a Citizenry stronghold, housing many of the tunnels and outposts scattered throughout the Undercity.

Alanna gripped the steering wheel, maneuvering around the foraging rats along the streets' edge and turning into an underground parking garage. She waved at the attendant to open the boom gate and followed the circling pathway inside. It spiraled deeper and deeper beneath the street, passing each parking level until reaching the foot of the garage. Atlas lowered his window, hoping for a rush of air to soothe his churning insides. He closed his eyes and clenched his teeth, awaiting the relief. But only a warm whisper of staleness trickled in. Alanna continued toward a large aluminum gate hanging from the ceiling at the end of the drive. Folding inward with crashes of metal on metal, it opened to a long tunnel hand-dug in the earth.

The tunnel stretched for miles, with wooden supports placed throughout, propping open the cavernous roadway. The light from the electric lanterns affixed to the dirt walls waned as they traveled deeper. Soon, only the car's headlamps were left lighting the path ahead, and small fragments of dirt began pattering atop the car's roof as the tunnel narrowed. Alanna briefly caught the side of the shaft with her passenger mirror, and tufts of clay and rock exploded across the windshield. Atlas's heart was in his throat, claustrophobia squeezing at his chest.

"What if somebody comes in the other way?" he asked.

"I guess one of us will have to reverse," she said, laying on the gas, the tunnel hum swelling into a rumble.

After several miles, a faint opening appeared in the distance, growing larger as they rushed toward it. The wall lanterns reignited and the shaft expanded, opening into a large, empty barn with Citizenry officials manning the pass. Alanna slowed to a stop when they reached beyond the tunnel's edge. She waved to the guard through the dirt-coated windshield before the large barn doors creaked open to the frost-kissed fields of a successful harvest. She pressed on the gas, easing from the barn to the winding gravel driveway.

Atlas looked out over the fields, brown and rotting. Blackbirds pecked at the dried wheat remnants as the glow of the sun's setting rays peaked between the hills in the distance. The fields evaporated to crust when they reached the Midian outer boundaries. Remnants of the previous world peppered the crumbling earth. Rusted-out vehicles sat frozen atop the pulverized roads that dipped beneath the ground's surface, edged by broken buildings and collapsed metal towers. Scavenger birds ducked in and out through shattered glass windows of old homes and stalled cars, clutching rotting carcasses and fill for their nests. Beyond the memories of the past, long stretches of dry land with frost-coated peaks of dirt littered the landscape for miles.

The Barrens. The vast sea of apocalyptic terrain between city-states. Although pockets of viable land still existed across the stretches of nothingness, only the most capable survivors could weather the intense isolation to tame them. In school, Atlas had learned that before the Fall, before the earth rebelled against the invasive organisms atop its crust, most of the Barrens were lush and green. Harvestable land was plentiful, and small communities would often serve the large, populous city centers with crops and other resources. Cities were not the farming powerhouses that existed today. But after the earthquakes, the tornados, the rising oceans, most of the land grew sterile. Arid. And migrations pushed the remaining people to large clusters of viable land, building entire new cities around them and leaving the previous world in ruins.

"I hate it out here," said Alanna. "I can't help but think of all the people that used to live in those buildings. It's so sad."

Atlas never considered it before. He was too preoccupied with his own shitty existence to be concerned with people from hundreds of years ago.

"Tell me something," she said. "Something happy."

He stared out into the blackness beyond the headlamps, sifting through happy tales of his childhood that might lighten the mood. There were plenty from the Home: the holiday gatherings with the other children, driftball tournaments on their makeshift pitch, bike riding through the Upper Midian streets. His childhood friendships had filled the void left by his parents—for the most part, at least. It wasn't until he was a little older, when his curiosity ballooned, that he worked to piece together his story. In the end, he hadn't learned much, but it was enough to have one thought nag at him through the years.

"I think my dad was a clown—"

Alanna's boisterous laugh shook the vehicle, jerking the car briefly before she regained control.

"That's such a curveball," she said, still catching her breath.

Atlas hadn't expected such a large response. But the joy on her face melted his momentary embarrassment, and a smile breached his lips.

"Most of the kids in the Home would make up stories about their parents. What they looked like. What they did for a living. If they were still alive. No one actually knew, of course, but they liked to pretend. This one kid, Ruben, was always getting mystery presents and extra mash at lunch. So, naturally, his dad must have been the chairman. He did kinda look like him a bit. Round and gruff-looking. But it was annoying to hear him brag constantly. So, one night, we broke into the head administrator's office to prove it wasn't true. She kept that office triple locked but never considered the window above her door. We built a ladder with our bodies, each of us kneeling on one another, and I climbed up through the open window and let the others in. She had this large metal cabinet covering an entire wall, full of all our profiles. It was locked, of course. But nothing we couldn't handle. We'd become experts over the years picking locks. Sneaking a few more treats from the commissary each night. We had that thing open in seconds using only a small pocketknife. But when the drawer slid toward us, Ruben's dad was the last thing on our minds.

"Jason's paperwork was completely redacted—nothing but his name and black bars covering the good bits. Nick's mother had been a nurse working with the elderly until her death when he was two. And my mother…was still alive. A trapeze artist in the traveling circus. Her name was Madeline. Madeline Ramsay. Nothing about my dad at all, but that was okay. I was just happy to have learned something about who I was.

"I waited years for the circus to come back to Midian after that—I'm still waiting. I wonder if she's still around. I'm pretty sure I could pick her out. But the one thing I worry about, the only thing I worry about when I think about seeing her…talking to her…is the possible news that my father was a clown."

Alanna did her best to hold back her laughter, but it erupted from her pressed lips, sending spittle to the underside of the windshield. "I'm sorry," she said between outbreaks of laughter. "It's just…it's…"

Atlas chuckled alongside her. "Yeah, I know it's dumb. But could you imagine? What if you found out your—"

Stupid…fucking…idiot. He clammed up instantly. His abrupt stillness extinguished Alanna's laughter. She sat quietly staring out to the darkened road ahead. How could he be so thoughtless?

"I wonder if it's easier not to have known your parents than to have lost them," she said. "It's a weird thought, but I question it sometimes… I was eight when mine died."

Atlas's chest tightened, anticipating her next words.

"At the Independence Day parade…"

He wished he could turn up the engine's rumble to drown out the softness of her voice. Or fling himself into the darkness of the Barrens. But she was opening up. And although the words from her lips were like barbs from a jelly's stinger, he had no choice but to let her speak.

"It was our first time going. I begged them to take me. I remember watching the floats and seeing the balloons from our apartment the year before. There was cheering and laughter and music. It seemed like a whole other world. I so badly wanted to go.

"My dad had just come home from a double shift. I could see he was tired, but as a kid, you don't really understand. To me, he was indestructible. Why couldn't he take me to the parade?

"My mother packed us some sandwiches and juice boxes—nothing special, just enough to hold us over while we were caught in the crowd. Cucumbers and cheese—I hated them, but I was so excited to go, I wasn't even thinking of food.

"I wore my best dress and stockings. And even put a bow in my hair. I had this little pink purse my nana gave me. I had never had any place to wear it before, so I filled it with rubber bands and candy wrappers—you know what every woman carries in their purse—and hung it off my shoulder so proudly.

"My stomach was in knots when the Mantle lamps dimmed. I was so excited. We tried pushing through the crowds to the roadway, but there were too many people. I remember my dad looking down at me with his tired eyes before lifting me in his arms and wrapping his hands around my legs. And like that, I was on top of the world.

"I watched as the marching band led the dancers down the road, the streetlights shimmering off their sequined outfits like diamonds, and they moved with such grace. That was the moment I wanted to be a dancer. I'd already asked my parents for too much that day, so I planned on asking them in the morning.

"Then came the balloons. They had all sorts. Large shapes and colors. Hundreds of them. Some were even made to look like animals. My favorite was the elephant. I swear it was the size of my school. It had a long trunk that sprayed water out over the crowd. My dad nearly dropped me when the crowd got drenched. My mom was laughing so hard at him, standing there soaking and miserable.

"And then came the floats. Large, beautiful creations, with lights and pyrotechnics. Each telling a story of Midian's history. From the city's founding to the building of the Mantle…and then the Syndicate. Why they forced their way into the parade, I'll never understand. It was a mammoth of a float covered in corporate slogans and symbols. And a large Syndicate logo in gold as the centerpiece; even then I thought it looked like a snake. And on each side of that monstrosity was a Guardian clutching a rifle… It was so out of place. Rifles in a parade.

"People started throwing whatever they could at them. I saw food fly. Toys. A baby's bottle. Then came the stones. The guards tried shielding themselves until one was hit with a brick. Gunfire rang out. They shot up to the Mantle, and everyone scattered. My dad was shoved to the ground, and I fell from his arms. All I could see were legs everywhere. I was lucky not to get trampled. I remember being so scared. I just wanted to get out from under the crowd. So, I squeezed my way past to the roadway…right in front of the stalled Syndicate float. The guards looked panicked, waving their guns all around. I heard my mom call out. I turned and saw her reaching for me before a loud clap shook me to the ground. When I looked up, she was on the pavement, writhing in pain. I didn't know what happened. My dad pushed his way out of the crowd and huddled over her. I'd never seen him so panicked before. He didn't know what to do. My dad always knew what to do. When he looked up, I saw rage. Pure anger. He looked past me and charged at the float. More claps. Louder. Scarier. I clenched my eyes and screamed. I screamed as loud as I could, hoping the scream would somehow take me back home to my bed. But when

I opened my eyes, I was still there. Most of the crowd was gone, and my parents lay on the roadway, lifeless. I just stood there, staring at the pooled blood in the grooves of the road. There was so much blood…and the golden Syndicate emblem reflecting off its surface."

Atlas felt the self-loathing wash over him with each word as she recounted the story. He remembered the crowd closing in. The hatred in their eyes. As if he had wronged them. As if he had walled them in. Fear overtook him. Fear had overtaken his bunkmate. It was his bunkmate's shot that ricocheted, striking her mother. Atlas had kept his cool the best he could, but he had no choice when her father charged him. Kill or be killed—or so Atlas had figured at the time. Just two scared teenagers with guns in a bad situation.

He mustered all the will he could to push through his shame. Sitting silent would do nothing to help, to earn her forgiveness. That was what his life was about now. Her forgiveness. Doing what she needed. Maybe then he could finally unlatch the rope from his leg.

"It must have been terrifying… I'm so sorry." He had never uttered truer words.

Alanna sat stoically, lost in her memories. The howling wind rushed past their windows, piercing the silence inside. Atlas watched her lips as they moved to speak. But only a soft sigh escaped.

A quiet distance later, Alanna turned off the main

highway down a gravel road leading to a small one-street town. The area appeared to have been spared from the devastation that laid waste to most of the world. Long brick buildings flanked each side of the road, splitting through the small village. Storefronts adorned the facades at street level, and apartment windows littered the upper halves. The car's headlamps beamed off the store windows, making it difficult for Atlas to see inside through the darkness. But even without the reassurance of seeing nothing inside, he was certain the town was abandoned, miles away from the rest of civilization, with arid land unable to farm. It would prove too difficult a challenge for even the most capable Barrens survivors. There should be little trouble here.

They stepped out of the car at the back of an old gas station near the end of town, locking the car's high-beams in place to light their surroundings. The sharpness of the Barrens wind cut through Atlas's clothes. Even in the late summer, it stung fiercely. Undampened, without any buildings to dull its blow or Mantle heaters to lift away the chill, the force of the wind squeezed the breath from his lungs. It wasn't until they made their way through the gas station's unlocked back entrance that the air softened.

It was dark, but his eyes soon adjusted. Old signs and posters hung from the ceiling, advertising discounted coffee and donuts. The filthy tile floors held the tracks of scavengers and the store shelves still stood tall, hundreds of years since they'd been picked clean. Alanna opened a door off to the side, and Atlas followed her inside. Stacked in the storage room among old buckets of sand and wide-headed brooms sat several plain boxes, each no taller than half a foot.

"Come on. Let's get these in the car," she said.

"What are they?"

"Medication for the rehab centers. The Syndicate charges too much, so we have to smuggle in most of our supply to meet the demand. Our people in New Manhattan scored this for us."

Alanna grabbed the first load and headed to the car. Quick to follow, Atlas reached down, gripping multiple boxes at once. But as he rose, the weight forced them from his grip. The sharp corner of the top box tore at his hand, leaving a small gash in his palm and blood dripping on the fallen boxes. He propped open the back door, bathing his hand in the car's light to examine the cut, when he heard Alanna's screams.

Atlas raced outside, stepping out into the headlamps. He could make out the silhouette of a man grabbing at Alanna as she struggled to shake free.

"Don't worry, sweetheart," said the man between her screams. "This won't take long."

The man shifted behind Alanna after hearing Atlas's feet shuffle against the dirt. His one arm outstretched across her chest, clasping her breast. The other pressed a pistol to her temple.

"Whoa, whoa, whoa," the man said. "Stop right there."

Atlas slowed and raised his hands.

"Atlas! Please!" Alanna called out.

He was frozen. Numb from the cold. Scared from the

gun. And no means to overcome the obvious lunatic pressing his pelvis into Alanna's backside.

"Good boy...good boy," the man said, slowly maneuvering around the car.

The overcast of the man's face soon dissolved under the headlamp lights when he shimmied outside of the direct glare. He was small, thin, and dirty, with a horse face and long oily hair that hung over his beady eyes. He wiped back his bangs with the barrel of his pistol, and Atlas saw the face of a boy he once knew.

"Tommy?"

The man stilled, weakening his embrace on Alanna and loosening the pistol's focus.

Alanna twisted the gun from his hand, catching him on the chin with her elbow. The man stumbled to the frozen ground, and she stood over him with the pistol shaking in her hands. Atlas rushed to her side. He watched a tear slip from her frightened gaze before he placed his hand over the outstretched gun. He pulled it from her grip and wrapped his other arm around her shoulders.

"It's okay...it's okay," Atlas whispered.

She pressed her now trembling body against his. But as if catching herself in a moment of weakness, she pushed off him abruptly, wiping the tears from her face.

"You know this fuck?" she said, her voice still quivering.

Atlas looked down at the man. His head hung, legs splayed, blood dripping from his face.

"Yeah..."

Tommy Tonsel was the runt of SyndiCares Home #3, loud-mouthed and stern-willed. Friendly as he was to the other kids, he wasn't much of a treat to the teachers, whom he tormented mercilessly. Atlas could remember the final straw for his French teacher, Ms. Lulliden, one spring afternoon. Tommy had been doodling nonsense on the chalkboard when poor Ms. Lulliden took the bait.

"Tommy, *qu'est-ce que c'est?*" she asked.

His devilish smirk said it all before a single word left his mouth. He pointed to a thick, straight line on the chalkboard. "*C'est une* YOUR MUSTACHE!"

The class erupted with laughter as Ms. Lulliden's pale skin shifted every shade of red through vermillion. Her eyes welled like two fishbowls, and the screech in her voice nearly shattered the windows, berating Tommy until collapsing to the floor.

Although Tommy had been a menace to the teachers and administrators of SyndiCares Home #3, he'd always been a good friend to the other kids—at least back then.

Atlas had taken a tumble one weekend morning during a driftball match with a group of older children. The dirt he kicked up from his fall scattered pellets and mud pies across half the field—a regular occurrence in any match worth interest. But unluckily for him, the end zone where he suffered his violent crash was, in fact, the freshly seeded garden of the head administrator. The ensuing punishment was a six-month ban on driftball—or any other *ball*—complete with the confiscation of all associated paraphernalia.

Tommy wasn't much for sports. He'd rather set fire to the toilet paper in the bathroom, flushing one end of the roll and seeing if the force of the flush was faster than the spread of the flames. But he was always up for a challenge—especially one that would relieve the suffering of his friends.

It had been about a week since the SyndiCares Gestapo had put an end to their fun when Ms. Lulliden's replacement had noticed she was one child short in the class.

"Has anyone seen Thomas?" she canvassed the room.

The class fell silent, except for a loud thumping in the ceiling above. She called down to the office to report his absence when the thumping grew faster and more pronounced. As she stepped from the room to investigate the noise, the clamor above shifted from loud clunks to small pings—hundreds of them. The register in the ceiling crashed to the floor, and scores of balls—of all shapes, sizes, and purposes—rained down over the class. The kids cheered, tossing the balls in the air as if they were dollar bills from a million-dollar windfall. But moments later, the scraping of steel and the bellow of a small child echoed through the vent of the small class. The teacher marched Tommy to the classroom with a twist of his ear. He stood in the doorway, hands bloodied and shirt in tatters, wearing a quiet smirk beneath the overhang of his blond bangs.

"Apologize now!" she demanded.

Tommy cleared his throat and glanced around the room

before shouting, "*Vive la résistance*!" and throwing his fist in the air. The class exploded again, and Tommy was pulled back into the hallway, never to be seen in the orphanage again.

For years, rumors of his whereabouts spread throughout the Home. Some said he'd been transferred. Others claimed he'd taken up runs with the Filth at an underside shelter. Even one rumor had him ground into sloppy joes. But after all the years of speculation and mystery, Tommy Tonsel now shuffled on the frozen dirt of an abandoned Barrens village, sobbing a plea for mercy.

Alanna's large, tearful eyes glistened in the headlamps. It was the same look she had as a child that night at the parade. The same look that had haunted him these many years. But this time, her eyes were fixed solely on him. Her frightened gaze cut through it all. The chill. The darkness. The memories of the little shitkicker from SyndiCares Home #3. Dousing Atlas with an overwhelming sense of duty.

Turning to Tommy, now scuttering his escape, Atlas raised the pistol. The barrel's line of sight locked in center mass. And he clenched his eyes before squeezing the trigger.

CHAPTER 8

SOLOMON'S GREED

Solomon huffed as he read the words on the page. Another foolish magus to be expelled. He turned to Sister Margaret as she sorted through a stack of letters on the sacristy table. "When was this received?"

"It should be on the envelope. I always write the date on the outside before tucking it away for your attention."

Solomon flipped over the envelope. *Three weeks ago.* He shifted a chair around the table next to Margaret's seat, tucking his long robe beneath his legs before easing in. He glared at her profile as she continued rifling through the unsorted mail. The sharp cut of her pointed nose and slim jawline reminded him of the large sea birds he used to feed as a child. The whole fish bubbling from their gullet after snatching it from the sky and sucking it down. It was an image he could never shake on the odd occasion Margaret would join him for dinner, forcing him to set his eyes on the decent-sized lumps protruding beneath her long black dress, just to make it through the meal. For all the disgust her face would herald, her body often made up for it in spades. Her round ass that would catch his attention as it jostled back and forth when she put in a little extra effort mopping the nave floor. The bob of her breasts as she walked the aisle, helping people into the pews. All images anchored further by the memory of her changing, stripped down to nothing but her panties, preparing for the Faith annual banquet. It was a terrible mistake Solomon had made, assuming her quarters were empty when he barged through the door. But the vision of her tight body improved relations between them almost instantly. The knowledge of her body being far shapelier than her habits could ever reveal pulled on his loins, overshadowing her faults. It was the only reason he continued to keep her around. It was just too bad that her face ruined it all. Spoiled like a spot of mold on an otherwise scrumptious roll.

Solomon reached across the table, slipping the long steel letter opener toward him from beneath the stack of envelopes. Clutching the flat end in one hand, he ran his fingertips over the shiny spike of the other end. The cool touch of metal soothed the radiating heat from his palm.

"Oh, here's one more from the mother," she said, pulling another letter from the stack and turning toward him with her vacant eyes of idiocy.

Solomon clasped the metal spike, pulling the letter opener from his other hand, before swiping the flat end through the air and clapping it against her cheek. The shock in Margaret's eyes only held for a moment, her tears quickly reshaping the surprise into a morose fear. Solomon watched the blood rush to the surface of her cheek, coating her pale skin a scarlet red, the air of fright dancing around her, coursing a rumor of passion beneath his waist.

He placed the letter opener on the table before extending his hand gently to her cheek. Margaret flinched as the back of his fingers softly brushed against the now throbbing welt, a tear streaming down her cheek.

"God loves not the loafer," said Solomon in a whisper. "The restrainer of news risks the damnation of the Faith."

"Yes, Your Worship." Her lips trembled.

Solomon stood and stepped to the kitchenette. "You see, Sister…we are not as flush with resources as we had been during the blessed times." He turned on the faucet and pulled a spoon from the drawer. "So, we have to make every dollar stretch." He held the spoon under the cold, rushing water, droplets splattering atop the countertop. "When news of a magus's…impropriety is revealed, we must act swiftly. Decisively." Solomon turned closed the faucet and stepped back toward Sister Margaret. "Your delay has cost us three weeks of the magus's salary." He pressed the cold spoon against her cheek. "Hold this here, my dear."

Margaret cautiously replaced Solomon's hand, pressing the spoon to her cheek as he returned to his seat.

"This man has committed a great sin in the eyes of the Lord," said Solomon. "Fathering a Filth child with a woman of his flock. A woman who had placed her trust in him. In God. And he has taken advantage. Advantage of his status. His position as an emissary of God. This cannot stand." He leaned in toward Margaret, elbows on his knees, the bitter scent of coffee staining her breath. "And we cannot sit around for weeks while he collects a check and leads countless more astray."

Margaret wiped the tears pooling beneath her eyes with her free hand before standing. "Yes, Your Worship. I will make sure his pay is ceased immediately."

"And?" Solomon asked.

"And…the child is removed. Placed at the shelter."

"And?" His frustration now caught in his throat.

A blank stare crossed the sister's eyes.

Solomon rose and placed his hands on her shoulders. "And you will have Magus Benka report to me immediately."

"Ah, yes, Your Worship."

The tremble in Margaret's arms stirred his manhood once again. He could feel it grow beneath his robe as he clutched her shoulders firmly. A quiet shriek escaped her lips as she subtly attempted to wriggle free. Solomon might have held her longer. Restrained her until his climax. But the fear in her eyes was not enough to overcome the distaste of her face. He released his grip, and Margaret quickly put distance between them.

"Thank you, Sister," he said with a large smile.

Margaret shuffled from the sacristy without another word.

Solomon pushed past the sacristy curtains and took a deep breath of the musty nave air. The scent of damp wood and incense acted as a balm for his angered soul. The smell was a reminder of the soothing peace he found in the Church after his mother's death, tied to the truth of God's promise and his ultimate salvation. He glanced about the empty central cathedral, the deafening quiet further stilling his nerves. He could feel the presence of God, even without the crowd. The power of the empty space tickling his skin. It was as if without the sins and filth of the people, the presence of God could exist wholly, uncrowded by the repugnance of man. A thought Solomon knew was blasphemous if spoken.

He stepped from the stage into the aisle, caressing the tops of the pews as he sauntered to the main church doors. The wood had become coarse and worn from use. Much of the dark chestnut stain was now diminished to a splotchy mess of pale brown streaks. Solomon had delayed the refinishing back when the Church was flush with money, opting to plate the church roof with brass tiles instead. The golden luster was magnificent for a while, until the thick underside air began tarnishing the tiles a rusted brown. Rather than a sight of God's majesty, the ugly roof of the central church now served as a reminder of the cost of vain pursuits. *I should have stained the pews.*

Solomon pushed the doors open and stepped into the street. Even with the church's proximity to the market walk, the roads lay mostly empty underneath the bright Mantle lights: the odd vagrant here and there, a stray animal scampering across the street. Solomon took in the meager surroundings, casually examining the church's stonework until his eyes reached the aging front doors. The dark red paint peeling from the thick wood accentuated sizeable slits growing lengthwise through the large planks. *The doors won't hold up much longer*, he thought. More maintenance work he had neglected, this time for a clergy trip to the Holy Land. *How we reap what we sow.*

"It's getting a little long in the tooth, ain't it?" A deep voice cut through the street silence.

Solomon felt a large body sidle up to him.

"I remember when she was a *beaut.* I didn't even mind getting dragged in every Friday as a kid just to get a glimpse of the old girl."

Solomon grinned derisively. "Yes. She has seen better years."

"She's like an old whore at the end of her days. Too many people going in and out. Not a one to show her a little tender love and care."

Solomon huffed and turned to the large wall of a man at his side. "How can I help you, Bass? Come for a personal prayer?"

Bass's grizzly laugh burst from his lips. "Yeah, sure. A prayer. That'll fix it all. How about this? You offer me a prayer, and I will help you find some leprechaun gold to fix up old faithful here." He directed his thumb toward the church.

Solomon shuddered. *The arrogance of man. Mocking the Creator and His creations.*

"Well, then. If there is nothing I can help you with, I must prepare for my sermon." Solomon stepped to the door when Bass's large paw clasped his shoulder.

"Now, now, Solomon. Just 'cause you can't help me,

doesn't mean I can't help you. Turns out, I already caught that damned leprechaun, and his gold is burnin' through my britches. I was thinkin' of makin' a donation…for all the good work you do in the Under Eastside."

CHAPTER 9
SAMI LEADS

It was Sami's first time beyond the lamps. And her first time seeing how much nicer everything was on the Mantle. She watched the calm topside streets from the back of the chairwoman's personal limousine. Cars glided across the smooth and unblemished roads as if floating on air. The buildings stretched high into the clouds like large crystal shards. There was a tranquil ambiance created by the rich vegetation ornamenting the streets. And the air was untainted and sweet, not a hint of fried potatoes. She reckoned only the air in the Faith's Paradise could rival it.

Jasper sat hunched beside her with his boot in his lap, picking remnants of dirt and debris from the grooves of his soles. Despite the opulence of everything they'd seen since arriving—the architectural wonders, rich green parks, lavish decor—he'd been most impressed with the footwear. The incessant nudges every time he spied a Guardian's shiny boot had driven her mad. She was thankful they had agreed beforehand to avoid speaking while in the limousine. It was originally intended to avoid the chairwoman's driver eavesdropping but now added the bonus of sparing her Jasper's dumbassery—even if for only a short while.

Despite her annoyance, Sami did appreciate Jasper coming along. Facing down the chairwoman and her goons might have been too much for her to handle alone. Rupert, Jon, and Marcus had all refused to be seen beyond the lamps. They assured her that the perception would be different once an agreement was in place. But until then, they were still the underbosses of many old-time undersiders, people who wouldn't get the subtleties and nuances involved in negotiations with the Syndicate. *Subtleties and nuances.* Sami laughed to herself. There was nothing subtle or nuanced about that meeting. Not with the chairwoman's right hand, Reginald Ottotop, at the table. His grease-slicked hair dripped onto the shoulders of his gaudy pin-striped suit as he ogled Sami's body when she spoke. It was as if her eyes had occasionally darted from her head and rested on her chest. Between the talks of cooperation and concessions was a parade of ribald comments and salacious innuendo. And although she had left with more than she'd expected to gain, some of that was a sense of defilement and loathing.

The limo pulled up to a park entrance at the Mantle's western edge, and they exited onto a long cobblestone walk. The sweet scent of petrichor filled the air as the pair strolled the path, edging the boundary overlook.

"Wow," whispered Jasper, stalling his feet and staring out to the horizon.

The evening sun was descending behind the distant hills, painting the ocean of the northwestern harbor a burnt coral. And beyond the few footsteps of passersby on the cobblestone, only the faint city sounds beneath their feet could be heard. Sami turned her ear to the ground, listening carefully to the Undercity life seeping through the boundary wall below.

"Jasper. This deal will change everything," she said with eager excitement on her cheeks.

Jasper paused, bending over the cast-iron railing along the Mantle's edge. "Yes. Yes, it will."

It was the same hesitation and agreement she'd heard a thousand times before but usually reserved for conceding which film they'd see or what to have for dinner. Something was wrong.

"What is it?" she asked. The evening had been full of anger. None she had shown—burying it for the greater good. But as she pressed Jasper in the moment, she knew his answer would release the beast she was battling to keep quiet.

He continued to gaze out over the lookout. "Sami… I know what we're trying to accomplish…but is it right?"

Is it right? This had been the play since the beginning. She had discussed every detail of her plans with him, even before the meeting with the Locals. And now he questioned the morality of it all?

"After all this? Now?! You want to question this, now?!"

"I know, Sami. But you heard them in there. They want to kill the Citizenry. They're just using us."

"Have you considered that *we* are using *them*?" she shot back.

Jasper's deep sigh and averted face pushed her irritation to the limit. Over the last several weeks, she had wondered whether their relationship had run its course. Whether they had simply outgrown one another. It had pained her to consider the thought. But lately, she had caught herself searching for excuses to avoid him. He was just not the same man she had once loved. Or perhaps she was not the same woman that had fallen in love.

"C'mon. We should head back," she said softly.

They continued along the boundary walk, extending along the Mantle's edge. Lampposts and benches ornamented the path, winding through the lush green park, peppered with topiary. As if moved by the evening ambiance, Jasper reached for her hand. His icy touch was coarse, scraping at her soft palm.

"It's cold up here," she said, sliding her hand away and tucking it into her jacket pocket.

She could still remember her excitement that first night when he'd held her hand. After weeks of flirting back and forth, the anticipation had thickened the sexual tension between them. Simply looking into his eyes ignited a passion she couldn't shake. The touch of his hand on hers was like pouring oil on a small flame. It consumed her. And she was his, in any way he wanted. But now, his touch was like a burnt log being doused with cold water. It was over. And she knew now for certain.

At the park's edge, they came up on the Outer Limits Tavern, one of the few places in Upper Midian housing a private lift to the Undercity. Sami had refused both the tram and a private ride to the Mantle top. She couldn't risk being undercut by rumors of her Syndicate visit, and a private lift was the least conspicuous option.

Despite the tavern outwardly blending in with the surrounding businesses, the inside resembled a typical Undercity watering hole. The air was tainted with the pungent underside aroma, and the sound of a man vomiting added to the whispers of the few remaining patrons huddled in the corner. Anti-corporate propaganda was littered throughout, in between posters of a young Jericho in various heroic poses plastered along the walls. Emblazoned on a large sign hanging behind the bar was the Citizenry creed: *Justice Arises from Resistance*. Although anti-Syndicate in tone, the bar was permitted to operate under a theme license, intended to give topsiders a glimpse into the seedy underbelly of their glorious city.

The bartender nodded at the pair as they pushed through to the back room. Despite being a Citizenry sympathizer, the bartender was first and foremost Jon Denton's brother, and Sami had assurances they could rely on his discretion.

Fashioned out of an old fishing cage and rigged up to an electronic pulley system, the lift didn't inspire much confidence in its safety. But having successfully escaped its clutches earlier that day, Sami cast aside the doubts and climbed inside. The cage eased below the floorboards, and she could feel Jasper's body press against hers. She recoiled, pushing farther up against the cage, causing it to sway. The wayward motion threatened more than her nerve, and she pressed her eyes closed.

Jasper placed his hand on her shoulder.

"Please, Jasper. Don't," she said. "I'm fine."

The lift came down at the back of an old corporate outpost extending the height of the Mantle. Being repurposed as a grain silo in Agriville, the building housed large mounds of grain trucked in from the farms beyond the urban city limits. With her feet now on solid ground, Sami opened her eyes, thankful her queasiness didn't get the best of her.

"I think Marcus should rethink how the grain is stored here," Jasper said, stepping out of the cage. "Imagine someone was sick coming down from there? They'd rain vomit all over the food." He chuckled.

Sami cringed.

They rounded the first grain mound at the front of the silo and exited onto the Agriville streets just as the Mantle lamps buzzed off for the evening. The cold eastern wind flushed through almost instantly.

"Whoa!" said Jasper. "Let's hang back inside until the streets take over."

She pressed on as if the *whooshing* wind had stripped Jasper's words from her ears. She couldn't stand to be alone with him for another moment and would rather suffer through the chill's fury.

It wasn't long before the streets were animated with passing transports and tractors, and the air warmed under the glow of the streetlights. Agriville was Marcus's Local. And much like him, it was all about the gut. Large food storage facilities and freezers comprised most of the area, with a few hydroponic bays stationed throughout. A functional neighborhood with little housing beyond the group shelters that kept the farmers and their workers near the crops. It wasn't often Sami made it out this way. But now, with the food supply in the sole hands of her Faction, she knew it was an important neighborhood to monitor. They had decided against cutting distribution to Citizenry Locals; their fight was with Bass, not the people. But there was always a chance he'd try to make a move to take it back. No quicker way to snuff out dissent than starving it.

They came upon a fenced-off lot next to a large meat packing plant a few blocks from the silo. Two shadowy figures stood just beyond the lights illuminating the open lot. Sami and Jasper pushed past the fence gate, rattling the links out over the open space. She watched one figure peel away, exiting through the darkened path on the opposite end as the other made their approach. The shadow melted from Marcus's face when he stepped into the light.

"Who was that?" Sami asked.

"Randolph," said Marcus. "Just makin' sure we're all good with business as usual. Don't want any surprises, ya know. He's a good lad, despite bein' on the other side." He began shuffling across the lot toward the plant doors. "C'mon. Let's talk inside. Rupert and Jon are waiting."

Inside the plant, reams of butchered meat hung from the ceiling, the subtle chill tinting the exposed flesh an almost pastel red. The refrigerant pumped in through the vents gave the air a scentless, cold smell. Jasper appeared queasy navigating the suspended carcasses, and Sami couldn't help but wonder what she had ever seen in him.

Marcus led them into a small room off to the side. Jon was seated atop a large metal table in the center of the room, next to a book on animal anatomy. Rupert sat hunched in the corner, taking the only chair for himself. Adorning the walls was dried blood splatter intermingled with large meat cleavers and lengths of knives Sami had never seen before. If it weren't for her trust in these men, she would have been certain of her impending death.

"Nobody droppin' any eaves way the fuck in here," said Marcus, leaning against the wall of knives.

"You know, Marcus," Jasper said. "I think—"

"They're in," Sami interrupted.

"Well, that's good news," said Jon, turning to the others with surprised pleasure.

"Hmmm… It was that easy?" asked Marcus.

Sami beamed, looking at each of their faces. "Yes. But even better than easy." She could barely hold in her excitement. "They've agreed to tear down the Wall—on top of everything else. The Wall will fall."

Sami knew that these were all hardened men. Men who would be hard-pressed to crack a smile even after a pint of the underside's best and their foot up the chairwoman's ass. But she still hoped the news would have inspired a little more than the stunned silence that had overtaken the room. She watched them glance between each other before Rupert spoke.

"Samantha—"

"No," she interrupted defiantly. "No. We're not going to do this. Can't we celebrate a win without having to sweep for a Trojan horse? Or pull out a decoder ring to search for some hidden fucking agenda? I'm so sick of it. We got a win here. A pretty huge fucking win. Something Jericho wasn't able to accomplish for decades."

"That's the problem, Samantha—would you just relax!" Rupert's booming voice shook Sami to a halt. "We'd all love to rejoice. Drink in the success. But my dear, our scars ache at the thought of how easily they would give up the Wall. After everything we've sacrificed. It couldn't be this simple."

"But it is, Rupert. Times have changed. Chairwoman Shoehorn is in charge now. Not Lutz. The Wall was *his* crowning jewel. Not hers. She couldn't care less. And besides, we're no longer at odds with them. We're working with them, hand-in-glove."

"Hand-in-glove is right," said Marcus. "Their hand up our ass."

"I think they're right, Sami," said Jasper.

Her blood steamed. She clicked her tongue and ordered through her gritted teeth, "Jasper. Wait outside." She fixed her eyes on the other men in the room as the silence swelled. A few moments passed, and she heard the door creak before it slammed shut.

"Rupert, I get it. I've worked closely enough with Jericho to understand the games they play. But I'm telling you it's different. It feels different."

"Gentlemen. Let's give her the benefit of the doubt," said Jon. "Make us understand, Sami. We are open to the possibility, but we can't just take them at their word. We have a responsibility to the people."

"I very much get our responsibility, Jon," she said. "It was the whole reason for our little union here. But let's not forget we have a common enemy. Our commitment to ridding ourselves of that enemy forced a new perspective. Giving us a win with the Wall will weaken the Citizenry. The people will see us as the legitimate authority in Lower Midian. And the Syndicate can just ignore Bass and his threats."

"We gathered as much, Sami," said Marcus. "But there has to be more to it. There's somethin' they ain't telling us. That bloody wall has been the centerpiece of our struggle against those corporate fucks for as long as I can remember. There's no way Bass has them that hard by the balls that they'd lay down their hand. I'm not buyin' it."

Midian was flipped on its head with Jericho's death. And with Lutz busy playing pickleball in his retirement, the established rules of the past were no more. There was a rewrite underway, and she wasn't going to allow the same old ghostwriters to plot the same tired tropes as before. This would be a Samantha Salem original.

"You don't have to," said Sami. "None of you do. The only thing that matters is that *I* do." She felt the self-loathing dance on her skin as the words left her tongue. Their silent stares stung fiercely. She knew what they were thinking. *Who does she think she is?* But Sami didn't even seem to know anymore.

Rupert nodded in defeat. "Okay, Samantha. But excuse me if I don't celebrate until the Wall is rubble beneath my feet."

Marcus pushed off from his lean, and the others rose.

"If we're going to proceed, I'd like to make a suggestion," said Jon. "I think it's best if we keep the deal under wraps—for now. Until we know their true intentions. Best not get our people's hopes up, and best not give Bass any more reason to do something crazy. We may wake a partially sleeping giant if he feels backed into a corner. And we can't risk that until we have the people on our side."

Sami agreed and followed them back into the freezer.

Jericho had made it all look so easy. She'd sat by his side during many meetings with the Locals. Rarely did they push back on his plans. Not like they just did to her, at least. Sami knew that blind loyalty was not something these men could offer. But she had hoped that they'd have a higher opinion of her judgment. She had learned at Jericho's feet, after all. She could feel it in her bones that the chairwoman was genuine in her intentions. Shoehorn understood the risk of Bass keeping his support and knew something drastic was to be done. How the others couldn't see what Sami was seeing—what she knew—only proved that she was the right person to lead.

Jasper was waiting when she stepped outside into the vacant lot. "Sami, can we talk?"

She didn't have the energy for the conversation. But she also didn't have the energy to put it off any longer.

The others continued on, and Jasper pulled Sami aside, looking at her with his large, soft eyes. The way the light shone down behind him, casting a shadow across his face, reminded her of their first kiss at the Harvest Fair. She still remembered how nervous she was. It had taken her hours to get ready for the evening. She had worn a leather bomber with tight blue jeans and straightened her hair with her mother's old flat iron.

The fair was set up in part of the Midriff—after the area was cleared of squatters—to allow most of the Guard to attend in their off hours. It didn't bother Sami to see Guardians walking among them. She was too preoccupied with Jasper to care.

They rode the Ferris wheel and bumper cars, and Jasper won her a small stuffed lightning bolt—there hadn't been any animals for some reason. At the end of the night, he pulled her up against the back of one of the game tents. His face was shrouded in darkness as the colorful fair lights traced him with an iridescent glow. And he leaned in for a kiss.

Back then, his supple lips could seize her fear and loneliness, taking hold of the deepest part of her. And from that moment on, he had always been there, through both the darkest and happiest moments of her life. He was everything to her. Her closest friend. Her lover. Her family.

"Sami—"

"It's over, Jasper."

CHAPTER 10
ARVIN FEEDS

The stinging blast of the eastern chill arrived with a sharpness, numbing Arvin's bones and charring his flesh as his coarse woolen clothes brushed against his soft, youthful skin. But the worst of it was breathing. The cold wind colliding with the warm underside smog thickened the air, forcing Arvin to be more deliberate with each breath. Most nights, he'd await the dampening of the evening wind before venturing out. But not tonight. Time was not on his side tonight.

He pressed on into the chill, clasping the handle of his loaded wagon trailing behind him. The busyness of a typical evening started to unfold. Storefronts were uncaged and vehicles filled the roadway. The vacant streetlamps drummed on one by one along the walkway, as if his steps triggered unseen switches beneath the concrete. By the time he rounded the corner to the Uptown Grove, the streets were awash in a glow of lights that lined the Undercity. Escaping heat from the streetlights began melting away the heaviness in the air, and the subtle warmth radiating from the passing shop doors gave Arvin respite from the ire of the eastern chill. With his stride loosening, he steadied a faster pace with the wagon in tow, alternating hands regularly to avoid jostling the load with a jerky tug of a tired arm. He was happy he'd left some of the load beneath his bed. Balancing it all while traveling the underside streets would have only slowed him down—and paint a large invitation for thieves looming in the Midriff.

Arvin approached the Under Eastside gates, paying no mind to the spectacle of foreboding warnings affixed to the nearly one-hundred-foot-high cast-iron fence. The fear of being shot, detained, or subject to another half-dozen threatened fates had been lost since his first trip to the city's military wing several months earlier. That first time had roused enough fear to cover a life's worth of crossings. Arvin could remember how shaky his hand had been presenting the missive to the hulking Guardian. A warm nervousness coated his thin, achy legs as flashes of the terrifying signs adorning the gates paraded through his thoughts. What felt like hours had passed until the guard returned the note with a smile and a nod. But by then, the puddle beneath Arvin had already crept to the soles of the guard's pristine leather boots.

Each approach to the military gates from there on had grown less intimidating, with the guards cracking wise and proving more friendly than frightening. But despite Arvin's confidence in getting beyond the Guardians during past runs, a nagging voice deep in his mind wouldn't let him forget how different this trip was from the others. Even though he'd received a missive from the Grand Magus himself for the evening's run beyond the gates, what he had stacked in the belly of his little red wagon would rouse more from the guards than a joke. He didn't know for certain what was in the boxes, but he gathered from his instructions that it was something a little less innocuous than Sister Mary Anne's beef rump stew.

With his nerve still holding, Arvin stepped closer to the gates, his wagon on his heels.

"I have to stop you there, little buddy," said an approaching Guardian, removing his rifle from his back. "I need to check your wagon."

Arvin stood boulder-still, gripping the wagon's handle, his confidence now melting with each step the guard took toward him.

"I've heard that you might be hauling contraband."

Arvin's knees buckled. This wasn't supposed to be happening. He'd been assured. He felt the blood drain from his face and pool in the pit of his stomach. *Was it a setup? A Citizenry trick,* he wondered, his thoughts drowning under the crushing weight of each heartbeat.

The guard flipped open the latch on the canvas bag wedged at the front of the wagon and peered inside. "Well, what do we have here?" he mused. Reaching into the bag, the guard eyed Arvin with an almost joyful triumph and pulled out a cellophane-wrapped slice of lemon loaf. "Now, these should be illegal," he said. "Addictive as skeet. You got the entire Guard itching for these."

Arvin's legs stiffened as the blood returned to his limbs. He was usually methodical about emptying his sack of leftovers after each run, a habit he had formed well before his adoption, when squirreling away extra snacks meant the difference between going to bed hungry or sated. But after arriving home late last night, his mother had forced his chores, and it had slipped his mind. In no scenario before now would he ever have been thankful for a sink full of dishes.

Arvin smirked politely and handed the Guardian the missive he pulled from his pocket, hoping to hurry along the charade. Time was of the essence.

The guard glanced briefly at the note before taking a second helping and signaled to his partner to open the gate. "Let the Faith runner in!"

Being home to only the SyndiGuard and the city's military defenses, the Under Eastside was not as large as the rest of the Undercity. But it was still vast enough to dwarf most underside neighborhoods beyond the gates. Guard residences and warehouses made up most structures, with a few venues for entertainment and shopping sprinkled throughout. The brown brick buildings clashed with the dark green armored vehicles littering the roadway, and the streetlights struggled to breathe any semblance of soul into the listless ambiance. Only the stars beyond the Mantle's shadow adorned the drab twilight beneath the muted Undercity lamps. But for Arvin, the stars were more than enough. He gazed past the city's edge to the blackened sky, fixing his eyes on the penetrating lights. Having grown up in the confines of the Under Westside, it was a joy he had never considered until his first run beyond the gates. And when finally struck by the possibility of witnessing a shooting star this close to the Mantle's edge, his focus rarely shifted from the night sky on his Under Eastside runs.

When Arvin was younger, some kids at the shelter swore they'd witnessed one, peering through a near-miraculous alignment of building alleyways and fence holes to see the magnificent trailing light in the sky. Arvin's jealousy consumed him for days after hearing them gush, pushing him into the shelter lot after lamps-off in hopes of lining up a similar view. But after countless tries and attempts to reconcile their story, the truth of the lie was clear. Growing up with nothing, Arvin knew only experiences had any worth, a harsh reality that often forced many of the other Filth to dream up fantastical tales to separate themselves from everyone else. This story was no different. But having felt the sting of its envy, even as a lie, Arvin now reserved a permanent seat in his thoughts for the wonder of a shooting star. A one-in-a-million view, if he was ever so lucky.

He stopped along a stretch of excavated land next to one of the Mantle's support pillars. Although not wide, the pit stretched nearly a block along the roadway, leading from a freshly filled site where the dirt had recently settled. Unable to see into the depths of the furrow, he waited patiently, taking in his surroundings. He gazed in amazement at the enormity of the Mantle pillar, at least twenty cars wide and stretching to the top of the platformed sky. Arvin tried tracing its height with his eyes, but the ground beneath him swayed.

"You're gonna get sick, kid!" a voice called out. "I always get woozy looking up like that."

Arvin looked down to see a man climbing from the darkened pit. Wearing a hard hat and reflective vest, the man brushed the dirt from his gloves before tucking them into his back pocket. He had the look of someone raised from the dirt, brown smears darkening his pale skin and large globs of mud hanging off his coated work boots. His eyes appeared vacant, as if someone was behind the wheel but wasn't sure how to drive. He reminded Arvin of the feeble man, Logan, who sat staring in front of the shelter for hours on end.

"You the Faith Runner?" the man asked, glancing toward Arvin's wagon. "Yeah, of course you are." He laughed to himself. "I'm really losing it. I guess working fourteen-hour days will do that to ya. This new fucking main is gonna be the end of me. But hell, what would the rich folks up top do if they were forced to keep drinking the same shitty water as the rest of us peasants? Perish the fuckin thought, eh?"

The man stepped forward with a tilt in his back and short, bowed steps. He gently shoved Arvin aside and began rummaging around the wagon, half-opening the neatly stacked cardboard boxes.

"Yup. This will do just fine," he said. "You didn't look in any of these, did ya?"

Arvin's eyes widened, shaking his head adamantly.

"Good. This is the sorta trouble you don't want any part

of, kid."

The man retrieved a nearby wheelbarrow and began unloading the wagon slowly, box by box. The monotony of his slow pace sent nervous jitters through Arvin's legs. He bounced in place to mask the stinging nerves, but the echoing clang of the mid-hour church bell beyond the gates invigorated the bastards further. Time was slipping away. He reached over to help the man along but was met by an outstretched arm and a stern stare. For a moment, Arvin considered abandoning the wagon altogether and heading on his way. But the wagon had been a gift from his adopted parents and made him the envy of the shelter when he'd pull up for a visit. The bright red paint and smooth wheel bearings were a far cry from the rusted-out bed and loose wheels of the old shelter haulers—or holey rollers, as they were affectionately named. His arm ached at the mere thought of finishing up runs with those three-wheel wonders. The Filth may be destined for torment and misery, but that didn't mean Arvin would volunteer himself for extra credit.

As the man finally lifted the last box from the wagon, Arvin pulled on the handle and sprinted through the excavation site back to the roadway. He could hear a faint cry from the man as he fled the site, but there was nothing he could say to slow Arvin's pace. He had wasted enough time watching the man unload with the urgency of a retiree planting their begonias. He wasn't about to spare another second for any more pleasantries.

Keeping a steady sprint, Arvin weaved up and down the dimly lit streets, relying solely on his memory of landmarks to guide him. He outstretched his neck, rounding the last corner of a large residential complex, hoping to glimpse the Under Eastside Memorial Park a moment sooner. The sharp turn brought the wagon up on two wheels before tipping over and spilling his bag onto the sidewalk. Arvin's enthusiasm instantly waned as he took in the utter stillness of the empty park. He was too late.

He dropped the handle of the overturned wagon and collapsed to the street. Pulling his knees to his chest, he fought to hold back his tears when he felt a sharp clap against his neck.

SMACK!

The stinging pain cascaded down his shoulders, disorienting him for a moment before he regained his senses and turned with a bright smile.

"You're late," said his brother. "Clean this up, and let's go."

An eager energy pushed Arvin to his feet, and he rushed to gather the scattered food from the spilled bag. He pulled the bag off the concrete and shoved each item that had fallen back inside. As he returned the canvas to the wagon, he noticed a small box that had been missed, crammed between the wagon walls. He looked to his brother patiently waiting a few steps away and decided to place the bag neatly over the remaining box.

Arvin struggled to conceal his excitement, trailing closely behind his brother into the desolate park. It had been only six months since his brother had left for his placement in the Guard, but there was already a new firmness to his voice, a new bounce to his step. Arvin tried mimicking his brother's stride, walking behind him to the steps of an old monument. The large statue of a former Guardian General was speckled white by the pigeons still sniffing around for a late-evening meal. It leered down at them with disdain as his brother poked fun at its exaggerated bulge.

"I can just imagine the meetings they had to sort that out," his brother joked, taking a seat on the step. "Good thing you snagged a run past the gates tonight. It's the only night I have free for the next few weeks."

"Yeah. Lucky," Arvin replied, unable to share how it had all played out. The Citizenry request. The promise of their help. And a signed missive from the Grand Magus of Midian. His brother would never understand the lengths Arvin had gone through for the evening to have him by his side once again.

It had been like the hand of God reaching down when Arvin was whisked from the shelter and given a bed in his new brother's home a couple of years ago. Despite the age difference, they bonded instantly, staying up through the night, sifting through his brother's comics. Debating the ingredients to their mother's wretched meatloaf casserole. It was as if he'd been forgiven for being a Filth, getting to enjoy the best parts of life. At least until the day of his brother's placement.

Arvin was certain his brother could have escaped it. Most underside Guard recruits rejected their obligation to the city, choosing Citizenry service instead. The Syndicate hadn't even batted an eye in those cases, not willing to risk an incursion into

Citizenry turf for the likes of a teenager with little to offer. But still, his brother had chosen his duty. And in doing so he left Arvin alone to plot his way back to his brother's company.

The evening continued on in a flash of words and laughter as they shared the details of the months they'd been apart. Arvin sat at his brother's feet, ensnared by the most mundane of stories. The lost retainer in the commissary. The misplaced boots recovered from the clutches of a raccoon beneath the barracks. The simple act of being alone with his brother again made it all worth it. Made it all worth the agreement Arvin had made with the Citizenry. His sneaky secret tickled the back of his mind the entire evening. The vision of his brother overjoyed to be released from his mandatory placement. All the memories they could share once again. It was almost too much to keep to himself, but Arvin knew the surprise would be that much sweeter if he waited to share the news.

After his brother returned to his barracks for the night, the excitement of seeing him again carried Arvin through the empty Under Eastside streets. His heart soared envisioning their time together and the countless hours they would spend once his brother was freed from his duties. And regardless of what the Citizenry had asked of Arvin, it paled in comparison to having his family by his side.

The squeal of the gates back to the Under Westside scraped at Arvin's bones, the sound cutting through him like the chill of the evening wind. On the other side of the gate, the guard from earlier was seated comfortably, legs outstretched against the pavement.

"Hey!" the guard cried out.

Arvin's heart sank, more out of annoyance than fear.

The guard climbed from his seat and shouldered his rifle. "You wouldn't have any more of that bread, would ya? Both loaves were gone quicker than my wife's chastity on our first night."

"…I should," said Arvin, removing the bag from the wagon.

"Watcha got there? Extras?"

Arvin looked up to see the remaining cardboard box dabbed with apparent bloodstains and crunched edges from the wagon walls.

The guard stepped closer, eyes fixed on the lonely box. Arvin rummaged frantically, his sweat shimmering in the gate lights dripping into the bag's blackened void. With his heart hammering at his chest, he fumbled for a few more seconds before dumping the contents to the ground. Reaching for the last loaf with his now trembling hand, he looked back to the guard now standing over his wagon. The top flap of the remaining box stood upright, flashing the drops of dried blood along its edge. And Arvin could no longer see the guard's face beyond the barrel of his gun.

CHAPTER 11
ATLAS PLEASED

Atlas's neck ached at the sight of Bass's monstrous mitts. They somehow looked larger than before. As did his arms, hulking through his sleeveless tee, more meaty and white. His pale pink skin looked washed-out and sickly, as if he'd blanketed himself in the shadows these past months, fueling his body with nothing but raw meat and anger.

Atlas trailed the brute, lumbering through the tight club corridor. The rush of air passing through Bass's underarms mingled with the scent of sex seeping from the open rooms lining their narrow path. Each doorway was shrouded with bead partitions, providing the guests with as much privacy as a rain-trickled window in the early spring. Atlas could see the nearly naked women toying with their evening clients through the beaded barriers, topside men dressed in corporate getups with a few underside drunkards sprinkled in the mix.

The end of the corridor opened to a large lounge area littered with plush, colorful couches and mirrored walls reflecting a pageantry of fluorescent lights through the smoke-laden space. Incense burned on the side tables, masking any remaining stink from the previous guests, and hot coals sat atop towering silver hookahs resting at the feet of broad decorative chairs flanking each side of the room. Several half-clothed women streamed in as Bass sprawled out on one of the larger daybeds.

"Relax!" he bellowed. "You've earned it. Might as well enjoy your spoils."

Atlas sat on the edge of one of the cushioned chairs, wary of the dried fluids that stained the dark fabric.

"How's the new digs, by the way?" asked Bass.

Jericho's sprawling penthouse was given to Atlas after Bass learned of the night he and Alanna had been through in the Barrens. It was a generous gesture that he'd have loved to turn down when Stixx brought him the keys. But unable to afford any more nights at the motel, Atlas no longer had the luxury of his pride.

"It's good," said Atlas. "Thank you." He didn't really want to get into the haunting images of death that plagued him each night. Or the faint scent of rotting flesh he convinced himself was wafting up from the elevator shaft. But despite the flashes of horror engrained in his exhausted mind, the flat was quite a step up from an hourly rental on the fringes of the Lower Midian ghetto.

Since moving in, Atlas had spent hours staring out through the wall-sized window overlooking the Undercity, wondering how he'd escaped the lonesome end he assumed was inevitable. If it hadn't been for Tommy's death, he'd have believed things were finally looking up. An earned respite from the years-long torment. But just as Atlas had started to stitch up the putrefying wound of his adolescence, another gash had been torn across the only unscathed portion of his being. One more self-inflicted wound to drain the remaining wisps of life that had been keeping him going. Atlas had no happy memories beyond his childhood, only regret and loathing. And now Tommy's death had tarnished the few years of joy he'd ever known. He could no longer revisit a memory without the clap of the pistol echoing in his head, every image tinged red by the pints of blood that seeped from Tommy's wound. He tried reassuring himself that Tommy was responsible for his own actions. He had forced Atlas's hand. Barrens justice was known to all who trod beyond the safety of city-states. But no matter how much he tried to convince himself, the guilt was ceaseless.

The entire ride home from the Barrens was consumed with could-haves and should-haves, the quiet between him and Alanna amplifying their calls. The evening had been too heavy for small talk. It wasn't until they arrived back at the Hall that Alanna broke the silence. She placed her hand on his with a warmth that radiated across his body, rushing over his skin and muting the deafening guilt ringing in his thoughts. And when she clutched him tightly, he could feel her heart racing, pounding through the layers of clothes between them. Her voice was choked with emotion as she whispered her thanks before pushing to her toes and kissing his cheek. The moisture from her lips settled on his wind-dried skin. And despite the blood and terror of the evening, he couldn't hold back the stirring in his loins. It took every ounce of will to restrain himself. The fear. The sorrow. The guilt. All ingredients in a perfect late-night cocktail, pressing the lonely to seek companionship in the most foolish places.

But since that night, Atlas had noticed a change. A kindness in her words that hadn't been there before. Her smile shined with pleasure when he spoke, and her eyes beamed when he entered the room. It was the only redeeming consequence of Tommy's execution. His gifted flat and newfound placement in the Citizenry ranks were added bonuses he could do without. Alanna's company was all that mattered.

"My friend's lonely there," said Bass to one of the scantily clad women lying on an empty couch.

Her smooth alabaster skin shimmered in the fluorescent lights, her large breasts bubbling behind her tight lace brassiere. Atlas stiffened on her approach—everywhere else than where was expected. The woman pressed up against him, working her way into his seat, gently rubbing his chest before sliding her hand to his lap.

Atlas shot up as her fingers grazed the crotch of his pants. "Sorry, I can't."

"Whoa! I just figured she'd be your type," said Bass. "Didn't think you swung the other way. They got dudes here too, if that's what you're into. But you're gonna have to find another room. Nothin' droops me quicker than two hanging chads."

"No, that's not it," said Atlas. "I'm just...not in the

mood."

"Not in the mood with heavies like that? That right there is what we call a mood maker. Ain't no getting a standing ovation if that doesn't do it for ya."

"Just got a lot on my mind."

Bass grinned, pushing the girls on his arms to the side before sitting upright in his seat. "Yeah, I bet you do. You're sweet on her, aren't ya?"

Atlas's cheeks warmed, and he cut his eyes to his shoes. Without even the mention of her name, he knew Bass was talking about Alanna. Atlas crossed the room and sat on the only couch void of any temptation, keeping his eyes fixed on the floor.

Bass snickered and lay back on the daybed, pulling the two women back to his sides. "Well, lots of guys have tried. Not me, of course. She's more like a little sister. But I've seen her lay waste to the hearts—and chubbies—of all who've tried. She's a good egg but hard-boiled. I'll tell ya, though, your efforts ain't been for nothin'. I've never seen her so smitten before you came around. Whatever you're doin' seems to have warmed that chilled blood of hers."

The words brought a smile to Atlas's lips, an involuntary show of joy he'd rather have kept hidden. He'd done his best to resist the temptation, focusing on nothing but her forgiveness. But each night, he found himself picturing her on his arm, going over their talks in his mind, again and again, until drifting to sleep. The thoughts replacing the drink with a much sweeter bedtime story.

Her horrid scream still pealed through his dreams, but the vision of her smile, her longing eyes, had softened its piercing edges.

The server returned with a tall bottle of champagne buried in a large ice bucket and two crystal flutes clenched between her fingers.

"Let the party begin!" hollered Bass, shooting up from his bed of now-naked consorts.

The celebration, such as it was, had been Bass's idea. Despite the slow drip of support seeping past the Citizenry levies, emboldening Sami's new Faction, Bass appeared downright giddy.

"Atlas! Come grab this." He stretched out his hand with an overflowing glass.

"Don't mind if I do!"

A cloud of silver hair pushed into the room with a rattle of beads trailing a thick mahogany cane. The man's wild mane enveloped his face, crowding the top of his worn old overcoat. Only his piercing green eyes proved he was anything but a bear dressed in men's clothing. He tore the glass from Bass's hand and hobbled toward Atlas before easing into the seat next to him.

"Didn't know topside boys won your fancy," the man said to Bass.

"Rupert! Good to see you! That there's—"

"Enough," Rupert cut in. "Unless he's willing to service my wife for me, I don't give a shit who he is." He downed the flute of champagne. "You wanna talk about the horrors underside? You should see the old battle-axe in her nightgown."

Bass slipped a few laughs, sauntering back to his web of naked women.

"Whatcha celebratin', anyway?" Rupert asked. "The way I see it, we're kicking your ass up and down the Mantle pillars. The only thing you should be toasting is the prospect of an early retirement. Or is this here one of those masochism parties?"

Bass grinned and squeezed a bare cheek lying next to him. Goosebumps stiffened Atlas's skin when he saw Bass's eyes go cold. It was the same steely look he'd worn the moment before Jericho's death.

"Well, Rupert…you win some…you lose some. You gotta stay positive. Even in the worst of times." Bass snatched another handful.

Rupert's spirited demeanor shifted under Bass's playful tone, and he nodded gently as if understanding a hidden meaning in the words. He climbed his cane and doddered over to the table with the champagne. "Twenty years ago, wasn't it?" he started, topping off his flute. "You were tough back then, too—nowhere near the callused foreskin you are today. But tough nonetheless." He eased back into one of the hefty chairs, clanking his cane against the hookah at its side and tumbling hot embers to the steel catch beneath its bowl. "You had a lot of potential. Brave. Like no one I'd ever seen. But also dumb. Fuck, you were so dumb. You reminded me of those *special* kids trying to put out the Mantle lamps with water balloons. Well-intentioned but in grave need of a short bus."

Bass sat unimpressed with a snarl, rubbing his swollen hands over the naked flesh at his sides.

"The Caravan made their way to our borders, remember? Looking for trades. New Citizens. And you had the bright idea of robbin' their armory. The armory of the only nomadic mercenaries on the entire continent. You know why they're the only ones? Because they ass-fucked every other state that tried. Enslaving their women. Executing their men. Indoctrinating their children. They're fuckin' savages. They'd have pinned you up in the vanguard, keeping you alive for years on sips of piss and stale crackers, just to send a message to anyone else who tried. I had to spend a year's worth of my Local's earnings to save your sorry ass. You're just lucky the guards that busted you were more corrupt than a democratic politician."

"Yeah, and what of it?" said Bass, shifting his gaze—and hands—to a pair of naked breasts.

"What of it? I'm at the end of my line here. Probably got half a winter before I see if the Faith's promise is true. So, I'm here to collect the debt owed before I give up the ghost."

"Hmph. What's money gonna do for you now, old man?"

"I didn't say anything about money, now did I?"

Bass looked up from his evening's entertainment to a heated glare cutting through Rupert's mane.

"I ain't stoppin' my fight," said Bass. "I appreciate your help all those years ago. And like I promised then, I'll make it up to you the best I can. But this…this is bigger than any of us. My life pales in comparison."

Rupert finished his drink. "Then, how about a life…for a life?"

*

It took Atlas hours to weasel his way out from the debauched evening. After Bass's reunion with Rupert, Stixx arrived with more drinks and several other Local underbosses. It wasn't until the fog of drink had overtaken the party that Atlas was confident enough in his escape. But by then, the blinding sights and fusty scents had been permanently seared into his mind—and nose.

Atlas stepped out of the quiet calm of the underside streets into the Mantle's Shade. The commotion of howling patrons enthralled by the driftball semifinals on TV had the pub roaring. The tables overflowed with people and drinks, while the bar sat empty—except for Alanna. She sipped her drink alone, seemingly unaware of the ruckus a few steps away. She wore a white halter and low-rise jeans, torn in provocative places. Her chestnut hair was braided to one side and sat atop her shoulder, exposing the fair skin of her neck and upper back. The milky smoothness wiped the disgusting visions of the evening clear from Atlas's mind. He took a breath and pulled up the stool next to her, placing his hand softly on the small of her back.

"How was your night?" she said, cutting her eyes toward him.

Atlas wanted to crawl behind the bar. His cheeks filled with embarrassment, and he removed his hand from Alanna's back. "Dull. Not my sort of scene."

A muted smirk breached her lips.

Atlas gestured to the woman behind the bar, signaling that he'd have whatever Alanna was having. The bartender poured a shot of brown and slid it across the bar. Atlas took a slow sip and felt the warm petrol run down his gullet.

"So, what is this? Our sixth date?" he asked Alanna cheekily, a playful jest he'd have never had the confidence to let slip if it hadn't been for Bass's loose lips.

She grinned. "When was our first?"

"I don't know. You taking me home to introduce me to your grandmother? Seemed a little forthright for a first date, but I dug it," he joked.

Her melodic laugh carried above the rest of the clamor in the bar. It was the type of laugh that could squeeze a smile from the meanest, stone-faced savage.

"*That* was not a date," she protested.

Her playful tone only fed his confidence, and he exposed his palms by his chest in a *don't shoot me* gesture, wearing a large smile he couldn't contain. Atlas watched her eyes as they filled with laughter. Until earlier that evening, the dreams of Alanna he'd worked so hard to bury had been just that: dreams. Wishes. But now he could see beyond his insecurities and fear. Her flushed cheeks. Dilated pupils. Playful banter. She was showing an openness to him. An openness to *them.*

The glass panes rattling in the pub doors shook away the moment as they crashed inwards against the wall, quieting the pub.

"Be ever mindful of the distractions of this world! The flowing of drink! The grip of sport! All creations of evil to spellbind and lead astray!"

The long black coat of the preacher who thrust himself inside was littered with stains and wet blotches. His large ceremonial hat struck the top of the doorway, plopping to the floor with heft as if having been soaked in a rainstorm.

"I come only with glad tidings," the preacher continued.

The commentators on the television burst into a delirium of joy when one of Midian's finest scored the game-winning goal. The bar shook with rage, having missed the nearly miraculous score for the preacher's cries of damnation.

The woman behind the bar stepped around the counter and approached the preacher. "You're gonna have to leave now," she said firmly.

"I shall go where my Lord takes me, my dear. And he has brought me here."

She placed her arm across the preacher's body, and he recoiled like a worm being touched by the dry finger of a curious child.

"My dear, women and men should not touch so casually, lest we succumb to evil's embrace."

"Well, if you don't want me to touch you, you'll have to

leave. I'll grab your nuts next if you don't step to it," she responded.

A hint of a smile crossed the preacher's lips before he bent down and retrieved his hat from the floor. He brushed the shells clinging to the sticky coating and forced a stern stare. "For the sake of your soul, I will leave of my own accord. I will not have you suffer on account of my magnetism."

"How noble," she responded.

The preacher left the bar with the door crashing shut behind him.

Atlas laughed and turned to Alanna. "Can you believe that guy?"

She fidgeted with her glass for a moment and took a sip before responding. "Yeah. I can."

Atlas watched her face carefully, searching for a hint of sarcasm. She was stone serious.

"I didn't take you for a believer," he said.

The sounds of the bar melted into silence as the room cleared out following Midian's upset win.

Alanna turned to Atlas with a question in her eyes. "Do you know about the Filth?"

"Not really." Most of his religious knowledge had been gained in the halls of the Home from the other kids' third- or fourth-hand accounts. He wasn't about to hold up the story of Franky Filth as knowledge.

"The Filth are the children of clergymen, born illegitimately," she said. "The clergy of the Faith are not allowed to marry or have sex. So, it's said that any child born to them is a manifestation of their sin. A reminder of their weakness. These kids are said to be doomed. Forced to live a life of shit and suffering. Another bonus for the transgressions of someone sworn to serve God and God alone.

"When I was little, it all fascinated me. I'd visit the Filth shelter just to hang out. There wasn't much supervision, just some shriveled-up Faith sisters, preoccupied with Church gossip and soul-saving. So, nobody cared I was there.

"There was one boy, Logan. He was a few years older than me but didn't mind me tagging along on his Faith runs—mostly delivering food around the city. I liked it. Everyone we passed assumed I was a Filth, too. I may well have been with the shit I was dealing with. But regardless, everyone was so nice to us. And every so often, someone would pity us and toss us a dollar or two. We'd rush to the store and stock up on sour candies and bubble gum. Logan always let me pick what we got. I guess it really didn't matter to him. He was just happy to have any candy. We had to rinse our mouths out raw in the washrooms of the Centers, or a restaurant—wherever we could—before we headed back to the shelter. Logan wasn't sure the Faith sisters would care if they saw his blue or purple tongue after downing a fistful of sours. But he wasn't looking to find out.

"It was all quite fun—which surprised and relieved me. I didn't think it was fair that these kids had to carry the faults of their fathers. They did nothing wrong. So, it was nice to see the stories of them suffering were just myths. Until…they weren't.

"Over the years, each shelter kid faced some absurd horror. One kid had half his body crushed between a dumpster and a brick wall, trying to shimmy his way past at the exact moment the garbage truck was backing up for the load. His entire right side was paralyzed. He couldn't walk and could barely talk. The sisters had to feed him through a straw until he died a few years later.

"They loaned another kid out to one of the pig farmers on the outside of the Wall. That's when I learned there were certain types of jobs that just stank too much to be locked in under the Mantle. I guess the farmer made a big donation or something—enough to get a Filth on loan, at least. We all thought how lucky she was to see outside the city. But a couple days later, she came back comatose after almost drowning in the waste pond at the back of the farmer's barn, a deep, dark pit full of pig shit and filthy barn water. I don't even know if she's ever recovered. They ended up transferring her to a Filth hospital in the north.

"And Logan…he was the one that seemed to break the curse…for a time. He went on with his runs and the occasional candy spree until he was eighteen. Then one day, on a free day no less, he was struck by a tire that had come loose from a stolen car skidding around a corner, running from the Citizenry Patrol. It hit him from behind. I can't help but picture it rolling over him like a rolling pin over dough. Pressing his face into the concrete. His spine snapped in three places, and his forehead collapsed inward. He couldn't walk. He couldn't talk. They said he lost all sight too.

I still go visit him now and again. He sits in front of the shelter underneath the streetlights and just stares. I think he knows it's me when I'm there. But I don't know. I just talk to him. He seems to like it.

"After all that. All the pain. The senseless suffering. It's said that the Filth will have *the run of Paradise* when the trumpets of the end sound and pearly gates open. A reward for their endurance in this world. I don't know if that's true…but what I do know is the curse of the Filth is as real as the Mantle is large. Nobody escapes it. No Filth can be saved from it. Some may dodge it for a few years, but it will eventually catch up to them. So, when I see a man commit his entire life to a book of myths—a book that calls for the damnation of everyone from a single group—I understand the motivation to believe it. Even if it's only to save themselves from the same fate as the damned."

Atlas tried sipping the remaining drops of moisture from his empty glass. Anything to detract from the dark shift in the conversation. Other than the first time they met, every conversation seemed to trudge through the torture chamber of Alanna's mind. A place where the horrors of her life had settled and the roots had taken hold. It didn't scare Atlas at all. If anything, it endeared her more to him.

"Let me get the next round," he said.

"It's okay. I have to get going anyway. This was a fun *sixth* date," she joked and kissed Atlas on the cheek before heading to the doors.

The feeling of her soft lips pressed against his cheek hung in his mind well past the *whish* of the closing pub door. He was committed to making it work. Making them work. Even if that meant navigating the truths about his past. He'd just have to be delicate in his approach, making certain the skeletons were moved from the closet to the attic—and no bones were dropped along the way. It wouldn't be fair to Alanna to rest his past at her feet. She had suffered enough. And besides, they were both broken dolls in the toy box of life. It didn't really matter who had done the breaking.

CHAPTER 12
SAMI BLEEDS

The nervous excitement had been building with the day fast approaching. Sami felt it run through her body, starting as a gentle weight in her chest until spilling over into a flutter in her stomach. But as the hour drew near, it punched deeper and now resonated in her bones.

She dashed about her small two-room house, tearing through the piles of clothes scattered on the floor. She had gone through three or four outfits, but nothing felt right for the occasion. Lenora sat in the corner amid the faded scent of her onetime street trophy collection, half-hidden under one of Sami's worn leather jackets. She hummed a quiet growl, making sure her presence was known beneath the chaos that had overtaken the cozy estate. At least, that's what Sami hoped she was doing. It was more likely Lenora was venting her frustrations with Sami's recent absences.

The preparations had taken weeks, and she'd been forced to make multiple trips above the lamps, leaving Lenora home to fend for herself. She had Mrs. Shields pop in every so often to make sure Lenora was given her medicine and some food—and a belly rub now and again. But Sami learned it wasn't enough to stop Lenora from thinking the worst. Starting after the first couple of trips, Lenora would greet Sami at the door with the energy of her youth, chasing her tail or trying to jump up on Sami's legs. At the time, she was overjoyed to see Lenora's condition improving, vindication for all the medicine she'd been pumping into her these last several months. But after noticing the listless hours and days that followed that small display of youthfulness, she could tell Lenora was forcing the show through her pain. An effort to get Sami to love her again.

If only there was more time. It broke her heart to know Lenora was feeling abandoned. But the future of the city was far too important. She committed to making it up to her, though, promising a celebratory trip to the Mantle after the evening's ceremony. They would ride the streetcar, and she'd perch Lenora on the guardrail to feel the fresh air wash over her with the force of a hundred beat-up red wagons. Then, they'd take in the breathtaking views from the boundary overlook and rest on the lush green grass in the park before heading home. A night like that together should offer Lenora a little more reassurance.

Sami noticed the hour on the small clock radio at her bedside. She was out of time. She pulled a wrinkled pair of darkened pants from one of the clothes piles on the floor. It was the clean pile—or so she hoped. She paired it with one of her black leather bomber jackets and a plain dark tee. Then she poured some conditioner into her hands and pulled it through her hair, letting her long, thick locks flow beyond her shoulders before glancing in the mirror. *This will do just fine*, she thought.

Sami emptied her mug of the last sip of coffee and tucked her small book of notes for the event into her shoulder bag. Lenora had stopped her grumbling and was now nowhere to be seen. Sami hated to leave without offering her a word or two of comfort, but there was no time to search through the devastation to find her.

She stepped from her house and headed on foot to Big Town, the Undercity neighborhood that was to host the evening's celebration. Although still under Citizenry control, Big Town had informally been run by Marcus and his Local. With the transport of grain and meats to and from the outside, through Big Town to Agriville, it had always been easier to allow Marcus full control of the transport route. Even now, with the Citizenry clamping down enforcement on their borders, Marcus was still confident there would be no bother. Big Town's official underboss, Randolph Stintz, had become an absent steward, ignoring his Local for other personal matters. Most assumed it was his new relationship with Jon's eldest daughter—a woman known to tear through men, stringing them along, demanding all their time and money. But Sami knew Randolph's slide had nothing to do with the man-eater. She'd seen the deadened eyes of an addict a thousand times before. And now, with Randolph preoccupied, Big Town lay open for her grand announcement.

Sami had spent days arranging her show of victory, the announcement of the Wall's upcoming destruction. But she needed more than just a speech. Jericho had always spoken of the power of imagery. How to imprint a vision on the hearts of the people. The Marketplace featurettes. The graffiti in the streets calling him a savior. All his ideas. A necessary show for the greater good. He could only govern if the people supported him. That meant showing them exactly why they should. Let the legends dovetail from the images. And now Sami needed an image of her own to cement her legend. Something to show them she was a woman of action.

In the end, the idea was Rupert's. A means to prove the Syndicate's intent behind the Wall's demolition: holding a large ceremony in the streets, where the crash of a wrecking ball would bring down a portion of the Wall. Just enough to break open a gaping hole, giving the people a glimpse of the outside world—and their future with her in charge. The chairwoman was reluctant to allow it at first, with the city engineers not yet having cleared the Wall's removal. But she came around when Sami pointed to Big Town as the spot of the show—the only place underside where the Wall separated slightly from the Mantle's edge. The crash of the ball would do little more than rouse the crowd's excitement and crumble a bit of concrete—at least in the eyes of the Syndicate.

Sami could hear a faint commotion off in the distance, riding the afternoon calm. With the site not too far off, she assumed it was her people putting the final touches on the event. She'd taken little risk in protecting the secrecy of the announcement. Only her close inner circle of Rupert, Jon, and

Marcus had been in the know about all the preparations—or what the preparations were regarding, at least. She even made sure the event wasn't advertised until earlier that afternoon. Runners were given flyers to distribute across the Undercity, inviting everyone to attend the neighborhood celebration featuring live entertainment, free food, and, of course, clowns. Although Sami knew the Citizenry would attend, they'd be hard-pressed to break off the type of block party so beloved by the people. And with such short notice, it would be nearly impossible to figure out the real motivation before it was too late. Bass would just have to watch as she snatched control from his hands.

Walking through Big Town always made Sami feel as if she'd stepped through a portal into a world of giants, torn right from the pages of one of Mrs. Shield's recovered gems. It was unlike any other Undercity borough. Each building sat atop two or more regular city blocks, littered with hundreds of windows and roofs that appeared to tickle the Mantle's underside. The structures were so large, many buildings contained their own little city within, complete with shopping centers, schools, apartment flats, and, in some cases, indoor parks. Even the streetlamps that lined the sidewalk were larger than anywhere else in Lower Midian. The hefty black poles stretched halfway up the buildings with light heads as blocky and wide as the ice cream trucks that cruised the area in the summer. The large shadows they'd cast during the day checkered the roadway, blotting out the light from the Mantle lamps above. With its wide streets next to the Wall and plenty of room for onlookers, Big Town was the perfect spot to usher in a new era.

Sami arrived at the site still very much in the throes of being prepared, workers scurrying back and forth across the double-wide roadway. The stage for her announcement was erected parallel to the Wall, right before the roadway that ran alongside it, blocking the intersecting street. Flanking both sides were two of Big Town's largest residential buildings, extending several blocks inward and making it appear as if the stage was the last stop along a stretch of tunnel. Sami could see children on balconies and in the windows staring down with eager anticipation, spying the clown troupe putting the final touches on their costumes and packing balloons into their pockets. Across the road, one of the clowns leaned against a building, sipping on a cigarette while resting his arm on what appeared to be a large guitar case. His curly green wig sat precariously atop his head, with his short brown hair underneath spilling out. He looked at Sami, unamused, before returning to his half-burned cigarette. For a moment, she thought she recognized the man beneath the white and red painted face. But she figured it would be just as easy to mistake someone underneath that much makeup.

At the foot of the stage, Marcus sat on the steps, redder and more flustered than usual.

"Everything okay?" Sami asked, making her approach.

"Do I look like a party planner to you? I love ya, dear, but if you ask me to help out with some shit like this again, I swear I'll show up on Bass's doorstep with a bouquet of roses, beggin' for him to take me back!"

"Where's Jon and Rupert?"

"Jon's been off securin' the area since mornin'. Haven't seen him in hours. And Rupert…well, you hear that hummin'?"

Sami listened carefully but could hear nothing but the Mantle lamps buzzing above. "The lamps?"

"No, no. That there is Rupert's snoring vibrating the goddamned Mantle. I saw him passed out by the food carts on the other side of that there crane." The large crane that hung the wrecking ball from its grasp rested behind the building to the right of the stage, just out of view of the attendees. Marcus pointed past it to a row of stainless-steel food carts.

Sami's mind drifted back to Rupert's head buried in the butt of his cane during her call to mutiny back at the Mantle's Shade. He was more weathered than in his younger years. Less vibrant. But something didn't sit well with her. Even with his age, it wasn't much like Rupert to be resting his eyes during the early evening. Sami felt a small pit sprout in her stomach but shook it off as hunger pangs. She hadn't eaten much that day except for a few crumbled crackers and a slice of cold cheese.

"I should check on him," she said.

"You do that darlin'. And you tell that son of a bitch he owes me for pullin' his weight. I just might have him come out to the pig farms for a day."

Sami walked past the scarred steel ball to a bevy of shiny

silver carts, all lined up neatly against the brick wall. The scent of food emanating from the bellies of each roused a deep hunger. She would have loved nothing more than to rip the top off one of the carts and bury her hunger under a mound of pulled pork and sauced beans. She could almost hear her mother's stern disapproval. *Beans are for men and married women. It won't do you any good to be single and bloated.* But as Sami rounded the end of the row, her appetite dissolved under the crushing heft of her dread. Rupert lay against the wall with his head resting on the cart next to him, paler than usual. He sat still and heavy.

*

Sami curled up behind the stage, clutching her knees to her chest. She did her best to choke the tears in her eyes, but a few trickled out as if escaping the rusted joint of an old pipe. Her chest was like a bellows in the hands of an overexcited child, rapidly pumping, stoking the fire of her pain with little concern for how high the flames soared. She could hear the clamor of attendees piling in on the other side of the stage. The laughter of children—no doubt enthralled by the clowns and balloon animals—weakened her further. It reminded her of the days when Rupert would lift her on his shoulders, holding out her hands as they strolled the annual Harvest Fair. She remembered how giddy she'd been watching the other children beneath her feet try to slip past Rupert's trunk-sized legs. How he'd stop at nearly every food hut and ice cream cart. In her mind's eye, she could still see his large, furry hand reaching up with one treat or another. She knew her mother wasn't too pleased with Rupert's overindulgence, but she rarely peeped a word about it back then.

Looking back, Sami could see it was those days her mother had cherished the most. In her later years, she would recount those stories with a glow on her cheeks and a smile in her eyes. The thought of her mother's laughter at the memories of Rupert hammered at the dams Sami built to keep her tears at bay. But it was all too much, and the tears broke free. She clutched her knees tighter, burying her face as the pain coursed through her. She felt her soul wanting to leap from her chest to escape. It stung almost as fiercely as the day her mother died. Rupert was the closest thing she'd ever had to a father, and his death was as unexpected as Jericho's murder.

Sami had seen her mother's death coming. The weeks of her lying in bed, frail and fatigued, had been like a train conductor warning of an impending departure. But Rupert seemed as strong as the days he'd toss her on his shoulders. Her first thought coming across his colorless body was that he'd been murdered. But after the medics arrived, it was clear his heart simply gave way. It was his time.

The swell of the crowd shook her from her emotions. The end of the Citizenry was near and was bigger than any one person—or any one death. Despite her sorrow, the announcement couldn't be delayed. By now, many would have seen the wrecking ball tucked behind the building, and rumors would be swirling. If she wanted history to mark the liberation of the Undercity with the Wall crumbling beneath the weight of their resistance, this was her only chance to do so. *Words create a following. Actions create an army. Symbols create legends.*

She wrestled her breathing to a slow crawl and rose to her feet. She straightened herself out, wiping the moisture from her face, and worked to rub the wetness of her tears dry from her pants. The loud clunk of the Mantle lamps deadening reverberated beneath the platformed sky. With Marcus having left to share the news of Rupert's death with Mrs. Umber, and Jon yet to be seen, Sami climbed the steps to the stage alone.

The early autumn breath struck her hard as she stood center-stage beneath the darkness of the lamps. The large Big Town buildings narrowed the path of the evening chill, tunneling it over the throng and charring Sami's skin. She could feel her tear-stained pants stiffen as the cold frosted the remaining moisture around her knees. She had forgotten how hard the chill could strike, having spent the last several nights on the heated Mantle streets above. In the distance, the twinkling of the streetlights ramping on in succession were like fireflies dancing over the blackened Undercity, making their way to the oversized floodlights littered throughout Big Town. One by one, they revved and popped on like spotlights on a theater stage. Sami looked out and watched as the heat from the lights melted away the shivers and tightness of the crowd. It was as if the people collectively exhaled, and the crowd loosened across the roadway.

The murmur of the people brought Sami back to the Mantle's Shade and how Rupert's grizzled roar had silenced everyone to attention. She felt the vapors climbing and shook them away. Swallowing her fresh pain, Sami opened with gratitude. "Thank you all for coming." The crowd quieted, and all eyes were now watching.

"I stand here before you all with a message. A message of hope for the future of our children. A message of peace for the old and tired. And a message of prosperity for those of us who have worked hard over these many years. My message stands in stark contrast to the new leadership of the Citizenry.

"By now, you may have heard that Jericho Sands is dead. I won't get into how he died…but rest assured, we will hold the perpetrators accountable once the Faction has won your support and is installed as the true caretakers beneath the Mantle. But now, without Jericho's measured hand to guide the peace and prosperity of the Undercity, the new Citizenry leadership would have us take the fight to the Syndicate. Sacrificing all we've gained in a struggle we don't stand to win. We all know the history of the Underside Wars. We don't need to go back to that nightmare.

"My message for you all is a promise that under the Faction we will never return to the death and violence of the past. We will continue to work together in the best interests of the people. A people who are tired of fighting. Frightened by the drugs flooding the streets. And starved of the light of day. It may take us time to tackle all the problems we face as a people, but I promise you we're up to the challenge."

The deep rumble of the crane bounced between the buildings and over the crowd as it maneuvered into view behind the stage.

"One by one, we will take on these challenges together." Sami pushed the words out louder and more forcefully to avoid being drowned out by the din of the crane. "And as we all stand here gathered, let's tackle the first challenge…together."

Sami turned to the crane and nodded conspicuously. It revved, and its long arm shifted. The shriek of metal pierced the deep thrum of the engine as the wrecking ball first eased beside the left of the stage before being thrust toward the large concrete slab. But as chunks of concrete crumbled from the impact, a series of loud pops and screams erupted. Sami turned back to see muzzle flashes tracing the crowd and was shaken to the stage floor. Ropes fell from the tops of the buildings, whistling through the screams and gunshots. Men wrapped in black Guardian body armor rappelled down the building faces, the glint of muzzle flashes reflecting off their tinted facemasks. The shattering of glass spun Sami back to the crane. Bullet holes exploded in the cabin windows, and the crane operator shoved the heavy door open, crawling to the ground with blood spouting from his arm. He shimmied on the concrete as bullets skidded off the pavement next to him. The sound of lead puncturing the metal crane echoed until it bellowed a final squeal, like a pig during slaughter. And the large steel ball, still swinging from the force of its initial blow, broke free, landing with a crunch of bones. Sami watched a flush of blood splatter beneath the streetlights, and numbness overtook her. She sat defeated, gazing vacantly at the stage between her splayed legs, ignoring the filthy Guardian boots now surrounding her.

CHAPTER 13

SOLOMON TEASED

It hardly appeared as if a tragedy had just taken place. The scarlet-tinged concrete might well have been from the neighborhood children's street paints. A mere inkblot test of artwork that every parent with school-aged children knew well. But the faded stains coating the roadway hadn't come from children. Just several poor souls sacrificed in the name of one's misguided attempt at seizing control. *The naiveté of that poor girl.* Solomon was not one to believe that good intentions lined the road to Hell. Rather, his faith had taught that intentions were the only measuring stick by which someone should be judged. The road to Paradise was paved with good intentions; however, the traveler need be warned of the highwaymen and rapists along the way.

Solomon walked past the flower bouquets resting against the Wall. The rubble beneath his feet scraped along the pavement as he stepped beyond the splattered crimson steel ball to the stage. Climbing the stairs, he looked out over the crowd of memorial attendees gathered silently, the Mantle lamps illuminating their long and somber faces. He took his spot in the center and started with a silent prayer before opening the service.

"In the name of our Lord..."

Over the years, he had said the introductory prayer so many times, it had lost all meaning. Not in the sense that the words were of no consequence—they certainly were. But it would simply roll off his tongue without a second thought. It was automatic. So much so, he had found that if he consciously tried to recite the prayer word by word, he would often forget and be forced back into his trance-like regurgitation for the words to flow correctly.

"Today is a solemn day beneath the Mantle. A day of remembrance and reflection. We are gathered here not only to pray and mourn, but also to shine a light on the souls of the victims. To tell their stories so that we may be inspired and hold them in our hearts."

Solomon refused to wade into the flood of rumors swirling since the attack. The streets had been awash with accusations, conspiracies, and flat-out fantasies from all sides. Some claimed it was a show of dominance by the Syndicate to beat the Undercity into submission. Others claimed it was a Faction ruse to rally bleeding hearts to their cause. The most salacious of the rumors had been that the chairwoman had ordered the strike in a fit of rage after Sami ended their torrid love affair. All nonsense, of course. Anyone who'd ever played the game of power could nose the stinking red herring through the gossip and whispers. Although Solomon liked to think of the Faith as an institution above the squabbles and power struggles of the less refined, the history of the Church had proven otherwise. Even his ascent to Grand Magus in Midian had not been without controversy. Not of his own doing, necessarily, but he had a hand in placing the crown within reach. Opportunity knocks, and the ambitious answer the call.

Solomon had his own suspicions about who was behind the attack in Big Town. But airing them publicly, or even alluding to the motivations, would do nothing to serve the Faith or the victims. Not to mention he'd rather not get caught up in the shitstorm of it all. No sense in having the Faith dragged in with the rest of the cuckoos' cries. He wasn't sure how he'd even address the High Council if someone accused him of being behind a highly trained team of Filth assassins and femme fatale Faith sisters. No, he would not be commenting on the attack. It was during times of hardship and tragedy that people sought out the Faith for comfort and to make sense of the senseless, an invariable recruiting ground for those seeking answers and light. And Solomon was not about to let the tragedy go to waste.

"Ronald Harmkipper." It was a funny name, but over the last year Solomon had gotten used to how it fell on his ear. Ron had sought Solomon for counsel on many spiritual matters that he'd hoped would not only open a path to salvation with the Lord, but also with his wife—should those matters be made public.

"He was a family man with eight children and a loving wife." He also had a mistress, but the masses would hardly find the mention of that in good taste. "A working man, recently retired, Ronald had committed his life to the building of our good city."

He also committed half his pension to keep his mistress's lips pressed closed about their bastard. Solomon doubted Mrs. Harmkipper would be so inclined to continue the payments once word got out about his infidelity. She was a soft woman but one of those no-nonsense types. A woman who could easily have dropped the wrecking ball on top of him herself, if she had known. A conspiracy Solomon could actually get behind.

"Ronald was one of several who fell during the cowardly attack, and we ask God to grant mercy on his soul and place peace in the hearts of his wife and eight," *nine*, "children."

An audible "Amen" washed up from the crowd.

"Jonathan Denton."

The cry of Jon's youngest daughter, a girl of fifteen, carried through the building-lined corridor. Her two sisters huddled around her for comfort. Jon's death had been a shock, not discovered until lamps-on the next day. His body was left on the roof of one of the overlooking buildings, lying in a gap between two exhaust vents. He had taken a nasty hit to the back of his head and bled out through the gaping wound. The doctor told Jon's daughters that he had died without pain from the sudden blow. But having been acquainted with death for the better part of three decades, Solomon had learned that doctors often softened the truth with pseudoscience and medical jargon. From just the markings on his face, hands, and clothes, Solomon gathered that he probably lay convulsing on the gravel rooftop for hours before his death.

"A man whose tale will echo beneath the Mantle for ages

to come. A giant among men, he always stood for what was right, even when it was hard. Even when his life was on the line. He made his stand during Midian's darkest hours. The Year of Shadows. A year when young Black men were used as pawns in the fight for underside control. And because of him, the Undercity flourished, unleashing the strength of our differences by unifying the people as one. He will be greatly missed. May God shower his soul with mercy."

Solomon continued the service, listing name after name of those who had died during the attack. There were ten deaths in total, mostly from Jon's security team, killed well before the event even started. And then there was Rupert Umber, another well-known Citizenry leader who appeared to have died of old age and fried chicken rather than a conspiratorial plot against Sami's outstretched hand.

Had she merely asked, Solomon thought. He could have guided her hand through the scorpions and pythons as she grasped at the hilt of power. At least then Ron's bastard would have been less likely to starve of poverty, and Jon's youngest may have continued the self-important musings of a teenage girl on the path to womanhood. Someone as idealistic as Sami could never see the chessboard beyond the pieces. In that arena, the echo of the slightest move could shake mountains. Even a sneeze could kill hundreds if the board was set just so. But as Solomon had seen, time and time again, arrogance and self-righteousness strip the eyes of sight and mind of reason.

"During these times," Solomon continued, "we ask that you all dig deep, both in your soul while you offer your supplications to the Lord, and into your pockets so that we may help the families suffering such unimaginable hardships."

Solomon left the stage to the sound of change rattling inside the donation bins passing through the crowd. Many people surrounded the landing for a private blessing. He placed his hand atop their heads, one by one, and whispered a prayer with his eyes closed, working his way through the dozens that stood in wait. The monotony of reciting the Blessed Pilgrim countless times was undercut by Solomon's excitement to see the enthusiasm flowing in the people once again. It was years since he'd been approached for so many blessings. And seeing the devout faces rejoice after he offered a personal prayer made him yearn more for the Church's revival.

"Can you do the Incontinent Pilgrim?" A sweet voice floated above the murmur of attendees.

Recognizing the old Faith joke peddled by new magi and sisters in training, Solomon turned to see the darling face of his former pupil, Alanna Thistle, a young beauty who had tried the path of Faith sister a while back—despite Solomon's caution against it. Sisters were typically of two types: ugly or lesbian. Alanna, on the other hand, was blessed with far more potential to have wasted away among the Filth and sickly. If she had stuck around a little while longer, he would have steered her toward a more central role in the Faith administration. But she had announced her departure from the convent after only a few short months.

Alanna's sorrowful eyes almost went unnoticed after the playful joke and welcoming smile. Her full lips rested with a slight pucker, and her firm breasts pushed out through her airy-thin tee—much farther than he had remembered. She'd always been a stunner, but now she exuded a sexual magnetism no right-set man could ignore. She was more seductress than sister.

"Come, my dear," said Solomon, ushering her away from the service.

The rumble of the crowd faded to a hum as they strolled along the walk next to the Wall. Solomon did his best to keep his gaze lowered during the back-and-forth of pleasantries. Alanna's beauty was a danger to be alone with, and only the banal view of the passing Wall could stifle his passion. Up close, the Wall had a rippled texture, like tiny waves frozen in a disturbed lake. Lining its bottom were small plants poking at its seam, giving people a glimpse into the lush vegetation on the other side. Solomon couldn't help but laugh when undersiders referred to the walk as a nature stroll. As a child, he'd get lost in the large crop fields beyond the city's edge, marching through tall greenery twice his height. He'd find a clearing, lie out with a stolen tomato or two, and stare up at the sky, watching the cloud formations as they blew by. That was a nature stroll. But he could hardly blame others for the changed meaning. It wasn't as if they'd seen much more natural growth than the few weeds peeking in from behind the Wall.

When the small talk devolved into awkward silences, Alanna's tone shifted, and she unloaded her worries. "Your Worship… I've been struggling lately. Working through the pain to achieve a higher purpose. But I feel…lost. I know everything has a place in God's plan, even the smallest gesture…or biggest tragedy. But I'm having trouble seeing what that plan is. What's the end goal? What's the purpose of it all?"

A common question from mourners. Solomon would typically have a canned response at the ready, something speaking to the tests God uses to try one's faith. And then he'd finish with a parable on how tribulation helps one recognize and appreciate the good times. But Alanna knew all this. She had been a tremendous student at the convent, even diving deep into some of the more spurious sources after mastering the canon. Solomon once thought she'd have made an excellent magus—if women were permitted into the clergy. Talking her down now as he would a layperson would do nothing to put her mind at ease.

"What is the purpose of any of it?" he said. "What is the purpose of you here with me? Or me standing on that stage a few moments ago? Or a stray wandering the streets, searching for scraps until he dies?" He stopped walking and turned to Alanna. "I don't have the foggiest idea. And that's because I am not meant to know." Solomon reached for her hands. "The will of God is not for any of us to know. Divine providence is the realm of the Creator and not for pissants like us. We are to go about our lives the best we can, obliging His rules and trying not too badly to muck it all up. That right there is the secret of life—and I won't even charge you for having divulged it." He smiled, and her eyes warmed. "Don't you dwell on it, my dear. Just have your purpose and keep working toward it, knowing full well that it's all in God's hands."

Alanna reached out and hugged him. He jerked his waist back slightly to avoid her feeling the rising tide in his robes. But she pulled him closer, and his now fully swollen appendage was pressing into her midriff. Solomon felt the embarrassment flood his face and inched away from her embrace.

"Best not dwell with such open affection—regardless of how platonic," said Solomon.

"Yes. You're right. My emotions sometimes make me forget."

They turned and headed back to the memorial at the same strolling pace as before.

"Your Worship?"

"Yes, dear."

"I can't tell you how much your guidance means to me. It's been tough without Jericho around."

Jericho, the savior, he derisively mused.

"Bass tries his best. He truly cares about the people and what happens beneath the Mantle. But...he lacks wisdom. He's all or nothing. No nuance. I can't trust his guidance. And that's where I need you."

The tide had waned but began waxing once again.

"Your Worship. Please don't take what I am about to say

as heretical, but…Jericho was like our prophet. Most undersiders would agree. Not a prophet in a spiritual sense, but still a prophet. He kept us safe and prosperous. He guided us. And cared for us. And we looked to him to lead. But now he's gone. And we're slowly losing our way."

Solomon walked with measured steps, clasping his hands behind his back while focusing on the sculpt of his face, trying to convey a look of thoughtful consideration instead of the anger that was swirling within.

"The attack only made it more complicated," she continued. "People don't know who to trust. Where to go. I heard that before the attack, the Syndicate had thrown their support behind Sami instead of Bass. But after what happened… I just don't know. I'm worried about the Undercity. Without the right leader. Without our prophet." Alanna stopped, looking intently into his eyes. "I just wish…" She hesitated and looked to the ground. "Never mind."

"What is it, my dear?"

She turned her face toward his, her large emerald eyes holding a look of pain. "Nothing," she said. "Just…you Sands have a gift."

*

Alanna's words trudged through his thoughts long after he left the memorial, as if the message had been sent from on high through a messenger of God's choosing. He couldn't shake its resonance. He couldn't shake his duty to spread God's gift. *The time for patience may be over.*

Solomon stepped through the newly ornamented front doors of the central church to find the pews more than half full. Mixed among the regulars and long-time parishioners sat a host of unfamiliar faces. Faces he'd never seen even at the high holidays. He continued down the aisle, past the crowd, into the sacristy to prepare for the evening sermon. He couldn't constrain his excitement. He also couldn't help being thankful for the sacrifice of Ronald and the others. Death was a necessary reminder of the hereafter. Solomon had long wondered whether the relative comfort of life had kept the masses from his halls. Jericho had pushed them past the fear of war and death, where they could rest in comfort and ignorance of their impending doom. But the attack had shaken people from their slumber. And now eyes were wide open.

Jericho the prophet. The blasphemous words rang in his mind. He was a false prophet, if anything. Jericho had led them astray, and Alanna spoke of him as if he'd been born of an immaculate conception. If only she'd met Gia Sands. She'd have learned real quick that the only thing miraculous about Jericho's conception was how their mother convinced three different men to pony up child support payments after his birth.

Solomon regretted letting Alanna blather on, using Jericho's name in the same breath as prophethood. It was heresy.

He should have stopped her. Interrupted with a cough or a parable. Or maybe place a finger on her soft lips. Or even… Solomon's thoughts shifted to the feeling of his manhood pressed against Alanna's tight body. She hadn't pulled away. She'd pulled him closer, in fact. He could feel the blood rush below his waist yet again. "*…you Sands have a gift.*" He questioned whether he had enough time to relieve the passion coursing inside. But the nave was almost full, and the stir of a sermon tickled the back of his tongue.

Solomon took a sip of water from a glass resting on the kitchenette and wiped his hands through his hair. After smoothing out his beard, he grabbed a copy of the Good Book and stepped to the curtain separating him from the crowd. *If they need a prophet, I will give them a prophet.*

CHAPTER 14

ATLAS'S UNEASE

The War Room was unlike any other in the Citizenry Hall. Walls draped with sound-dampening coverings, devoid of any windows, and heavy metal doors that clunked loudly when closed. A long wooden table stretched the length of the room, with broad leather seats on each side. The room usually supported large gatherings of Local leadership, but after several notable exits, it dwarfed the small crowd sitting around the table. Bass had replaced several underbosses of the remaining Locals, installing only those he had known since childhood in positions of authority, his attempt at weeding out Sami's loyalists still in his midst. He even went as far as changing the governing rules in case he ended up sacking most of the leadership, trying his best to get the voting quorum down to two, but settled at five when the rest objected.

Atlas had done his best to keep up with all the names, but it almost didn't seem worth it. He knew some, like Jonah Turret and Derick Lowder, from his brief time at the Hall before Jericho's death. They seemed to be in well enough to keep Bass's trust. And then there was Amelia Stintz, a recent addition whose name Atlas remembered as the only female underboss among the lot. But for the rest, the revolving door of Citizenry leadership was moving too fast for him to put in the effort. And really, he was only there for Alanna. He couldn't care less about the who's-who around the table.

Atlas turned to his left. The high back of Alanna's broad chair towered over her petite frame. They had arrived together moments earlier, but the smile in her eyes when she caught his glance felt as if she'd been starved of his presence for days.

Alanna had become a regular in his swanky new pad. Dinners and movies on his new TV. Lying together atop his plush cashmere sofa among an assortment of tropical plants and hand-crafted crystal trinkets she had him bring in to spruce up the place. There had been several moments when the urge to feel her soft lips overtook his better judgment. His yearning to hold her close, breathe in her sweet perfume. But every slight move, every hint of a gesture toward her, seemed to shake her from her comfort. He could see her airy movements stiffen, like a doe frozen by fear. It would only happen for the briefest moment, but it was enough to shake his nerve, forcing him to mask his movements with a reach for the popcorn or to grab a pillow. And on nights when she'd opted to sleep in his spare room, the thought of Alanna dressed down, sleeping alone steps from his bed, only added to his tortuous urges. The thought of inviting her into his bed—if only to sleep—had crossed his mind, but his recent sleep terrors had given him pause. He wasn't certain how she would react to the nighttime theatrics of him thrashing about with Tommy's name on his lips.

Things were going so well. Best not tempt fate, he figured. Not yet, at least.

The heavy doors to the War Room clunked shut as Bass lumbered in with Stixx by his side. Atlas always found it amusing seeing the two walking together. Stixx was tall and lanky, with long arms and a slim waist. Atlas couldn't help but picture the number ten when he saw them side-by-side.

"There ain't no reason to sugar-coat it," said Bass to the half-filled room. "We're anemic. Even after the shit-show Sami and her clowns tried to pull off. We haven't gained any more support. The people seemed to have forgotten everything we've done for their asses and have climbed so far up Sami's cunt, they can't find their way out. We're even getting' complaints about the videos we have playin' in the market—Turret?" Bass searched for Jonah Turret among the faces at the table.

"I'm here."

"What the fuck is that shit you have broadcasting in the market?"

Jonah gave a weaselly glance around the table. "Just the truth, Bass," he answered smugly.

"Truth? The only fuckin' truth is you're half-retarded," Bass fired back. "How about you broadcast that over the Marketplace? Maybe throw in a montage of your wedding to your cousin?"

A smattering of soft chuckles rounded the table as Jonah sank into his chair.

"I don't wanna hear any more about her sexual escapades with the chairwoman, or whatever the fuck you and your inbred team of monkeys have cooked up for the next video."

"Excuse my interruption."

On the other end of the room sat a man Atlas had known from his time in the Guard. Not in any official capacity but knew him nonetheless. Asher Punsch had his tentacles so intertwined with the SyndiGuard that nearly all Guardians working the Under Eastside gates had taken at least one order from him—if only indirectly.

Asher rose to his feet, draped in a fine silk suit with his silver hair slicked back and one dead eye seemingly fixed on Jonah's flushed face. Quiet rumbles could be heard from the underbosses as they whispered under their breath.

"From my understanding, you have a much bigger problem than mere public relations," said Asher.

"I was gettin' to it," said Bass.

"Well, don't bury the lede. I need to make sure I didn't back a loser… Or did I?"

"Yeah. Wouldn't want to hurt your pristine reputation, now would we?"

Asher smirked derisively before returning to his seat next to the several large men of his entourage.

"And that brings us to our main problem," Bass continued. "We need cash. And now. These goddamned cockroaches are eating our lunch, and we need more than loose meat sandwiches and pocket cheese if we're gonna push through. We can't take on the Syndicate with only half a war chest. They have eleven corporate mules pulling their weight. We need our coffers full. And it's on y'all to figure out how we're gonna do this."

"We can always start a tax," said Derick Lowder.

Bass wasted little time with the suggestion. "Yeah? We could also lock you ass-naked in a pillory on the market walk. Charge twenty a pop to stick it between your cheeks. Hell, ten for a blowjob."

A nervous laughter rippled through the room. Derick slumped in his seat, folding his arms.

"No fuckin' ideas that will push people away," said Bass. "We need to draw these people from Sami's teat. If we offer a rancid bottle, they'll just assume her soft pillows are the best they can get, and the Citizenry will be a stale fart in the chill."

Alanna turned to Atlas, eyes wide, nodding toward Bass as if pushing him to jump in. He shot her a perplexed look before turning back to the conversation around the table.

She tugged on his arm. "What we discussed. The businesses," she whispered.

It was a conversation he vaguely remembered from the night before at his apartment. But she'd been the one speaking. Atlas was busy watching her, doing his best to tame the carnal urges struggling to break free. It was as if everything she did throughout the night had whispered a lusty invitation, exposing her smooth, toned legs from beneath the short blanket she would place over her midriff. Her painted toes pressed firmly into the soft cushion, leaving imprints in the velvety fabric when she shuffled her feet. And the slight push of her thick lips when she spoke. The last thing on his mind was Citizenry finances.

Atlas shook his head subtly. He wasn't about to speak. He was only here for her, not to play strategist in the Undercity politicking. But as he turned his head back to the table, Alanna's heel struck his shin with the force of a shotgun blast.

The sharp sting of her boot jolted the words from his mouth: "Sell the casino!" All eyes turned his way, and he could see Alanna beam in his periphery. "All Citizenry businesses," he continued. "Profits are down across them all. Faction sympathizers don't want to be seen supporting Citizenry business, so they go elsewhere. Why not dump the lot of them?"

Bass sat quietly for a moment as the room hummed with discussion. A sneaky smile crept to Derick's lips, as if the idiocy had been passed along to Atlas, and he was no longer the only half-wit at the table.

"That's a terrible idea," said Derick. "We don't want to handicap ourselves in the future."

Atlas could feel the sweat drip from his armpits down his sides, bracing for Bass to pile on. Why did he open his mouth? A parade of possible insults flooded his head. *Your shit for brains is spilling out of your mouth. The wheel is turnin', but the hamster's dead. I thought that level of stupid died out with the ostrich.* Which one would it be?

"It's brilliant," Amelia Stintz called out.

Amelia was a stout older woman with short, curly brown hair. Her white round face was flush from the drink, and her plump, pale hands were covered in cuts and bruises. She ran an auto repair shop in Big Town, specializing in big rigs and tractors. For the blue-collar type, she always came across as exceptionally calculated. Amelia had recently taken over her brother's charge of Big Town after Bass found out Randolph was caught up with the daughter of one of Sami's closest confidants. Bass had known Randolph for years but couldn't trust that he wasn't compromised. "Pussy is a powerful influencer. That's probably how the Faction got the jump on you in Big Town," he had said right before he ousted Randolph and called on Amelia to take his spot.

Amelia continued. "And once we take the city, we can force the buyback of our businesses and thank the good folks for the loan and their stewardship."

With Amelia co-signing the idea, most around the table now seemed open to it. Atlas looked to Alanna, who was wearing a smug look of superiority. She didn't need to say anything for Atlas to know exactly what she was thinking behind her pretty green eyes.

"An inspired suggestion." Asher rose again from his seat. "In fact, I'm certain I could round up the funds for your little fire sale. With a little help from my friends, of course."

The faces in the hushed room matched the feeling throughout.

"However, if I commit to this plan, there will be no buyback of the casino. That will be mine, in perpetuity."

Bass's demeanor shifted to humbled fright. The faces across the table cycled through various shades of red. Taking note of the room's swelter, Bass started, "Well, I don't know—"

"You don't know what?" Asher interrupted. "If you need the money? If you could let the crown jewel of the Undercity fall into my *skeevy* little hands? If you really don't know, maybe I'll just call in the Citizenry's debt now. Take everything in your coffers…and the casino for good measure."

Half the room pushed to their feet. Asher's men followed.

Bass reached out his arms with open palms and yelled, "SIT DOWN! Everyone!"

It took a moment, but the room eventually stilled and the seats filled once again.

"We're on the same goddamned side, you fucks! This ain't how any of us would've liked to see it workin' out, but our dicks are floppin' in the wind. We need some support. Asher." Bass looked to the back of the room. "Let us sort this out among ourselves. Alone, if you don't mind."

"Certainly. Take your time."

The door slammed behind Asher and his men as they stepped into the hall. Atlas sat quietly and watched the fury set the quiet calm of the room aflame. When he had first entered, the soundproof room created a tranquil space to block out the humming Mantle lamps and occasional engine clunk of a passing car. But now the tightly sealed chamber, chock full of seething undersiders with years of harbored pain, felt more akin to a pressure cooker. The rumble of the deep yells and angry expressions had Atlas praying that Alanna wouldn't push him further to get involved. She sat with a simper as frustrations pushed Bass to his limit.

"WE MAY NOT HAVE ANY OTHER CHOICE!" Bass's voice boomed, quieting the din of rage. "We can't waste time searchin' for buyers. And then negotiating. And then waiting for the cash to move hands. We'd have already bled out by then. And I can't squeeze another penny out of that fuck without some collateral. We've blown through most of his cash already."

The rabid anger cured, reducing everyone in the room to a somber stillness when the War Room doors heaved open. Bass glanced over, confusion washing away the defeat in his eyes. He rose from his seat and stepped out into the hall.

The tranquility returned while everyone sat stewing in the emotions of the meeting. People stared, but no one spoke. In the calm of the silence, Atlas was suddenly struck by Alanna's earlier insistence. Why hadn't she shared the idea herself? It was hers, after all. And even though she wasn't an underboss, she was high enough in the central ranks to have been heard.

Atlas had never been much for ideas. He was more the doing type. Tell him to scale a large tree to shake out a lost driftball—no problem. There was a junkie from the Midriff setting up camp next to the Under Eastside gates? Give Atlas a gun and some gloves and he'd clear the tent faster than a day-old egg salad sandwich. But ask him to opine on anything beyond the quality of some thirty-year-old import, and he'd be less coherent than an addict on a bender.

Soon, the War Room doors *swooshed* open, and Bass trotted back in, looking out over the room with a menacing confidence.

"Like a thousand-dollar whore added to a lineup of ten-dollar lot lizards, looks like we have another fuckin' option!"

CHAPTER 15

SAMI SHEATHES

Her shovel punctured the dirt like a syringe through callused flesh. With some effort, she made it nearly three feet and was thankful the winter frost was still several weeks away. One of the few things she'd been grateful for as of late.

Sami climbed out of the hole and wiped her brow with the sleeve of her sweater. The yellow glow from the surrounding streetlamps gave just enough light to move around her small backyard without the risk of plunging into the gaping pit. She rested her shovel against the porch swing and turned to the wooden box at the foot of her evening's labor. The crate had been lying around her home for years. Rupert had used it to haul fresh produce from the farms when he'd go out with Marcus for a visit. When her mother died, Sami used it to store her personal effects until eventually donating them to a Faith Center in the Bottoms. And now the box held what was left of Sami's oldest friend. Had it been a couple years ago, she would have needed a box twice its size to hold Lenora's remains.

Sami stepped to the crate and kneeled beside it, her knees squishing into the mound of loose dirt surrounding the open earth.

She lifted the box a few inches from the ground and placed it into the hole. Despite her tired arms, the box felt no heavier than a laundry basket full of clothes. She had wrapped Lenora in one of her old sweatshirts and wedged some rags between her and the wooden walls to prevent any jostling. To keep her from being alone, Sami placed the rubber mouse Jasper had bought next to her snout for company. But even with the toy for comfort, Sami could still picture Lenora howling from loneliness, wondering why she'd been abandoned.

Sami's mother had brought Lenora home soon after Rupert stopped coming around the house—no doubt to replace his fuzzy arm with something else to snuggle. Sami had slipped several tears of happiness when she first came home to the rambunctious little pup. Lenora was the cutest thing she'd ever seen, with long, floppy ears and big brown eyes. She could still remember all the mischief Lenora had caused her first year in the Salem household, confusing her mother's personal massager for a bone. Tearing through the streets of Plainsview with Sami's padded bra dragging from her clenched jaw. The terror Lenora unleashed was both horrific and amusing—at least after the years had dulled the embarrassment.

But despite all the memories and joy and the vision of Lenora crying out from the belly of the earth for cuddles, Sami was unable to shed a single tear. Even when she found Lenora dead beneath her old leather jacket in the corner of the main room, she hadn't cried. It was just another drip in her overflowing bucket of sorrow.

She pushed the dirt with her hands into the gaping furrow atop Lenora's crate. The sound of the dirt pattering on the wooden box reminded her of the energetic little pup's paws clawing at the tile, racing around her home. And just as that sound had slowly disappeared over recent months, so too did the pattering as the box became fully enveloped in earth.

Sami pushed herself up with her blackened hands and stared at the broken hill of dirt. She closed her eyes. Her mother would have let loose a word or two for Lenora's soul. Jasper might have offered a praise of thanks for how much more life she'd gained from the treatments. But Sami could think of nothing else than the easing of Lenora's pain and that her selfishness had done little but prolong it these many months.

Sami peeled the mud-crusted sweater and jeans from her body and tossed them next to the bathtub. Crammed beneath her bosom were more trinkets of her dig that fell to the washroom floor after she unclasped her bra. She removed her socks and underwear before stepping into the tub. A long soak would give her time to reflect on the last few days. But as she rinsed off in the shower, the chaos of the water streaming down and splashing against the tile wall seemed more appropriate for reflecting than a still pool. Her life had descended into a never-ending frenzy of death and failure. The calmness of a quiet soak would do nothing but feed her anxiety. If she was destined to remain in the heart of the storm, she was going to embrace the chaos.

The weight of all the death hung around her neck like a five-hundred-pound chain—or steel wrecking ball. Lenora. Rupert. Jon. Ron. Ronald hadn't even wanted to be there. Sami had known him from her work constructing the new rehab centers. He had helped tear down the previous dilapidated buildings occupying the land, and every now and then, she would visit the site and chat him up. He was a sweet man who would often go on about his wife and how he wanted to do good by her. So, when Sami's little plan had formed, she convinced him to help, promising a romantic evening for him and his wife on the Mantle afterward. Ron had turned it down at first but after some thought figured the missus would enjoy an evening beyond the lamps. It hadn't struck her until after his death that she'd taken advantage of his confidence. She needed a crane operator, after all.

Sami turned up the heat on the faucet and looked up to the shower head. The scalding water streaming out scraped at her face. She could feel a slight burn on her forehead and cheeks, but not enough to cower from the pain.

Jon had survived the darkness of Midian's race riots, even after the Citizenry had sent him to his death during the Year of Shadows. But Sami's idealistic wet dream was a bridge too far. One of the Undercity's true heroes, snuffed out alongside several others because she'd been too naive to think someone else might have plans for *their* plans.

She reached again to the faucet. It wouldn't turn anymore. The steam billowed in the shower, spilling over the top of the curtain and engulfing the small washroom.

Rupert's death may have been from natural causes, but that didn't assuage Sami's guilt. Marcus had mentioned he'd been on his last legs with the Citizenry before he jumped to Sami's side. She couldn't help but think he'd still be around if she hadn't needed him to shoulder her inexperience.

The water splashed against her body and trickled to the pool forming in the bottom of the tub. She looked at the tangled mess of hair swirling above the drain and plopped herself down as the water continued to rain from the shower spout above. Droplets escaped the streaming water as it reached farther from the spout, transforming the steady flow into a stinging barrage of tiny wet slaps. But the heat of the bath had numbed her skin to the sharpness of the racing droplets, and she could no longer feel any pain. She could no longer feel anything. An all-encompassing numbness had overtaken her, submerging her pain and desires beneath a heavy compress of defeat and apathy. Perhaps that was why it had taken her days to bury Lenora. She knew it needed to be done but couldn't muster the energy. And now, not even a hint of guilt could pierce the suffocating compress.

Sami almost wished the Guardians, or whoever they were, had hauled her away after their attack. Strung her up. Put an end to her now muted life. But they hadn't. They seemed almost indifferent surrounding her on the stage. And after the chaos simmered, they simply walked away. Away from her. Away from Ron. Away from the panic and carnage. They just stomped off with their filth-ridden boots, kicking up dry mud pellets along the way.

Through the splatter of droplets hammering at her face and plinking atop the steaming bath, Sami could make out a sharp rattle from her front screen door. She closed her eyes and sank deeper into her water coffin, hoping to lose the sound. But the rattle grew louder.

It was several minutes before the knocking quieted and nearly an hour before Sami stepped out of the tub. She dried off and wrapped herself in a thick white bathrobe before stepping into the hall. Walking over the clothes lining the floor, she entered the main room, still disheveled from weeks of neglect. Garment piles rivaled the height of the leaf-green couch against the main room wall, and a subtle whiff of Lenora's decomposing carcass floated about the room. It was a smell she hadn't noticed until now, likely hidden behind her own unshowered scent.

Sami stepped to the front window and pulled open the blinds. Reaching for the window latch, her eyes met Jasper's swollen browns as he leaned patiently against her front railing. He lifted his palm to a slight wave but made no immediate gesture to come inside.

She opened the window and reached for the front door. She hadn't wanted to see anyone since the attack but found herself open to Jasper's company in the moment. She took a deep breath before swinging the door to the side and pushing open the screen.

Jasper entered with a somber gaze and hugged her without a word. His warm, tight embrace stirred emotions she thought had died with Rupert and the others. He smelled of the cologne she'd bought him for their anniversary a few months back. The rich scent overtook the room, masking the death still lingering in the air.

"I missed you," he whispered in her ear.

The feeling of his breath on her ear tingled, sending a shiver down her spine and goosebumps across her body. She had missed him too but didn't speak.

He kissed her cheek before taking her by the hand to the couch. They sat close, legs pressed against each other's. Almost by habit, Sami nestled against his body and rested her head on his chest. Jasper untucked his arm and wrapped it around her. It had been a while since she'd felt safe. But she did then. She could actually feel…something. The familiarity of his body. The warmth of his embrace. The kindness of his heart. That she was loved. The leaking of her feelings, drip by drip, soon gave way to a flood of emotion, rousing the typhoon buried within. And she wept.

CHAPTER 16

SOLOMON WEAVES

If there was one thing Solomon had learned from his post as Grand Magus, it was that myths held tremendous influence with common folk. Primed with the innate belief of an omnipotent creator, the part of the mind open to myth was a powerful influencer if hijacked with the right message. It was a trick many charlatans had used to implant certain beliefs, enriching themselves through the vulnerability God had placed for his purposes alone. But now Solomon was planning to restore the true aim of the mind's propensity for faith, renewing its yearning for the promise of salvation. Even if that meant treading dangerously close to the footprints swindlers had pressed before him.

Solomon stood on the concrete edge of the wharf with the open ocean at his back and two long wooden piers reaching deep into the water, flanking each of his sides, his knees trembled behind his robes from the autumn cold. He'd made certain to wear a layer of clothes underneath to prevent the cutting ocean wind from rattling him during his grand sermon. But there was only so much room beneath his ceremonial robes before he'd balloon. Solomon would rather freeze than present as puffy and weak. A criticism he had of his predecessor, Grand Magus Lucious, an overly plump man with poor circulation and even a poorer sense of his image, often needing a chair to get through his entire sermon. Perhaps Solomon would have been more inclined to aid Lucious in his final controversy if he'd carried himself with more dignity befitting his stature. The man, after all, had possessed one of the sharpest religious minds the Faith had seen in generations, regularly overturning decades-long understanding of scripture with modern exegesis, particularly as it came to the Filth.

In the early Faith foundations, the Filth were believed to enter a celestial purgatory after death, adorning the night sky as star-like beings to watch over humanity as caretakers. But Lucious had dismissed this understanding, reinterpreting the passages as metaphorical, merely reflecting the Filths' status as heavenly overseers in the hereafter, granting them the run of Paradise to make up for their suffering in this world. A change the High Council was quick to adopt to satiate the skeptics threatening the spread of the blessed word. Solomon doubted the Council would be as eager to canonize the contribution *he* had in store for the evening's oceanfront sermon. But it wasn't the Council he was trying to convince. All he needed was his parish.

Bathing in the stares of his people, Solomon looked out beyond the throng to the evening dock workers, ignoring their nightly tasks to eavesdrop on the show. Their added scrutiny was starting to rouse his nerves. All the effort he'd put into organizing his revelational sermon would all be for naught if the hardened men of the docks mocked his message openly with his people in earshot. Solomon whispered a private prayer for God's protection from their skepticism before pushing the thought from his mind. He had come too far to allow the meaty and mindless to dictate the Church's future.

It had been a challenge organizing the sermon. The dock supervisor was easy enough to pay off, but getting permission from the chairwoman to allow dozens from his congregation beyond the Wall took far more convincing.

"It poses a security threat," the walrus masquerading as the chairwoman had said, as if the elderly and half-wits among his regular flock were to smuggle in Caravan raiders beneath their hats and shawls.

Solomon had wanted the full weight of his recently bloated church to witness his words. But to compromise with the chairwoman, he reduced his request to just the core group of regulars.

"Even still," the chairwoman said. "We have no way of knowing what could result from allowing that many people access to the docks. The city's northern wharf is our primary point of entry for shipments. It needs to remain highly secure."

"From my understanding, there are many dock workers," said Solomon. "Do you not risk having them on the wharf?"

"Each worker has undergone thorough background screenings and is a former SyndiGuard recruit. We cannot know from where your members have come, and it would take months for us to screen them all."

"Oh, that's unnecessary," said Solomon. "I know exactly where they come from. They are all from God. As are you."

The chairwoman rolled her eyes. "It is done, Solomon. Please show yourself out."

Solomon smiled and stepped to his feet.

The chairwoman had redecorated the office since Lutz's retirement. Gone were the deep wooden tones and vile nude paintings that had passed as art. She had lightened the overall mood, opting for softer grays with white accents. Even the dark mahogany desk Lutz had hauled in from the artisan carpenters of the southern states had been replaced. Now reduced to a thinly framed white table, the chairwoman's monstrous tree trunks were visible from all sides.

There was something to be said about how someone kept their surroundings. A window into their soul. Lutz's style was strength. Broad and boisterous. Firm and resolved. While the chairwoman was more welcoming. Accommodating with more neutral pieces. Less obtrusive. More open. As if creating a tranquil space for others to spend their time. Or with the hope of it, at least.

Solomon stretched out his hand. "God be with you."

The chairwoman's hand was soft, clammy. Like clasping dough. "I suppose I won't be seeing you at the ceremony next week, will I?" asked Solomon.

A confused wrinkle dimpled her brow as Solomon pulled back his hand.

"Oh. You weren't aware?" he said. "Such joyous news. Your husband—ex-husband, my apologies—is set to marry that darling sweetheart of his. I am personally to officiate the wedding."

Solomon watched as rage spilled across her spongy cheeks, burying the parchment paleness under a deep sea of red.

"I am lucky, I guess, that you denied my request," he continued. "The sermon was planned for that very evening. The moon, you know, will be its most luminous that night. Perfect for my grand sermon. But no matter. At least I will get to enjoy the festivities of their loving union. A chance I would not otherwise be able to facilitate with our current demands. Can you believe the entire Midian diocese is fully booked for nuptials for the next two years? What unfortunate circumstances would have befallen such a sweet and adoring couple if my sermon had delayed their evening."

At the seminary, many lessons centered around the influence of the fairer sex. Their ability to manipulate and besiege the will of man, shaking the most resolute from their iron-forged resolve. But Solomon saw something different in the cautionary tales the magi would often hold up as proof. He saw the underlying evil. The Achilles heel in the soul of most people: loneliness. And it was one hell of an influencer.

*

The evening soon reached peak darkness, with only the few wharf lamps and moonlight illuminating the shaded faces in the crowd.

Now was the time. Solomon raised his arms and spoke the Light of God.

"We are collected here on the edge of the city. On the edge of the vastness of the ocean. In the shadow of the great expanse of the heavens. Under the forever watchful eye of our Lord as a witness to my humility. Often, we need reminders of our insignificance in the vast playground of our universe. Taming our egos by recognizing how small we really are. And on this night, such a reminder will be essential to ensuring the sanctity of my faith and servility of my soul."

Sneers from a few of the dockworkers began warming Solomon's blood. *Lord, remove these heathens from our midst.*

"As you all know by now, my beloved brother recently passed, returning to the embrace of our Lord after the years of good works he'd committed his life to. In my days of mourning, I thought on his deeds and message. I revisited our childhood memories and exchanges. I spoke to many of you, listening to how he impacted each of you and your families. How he impacted the lives of so many, and their hopes for the future. And I was struck by something so clear…so obvious…that I can only blame the devil for its concealment from my eyes. Do you all recall the Testament of Purpose?"

Heads in the crowd nodded silently.

Of course they do. It was only the central teaching at the high holidays. But today, Solomon had other plans for its telling.

"Beyond the deep messages of servitude buried within its

pages, the Testament of Purpose speaks of a prophet whose acts transcended the outwardly spiritual. Acts of which, by their very nature, prove the divine providence inherent in each. The shepherding of souls. The dedication to the tribe. The casting out of evil oppressors. Much like the Unknown Prophet, Jericho committed his life to the people of our fair city in an almost step-by-step retelling of the exploits we read within the pages of Purpose. Neither he nor the prophet from the scripture spoke of God or His will. But in the end…it is clear to me…as it is clear to many of you, they were one and the same in status."

It wasn't much of a stretch with the legends of Jericho Sands having sowed the fields of his prophethood these last decades. And the soft murmurs and eager stares seemed to prove it. Even the dockworkers appeared open to the comparison. But it hadn't been this portion of the sermon that had kept him up the past several nights. It was easy enough to make a claim for the people to adopt as truth, less so when attempting to lead people to arrive at their own conclusions through innuendo and word association.

"My brother…a prophet. It's humbling to imagine. To know that we share the same blood. The same lineage." That part was dubious but not entirely dishonest. Their mother had always claimed they shared the same father. And despite the scores of different men that had frequented their small apartment through the years, Solomon had witnessed several repeating through the rotation. So, it wasn't entirely out of the realm of possibility. But it was certainly the story he had to sell if he was to lead his people to the watering hole. Whether they took a sip would be up to them.

"And we know from scripture that had Jericho had a son, he'd have continued the line of prophets after him. As prophets beget prophets. But alas, the line has been broken. For Jericho chose to commit himself wholly to the plight of the Undercity." And commit himself wholly to other sorts of holes. "With Jericho's prophethood now at an end, we must look to another shepherd to lead us. One that embodies the same heart, spirit, and dedication to the people. One who is not afraid to lead in times of crisis. One that steers us away from violence and slaughter. A protector. An advisor. A brother—"

"YOU ARE THE ONE!" a voice rang through the crowd.

Calls of agreement followed as Solomon bowed his head with humility. He couldn't have planned it any better.

"Thank you all." He paused as if to convey thoughtful consideration before looking back out over the congregation. "Although a debate still rages among scholars about how wide the net of prophethood may reach within a family, and although there have been past prophets that passed on their mantle to brothers and cousins, I simply may not be worthy. Only if God wills it shall it be done."

"BACK TO WORK!" another voice boomed over a loudspeaker, shaking the dockworkers back to their posts.

The servant asks, and the Master provides. The timing

couldn't have been more perfect. Solomon had arrived at his grand finale. And there was no room for anyone but the most devout if he was to pull it off.

"Brothers and sisters. Come. Let us congregate, unifying as one as we pray for the guidance of our Lord."

Solomon herded the crowd in toward him. The space between them narrowed until they stood shoulder to shoulder, toe to heel, with Solomon at the head of the crowd and the balls of his feet pressed to the wharf's concrete edge. The water kissed his sandaled heels as the waves splashed against the docks, and Solomon could feel his knees tremble, no longer from the cold. His heart throbbed in his neck and nerves danced atop his skin. After one final check, ensuring the workers had left, Solomon pivoted his feet to face the water before reaching toward the moonlit sky.

"My Lord has spoken!"

Solomon took a single step forward, carefully reaching his foot down the several inches to the blackened water surface. Then, pushing the entirety of his weight forward, he pulled his back foot from the wharf and stepped down to gasps from the crowd.

"PRAISE BE!"

"GOD IS GREAT!"

"HALLELUJAH!"

The calls of God's praise echoed out over the open ocean as Solomon's footfalls splashed forward atop the water's surface. On his fifth step, his footing gave way, and he plunged into the frigid darkness.

CHAPTER 17

ARVIN'S FEES

"I bet it's a mile high."

"A mile? No way! It's a mile from my house to the market. There's no way it's that high."

The rusted hood of the broken-down school bus scraped at the seat of Arvin's jeans as he gazed up at the darkened metal platform. Miron lay next to him on the smooth, unblemished side, shifting his weight and adjusting his footing to avoid slipping off the edge, something Arvin had experienced on his first go-around after scaling the stalled eyesore. Only he'd fallen from the roof, learning quickly that the rust stains on his clothes were far better than a broken arm.

"Why is it called the Mantle?" asked Miron as he struggled to find a perfect balance.

"I dunno. Probably because it has important things on it. My mom puts my brother's trophies and pictures on our mantle."

"We don't have a mantle... We have a shelf, though. That's where our pictures are."

"A shelf *is not* a mantle," Arvin responded derisively.

Miron was a few years younger but lived in the apartment

complex just down the street from Arvin's adopted home. With most of his time spent on schooling, runs, and visits to the shelter, Arvin's friendship with Miron was more out of convenience than shared interests. He was a nice enough kid but often annoying with his childish understandings of the world.

"What do you think is on it?" Miron asked.

"People. Businesses. It's like down here, but they get to see the stars."

"Really? I wouldn't want to live up there. What if you fell off?"

"You can't fall off."

"How do you know?"

"I just do," said Arvin.

Miron paused a second before turning to Arvin. "So, you'd want to live there?"

"Hell, yeah. The stars. The sunsets."

"You've seen the stars a bunch," said Miron.

Arvin slid from the hood. "Only on runs. But even still, I haven't ever seen a sunset." He reached down and dusted the orange stains from his pants.

Miron stumbled after him less gracefully, thudding to the ground and kicking up a plume of dirt before climbing back to his feet and adjusting his thick glasses. "Do you think the people up there are important?"

"I dunno."

"If a mantle is where they put important things, wouldn't

important people live there?"

"I guess."

Arvin curled back the scrapyard fence, and the boys slipped through to the other side. Across the street sat an abandoned brick building, half-collapsed with boarded-up windows and scrawls of graffiti praising *the great* Jericho Sands. Arvin had seen it sit dormant for years but only recently noticed the yellow caution tape around its perimeter.

"Whoa!" said Miron. "Does that mean they're going to blow that up?"

"I dunno."

"Man, I would love to see that. Watching the bricks go everywhere. It would be awesome."

Arvin had to admit, he'd love to see it live as well. He had once watched a demolition on TV, and unlike what Miron was picturing, the bricks didn't go anywhere but down, appearing as if the building had collapsed on itself.

"I can ask my brother," Arvin said.

"Really? He does that stuff?"

"Well...no. But I'm sure he knows somebody that does."

"Cool," said Miron. "Hey, did you hear about the magus that walked on water?"

Arvin had. It was all anyone was talking about at the shelter. But having met the Grand Magus several times, Arvin struggled to believe it was true. The man came across more sour than saintly, and even the shelter sisters couldn't believe it.

"*If Solomon had performed a miracle, it would have been disappearing all those whores he has cycling through the church regularly,*" Arvin overheard Sister Mary Anne say.

"*And despite how many shots of the cleanse he's gone through over the years, I doubt it was enough to purify him to that level,*" Sister Sabrina followed up, to giggles from the others.

"I heard he walked out into the middle of the sea," said Miron. "That'd be so cool! I'd catch so many fish. They would never suspect someone being all the way out there without a boat."

Arvin ignored the comment and kept his pace toward the Marketplace, his new stomping grounds for runs of a different kind. He had stopped all runs beyond the gates since his little brush with the Guard. They had hauled him into a blank, windowless room with only six concrete slabs and a locked door to keep him company. Arvin was left to sleep alone on the cold floor for hours before waking to an unusual man with a lazy eye. Certainly not a Guardian—at least, if he had been, he wasn't dressed like one. The man wore a black suit and tie, and despite appearing fairly young, his silver hair slicked back to curls behind his ears told a different tale of his age.

"You are in quite the predicament," said the man in black. "What do you think your brother would say if he heard about this?"

It was all Arvin needed to hear before completely folding.

The evenings in the Marketplace were varying spectacles of street performances, Faith preachers, and crowds unseen anywhere else in the city. Unlike the day when the streets fell quiet, with only a rat or two gallivanting through the roadway to cut the eerie stillness, the nights were painted with a pageantry of colorful characters, each adding their own impression to the tapestry of the market streets.

Outside Jensen's Beardery, a nude contortionist performed an interpretative recreation of life beneath the Mantle. With his rubber limbs and limber movements, the performer had become a staple of the market core, attracting many from across the Undercity to witness "the man with no bones." Arvin had seen the performance at least a dozen times since his new placement. Being an ideal landmark for his clientele to congregate, he would often take in the show while he awaited his meet-ups.

The boys stood on the periphery, the surrounding crowd's attention directed to the hand-standing artist, his manhood flopping with his airy movements. Miron shielded his eyes while Arvin kept watch on the area. It wasn't long before the flailing arms of a tall man across the road seized Arvin's attention.

"Go get us some Icers," he said to Miron, reaching into his pocket.

"What kind?"

He clinked the handful of change into Miron's palm. "I dunno. Lemonade?"

"What if they don't have lemonade?"

"It doesn't matter. Get anything."

Arvin tipped his head to the man waving furiously and stepped into the street, cutting through the thick exhaust fumes sputtering from the stalled cars collected along the road. Approaching the other side, he watched his hailer direct him with a tilt of his neck before evaporating into the darkness of an alleyway. Since his little agreement with the man in black, Arvin had been forced into decrepit drug dens, filthy alleys, and seedy bars throughout the Marketplace. And despite the number of times he'd serviced the often dank and foul-scented locales, he could never shake the chill that rode his spine on each go. He'd have much preferred the long and weary shelter runs, even with a payload stacked high in one of the old holey rollers. But he wasn't given much choice when the man in black mentioned his brother. Arvin understood what was implied, and it wasn't a simple tattling on what he'd been up to. If he didn't do what he was now being asked—pushing skeet for the man in black as punishment—his brother would face the consequences.

As a Filth, Arvin always expected misery in some form or another. It wasn't anything that could be threatened upon him. It was his destiny. But his brother wasn't doomed with the same fate, and Arvin couldn't allow his foolishness to harm him. The hefty chains of love and family had stolen his freedom. And although he'd have gladly made the trade a thousand times again, Arvin had inadvertently opened the door of true suffering the Filth were never meant to experience: the risk of loss.

Peering through the long alleyway, Arvin noticed a figure tucked behind a large metal dumpster, jostling back and forth in the faint light leaking through from the street. Steeling his nerves, he approached slowly, only to be thrust violently against the alley wall as he rounded past the dumpster.

"Whatcha doin', man?! You're bringing heat!"

Arvin froze against the wall as the man's large, filthy hand pressed against his small chest. Crouching behind the mound of trash heaping from the open bin, the man darted his head up and down, eyeing the street as if an army of pursuers were about to push through.

"I wasn't followed," said Arvin. He wasn't exactly certain of that, but he figured the assurance might take the edge off.

After rubbernecking a moment longer, the man turned to Arvin with a curious glare, squinching his eyes as if to bring them into focus. "You're the Filth boy."

He was *a* Filth boy, but wasn't sure what he meant by *the* Filth boy.

"The one moving the shit to the Under Eastside."

Arvin didn't know how to respond—or even if he should. Instead, he pulled the baggie from his pocket into view, and the man snatched it from his fingertips.

"Fuck 'em is all I have to say. You shouldn't do a thing they ask," the man said as he handed Arvin a wad of filthy bills. "I've known the fuckin' guy my whole life. And he thinks some chick's got me so turned around, I don't know what's up in my own Local. Fuck Bass. Wait until he has Amelia rubbin' up on his women. See if he doesn't come beggin' for me to come back."

Even during Faith runs, Arvin had learned not to hang

around too long after a delivery. The sisters would often require his help with other tasks around the Center if he didn't appear busy. Once, he'd even been tasked to scrub the tile floors of a church nave with a small brush and bucket of soapy water. His knees were raw by the time he'd finished. And after pushing to his feet, he turned to see the church magus sitting atop the stage with a smirk, reveling in his anguish. But now, with Arvin's deliveries being made to less reputable sorts (*debatable, really*), the risks were much higher. Indulging addicts with any more than the simple exchange of cash and drugs had already proven to be dangerous. Not only to his sense of smell—most carried a putrid odor of sweat and urine—but also to the safety of his brother. It was on his second run for the man in black that he'd been robbed after lingering for too long. Thankfully, the debt was forgiven. But Barrel, the brick house of a man who served his lazy-eyed employer, had warned Arvin that it wouldn't be if it happened again.

Eager to escape the raving addict now frothing with anger at the Citizenry, Arvin nodded and slipped away to the safety of the crowded street. His swift exit didn't seem to bother the man very much; he could still make out every second word of the addict's rant, even after rounding the corner into the bustle of the market core. *And I'm the one bringing heat.*

Looking across the street to the sea of people surrounding the nude performer, Arvin spotted Miron cowering several feet from the crowd, hiding his eyes with an overflowing Icer in his clenched fist.

"You can have the melted one," Arvin said to Miron as he sidled up to him.

"Okay. But can we go? I hate this part."

"Why? It's the best—"

"INFIDELS!"

A street preacher pushed through the audience, spreading his long trench coat to shield the man's nakedness as it thrust high in the air.

"Shield your eyes! Lower your gaze! Or burn in the fire for eternity!"

Groans bubbled from the crowd as people dispersed with rounding eyes and shaking heads. The performer swung to his feet and lunged at the preacher, pushing him to the ground.

"This is how I make a living!" he yelled. "I let you preach your bullshit on the corner all day. I never bother you. But then you come here and ruin my finale—where I make the most tips. Are you going to fill my pockets?"

Climbing to his feet, the preacher smirked. "First pray for some pockets, and then God will provide."

The light from the Beardery's storefront sheened off the performer's bald head as he rushed the preacher again. They locked in an arm's-length grapple, shoving each other from side to side. The crowd returned with a roar of cheers and jeers. Arvin stumbled forward after the rising tide of onlookers shoved him from behind, knocking the cup from his hand and scattering the crushed ice at the feet of the crowd. Miron reached out and clutched Arvin, keeping him upright briefly before another wave swept them both to the ground. Arvin tugged on Miron's shirt as he led him forward through the forest of legs, shimmying atop the spilled ice until escaping beyond the chaos.

Dusted in street filth with wet blotches from the spilled Icers peppering his clothes, Miron looked at Arvin with a crack spidering one of his lenses. "I still have a bit left." He held up a clenched cup with half-melted shavings spilling out over the sides. "You can have it."

Arvin smiled, remembering why he continued to keep him around.

Walking back to Plainsview, the boys went back and forth on who they thought had won the fight, the battle still raging when they stepped away from the ruckus.

"The bald guy is squirmy," said Miron. "He's too hard to hit."

"Yeah, but street preachers have people pushing and spitting on them all day. That'd toughen anyone up. Faith folks are usually not to be reckoned with." Images of Sister Mary Anne raining down blows with her thick leather belt flashed in his mind. The worst was when she'd tear strips into his bare thighs, leaving dark red welts that would take weeks to heal. Arvin rubbed the spot on his leg where the memory had ghosted an imprint. But as his hands brushed the front of his pants, a far worse image bloomed.

"The money!"

He turned his pockets inside out, searching for a fold or

hidden crevice concealing the wad.

"We have to go back," said Arvin.

They retraced their footsteps with the urgency of a washroom run after a hefty helping of his mother's meatloaf. But the money was gone. Arvin's stomach sank. He had spent his last few pennies on the Icers now coating the soles of marketgoers. He didn't even have a cent to pay back. Arvin's knees crumbled beneath him.

"I don't have any money, but I can probably sell my Jericho action figure for a few dollars," said Miron. "It's a first edition."

Arvin wondered why Miron, someone with a heart as pure as the Mantle air, would ever want to be friends with a degenerate like him. He was a Filth. A skeet-pushing Filth at that. With nothing to offer the world but a pull of his little red wagon.

Arvin looked to Miron. "Thank you. But you don't have to. I know what I can sell to make back the money."

CHAPTER 18
ATLAS'S BREED

Atlas couldn't understand the words at first. It might as well have been a toddler's first attempt at stringing together a sentence. Incoherent. Nonsensical. It just wasn't possible for the words to mean how they sounded. The meaning was absurd. Impossible. And even though it was a dream any SyndiCares kid could have only wished to be true, he couldn't believe it.

Atlas looked deep into Alanna's lustrous green eyes, watching her pupils wax and wane under the streetlights. Her plush cheeks firmed with the solemn truth of her words. Even when she clasped his hand, he felt no tremble. Not even the faint thrum of a hastened heartbeat. Only a softness to ease him gently past his disbelief.

The evening had started out unlike any other. A match for the ages. The final minutes of the National Driftball Finals hushed the entire Undercity until the roar from Midian's game-winning score shook the Mantle from beneath, reverberating cheers off the Wall, cascading the rumble through the steel sky and out across the eastern ocean.

Atlas shot up from his seat as the ball crossed into the end zone, triggering memories of his childhood victories. The rush of immense joy. The relief of suspense. The firm clutches of his housemates. The SyndiCares Cup was the achievement of all achievements back at the Home; the winning house was awarded an old trophy with the year and home number of the victor engraved on its base. Atlas recalled seeing at least thirty carvings haphazardly etched into the large square block beneath the tarnished silver goblet. SyndiCares Home #3 had won only once during his time at the orphanage, and he'd been a part of it.

Atlas was not the best player on the team, but he wasn't the worst either. He had held his own during the tournament, with several scores over the month-long event. He was even given the honor of housing the trophy for a couple of weeks. The pride he wore with the trophy at his bedside was much like the pride he'd felt walking into the Mantle's Shade with Alanna on his arm. But now, gripping her in celebration to the cheers of the pub, the feeling slipped beneath a cloud of immense shame. The flood of memories were stained crimson from Tommy's death. Tommy hadn't even been part of the Cup celebration back at the Home, off melting ants with a looking glass or battling crayfish from the small stream next to the administration offices. But even still, Tommy's inescapable presence in Atlas's youth now sullied the once-happy memory.

"Everything okay?" Alanna yelled over the clamor after he loosened his embrace.

"Yeah. Just too crowded. Can we leave?"

Alanna took his hand, leading him through the riotous celebration to the top of the pub steps outside. People began pouring out from the surrounding buildings, chanting a limerick in unison that shook the streetlights with its reverb.

The Chair sits up on high steel.
Pushing the wee men to heel.
But out on the pitch.
We make them our bitch.
Pushing it deep till they squeal.

With the recent flood of homeless and thousands of drunken driftball fans now caroling through the streets, the Grove bulged with the forgotten and revelrous. The destitute, caught in the whirlwind of Midian's championship win, pushed farther into the alleyways, while the drunks among them celebrated with beer passed from person to person. Atlas tried to enjoy the moment, but Tommy's face was everywhere in the crowd. He watched Alanna's eyes ignite with the joy of the mob as she joined in the now thundering chorus.

The Chair sits up on high steel.
Pushing the wee men to heel.
But out on the pitch.
We make them our bitch.
Pushing it deep till they squeal.

The bliss in Alanna's smile seemed to tame his ravenous anxiety, his heart calming, breath easing. But even with his guilt still blooming from the joy playing out in the streets, he knew he couldn't steal the moment from her any longer.

Atlas forced a blur on his eyes and pulled her down the steps, squeezing into the streaming sea of fans marching through the streets. Her laughter climbed above the noise. Her delight pushing him farther into the beer and vomit-scented crowd until a soft tug on his arm stalled his feet. Turning back, he saw Alanna being pulled by a large, shirtless man into a group of circling fans. Painted head-to-toe in the gold and brown Midian colors, the man raised Alanna onto his shoulders, stretching her hands over the crowd. Atlas felt a punch of jealousy as her pleasure radiated across the sea of people. But after she leaned in to the large buffoon's ear, the excitement melted from Alanna's eyes. Ignoring her whispers, the man continued his drunken dance, shouting the chant to the Mantle above.

The Chair sits up on high steel.
Pushing the wee men to heel.
But out on the pitch.
We make them our bitch.
Pushing it deep till they squeal.

With the chaos of the celebration distracting the crowd,

only Atlas noticed the buffoon slowly drop to his knees, scratching at his neck. He struggled a yell as his painted gold face now burned a deep, fiery orange. Anchored with her locked feet, Alanna's legs wrapped tightly around his neck, sealing the breath in his lungs. Lurching forward like a camel relieving its rider, the buffoon collapsed, and Alanna dismounted from his shoulders.

She reached for Atlas's hand, pulling him through the pressed bodies and up a building stoop edging the parade. Atop the several steps, Atlas looked out to where the large man had collapsed. It was as if he hadn't existed, now swallowed up by the throng.

"You okay?" he said to Alanna, leaning into her ear. It was clear she was, staring out over the crowd with a smile in her eyes. But the question was more for him, making certain he hadn't imagined the image of a man collapsing at her feet.

"Yup," she said, reaching for his hand.

"Sorry about that back there. I didn't notice what happened until you were already on his shoulders."

She looked out to the slow-moving stream of people. "Oh, that's okay. I didn't mind at first. Until he didn't want to put me down. My whole life, I've had to deal with men like him. The Bottoms is filled with them. They think they can just take what they want. As if I'm some helpless girl." She turned back to Atlas with a glint in her eye. "I'm not."

They sat on the steps until the celebration died out. From the rowdy chants. To the drunken cheers. To the hobble of the exhausted. Slowly, reams of people began peeling away until the nearly vacant street exposed the aftermath. Vomit and spilled drinks were splotched across the pavement. Torn clothes and debris swept to the curbs from the thousands of marching feet. And the lingering scent of beer masked the fried Undercity air. As if tired from the spectacle of the evening, Alanna rested her head on Atlas's shoulder, gazing out to the filth-ridden street. With her warmth pressed up against him, Atlas's mind drifted back to the meaningless existence he'd suffered through for so many years. It seemed so far away. Like another lifetime ago. He couldn't imagine having to wrestle away those demons again. Not now. Not with everything going so well. Not with Alanna by his side.

It had been a while since Atlas realized his feelings for her. A while since he'd fallen hopelessly in love. She'd always been his future. He'd known that since the death of her parents. But instead of a future of service he'd always planned, it was now one with a promise of joy.

There'd been many chances to tell her how much he cared. At his apartment while lazily enjoying a movie together. At the Hall, working side-by-side in her office, sorting through paperwork. But as the quiet calm of the street pushed the chaos of the celebration into neighboring boroughs, the distant cheers massaging the silence tuned the ambiance just so.

Atlas shook away his nerves and parted his lips, eager to say the words. But she spoke first.

"Atlas. I have to tell you something."

A tightness clasped his throat. His breathing hurried. *Is she about to say it, too?*

"But before I do, you have to know… I only just learned about it. It wasn't anything I was concealing—I would never hide anything from you."

Alanna lifted her head off his shoulder, her face sculpted with worry. The softness of her cheek now firm, unyielding. As if her words were going to cut deep. Atlas had never seen her eyes so still. Not even recounting her parents' death. It felt ominous. Weighty. And his hope for her proclamation of love melted beneath the sense of foreboding creeping beneath his skin.

"Jericho was your father."

The words fell on the air as if spoken in tongues. Atlas's mind struggled to assemble the true meaning of the sounds. But the sincerity in Alanna's face soon washed away the disbelief, and he forced out the only words he could think of in the moment.

"At least he wasn't a clown."

Alanna's cheeks filled, but she maintained a quiet stare, searching his eyes for a reaction. But Atlas could barely process the information, let alone determine his feelings. As a child, he'd have been overjoyed to know his father was someone of importance. One more thing to own that set himself apart from the sameness of everyone else. A hero's son—or the progeny of infamy. But now, his feelings were far more complicated.

"How…do you know, for sure?" he asked.

"Bass," Alanna said softly. "The chairman, actually. He

made it known before Shoehorn took over. I don't know why. What his purpose was. But when Bass heard, he needed to know if it was true. He figured it was probably why Jericho was so open to working with them. To protect you. And…"

Alanna paused as if the next words pained her to speak. Her eyes fell to her lap. Atlas squeezed her hand to let her know it was okay. He'd be okay. Even if he wasn't certain what it all could mean in the moment.

She took a breath and raised her eyes back to his. "And, when Jericho turned you away…Bass knew it was true. It didn't make sense otherwise. Why refuse someone with all the training and experience of a Guardian? And it wasn't because he was afraid you were still one of them. He would have had Bass look into it. Keep you at arm's length until we were certain. But he just said no. Sending up a red flag. Pushing Bass to do…what Bass does."

Atlas had watched—even helped—Bass choke the life from the man she claimed was his father. He thought on the different looks, the peculiar expressions Jericho shot at Sami during that night. There was something between them not shared openly. Something he hadn't seen until now. *Did Sami know?* Was that what she was mumbling when he'd left her on her porch all those months ago? The questions surged like the rush of rapids through a punctured dam, drowning his thoughts in a sea of possibilities. He'd always wished to discover his truth. And after learning of his mother, he was certain he'd pieced together his past with enough confidence to know his story. But now, if what Alanna had told him was true, if Jericho Sands was his father, the simple story of the trapeze artist unable to care for her child was merely the fin of the beast splashing atop the water's surface.

He took a breath and stared vacantly over the street, a million questions dancing in his head. None seemed to rise above the rest with any urgency. But he had to ask her something. She had known his father more than most, and this was his chance to learn…something.

"Did…he like driftball?"

"Not really," said Alanna. "He was always too busy…but he still wanted everyone to enjoy themselves. And he knew the value of rooting for something outside ourselves. Unifying the city under one team. So, he encouraged us to take in a game every now and then. He came with us once in a while. Even tried talking to us about league news or what happened in the match the day before. But it was easy to see he had no idea what he was talking about." A small laugh escaped her lips. "It was endearing, though."

She clutched Atlas's arm and nestled her head closer to his neck. He felt a trickle of excitement wriggle down his spine, a mixture of her affection with a twist of his alleged father's exposed humanity.

"You trust me, right?" she asked.

In the moment, Atlas wasn't even sure he could trust his ears. His mind was racing through a string of what-ifs and what-abouts. He could hardly form a thought with the jumbled mess rattling around in his brain. But he had to respond to the question.

And only moments ago, it would have been as easy a yes as an invitation to share her bed.

"Yeah. Of course."

"Okay," she said. "I know it's a lot. But you needed to know—I would want to know. And…" Alanna took a breath before squeezing his arm tighter. "Something's coming, Atlas. Something big. I can't tell you now because you'd just overthink it. But you have to trust me. Okay?"

Something big. As if learning his father was Jericho Sands had not been big enough.

"The Lord's Messenger has arrived!" a preacher cried out, rushing through the streets, chasing the now evaporated crowd. "He calls us to him, and we shall obey!"

Alanna sat up and pressed her lips softly on Atlas's cheek before pulling him to his feet and leading him home.

CHAPTER 19
SAMI DECEIVED

It was hard for Sami to laugh, even with the crowded theater convulsing with pleasure from the torrent of comedic gems that scrolled across the screen. Jasper had suggested a comedy to help boost her spirits. And although she resisted at first, suggesting a dark romance entitled *The Witch's Keeper* instead, she figured Jasper needed the laughs more than her. Sami recognized she hadn't been much of a delight these past weeks, and there was only so much sadness a person watching the tempest from the outside could take. He needed at least a few smiles to store away if he was to make it through the storm of her company. And judging by the previews, *The Witch's Keeper* appeared scant of happy moments. It was a tale of unrequited love between an ordinary farm boy and a country girl with hidden supernatural powers, on a journey to discover the truth of her parentage, all the while stringing the boy along as he served her devious needs. Sami doubted a happy ending to the tale. But nonetheless, the darkness of the story matched her mood and made it all the more enticing a couple of hours to sit through.

Another burst of laughter echoed through the theater.

Jasper's loud bellow cut through the roar, drumming at her ear. Nothing particularly funny happened on screen—that she had seen. But then again, she doubted *Eyebrows Aplenty* had been created with her sense of humor in mind.

Sami worked to shake free the nerves climbing her leg, bouncing her foot slightly at first but ramping up more aggressively as it spread to her thighs. The cut of the actors' voices shrieked in her ear, and she could feel the crowded breaths in the theater suck the oxygen from her lungs.

"I'm going to step out for a moment," she whispered to Jasper.

He nodded without shaking his focus, enthralled by the slapstick playing out on the silver screen.

The theater exited to a quiet Plainsview street. Even though the lamps had long deadened for the evening, only a sparse gathering in front of a local bar breathed any life into the once-busy entertainment district. When she was younger, she'd stroll the lively street with Rupert and her mother, bouncing from theater to theater, debating which movie or play to see. They'd clutch her hands, swinging her from sidewalk tile to sidewalk tile to avoid the rushing lava bubbling up from each crack, skirting the large crowds gathered outside ticket booths and outdoor patios, slipping by lines of people, awaiting a table at the many restaurants teeming with diners. Simply being out on the busy street was enough to fill her night with happy memories. But now, the cold chains of shuttered businesses and boarded-up restaurants had ripped the soul from her childhood memories.

Sami stared at the movie poster clinging to the theater doors. An image of a young woman's long, dark hair cascaded atop the back of a soiled white dress amid a darkened forest, cropped to emphasize the thin white hand stretching down from her bodice, with flickers of orange flame rising from her fingertips. *The Witch's Keeper,* it read. *Love's Sacrifice for the Pursuit of Revenge.* She so wanted to see that movie.

Steps away, a large rat scurried along the sidewalk, hauling a chunk of discarded pizza from a tipped trash bin next to the theater. He paid no mind to the girl entranced by a movie poster, only living to serve his own needs. Not concerned with the opinions or wants of others. A selfish existence, where his appetites were all that mattered. Sami felt a pang of envy. What she would give to be that rat, even for a day.

The movie let out, and scores of people spilled into the street. Sami watched as Jasper stepped through the doors, searching the faces of the emptying theater. She wished she could duck, slip away into the night among a group of friends that didn't mind her tagging along. She wouldn't say much. Just enjoy the camaraderie of ordinary people going through their ordinary lives without the weight of responsibility crushing their souls. Maybe that was all she needed to feel like herself again. A simple existence where the fate of the entire city didn't lie on her shoulders. She could still work with the needy. All they needed was a helping hand. Not a leader. She almost wished she had taken Solomon's offer back at the church. Looking past the racist and homophobic teachings, ignoring the misogyny and forced child labor. Complicit in the abuse of brainwashed children, forced to think they were less human than everyone else. Sami's stomach churned. She could never. She'd rather suffer a thousand losses like the one in Big Town and live through a thousand more deaths than ever work under the banner of the Faith. What she would give to be that rat.

Sami waved her hand above her head.

The walk home was filled with commentary and dramatic recreations of *Eyebrows Aplenty*, starring the one and only Jasper Keep. His boisterous impressions rang out through the streets, angering passersby out for a quiet walk and the homeless hunkered down in their tents for the evening.

"Keep it down," she whispered after he startled awake a man lying atop a steel grate.

"Lighten up," Jasper said playfully. He reached for her gloved hand and raised it toward the Mantle, shouting, "We have come upon a fork in the road and have chosen to take it!" Another gem from the film.

"You're waking people," she said, pulling her hand away.

"Well, what are they doing here anyway?"

What were they doing here? Plainsview was now awash with tents and makeshift shelters, mostly tucked away between buildings and recessed lots, but several lay openly edging the sidewalk, cloaked in filth-ridden sheets and flattened boxes.

On the best of days, Plainsview was home to only a

smattering of homeless, those who had grown up in the quiet neighborhood and had fallen on hard times. But now it appeared as if a migration of homeless had gripped the once vibrant community, and Sami was horrified she'd been so self-consumed to have not noticed the suffering.

"How long has it been like this?" she asked Jasper.

"Honestly, I just noticed earlier today."

For a moment, Sami wondered if they'd been caught up in the street celebrations and hunkered down afterward. But she quickly dismissed the thought. The homeless were not the sort to mingle with large groups of people, a survival instinct most learned early on.

"Do you know what's happened?" she asked.

"No. I've been so preoccupied with making sure you're okay, I haven't even had a chance to get back to the Hall."

The words fell on her ears like a cinderblock. "The *Hall*?"

"C'mon, Sami. Let's not do this now."

Her lips tightened. She could feel the heat radiate beneath her thick coat. He'd still been going to the Hall. Still been seeing Bass. Sami was certain they were behind the attack at Big Town, but it hadn't made sense how they'd arranged it without having advance notice. She'd been so careful. Was Jasper the reason?

Refusing the demons further, she pushed aside the haunting thoughts. She couldn't let her anger turn to paranoia. Jasper had been there for her through it all. It was impossible that he had caused all the suffering.

Sami and Jasper soon rounded the corner to her street. The homeless had pushed into the residential areas as well, setting up camp in the back alleys, with some opting for the front sidewalks instead. None appeared bold enough to push onto private property—except one, on the steps of Sami's home. A large, cloaked mass sat silently as they approached. The thick brown burlap slumped against her thin metal handrail like a folded sack of Barrens potatoes.

"Can I help you?" said Sami uneasily, slowing her steps. It wasn't as if she feared the needy and homeless, but she wasn't sure this person was either. Since Big Town, she'd been on edge, careful about her surroundings. And this was the only migrant that had inched onto any of the properties on her street.

The large sack blossomed with her words, and the blazing ginger mane of Marcus Bertram irradiated the darkened step.

"Geez! You want two heart attacks on your conscience, honey?" said Marcus, shooting to his feet.

The barb should have sank deeper, but her surprise dulled its blow.

"Marcus. What are you doing here?" said Sami.

"Waitin' for your ass. How late do you kids stay out? The goddamned lamps will be roaring in a couple of hours."

"Come in." Sami tried ushering Marcus inside, but he stepped from her porch and waved her off.

"No, no. It's too late for that. How about you send *sweet lips* inside and we talk for a moment?"

Jasper slipped inside to the squeal of her screen door cutting the early morning calm. Sami took a seat on the step, Marcus's warmth still radiating from its surface.

"How've you been, dear?" The squint of his left eye forced his right to consume her entirely, as if only the one eye could read the truth in her face.

Sami exhaled a quiet breath. "Not good, if I'm honest."

"I figured as much. Done my best to keep our people in line with you on the sidelines. Givin' you space, is all. But dear… I'm old. I can't hold down the fort much longer. People need to know where we're headin'. Especially after the shit went down. They're ravenous. They need a leader. I've done my best with distractions, but I ain't pretty enough to keep their heads spinnin' for long."

Sami stared out to the darkened homes across the street. At one time, she'd known everyone in the neighborhood. What they did for a living. Their hobbies. Even their ailments. But many had moved on over the years, and only a few familiar faces had stayed. There was Mr. and Mrs. Shields, of course, who'd sooner storm the Syndicate halls than leave the only home they'd ever known. Nasir Naroo and his wife, Anya, had almost purchased a new home in Uptown Grove. But after learning of the Citizenry's influence in the area, much preferred the Plainsview school district for their future kids. Sami didn't blame them for avoiding the indoctrination camps of Grove schools; she'd probably do the same if she were to have children. And then there were the Mastersons and their son Jacob, who had taken in a shelter child from the Faith a few years back. She had planned a visit before Jericho's death but hadn't found the time in recent months with chaos following her every move.

Much like the crowds in the entertainment district, the rest had chosen change. Growing. Evolving. And there she was, clutching to the past. Fearful of the future. Convincing thousands that they'd reached the best they could beneath the metal sky. A perfect state that needed shielding. From the likes of Bass. From the winds of change. But she was no longer sure that she'd been right. Thousands still suffered under Jericho's "utopia." Maybe more needed to be done than tearing down an old wall. Force the Syndicate's hand further. Perhaps she'd been wrong all along.

"Marcus, why are the homeless migrating?"

"They're leaving the Midriff. Not sure why. But folks have seen the Guard clearing them out. The Bottoms have been overrun. No more room at the inn. They gotta go somewhere. Something we can fix if you come back. Give us something else to focus our time."

"Marcus…I—"

"Don't say it! No fuckin' way you're gonna say it! Jon and his men didn't die for you to say you're fuckin' off. And I ain't been leadin' half the goddamn Undercity in your stead, with this hole burning in my stomach, screaming for you to come back, just to hear you've up and quit."

Pain seared her chest at the thought of her words leading

people to their deaths. The shame of it flooded her body with a tingling warmth as blood flushed her caramel skin. She'd forced Rupert and Jon to their deaths, all to keep her grip on the past. To stop the city from moving on. And now all she wanted to do was run. Forget the torturous thoughts. Bury the pain. But how could she now, with her hands steeped in blood?

"I know," she said, feigning a smile. "I wasn't going to say that. I just need a little more time." What she would give to be that rat.

"Okay. Fair enough. It mustn't be easy losin' so much, so quickly. I get it. But you have to understand that people need you. They've always needed you. You may think that you convinced us to join your side, but the truth is, all you did was wake us to the reality of our situation. We were sleepin'. Not considerin' what we had goin' for us. In the end…remember…we chose you."

Sami pulled the screen door closed after watching Marcus limp away toward the tram station. She wondered how much more time she had bought herself before he would return. How much longer she could delay the truth. That, or regain her nerve.

"What'd he want?" asked Jasper, lounging on the couch with a spread book on his chest.

"Just seeing how I'm doing."

"Okay. As long as he doesn't expect you to go back to the Faction," he said.

Sami cut her eyes at Jasper. *As if it's his choice.*

She snarled. "And what if I do?" Even though it was the

furthest thing from her mind, the thought of Jasper "putting his foot down" sparked a blaze fueled by exhaustion, fear, and guilt: the soak of her spirit.

"C'mon, Sami!" Jasper rose to his feet, tossing his book to the side. "You're kidding me, right? You nearly killed yourself with this little rebellion! If Bass hadn't owed Rupert, you could've been right out there in the dirt with Lenora!"

The rage melted. Flames were extinguished. Disbelief smothering any hint of life animating her in the moment.

"Shit..." Jasper sighed, shaking his lowered head.

Had the entire world conspired against her? Bass. Rupert. Jasper. What had she been doing? Pushing a loaded wagon uphill, thinking her hard work was making progress, each step forward bringing them closer to the hilltop. But what she hadn't seen in front of the large boxes weighing down the wagon bed were the forces making certain she'd fail. Making absolutely sure she'd never make it. The slips of her feet were not from the pull of gravity. It was from the added weight of betrayal she couldn't see from the other side of the wagon. If only she'd stopped for a moment to look around. Mapped her progress against her efforts. Maybe Jon and the others would still be alive. Maybe she could have taken Lenora to the Upper Midian parks before her death. And maybe still caring wouldn't have been so hard.

Sami thought of the rat back at the theater. She had wished to switch places. Selfish and free. But as she stood despondent from disbelief, defeated from the truth of her betrayal, the reality was as clear as her wasted efforts. She was never meant to be that rat. She was just the leftover pizza clutched in its jaws.

CHAPTER 20

ARVIN PLEADS

Arvin sprawled out on his brother's sheetless mattress, looking fearfully across the room at the cardboard box peeking out from under his bed. It was a portion of the Citizenry load he'd tucked away to avoid the scavengers in the Midriff. Arvin figured whatever was inside was valuable enough to sell, and he could use the money to cover the payment he'd lost during the street brawl. But after prying open the top, all he found was more grief.

At first, he wasn't sure what his eyes were showing him. Several gray rectangular bricks, soft as plasticine, were wrapped in a thin translucent film and packed tightly against each other between the flimsy box walls. But when he pulled one from the spread, spying the hazard label on the underside, his stomach hit the floor. *Explosive Plastic, Composition 4, Demolition Block.* It took his full attention not to drop it from shock. He gingerly placed it back in the box and sealed up the top.

The mattress screeched as Arvin shifted to his side. He could only imagine why the Citizenry would want to smuggle explosives into the Under Eastside. Visions of exploding buildings and maimed Guardians scrolled through his thoughts. Nausea twisted at his insides. He tried reasoning the idea away. Maybe there was some peaceful purpose. But no matter how he contorted his thoughts to figure out a reason beyond that of destruction, the simple fact that the Citizenry had him smuggle them in wiped clear any possibility of their legitimate use. No. The truth was as obvious as the homeless man rummaging through his garbage outside his window.

Arvin felt anger seep into his bones, as if the blood from his brain had carried his thoughts to the rest of his body. He'd been fooled. Slipping devastation beyond the Undercity's most secure boundaries. Risking his family's safety. All for a promise the Citizenry didn't appear to have any intention of keeping. He hadn't even heard a whisper about his brother's release since the delivery. And now he owed a dangerous man a sum of money he had no means to pay back.

As quickly as the rage overtook him in the moment, so too did a pervading sense of dread. The explosives. His brother. He couldn't be sure where or why they were to be used. But if it was going to be a Citizenry attack on the Guard, his brother might be caught in the blast. Arvin's legs ached at the thought, and his fear of the man in black paled in comparison.

Working to calm the anxiety climbing to his throat, Arvin glanced at the posters of musicians and supercars pinned up on the walls of his room. On his first night, his brother had cycled through each poster, explaining why each was so special, blasting his mixtape when Arvin admitted he hadn't heard of most of the bands—all of the bands. Then finally pulling free all the posters from Arvin's side of the room.

"That's your side now," he said. "You put up whatever you want. Just know, half-naked women will get Dad to come around more often. I had to pull mine down. He was always up here." They both had laughed hysterically.

Arvin had spent countless hours thinking up decor for his blank side of the room. But beyond the small photo of him and his brother affixed to the wall by his pillow, the rest had stayed barren since that first night.

He sat up against the headboard. The man in black would have to wait for now. He needed to make sure his brother was safe. He needed to do something about the beast he'd smuggled in before the carnage ripped through the Under Eastside. And he doubted the man in black would notice the missing money for at least a few more days.

Arvin leaped from the bed and retrieved a single brick from the cardboard box. Lugging them all through town was no longer a risk he was willing to take. After gently placing it into an old tin lunchbox, he stuffed a couple of shirts inside to keep it stable and clicked the metal box closed.

The Mantle lamps shone over the vagrant-filled streets of Plainsview as he scurried down the roadway to a path connecting his street with the back alley of the next. Arvin had considered all his options. The Faith wouldn't be of any help. They'd pull him from the Mastersons' home, and he'd be lashed for neglecting his duties. As for the Guard, they would probably call in the man in black again, and Arvin would have to explain what happened to his money. Besides, they had already caught him with a box of the stuff and did nothing about it, likely assuming he'd been smuggling it out of the Under Eastside rather than in. If he went back and admitted it was the other way around, God knows what they'd do to his brother. And his parents... He couldn't go to his parents. They'd placed all their faith and trust in him by accepting him into their family. He just couldn't break their hearts with how far down the shit hole he'd fallen. Arvin knew there was only one person who could help him.

After reaching the back alley, he hopped the short fence of a small property with the lunchbox in hand. Skirting a packed mound of dirt, he stepped to the half-broken back porch and rattled on the door. Impatiently waiting, he tried peering through the smudge-covered window above a rickety porch swing, but the grease-coated pane made it too difficult to see inside.

"Can I help you?" a voice said from behind him.

Arvin turned to see the toffee-brown skin of the only person in the Undercity he could still trust. Wearing her unkempt black hair above her head, she was cloaked in a long, thick afghan sweater that hung below her knees. She didn't look right. She wasn't the same put-together young woman he'd seen animating the streets with her laughter. But his parents had always said Samantha Salem was someone he could trust if something ever happened to them. A beacon of light if darkness ever consumed the Undercity. And what greater darkness was there than the threat of his brother's death?

"I need your help. Please."

CHAPTER 21

ATLAS ACCEDES

The clicks of the slots whirling and chimes of bells singing climbed above the cheers and groans of the busy casino. Atlas had always avoided the place. He'd witnessed too many older Guardians fall victim to its charms—and its bite.

Abe Rommi had been a top candidate for a senior Guard post before the hypnotic dance of the roulette ball two-stepped away his future beneath one too many black landings. Thirty-two was his "lucky number," an omen he'd often see in his encounters throughout the day. Once, it had been the address of a Midriff junkie he was tasked to round up. Another time, a page number of a book describing the fortunes of an emperor. Everywhere he'd turn, the number would appear, whispering an invitation back to the churning wheel of misfortune.

On the odd occasion, the number would strike as he suspected, and Abe would celebrate extravagantly with lavish meals and expensive gifts for his wife. But with each fall of the smooth rock on a darkened number, the distance between his losses and victories stretched further and further apart, until the chase became too great. The distance too far. They found him with thirty-two puncture holes in his chest when he couldn't pay back the loan he'd taken out.

The Guard wrote off Abe's death as a junkie ambush during his rounds. But everyone knew it was Asher Punsch. Atlas could still remember the pain his wife had worn when she stormed the gates. An underside beauty with long blonde hair and olive-tanned skin, she rivaled some of the most desirable women in the magazines—even with the mascara lines and dark circles beneath her sorrowful eyes. She didn't believe the official cause of death, screaming a plea for justice that seeped through the office walls. The howl of her cries echoed through the abandoned Midriff buildings. It wasn't until Asher's long black sedan arrived to retrieve her that quiet returned to the gates. But by then, scores of Midriff squatters had congregated outside like children looking for an after-school brawl. It took only one shot to the Mantle from a Guardian's pistol to scatter the junkies back to their holes. And it took only one sit-down with Asher Punsch for Abe's widow to forget the entire ordeal.

On his next visit to the gates, Asher wore the once-mourning beauty on his arm, her eyes stale, face bereft of life. A payment of sorts, in lieu of the debt Abe still owed.

Atlas figured tonight would be as much of a gamble as a spin on the roulette wheel. And judging by Alanna's secrecy, he was certain the stakes were much higher than a few dollars and a widowed wife. The *something big* she promised was happening now and involved several key members of the Citizenry. Amelia

Stintz, Derick Lowder, and Jonah Turret had met them out front of the casino and were now following along as Alanna led them through the casino floor. Atlas could hear Derick and Jonah bickering from behind the pack. It was obvious they were as much in the dark as he was.

Atlas had almost forgotten about Alanna's promise of *something big* and her plea to trust her, buried in his thoughts beneath the questions of his father. He'd been too busy piecing together what he knew about the once-great leader. Replaying the night of his death. Peppering Alanna with questions about the real man beneath the legend. What he was like. What traits they shared—certainly not their hair. Atlas must have gotten his black locks from his mother. But he could see himself in Jericho's eyes. Similar grays, almond-shaped.

The more he learned about the Citizenry giant, the more Atlas admired him. Most stories from the Mantle were overblown or complete lies, blooming from a tiny seed of truth to give the rumors an authentic feel. The evacuation of the Midriff all those years ago was not some calculated plan to distract the Guard; it was a retreat to prevent further fighting. A common thread in most true stories involving Jericho Sands. He was more a pacifist than a rebel—at least in his later years.

The early stories spoke of his ferocity. The kidnapping of Guardian patrol men in the Undercity. Overtaking Syndicate outposts. But something changed later on. He became more docile. More willing to partner with the Syndicate. Bass figured Atlas was to blame. A bargaining chip the Syndicate used to keep the dogs at bay. But it didn't make much sense to Atlas. If the man cared that much about him, why didn't he ever send a gift? A birthday card? Something?

The casino air was fresh, like a crisp breeze soaring off the calm, silky ocean in the spring. Atlas once heard that oxygen was pumped in through the vents to keep people awake and gambling. But without the thick underside air, the clean scent of the cool current seemed to lift away the Undercity angst, creating a tranquility that melted Atlas's muscles and had his mind searching for a quiet spot to sit. He figured it must be why all the noise was important. Keep the gamblers calm, but not enough to fall asleep.

They strolled past the table games and ringing slot machines to a small, sparsely filled lounge. Atop the wide stage, flanked by a glossy white grand piano, sang a tall blond beauty with short curls peeking out below a round sequined headpiece. Her long, velvety smooth leg peered through the waist-high slit in her tightly shaped gown. The singer's voice floated above the softened sounds that escaped from the casino floor before the strokes of the piano filled the room with a somber melody. She met Atlas's gaze briefly before darting her eyes away, as if he was unworthy of her attention.

On the other end of the lounge was an entrance to a side room, unmarked with a plain door. A large man sitting a few steps away stirred slightly as they approached but kept to his seat after recognizing Alanna. The door opened into an opulent room with masterful hand-painted artwork dressing the walls. An oversized chandelier hung above a single games table in the center, surrounded by several upholstered leather seats, all empty but three.

The dealer, dressed in a black waistcoat and white dress shirt, sat at a deep notch in the middle of the table with several decks of cards stacked to his side. Crossways from his seat sat Stixx, hunched over the table with cards on the green felt beneath his nose, examining each with the concentration of some deviant hiding in a thicket of brush at a playground. His broad, bony shoulders reached for the ceiling as if to escape his sunken traps dipping below his collar.

Sitting along the same edge of the resting oval, Bass crowded out the seats beside him. His trunk-sized legs stretched beneath the table, and his cards were buried deep in his monstrous paws, with tall stacks of casino chips piled in front of him.

"Whoa! Here comes the cavalry," said Bass, turning to greet them.

"Get lost," said Amelia to the dealer after he finished dealing a hand.

The dealer clapped his hands and stretched out his bare palms before leaving the table and exiting the room. Everyone but Atlas took a seat, with Alanna claiming the dealer's chair for herself.

"What the fuck, guys?" said Bass. "Can't you see we're in the middle of something?"

"That's the problem," said Amelia. "You've been too busy with your head up your ass to see the shit-show that's going on out there."

Bass waved his hand as if to swat away a fly. "Fuck that bitch, Solomon. Don't worry about him. I already sent Asher to talk him down from the clouds. Besides, the support we lost from his little magic trick was only enough to fill a short bus. And hell, those that believed it should be ridin' it anyway."

"We're not here about Solomon," said Amelia. "You step outside lately? The streets are overflowing with Midriff squatters. The Guard's been pushin' them out into the other neighborhoods. They're practically creating a new upper level in the Bottoms just to accommodate."

Bass toyed with his stacked chips. "Well, it's the Guard's land now. We got our fee. Asher got his five percent commission. They can do whatever the fuck they want."

"Bass, this is serious," said Alanna.

Amelia cut in, "Damn straight! People are scared. Nobody wants to leave their home. The squatters aren't hurtin' nobody, but still, the Under Westside is turnin' into an apocalyptic horror show. We're just lucky the people don't know it was your dumb ass that started it."

Atlas wasn't the only one taken aback by Amelia's forthrightness. He even caught Derick and Jonah sharing a glance of wide-eyed disbelief. The last two people Atlas had heard speak to Bass with such reckless abandon had died soon afterward. And in Jericho's case, not even the air of mythos could protect him from Bass's scorched-earth temperament.

Atlas couldn't see Amelia's face, but judging by how loose she appeared in her seat, with one arm stretched behind the backrest and the other resting on the tabletop, he sensed a confidence that neither Jonah nor Derick wore at that moment.

"There's something about pussy," said Bass in a low, casual tone. "It must be the secret well of machismo. How else do you get the balls to speak to me like that? You see, Turret and Lowder over here would never dream to come at me with such…vitriol. But then again…they don't get nearly half the pussy a bull dyke like you can pull in."

Alanna cut in calmly before the back-and-forth escalated. "Bass." She said nothing else. Atlas watched her stilled head until Bass shifted his gaze away from Amelia to the dealer's chair.

"Okay, darlin'. What is it?"

In a cold, monotonous tone, without even a hint of nerves, Alanna said, "I'm calling for a vote to officially remove you from Citizenry leadership."

"*What the fuck is this shit?*" Bass roared.

"Do I have someone to second this motion?"

"I second it," said Amelia.

"You fucks think this will fly? You think you can get rid of me? I *am* the fuckin Citizenry!"

"All who vote to remove Basson Tate from leadership, say aye."

"Say aye and lose an eye," Bass threatened.

"Aye," said Alanna.

"Aye," said Amelia.

Both Derick and Jonah were white with fear, sitting silently as if Bass held their tongues with invisible pincers. They glanced about the table but avoided the brute's cutting glare. The silence in the room reached its height until Bass's loud, hearty laugh broke the stillness.

"See, you dumb fucks!" said Bass. "You can't get rid—"

"Aye," said Stixx.

Bass's pale skin flushed scarlet as he stepped from his seat and towered over the table.

"The ayes have it," said Alanna. "Basson Tate, you are officially relieved of your duties."

The now fire-red beast rained his monstrous mitts onto the felt, snapping the table legs on one side and sending the stacked casino chips soaring across the room. Jonah fell to the floor as Derick scurried to the corner, far from Bass's reach. Unshaken by the show of force, Stixx rose to his feet and eyed the angry bear with a stoic stare.

Bass's demeanor shifted to reluctant defeat. He lumbered out of the room without saying another word.

Atlas couldn't help but feel sorry for Bass, leaving the room betrayed and deflated. He had committed his entire life to the cause. Everything he'd done was for the interests of the underside. Even killing Jericho. And despite it all, Atlas felt pity as if back then Jericho had not been his father, claiming that title only recently.

It was so much easier when Bass was just some feral savage, a brute with as much need of sympathy as a Barrens slaver. But as of late, Atlas had started to see the actual person. Someone with emotions and feelings. A family. Atlas had Alanna to thank for that, humanizing Bass by sharing the details of his past—the real past.

Like Jericho, Bass had earned his own myth. A battered runaway. A street kid who learned the Undercity ropes from hustles and shakedowns. But none of that was true. He was a child of the Midriff—before the evacuation, born to a middle-class family as one of two sons. Alanna mentioned nothing about his brother, but his father was a factory worker, pressing steel girders for the Syndicate construction businesses. Unlike Bass, he was a calm man, never raising a hand to his wife or children, simply showing his displeasure with a soft word or subtle glance—except when it came to Syndicate affairs. Bass had recounted to Alanna how angry his father was when he heard about the Wall's construction. Even though they lived deep in the belly of the Undercity, far from the sight of the setting sun, it still clawed at his insides. And although he wasn't in charge of the rebar, the skeletal bones of the Under Westside's soon-to-be seal, his father's factory was to have a hand in its supply.

The man spent weeks searching for new work, refusing to be a part of the Undercity's imprisonment. But the only industries hiring at the time were involved with the new wall contract. Even dockworkers were required to unload supplies to support the build. With nothing else available for an old steel worker with few skills, his father was forced to continue at the steel mill well beyond the Wall's completion. He despised every moment.

Bass hadn't been close with his father, the extent of their bonding lasting the length of any given driftball match. But watching his father look past his principles for a mere paycheck, resigned to be another cog in the wheel of the Syndicate machine, pushed Bass to lose all respect. He would often search for ways to rile the old man. Talking up the Guardians along the stretch of gate on his route home from school. Spending what little money he'd earned from his paper route on SyndiCape comics, making sure they were strewn about the apartment for his father to see. And to top it all off, enlisting in the SyndiGuard on his sixteenth birthday. Bass smirked proudly, watching his father's face fall when he saw him in his new cadet uniform. But the old man hadn't said a word.

It wasn't until the week before Bass was to attend formal Guard training that everything changed. It was in the blackened early morning after a long night of drinking. Bass and his new Guardian friends had come up behind a man in the darkness walking home. Dressed in matching shirt and pants, the man carried only a metal lunchbox.

Bass's Guardian friends pushed a rifle into his hands and ordered that he teach the man a lesson. "Only Citizenry rebels roam the streets this late," they had said. The man tried to run when they approached, but his legs gave way. He tripped forward, smashing his head on the sidewalk. Bass recounted how the Guardians' laugh echoed through the empty streets when they saw the man's blood-smeared face. But beneath the mask of blood, beneath the fear and exhaustion on the man's face, were the pale blue eyes of Bass's father.

Bass described what he felt in the moment as a switch. He could almost hear the click in his head. He had tormented and mocked his father for years. But watching the likes of two privileged topside button men howl with delight at his father's pain stirred the beast inside until it finally lashed out.

He caught the first Guardian with the rifle stock, buckling his knees and forcing him to the pavement. He then turned the gun on the other, pressing the muzzle to his forehead before tightening the trigger. The clap was loud and bloody as shards of the Guardian's skull and clots of brain blew across the roadway. He then waited until the other sat up, massaging his jaw, before placing another shot between the Guardian's eyes.

The unsolved deaths of the two Guardians tripled SyndiGuard incursions in the following weeks. Riots spread across the Midriff, and threats to the Under Eastside gates ramped up Guard presence. Nearing a full-on civil war, Jericho ordered a mass evacuation, leaving the Midriff to the vagrants and junkies and pushing Bass and his family from their home. It was then Bass joined the Citizenry, angered by the retreat. Even back then, he and Jericho were at odds. But he'd been careful not to show his disdain until after having built up support with the Locals, gaining recognition as head of the Citizenry Patrol. And by then, Jericho had no other option but to keep him close or risk mutiny. A strategy that only seemed to delay the inevitable.

*

Alanna reached out to invite everyone back to their seats.

"We need to appoint a new head," she said.

"G'tting' rid of that psychopath was the easy part," said Amelia. "Who do we got waitin' in the wings?" She looked around the table. "Stixx?"

Stixx sat as heavy as a statue, face firm as if carved of stone.

"I love the guy, but he doesn't really exude leadership," Amelia continued. "Maybe for an army of mutes."

"I nominate Atlas Ramsay to head the Allied Citizenry," said Alanna.

The words churned through Atlas's mind, awaiting his brain to catch up with his ears. He'd learned that anticipating Alanna's words would always prove a fool's errand. Her lips were too unpredictable. Her thoughts inexplicable. But this was beyond anything he could have guessed.

Stixx remained motionless, but Derick and Jonah appeared dumbfounded. Amelia shifted in her seat, glaring at Atlas as if he had bewitched Alanna's tongue.

He could feel his discomfort catch in his throat, trying to force out an objection. "Alanna, I—"

"Atlas is Jericho's son," she said.

As if a mystical enchantment had been spoken, the shocked expressions melted, and a look of understanding swept across Amelia's furrowed brow.

"He needn't make any decisions," Alanna continued. "He could be the figurehead. Jericho's true successor. The people would support it. Many still love Jericho, and Solomon kicked open the door for him by peddling Jericho as a prophet. The Faith parishioners would follow Atlas to the poisoned air of the Chemical Hills. He's the perfect choice for us to take back Lower Midian."

Was this the play all along? Why she had him claim her ideas as his own? Was she building his résumé?

"And how would decisions be made?" asked Amelia.

"Consensus," said Alanna. "Just the five of us. We can have the others provide their input. But in the end, it will be our decision. And Atlas will sell it as his."

No. She wasn't building his résumé. It was his audition for the role.

The back-and-forth continued as if Atlas wasn't in the room. Points of clarification. Strategies for Local reconciliation. Even a name change. Not for the Citizenry, but for Atlas. He was to be now known as Atlas Sands. His life was being decided without a whiff of his input. He was to simply go along with their wishes. A return to how his life had always been. At the Home. In the Guard. A vehicle to be driven by anyone with the keys.

When it reached a vote, the entire room committed their support. Even the silent steel pole that had once been Bass's right hand had agreed. Without a word of congratulations to the new head of the Allied Citizenry, everyone but Alanna and Atlas cleared the room. She sat with a muted smirk, and he took a seat next to her.

"So, Boss…" she said with a playful gleam.

"Alanna, what the hell was that? You didn't even ask me. I can't lead the Undercity. I can't even lead my own affairs without your help—"

"Exactly. I'll be with you every step of the way."

"That's not it. Who am I to—"

"Atlas. Stop." Her spirited smile fell as her gaze pressed deep into his eyes. "You said you trusted me, right?"

He did. But something inside was screaming for attention.

Atlas nodded.

"Then trust me. This is bigger than you, or me, or Bass, or the entire Citizenry. This is for the future of the city. We need you to be the face of our fight. It's the only choice if we're going to make it. We're divided as a people, and that's a dangerous place to be. The Syndicate will keep fingering the holes of the divide until we collapse. We need to unify. The Citizenry. The Faction. The Faith. And only you can do it all."

The immensity of her words struck Atlas like a tram. It was too heavy. They wanted too much. He was no leader. She hadn't asked. She hadn't warned. She simply expected him to go along with her plans. He was fomenting a slow, storming fury when she reached for his hands. Her soft touch did little to tame the rage.

"We need you, Atlas," she said.

Alanna leaned over the notch in the table, clutching Atlas's hands before pressing her soft lips to his. Instantly, intense passion overtook the anger. He could feel his loins stir. It was as if the sweet taste of her lips had overwhelmed the poisonous indignation coursing through his veins. And when he felt her warm tongue against his, all his fear and angst dissolved under the weight of pure bliss. He rose from his seat to hold her as their lips embraced. But roused from the passion, Alanna's grip strengthened, and her nails dug deep into his palms.

Atlas snatched his hands away, and Alanna pulled back in horror.

"Oh my God. I'm so sorry," she said. "I…it's just…"

"It's okay," said Atlas, examining the impressions in his palm.

"No, it's not. Atlas, I've never…done that with anyone. I just got carried away—I'm so sorry."

She'd never done what? Dig her nails into flesh? Kiss someone? He had always assumed her inexperienced because of her age, but he couldn't imagine someone like her going through their teenage years without a youthful indiscretion. Even Atlas had found a few willing lab partners for experimentation during his early years in the Guard. No one who had made him feel like Alanna, but as a teenager, love hadn't been the point. Casual *what-the-hells* were a part of the landscape, a rite of passage for maturing young adults exploring a new dimension to their lives.

"You've never…kissed anyone before?" he asked.

Alanna looked to her fidgeting hands. "No."

"Oh."

"Does that make me weird?"

It was unusual. But given her circumstances growing up, it could well have been expected.

"No. Not at all." He reached for her hand before taking his finger and lifting her chin to meet his eyes. "I get it. With all the…shit you were dealing with. I get it."

A slight smile of relief curled her lips. But just as the embarrassment left her cheeks, Atlas was overwhelmed by shame. He had judged her when he'd been the cause. He had stolen her youth, and everything that was to have gone along with it. And now he was questioning her need for him. She needed him to lead. She said as much. But he was protesting. Angry, even.

Burying his fear under his sense of duty, Atlas agreed. "I'm in," he said. "I'll lead. Whatever you need."

Atlas and Alanna exited into the lounge. A soothing ballad filled the room, spilling from the songstress's lips. Her seductive gaze and flirty smile caught Atlas's eye as her voice climbed the melody's crescendo. He remembered the almost disdainful glance she'd given him only moments earlier. It was as if she now knew he was someone of importance, someone worthy to share a glance with. It was as if everyone knew. He could feel all the other eyes in the lounge turning toward him. The rush of excitement was like a current in his bones, surging through his steps to the casino floor. He bounced in his shoes, his chin held high, when a voice cried out above the casino clamor, "Red, thirty-two!"

CHAPTER 22

SOLOMON HEEDS

Solomon sat at the table in the sacristy, scribbling in an open leather-bound notebook. Stacks of bills towered over his lowered head, swaying with the rhythm of his scratching pen as he went over the count for the third time that day. Since his Sermon on the Sea, the Church had been flush with donations. Not just from the parishioners of Midian, but word had also spread across the continent. He even received a sizable donation from the savages in the Caravan, asking for his intercession with God on the day of judgment. Solomon accepted the money, but any true believer knew you couldn't buy yourself out of your sins.

The maelstrom that followed his display of God's bestowed power had been everything he'd expected and more. Rumors out of the High Council even spoke of a sainthood after his death. Solomon's little showing had reinvigorated the masses across America. Pews everywhere were now bursting with believers, eager for a word or two on the Prophet of the Pillars—a title he had received from his diocese's local characteristics. Pilgrims had even made their way across the Barrens to hear him speak, stuffing his nave like a holiday turkey, forcing him to install loudspeakers on the outer church walls for the overflow to listen in from the streets. The second coming of the Church's golden age was here. And Solomon was solely responsible.

Since his days at the seminary, he had often imagined himself a seat on the High Council, draped in the finest black silk robes, sitting among such intellectual giants as Abdullah Bin Assissi or Vincenzo D'Orio. Men who had shaped modern Faith jurisprudence with their resounding mastery of the Testaments and deep spiritual wisdom. But what had at one time seemed a distant fantasy, a foolish dream sputtered from the lips of a child when confronted with the question, "*What do you want to do when you grow up?*" was a possibility now within reach. He had received letters from High Council members inquiring about his state of mind when he'd taken the walk. Had he recited any particular prayers? Any words of scripture? Fan mail from the vanguard of the Faith. An interesting turn of events. Especially with his letters to them having never received a response. Even High Magus D'Orio had acknowledged the "oversight" in his letter Solomon received today, claiming he'd only come to learn of Solomon's previous messages and had chastised his assistant for overlooking such essential communications. A twelve-page volume of responses to his long-awaited questions accompanied D'Orio's own inquiries, written in the apologetic tone typically reserved for decrees of past regrets. Solomon could almost hear the groveling of remorse intermingled among the well-formed prose of the seasoned jurist. Tonal wisps of contrition that, for a brief moment, infused him with a primal dominance that surged through his muscles and overtook the aches of his weary bones. He had never been so hard, not even after glimpsing the supple bodies of a young new batch of sisters through a break in the shower room door.

"Looking to rival the boundary wall, I see," said a voice from the entrance of the sacristy.

Solomon raised his head. A tightly groomed silver mane combed to perfect curls rose from behind the peak of the stacked cash encircling him. As his sights climbed further, Solomon could see the dead stare of a false eye glare past him. The other eye held a smile fringing its edges.

Solomon kicked back his seat in shock and pushed himself to his feet. He tied his long white robe closed before he approached the man dressed in a fitted black suit. Solomon's skin cascaded with gooseflesh as he reached forward and embraced his oldest friend.

"Punchy. It's so good to see you."

Growing up, Solomon and Asher Punsch had been inseparable. Stickball and bike riding as youths. Dame-hunting and street hustling as teens. With Jericho off engraving his legend in the streets of the Undercity, Asher became Solomon's *de facto* family, seeing him through some of the darkest times in his life.

After Solomon's mother had died from a cleanse-resistant strain of one of her many sexual infections, Asher covered the funeral costs and his rent until he was ready for the seminary. By that time, Asher had already made headway into the narcotics trade, a pastime he'd taken up to fill his days as Solomon's absence in the streets grew and his seat in the library warmed. Sometimes they'd attend the library together. The future Grand Magus with his ancient religious texts and his cyclopean friend thumbing through the sociology and psychology texts from before the Fall. But Asher often complained that reading put too much strain on his one good eye. Soon, the distance between the once close friends stretched beyond each other's reach, and their daily meet-ups were reduced to semi-annual reunions and fortuitous encounters.

"You still pulling this old trick?" asked Asher, pointing to the tray of figs on the kitchenette. "I thought we figured after the Mancini sisters that this shit is no more an aphrodisiac than a stick of gum."

Solomon chuckled, remembering the night the old friends had picked up twins in the market during their early teenage years.

"It wasn't the figs that were the problem," said Solomon. "If anything, you popping out that fake eye sealed up their panties for the night."

"Ah, yes. The horror on their faces." They both snickered.

Solomon could remember the first time he'd seen Punchy with the black eyepatch pressed to his vacant socket. The guilt was overwhelming. They'd both faced the same beatings from their schoolmates. But Solomon had escaped the permanent deformity his friend was forced to endure.

Long after they had rid the school of their tormentors with a few nudie mags, the damage Asher suffered to his eye from the beatings worsened. Blood seeped through the retina, spotting his vision with red blotches. And eventually, the nerve pain radiating from the damaged eye forced him to have it removed. The flood of guilt pushed Solomon to pain over questions of justice. Why his friend? Why not him? But just as guidance had descended in the darkness of a fusty locker, so too was he guided from his guilt-riddled despair. God had shielded him from the suffering. It was not written for him to endure the same hardship. He was to keep both his eyes for some greater purpose. A purpose he searched for in an old, tattered volume of the Testaments he found tucked away in his mother's room.

Solomon cleared the table, returning the stacks of cash into a large donation chest before the old friends took a seat together. He exhaled a grunt of age, collapsing into his chair as Asher's spry, lean body slid into his seat with one graceful movement. Sitting back from the table, Asher crossed his legs and rested his hands on his knee.

"So, you're performing miracles, I hear," said Asher.

Solomon couldn't restrain his smile. "Can you believe that? A kid from Bottoms Edge touched by God's hand. Skimming the water surface with nothing but my sandals and resolve."

"Well, I'm sure the transparent shrimper's mesh didn't hurt either."

Solomon felt his face flush with warmth. He never figured he could fool Asher with his little trick. But having it exposed so bluntly, so openly, when others accepted its truth without hesitation, made his skin tickle with diffidence. Until that moment, Solomon had all but forgotten the ruse, convincing himself he really had trod upon the water's surface.

"Yes…that too," he said reluctantly.

"I give you credit. It was clever having it stretched out between the piers. I bet it was impossible to see in the dark water. I may not have figured it out if my man on the dock hadn't been late with my shipment. He wailed like a child, complaining how you had him scaling the pier posts with the mesh clenched between his teeth, tearing at his gums. He blamed you for my delay, claiming you wouldn't let anyone else help tie it off."

"I couldn't have anyone else involved," said Solomon, annoyed with the complaint. "He was already one person too many. If the logistics of it all got out, I'd be cast from the Faith as a charlatan. I couldn't risk that."

Asher replied with a coy simper, "I know. And if he was so willing to share the details with me, it wouldn't have been long before the rest of the world heard the dockman's tale."

Solomon felt his body seep its strength through his seat. He had known Asher since they were very young. And through the years, he'd witnessed his best friend smirk with the same curled lips of requital at least a dozen times. Once, after Asher had taken care of a troublesome young girl with a big mouth, threatening to expose Solomon's advances. And another time after Solomon's predecessor had found himself mired in a public affair with the daughter of a Local Citizenry underboss. With every showing of

Asher's smug smile, uniquely twisted at its edges like a drying leaf, Solomon became certain of two immutable facts: Asher had taken action to aid his old friend, and Solomon would owe him a great debt.

"What did you do?" Solomon pushed out through his exasperation.

"Oh, lighten up," said Asher, rising to his feet. He stepped over to the tray of figs atop the kitchenette and pitched one into his mouth. "I do what you can't."

"But Asher… Of course, he'd tell you what I had him do. But just because you can coax people's secrets doesn't mean others would be able to. We can't assume he'd have shared it with anyone else. He assured me he wouldn't. He is a good, God-fearing man."

"Then he should be fine when he steps forward for his final judgment, no?" Asher surveyed the small room as he spoke, fingering some old texts lining the back of Solomon's open wardrobe. "Do you know what the problem is with the average man? I'm sure some of your texts will say it's the gaping hole of faith. A need to belong to something greater than our own individual worlds. But that's not it.

"There's a phenomenon that exists among the mediocre—the average joes of society. Where they feel they're somehow special. Deserving of something more. Those on the lower rung typically know their place. But a sort of cancer has popped up among the average. They delude themselves into believing they're more important than they actually are. Standing up to governments and corporations. Wrapping themselves in a banner of freedom and human rights. When in reality, they're baring their naked souls for attention. Yearning to be considered of the great men of history when they are merely the loudest of the mildly intelligent. The ego deludes.

"Back in the day, the average understood their mediocrity. They knew they were merely a single grain of sand among a billion others on the coast. But now…all people want is to feel important. Feel a sense of superiority. *All eyes on me.* A more potent drug than skeet itself—or any other I could ever procure.

"With that in mind, I want you to consider a man working a thankless job on the docks, arriving home each evening with the scent of dead fish and saltwater engrained in his skin. Being rejected by his wife for some late-evening action because of the smell that refuses to wash away. Returning to work the following day, where, due to the nature of his duties as supervisor, his coworkers despise him. Slowly being chiseled down from a man of honor to a child seeking validation. But how could he attract such reassuring attention? He's only a dockman, after all." Asher clicked his tongue. "And then he remembers…the little task he'd been asked to perform for the great Grand Magus Solomon. A task that resulted in Solomon's meteoric rise, an event known the world over. The benefits the Grand Magus had reaped were endless. But all the man received for his contribution was a few extra dollars he'd long spent on cheap whisky and cigarettes. But that could all change. He could have global attention at his doorstep. Famous. A hero. Like the ones in the history books millions pore over each year in their studies. All he needed to do was say the words. Tell his tale… No, Sol. He had to go. You know it's true."

Solomon's stomach churned. A heaving sensation climbed through his chest. *Lord, forgive me. Lord, forgive my friend.* With every ounce of strength he could muster, Solomon swallowed the beast scratching at his insides, scaling his throat. He took a breath, hoping to still his jittered limbs.

Asher returned to his seat and was now eyeing him curiously. "You seem…bothered, old friend," he said. "You never balked at the other things I've done to help you. Why is this one any different?"

Solomon struggled to get out his response. "Murder is of the greatest sins."

"Ah, I see. But murder is merely the taking of a life. We have taken many lives together, you and I."

"Never murder."

"No? The expulsion of our little friends from school. We stole the life they could have had, did we not? The girl who accused you of sexual advances. Where is she now? Strung out on skeet. Spread out on some filthy motel mattress with a john on each arm. Was that not the taking of a life? Your predecessor. Exposing his affair publicly so you could take his seat as Grand Magus. His suicide was certainly the taking of a life. One for which we were responsible."

Asher's words ricocheted off the reproachful cloud

crowding the room. Solomon glared at the table, unable to look across to his friend who spoke of taking life with such cavalier indiscretion.

"Besides, Sol, you're free and clear of this. It wasn't as if you asked me to do it. I did it of my own accord." Asher looked to the ceiling with his arms spread. "Do you hear that, Lord? Your humble servant had no part in this. I alone bear this sin."

Solomon closed his eyes to avoid witnessing Asher's mockery.

"My friend," said Asher. "We are not so different, you and I. We are both in positions atop a hierarchy. Both leaders of men feared for our judgment and wrath. Both selling something to ease the ache of this world. But where we diverge is the path of righteousness. You chose its confines and hypocrisy, whereas I forged a path of my own. One where I'm free to be me. Without judgment. Without the cage of righteousness. But together, we can run the gambit. You in the light. Me in the shadows. We can achieve something great…together. But you have to stop being such a pussy."

Asher's insult immediately stiffened Solomon's spine, overwhelming any guilt stirring within. He was right. Solomon hadn't asked for the dispatching of the dockman. And in the end, he may very well have brought ruin upon the Faith. Asher was merely acting in the interest of the greater good. An instrument in God's symphony, helping to carry the melody.

Solomon straightened his shoulders, pressing himself to

the chair's backrest. "Fair enough. How would you like me to repay your…generosity?"

Asher shot a playful smile as he crossed his legs. "We need the Citizenry to do themselves in. They're playing a dangerous game. They think I'm too blind to see what they're planning. But I see it all. And in the end, they'll bury themselves. We just need to make sure their plans go off without a hitch."

"And how does that involve me?"

"My friend, you are the linchpin in their plans… Did you know Jericho had a son?"

The words landed on Solomon's ear like a tickle, and he couldn't help but laugh.

"A *son*? Preposterous. My brother was more likely to have ground his manhood between stone boulders than the walls of a snatch."

"Perhaps you didn't know him as well as you think. It's true. He had a son."

Solomon's joyous disbelief slowly dissolved as he searched Asher's face for the truth. He wasn't lying. Solomon could always see the lie bursting from the fringes of Asher's glass eye. A throbbing vein splintering toward his temple. But now, the only lie the smooth, supple skin was proving was that of Asher's age.

"How?" The word escaped as a stunned mutter.

"Must I give you a lesson? I'll send over one of my girls to teach you. But for now, you must know that the Citizenry has appointed Atlas Sands as their new figurehead. And what I need of you is to support it. Throw your weight and the weight of your followers behind him."

From the shock grew intense anger. Solomon hadn't even supported Jericho's band of fools when he was alive. But now he was to back some bastard nephew as if he was the Savior's second coming? The influence of the Faith was to be used for God's purposes alone, not so that man could claim dominion over His creation. He would not.

"No. Certainly not," said Solomon. "I've worked too hard laying each brick in the path for the Faith's revival. And now you want me to tear it all up? Direct my followers to a boy who has done nothing to earn their trust? Someone whose belief is untested—unknown? Never."

"Come, Sol. You're not seeing the bigger picture. His appointment is a done deal. Do you really want to battle him for your parishioners' affection? You already laid the groundwork for him by claiming Jericho's prophethood. You won't win. Besides, the boy is an idiot. He'll bring the entire Mantle down on their heads. And when the Citizenry is a despised memory, languishing with only their most fervent supporters, who will be there to pick up the pieces? The only one left with any legitimate authority underside. You. God's chosen."

Solomon stroked his beard, working to drain the anger pulsing through his veins. He had cornered himself with the Sermon on the Sea, claiming Jericho as a servant of God. And now, despite Solomon's "miracle" on the water, Jericho's bastard had a stronger claim to the ears of his believers. Even the High Council would say as much. The inheritance of prophethood had been affixed in the Faith since its inception. It had been known even in the foundational monotheistic teachings from before the Faith. It wouldn't be something he could explain away. Nor could he go back on his praise of Jericho. His entire charade was supported atop the cornerstone of Jericho's divine endowment and the love of his people.

"I could deny his lineage," said Solomon.

"Yes, you could. But it was Chairman Lutz that slipped the news of Jericho's son, I suspect in defiance at being removed. But, regardless, the Citizenry could always trot him out once again to prove the truth of it. I'm certain he has documents somewhere—or at least his friends at SyndiCares do. If he was motivated before to leak it, I don't see why he would shut up now." Asher uncrossed his legs and leaned forward, unmasking his face from all emotion. "I've always had your best interests at heart. Never have I wavered. This is no different. I can't tell you what will happen—and trust me, you don't want to know. Just do as I ask. And in the end, you will stand alone. Atop it all."

Solomon sat quietly, working through it all. His ego. His loyalty to his friend. The truth of Jericho's son. It was too much to take in, clogging his mind and making it impossible to form a coherent thought. There was only one unimpeachable source that could guide him through the chaos: the law of God, Solomon's North Star.

"I will subdue my ego," he said but more to himself than to his friend. "I won't speak on matters of which I'm uncertain. I guess it is possible a woman seduced my brother at one time in his life. He would have experienced temptation beyond that of any normal man—especially in the early years. It may not be that far-fetched." Again, he spoke as if to convince himself. "I will concede this boy's status and will not stand in his way. But…I cannot urge my parish to follow him blindly. Not yet. Not until his mettle is tested."

Asher grinned, rising to his feet and buttoning his suit jacket. He stepped around the table and extended his hands. Solomon clasped them and stood from his seat.

"My friend," said Asher, "I couldn't ask for anything more." He pulled Solomon in for an embrace before clutching his shoulders and extending him at arm's length. "Thank you. You'll see."

Solomon felt a chill ride his spine as Asher's one good eye rested with the same dead stare as the other, a grin carved across his face. Solomon had never feared his friend, always questioning the alarm others would show when his name was mentioned. But standing there in the dimmed sacristy lighting that tainted Asher's face a rose-colored tinge, Solomon could feel the evil radiating like the dry heat pushed out from a furnace. *Satan never comes with a scowl. Always a smile.*

CHAPTER 23
ARVIN AGGRIEVED

Arvin tucked the wad of bills into his pocket, pushing down as deep as the stitching would allow before fastening the slit with a safety pin. He wasn't about to risk losing it again. Not after what he'd been forced to give up. The worst of it was the entire stack was to be handed over to a man that wouldn't even feel the loss. A loss Arvin would feel all over after one run with a shelter wagon.

He glanced back to his shiny red wagon one last time as the pawnbroker scribbled a label and hung it from its handle. Double. He was charging double what he had paid Arvin. Nausea bubbled beneath his breakfast, and Arvin stepped out from the shop to the busy market streets. He hadn't yet planned what to tell his parents. Perhaps it was stolen after he'd forgotten it outside a Faith Center in Bottoms Edge. Or maybe he gave it to one of the kids at the shelter. Someone with a handicap that would worsen each time they struggled with a holey roller. Maybe his parents would be so taken with his generosity that they'd get him a new one.

Arvin half-wished he had asked Samantha for a loan instead of wasting his request on his little discovery. She wasn't as helpful as his parents had always praised, dismissing his fear as an ordinary childhood worry. Like the bogey monster or being picked last for a pickup game of driftball. Maybe he was a bit crazy in his worry, coming to conclusions with very little proof. But then again, if there were a risk—even the size of an ant mandible—that he'd placed his brother in danger, he wouldn't be able to live with himself.

"How much you get?" asked Miron, pushing off from his post next to the shop doors.

"Enough."

Despite the teeming Marketplace streets, Arvin paid no heed to the crowd. He sauntered despondently through the rush of people. Miron followed closely, shouting something about the most recent episode of *The Deaf Detective*, his favorite TV show. Arvin would usually play along, humoring his friend with fake gasps and forced questions, just enough to fake his interest. But now, he wasn't paying any attention, bumping into every third or fourth person he passed.

He wondered if this was how he was supposed to have felt during breakfast when his mother shared the news of another shelter death. This time, it was Mack. One of the sisters had called his mother to let her know. For one reason or another, they believed Mack and Arvin were close. But Arvin was no closer to him than any other kid at the shelter.

Arvin's mother had approached him softly and put a tender hand on his back with a calming look in her eye. But the news hadn't stirred much inside. Filth death was inevitable. Arvin hadn't even questioned how Mack died. He just continued slurping down his cereal, dreading the moment he'd have to hand over his wagon.

The sense of loss was overwhelming, a new feeling he hadn't yet learned to navigate. At the shelter, he had nothing. No family. No possessions. Not even anyone close enough to be considered a friend. Loss was an impossibility.

The ordinary life of a Filth was a colorless existence, a daily grind of menial tasks intermingled with the self-aggrandizing conversation of the other kids and routine human rituals. Eating. Pissing. Shitting. Sleeping. Rinse. Repeat. And although the same could be said of his adopted life—although with better food and cleaner toilets—he could now have things beyond his own experiences. His own belongings. His own family. His own home. But with that came consequences he had never considered with all his dreams of want. The fine print nobody reads. Fear and loss. Fear of being on the edge of loss. The angst that still ran through him when thoughts of his brother crept in. The incessant worry that consumed him was a torturous hell. And with good reason—as he had learned at the pawnbroker's hand. Loss was a son of a bitch.

The fringes of Bottoms Edge were not as seedy as the rest of the neighborhood, large houses with expansive lots and the occasional concrete park caging in a playground and basketball court. The houses were old, and the parks were now overrun with homeless, but the fringes were nonetheless much nicer than the heart of Bottoms Edge.

Conspicuously absent anywhere in the neighborhood was a driftball pitch. With the need for turf, those were mostly spread out among the nicer neighborhoods. But it hadn't stopped the children in the area from repurposing a caged lot—at least before the tents had arrived.

Arvin had once played a match with his brother on a makeshift pitch, nearly ripping off his skin after an enthusiastic slide trying to steal the ball. The rubbing alcohol his brother had doused his leg with burned something fierce. He had never felt that level of pain before, not even after one of Sister Mary Anne's more liberal uses of the belt. Arvin had sworn off driftball after that, refusing even to play on one of the nicer turf pitches. But ever since Midian's championship win, he'd felt the urge to give it another go, if only to distract his thoughts for a short while.

Arvin wondered if his brother had caught Midian's upset win on television. *They would've had to have shown the match*, Arvin tried to convince himself. It was the championship, after all. He must have seen it. It had been exciting to watch. To see his parents scream with joy after that final score. To hear the street outside roar in celebration. The chants. The parade of people. He was certain his brother would at least have heard the spectacle in the streets. But with the thought that he may have missed out on such a miraculous score, being busy with Guard duties, Arvin could feel his frustration wrestle away the melancholy.

The Citizenry had promised to help. They said they had ways to get him out. But they did nothing. Arvin's anger surged. He wanted to lash out. Make them pay for their lies. But all he could do was take out his frustration on the large red door in front of him.

The loud bangs prompted a tall, skinny man with long blond hair to pull open the door. "Relax there, little man." He wore a stained undershirt that stretched over a pair of flowered shorts, almost complementing each other as well as the man's rubber sandals and socked feet. "Come in…both of you."

Both of you? *Miron.* Arvin had forgotten about Miron.

His heart sank. It wasn't like his friend to stay quiet for so long. Unless he hadn't been and Arvin had tuned him out while swimming in his despair. He'd done that before. But it hadn't been a big deal then. No consequences for his absentmindedness—only a partially annoyed Miron. But this time, he wouldn't be as lucky.

Before stepping inside, he turned to Miron. "You need to go home," Arvin said with a tremor in his voice.

"Why? It's the weekend. I don't have to be back until late."

There was no time to explain. Arvin reached out and clasped the shoulders of his little shadow. "Go. Home. Now!"

Miron's eyes widened behind his glasses. With his regular pair damaged, he was forced to wear an older set with arms that barely rested atop his ears. The lenses were also much thicker, swelling his eyes to twice their regular size.

"No, no," the skinny man interrupted. "*Littler* man here

now knows the spot. He's not going anywhere without Barrel's say-so."

Barrel. The man in black's "banker" and the largest man Arvin had ever seen. Nearly double the size of that huge ogre, Bass. Barrel's wrinkled and bald face often reminded Arvin of a knuckle, layered and lined with skin folds across his brow and neck, but smooth as a clenched fist when angry, the muscles in his face bulging to stretch out the loose skin. Arvin had only seen him angry once, but it was enough motivation to avoid another showing at all costs.

Still clutching Miron, Arvin turned toward the door and nodded before turning back to his friend.

"It's okay," he whispered. "It will be okay. I'll take care of it."

Miron's confused defiance was gone, replaced by a trembling lower lip and watery eyes. Arvin wasn't sure whether his fear was from being ordered to leave or being forced to stay. Regardless, he knew fear was the right emotion.

CHAPTER 24

ATLAS'S PRESTIGE

Chairwoman Shoehorn had a large round face with small eyes and slim pink lips. Her cheekbones protruded thin and hard from her dimpled, doughy cheeks, like steel rods hanging cattle carcasses in a slaughterhouse freezer. Her chin jutted from the folds of her neck, with several faint whiskers pinned to the center of a fingertip-sized mole on the end. Her oversized blue blazer fitted over her body like a hefty winter coat, and her knee-length pencil skirt exposed the large hams that sat atop her swollen feet, bursting from the top of her matching blue flats.

"I have to say, we were over the moon when we heard," she said, looking down at Atlas through the small glass lenses sitting at the end of her round nose. "After the attack in Big Town—certainly staged by your predecessor—and our purchase of the Midriff, we were concerned the aim was to rouse an underside mob against us. It wouldn't shake us from the purchase by any means; real estate is scarce these days. But still, it had Reg there sounding the alarm." She nodded toward a grease-slicked suit in the corner. He sat smirking, eyes fixed on Alanna as if Atlas wasn't in the room. "I'm just happy that we can continue the good work we did with your father."

It was weird how the word fell on Atlas's ear. *Father.* He'd gone his whole life without knowing his father, and now references to him were being made at least a dozen times a day. People spoke as if to let Atlas know how close they'd been to him. Like that would earn his favor. As if Atlas had grown up tossing the ball around with the old man, building soapbox racers, and going fishing. But something inside made him resent them instead. The thought that they held memories he never would. If anything, it was for their closeness, their encouragement, that he'd been abandoned. Maybe if Jericho hadn't known *them*, he'd have known Atlas.

"Just a few housekeeping matters..." The chairwoman fingered a stack of paper on her desk with her plump pointer, drawing it across the page before looking up to Atlas from the other side of her thin white desk. She sighed and snatched her glasses from her nose with a concerned grimace, reminding Atlas of the overacting in the SyndiCares production of *The Wizard of Oz.* Fraser had pulled off the role of Dorothy well, complete with the blue dress, brown wig, and red sparkling shoes. But when he spoke, the drawl he added to every other word smacked Atlas with cringe.

"The Wall," the chairwoman said. "Our engineers had a look at the plans to remove it." She sucked the air between her clenched teeth. "It turns out, over the years, the Mantle has settled on top and is now structurally supported by it. So, although we had made a commitment to Samantha, it isn't something we can promise any longer."

Atlas looked to Alanna. A slight curl around the fringe of her lips signaled he wasn't to make it an issue. He looked back at the chairwoman and nodded.

"Fantastic." Her eyes returned to the page. "And finally, there are several outstanding demolition requests from before…*ahem*…Jericho's disappearance. They've been on hold while we sorted out our…relationship. Didn't want the Guardian escorts to be mistaken as an incursion into the Undercity. Are we good to proceed now?"

Atlas stared blankly before turning back to Alanna.

"Yes," Alanna replied. "That will be fine. Do you have a copy of the plans?"

The chairwoman handed several sheets of paper to Alanna from across her desk. "There are several sites that need some work or another."

Alanna perused the stack briefly before handing them back.

"You can keep those," said Shoehorn.

"That's okay. I got it. Thank you."

The chairwoman placed the pages back on her desk and let out a deep breath. "Well, I think that's the lot of it. As long as we have your commitment, I don't see why we can't renew our funding."

"We'd like the back-payments as well," said Atlas. A sticking point Alanna had hammered home before arriving at the meeting. "The payments that were withheld these last few months."

The oily suit rose from his perch, wiping his hair back with his palm to keep it seated. As if there was any doubt with the wet dripping from its ends.

"That is not something we can accommodate," he said with an odd accent.

Alanna stood and stepped toward him. "Here. Let me get it." She clutched Reg's arm softly with one hand and raised the other to his head, sliding her hand over his hair before stepping back to admire her work. "There. Handsome as ever."

Atlas felt his insides twist. *Is she flirting with that slimeball?*

Reg's lips curled beneath his pencil-thin mustache. "Thank you, my dear." He reached out and caressed Alanna's shoulder.

"Why can't you accommodate?" Atlas squawked, hoping to snuff out whatever was playing out between his girl and the creepy oil stain.

"Well…we cannot reward the months of disdain…"

As he spoke, Alanna let out a soft moan, straightening her back and stretching her neck as if attempting to loosen her tight muscles. Reg's eyes darted to her now prominently displayed breasts.

"But the more I think of it… I guess it would be a gesture of good faith," he said, eyes still locked on her chest.

Alanna shook off the stretch before smiling and thanking him in the cute tone she usually reserved for nighttime banter.

Atlas squirmed in his seat until his discomfort forced him to his feet. "Okay, great. I think we're done here."

The chairwoman heaved herself out of her seat and extended her hand. "I am pleased with how it all turned out. Thank you again for coming, Atlas. It's been a pleasure. And we look forward to our lasting partnership."

Atlas's hand sank into the chairwoman's soft, moist palm, shaking it brusquely before pulling away. Turning to leave, he caught Reg placing two soft kisses on Alanna's cheeks.

"Perhaps we can get together, just the two of us," Reg said with an airy breath, both hands on her arms. "And see how best we can support our fearless leaders."

"That's an excellent idea," she replied.

Atlas stewed on the elevator ride down to the ground floor. A hundred floors of irritating dings. He could see Alanna watching him from the corner of his eye. She smirked but didn't say anything until they left the building and the car door slammed shut.

"You're such an idiot," she said before the driver turned the key in the ignition. A glass pane slid from between the driver and rear-facing seats, sealing closed with a satisfying thud.

Atlas was still agitated, staring out at the passing sights as the car pulled away from the Syndicate Tower.

"I know there were no girls back at the Home, but I

assumed you would have learned something about us since then," she said.

"And what would that be?" he asked, eyes still glued to the window.

"I dunno. Maybe that greasy men get us all riled up. Make us *burn* with desire. We just want to tear off our clothes—"

"Stop." She was mocking him, but he couldn't help how he felt.

"That man was gross. The fact that you're jealous—although cute—is disturbing. As if you think I'd be interested in…that."

She was right, of course. Atlas had known on some level what she was doing, using Reg's sleaziness against him. But his jealousy was still hard to tame.

Jealousy had been his constant companion of late, a swirling tempest of anxiety and fear at her slightest gesture toward another man. It was an odd feeling. An emotion he'd only ever sampled sparingly before her, watching the other Guardians go about their day carefree without the heft of guilt on their conscience. But even then, it had been watered down, more a longing than anything else. This was different. More visceral. And only strengthened by their growing fondness.

Since taking over the Citizenry, they'd been inseparable. She'd even spent a few nights in his bed, if only to sleep. The intimacy he craved was still miles away. But that first night was nonetheless special. A calm had enveloped him, as if she warded off the demons busying his thoughts. And the peaceful air, infused with her scent, slipping him into a deep, restful sleep. Like always, she'd still been the cause of him waking. But instead of her childhood screams, it was merely from her hand resting on his chest. It was as if her nearness was wiping clean his past. The weight, no longer crushing. The rope, light as a feather. There had been only one night of terror while she lay beside him, a horror-filled dream that had Tommy and Alanna falling from a blood-red sky, riding a shooting star with Alanna clutching its reins. Atlas tried to run toward them, but the road kept cycling beneath him like a treadmill. It wasn't until they were about to collide with the ground that he lurched forward in his bed, soaking in a cold sweat. Thankfully, Alanna was still fast asleep, grasping a pillow, making it easier for Atlas to drift back to sleep without embarrassment eating away at his thoughts. But even with that one relapse, Atlas knew he had found the cure he'd been searching for. A cure he could never risk losing.

He pulled his eyes from the road and turned to Alanna. "What was the whole demolition thing about?" he asked, hoping to shift from the embarrassment now cooling his anger.

She let out a deep sigh. "All demolitions have to be approved by the Syndicate," she said, leaning back in her seat. "Jericho tried bringing down the Wall a long time ago. The explosions did nothing but destroy some homes in the area. But it scared the Syndicate enough to ban explosives in the Undercity. They're now controlled by the Guard. Any structures that need to be brought down must be approved first, and a Guard escort will bring in what's needed."

Atlas remembered the Fire Team excursions leaving the Under Eastside. He could even recall the shockwaves afterward, reverberating beneath the Mantle. But he'd never considered that they were requests from the Citizenry. He just assumed they were part of some military operation.

The entrance to the Lower Midian roadway sat near the center of the Uppercity, beyond a large metal gate jutting from deep beneath the concrete, the road dipping through the Mantle. Atlas kept his eyes raised to the car's glass roof as they descended the large, spiraling roadway attached to the Mantle's core pillar. The majestic beauty of the cloudy sky was traded for the industrial feel of steel girders and wire ropes. It was only Atlas's second time on the core path—the first being earlier that day. Traveling between the Mantle and Lower Midian was typically undertaken by tram. But with the Citizenry's recent influx of cash and support, they could now afford a driver escort. And Alanna felt it would make a better impression than stepping off a crowded tram.

Everything had been different since that night at the casino. Cash was flooding in, and support for the Citizenry was at its highest peak in decades—at least according to Amelia. The Hall was now teeming with undersiders, people crowding outside on the pavement, awaiting a glimpse of their new leader. It was weird being cheered on everywhere he went, showered with praise and gifts. It might not have felt so strange if Atlas had done something to deserve it. But his meeting with the chairwoman moments ago had been his first act resembling leadership in the weeks since he'd been appointed.

The madness of Atlas's instant fame started a day or two after Bass was removed. A massive crowd swarmed his building, screaming and begging for his blessings, tears streaming down their cheeks, palms raised to the sky as if reaching out for something to grasp. A gift from his newfound uncle. The Grand Magus had called on all Faith believers to rally behind Atlas, and now people were claiming he was a prophet of God. An absurdity, of course. Atlas had no more connection to God than the random junkies animating the Grove streets. He'd never so much as prayed. But that was something he could hardly share with his admirers.

Atlas had yet to meet his new uncle, Solomon, and Alanna's description of him left much to the imagination. She had apparently known the Grand Magus well, having spent some time with the Church after the death of her parents. But she always pulled up just when a kind word was teetering on her tongue. Atlas couldn't decide exactly what that meant. It was usually a sign the person was no good. But then why wouldn't she just have said so? He figured she was probably trying to protect his feelings. Solomon was, after all, the only family he'd ever know. Perhaps she wanted him to form his own opinion. Whatever the reason, Atlas chose not to pry or hound her about Solomon as well as Jericho. He was still tempering the flood of questions about his father, spacing them out between long stretches of regular conversation. But even with his attempts to limit his curiosity, he'd seen the annoyance on Alanna's face the other night after one too many questions. She hadn't stayed over that night.

Atlas hoped his uncle was someone he could like. It would be nice to have a family for once. Not to be alone in the world anymore, knowing there was someone around who might actually care. He sank back into his seat, the headrest pressing against the nape of his neck. He rolled his head to face Alanna, who was now staring out through the glass divider to the roadway ahead. He still had her, he thought. Even if Solomon was an utter asshole, she'd still be there. Atlas watched silently as she strained to get a better look at the road ahead. His eyes landed on her soft cheek before falling to her exposed neck. The milky innocence, unblemished by the harsh sun. She was stunning. She was always stunning.

"Atlas, look." Alanna pointed to the roadway ahead.

A large crowd had bloomed across the front of the Citizenry Hall, spilling onto the street. Atlas could see signs waving in the air, children on their parents' shoulders. It was far more people than the day before. A trend he'd noticed ramping up with each passing day. He could hear screams intermingled with the pattering of hands on the windows as the crowd engulfed the car.

"This is getting nuts," he said, trying to hide the smile itching to break free. He was beginning to feel like a pro driftballer with the adoring fans and screaming women.

"They're excited. You give them hope. They just want to

see you. Meet you…" Alanna paused as the hammering outside grew louder. She turned to Atlas with a look of mischief, squinting, with a slight curve to her lips. "Which is why…we're going to have a rally." She plopped back into her seat, a simper where the muted smirk had been.

Panic sprouted in his gut. *A rally?* No. She couldn't be serious.

The car came to a stop at the back of the Hall. The pattering sounds ceased, and the screams grew distant as their new security ushered people away.

Alanna turned in her seat, pulling up her legs and crossing them beneath her. "Listen, I know it really isn't your thing, but don't worry. We will script everything. All you have to do is read and look pretty. I know you can do the second part," she said cheekily, anticipation flushing her cheeks. "It will be great. We'll even have your uncle there. A perfect chance for everyone to see you. To meet you. And for you to introduce yourself to the entire Undercity."

Atlas hated to be the wet blanket snuffing out her excitement, but he couldn't help but think of all that could go wrong. He was not a statesman. Or an entertainer. He was barely a decent Guardian. He'd never be able to pull off the charade she was leading under the scrutiny of all those eyes.

"Alanna, that's not me. I have trouble speaking to more than one person at a time. How am I going to do hundreds?"

"More like hundreds of thousands," she said.

"*Alanna*? Who do you think I am? I can't do that."

She reached for his hand and held it softly, her large doe-like eyes embracing him with calm. Atlas's fear dissolved, but his doubts still lingered.

"What if they grill me? Ask questions. What if the *Gazette* shows up and wants to know my plans for the city? I'm no good on my feet."

She firmed her grip on his hand. "Don't worry about that. We won't let anyone get close. You just go on the stage and read the words. That's it. Then you come down, and we head home."

Atlas had given a speech only once, back in school. A presentation for some group project about the different species on the Mantle. He couldn't stop his hands from shaking for hours afterward. And the memory of his cracking voice had been fodder for his self-loathing well into his time as a Guardian recruit. But Alanna's gentle tone and caring warmth offered a reassurance that seemed to smother his nervousness.

"Atlas," she said, looking at the seat between them. "Do you think I'd throw you up there if I didn't think you could do it?" She turned her eyes back to his face and lifted her hand to his cheek. "You need to believe in yourself more. The jealousy. Your confidence. Your complete unwillingness to believe you are someone special. You're not like everyone else. You are the Leader of the Citizenry. Trust yourself. Trust me."

Her thumb sliding across his cheek sent tingles to his toes, and he could feel an urging sprouting beneath his waist. She was right. He needed to get over his past and embrace his future. After all, she had more to lose than he did if things went awry. And she was still trusting in him, trusting he could do it.

Atlas leaned over and kissed her lips. "Okay. I'll do it," he whispered.

Joy exploded onto Alanna's face. She reached over and pulled Atlas in for a tight squeeze. "This will be perfect. You'll see. A historic moment for the Undercity. For us. And you'll be at the center of it all."

CHAPTER 25

SOLOMON SEETHES

His nephew was a twat, the first thought that crossed Solomon's mind when he shook the boy's hand among the pews. He had steely gray eyes, messy black hair, and a look on his face that had Solomon convinced he was permanently constipated.

The scream of the kettle whistled through the sacristy.

"The tea," said Solomon, stepping from his seat to the hotplate on the counter. "Do you take sugar?"

"Yes. Three, please," said Atlas.

Of course he does. Indulgent, with no self-restraint. The boy was less a prophet of the Book and more a leader of one of those infernal boy bands that had teenage girls swooning. A good-looking chap, but as vacant as a Barrens truck stop. All show and nothing to offer. No doubt a layover trait from the great Gia Sands. Even the resemblance was uncanny in the almond eyes and soft jaw of both Jericho and their mother. The boy was undeniably kin, a conclusion that pained Solomon to reach. Up until he'd stretched out his hand to his would-be nephew, he had held a quiet hope that it was all a ruse. A Citizenry plot to win over Lower Midian, executed well enough to have even Asher Punsch convinced. But that all dissolved after a mere moment with Atlas.

Atlas. What a dumb fucking name that was as well. A low-rent pagan god who couldn't escape the punishment of restraining the heavens. *Some god.* His nephew's mother must've been a moron because Jericho wouldn't have been that bloody oblivious, naming a child of the Undercity after a glorified support pillar.

Solomon could clearly remember the ditzes and groupies that had infiltrated the Citizenry in those early years. Their harem of tramps and whores clinging to the robes of power. But back then, there had always been just one found at Jericho's side, a tall seductress with long dark hair and breasts as perky and round as cantaloupes. Melanie…or Mallory, or something. The Citizenry's second-in-command. Without question, that was the imbecile's mother. But she'd never struck Solomon as someone vacuous. On the contrary, she'd been quite clever—cunning, in fact. The key architect of Jericho's ascension, convincing Marcus Bertram to step aside after Jon Denton handed off the reins. She'd known Marcus was next in line and sidled up to him early on, whispering in his ear and shaking that ass of hers. Many were convinced that she'd been the true strength behind Jericho's success, the brains of the operation. It was about when she disappeared that Jericho's aggression had waned. Coincidentally, around the time of Atlas's birth.

Solomon strained to remember what had happened to Jericho's onetime "confidante." But those years were a whirlwind of seminary training and cram sessions. His brain just hadn't had the capacity for frivolity. No matter. The only thing at hand now was how he'd completely fucked the Church with his Sermon on the Sea—or, rather, Sermon of the C (C being short for charlatan). Solomon had received word that members of the High Council were planning a visit to Midian to meet their new "prophet," an honor that hadn't been considered for him, even after the display of God's power so openly. All he'd received were a few letters and a title bearing a crude reference to the city: the Prophet of the Pillars. Which, as it turned out, was revoked after the news spread of Atlas's existence. There had never been two prophets existing at once, at least none in the post-Fall era of the Faith. And if it were through Jericho's bloodline that Solomon had received his prophethood—a story conjured from the depths of Solomon's ass—then prophethood would necessarily be bestowed upon his son. *Utter rubbish.*

The jig will soon be up, he thought. The Council would need only one brief conversation with Atlas to see God's blessings were nowhere to be found in this Godforsaken city. The boy was as dim as the Mantle's belly at night. And his knowledge of the Faith was no more evolved than a child's understanding of the basic tenets. *He had actually asked if the story of Franky Filth was canon.* With questions swirling about Atlas, the Council would no doubt extend the inquiry. Next would be an examination of the docks, seeking proof of Solomon's miracle. And with the veil of faith tarnished by his fool of a nephew, suspicion would seep in faster than sewage in the groundwater in the Bottoms. They'd be clever enough to suspect something had been tied between the piers, and all would be revealed when they learned of the dock supervisor's disappearance soon after.

Solomon's heart ached at the thought of all his years of study being washed away by his brother's youthful indiscretion. *Couldn't he have found a hairy asshole instead?* Lord knows he'd sampled many over the following years.

If only his brother's progeny was something he could work with. Someone with even a basic understanding of Faith teachings. At least then it might be possible to coach the boy on what to say when the Council came sniffing around. Solomon had made certain to mention their pending arrival while Alanna was within earshot. Having orchestrated Atlas's rise to the head of the Citizenry, she no doubt had cause to make sure he remained in good standing with the Council. And she would understand the implications of their visit without Solomon having to spell it out for her. Perhaps she might work her magic to get him brushed up on the basics, at least enough to sound somewhat intelligent on spiritual matters. If anyone were at all capable, it would be Alanna. Her mastery of persuasion was unlike any Solomon had witnessed in all his years, perhaps rivaling only Atlas's mother, another woman puppeting her man to the seat of power. *Oh, how history so often repeats.*

"Should we see if Alanna wishes a cup?" Solomon asked.

"No. I don't think that's necessary. I doubt she's waiting

around. A church really isn't her scene."

Alanna had slipped away nearly an hour ago to allow them time to get acquainted—or so she claimed. Solomon could see the annoyance in her furrowed brow at Atlas's incessant prodding about Jericho. Her pursed lips spoke volumes.

Solomon returned to the table with two small cups of tea resting atop a floral-patterned saucer holding a single biscuit. "You two have grown close, I see." He watched as Atlas's eyes danced with delight.

"Yes. Quite close." His face flushed red, eyes dilating the size of marbles.

"Well, she's a lovely girl, and quite bright." Too bright for the dim-witted buffoon dipping his biscuit in his steeped green tea. Solomon had even questioned whether Alanna's insinuations the last time they'd met were part of her grand plan to remove Bass from leadership. It made Solomon sick to think she could have manipulated him so easily. Like a puppy dog after a brief belly rub. But after considerable reflection, he dismissed the idea as too fantastical a plan ever to have fallen into place so simply. She never could have anticipated his next moves. His call for Jericho's prophethood. It would take a uniquely troubled mind to put all that in motion. Certainly not the mind of a half-broken nineteen-year-old girl.

"Yes. I'm a lucky guy. I know that much," said Atlas.

Solomon cringed at the mention of luck. The High Council would dismiss the boy on the spot for such blasphemy and lack of appreciation of the Lord's blessings. *I'm so fucked.*

"So, is it true you walked on water?" asked Atlas as casually as a neighbor asking about the weather.

The reminder of both Solomon's claim to fame and eventual downfall stuck deep in his chest. He could feel it pulsing with agony as he sipped on his tea.

"Ah, yes. This is true." *Why not keep up the charade until the very end.* He had so little time left to enjoy it. "It was quite miraculous. The Lord's power is truly something to behold."

"That's impressive," said Atlas with a huff of amazement.

Impressive? It was an act of the Almighty's power and grace, not some score in a high school driftball match.

"Yes. *Impressive*," responded Solomon.

"Do you think…I could ever pull that off?"

"Oh, I don't know. Perhaps," he replied. *Maybe I'll take him out to the middle of the ocean and we can see.*

Atlas gulped back the last sip of his tea before pushing the cup and saucer to the side. "Thank you. That was excellent. I've had a wonderful time. We should do this again."

Again? Solomon would rather reenact his water walk above a swarm of electric eels than spend another moment with his imbecilic nephew.

"God willing," he replied, pushing a smile to his cheeks.

"Before I go, I did…want to ask you something."

Hasn't he already asked everything? Solomon thought. *I guess the size of Jericho's briefs is still looming.*

"Alanna has suggested a rally. A gathering for the entire Undercity. She wants me to speak to everyone."

God help us all.

Atlas continued. "We're hoping to hold it in the Grove. Liberty Park, I believe. The Syndicate has okayed it for topside viewing, so it will be broadcast to everyone in the city. We…would like you there. To say a few words. Call me up to the stage, perhaps."

Solomon would ordinarily have jumped at any opportunity to speak to a gathering of hundreds, let alone millions. But to do so now would tangle his reins with Atlas's even more. If he were to introduce his nephew, it would be a citywide endorsement with global implications. Even though he'd already urged his followers to support the boy, he'd been careful not to imply anything beyond support for his leadership of the Undercity. The question of his prophethood had not even neared his lips. That was a conclusion drawn by the street preachers and junior magi and ultimately sanctioned by the Council. If there was to be any wiggle room left with the High Council after their visit, he could not be seen giving such a formal endorsement to someone so vapid.

"I would love to, but—"

"I'm kind of nervous about it," said Atlas. "It might make it easier if you were there. Speaking first to all those people. They all know you. And love you."

They do love me, Solomon thought. Solomon had been the darling of the city. The savior in waiting. The question of how he could use this status suddenly tickled the back of his mind. If he chose to speak, his face would be everywhere. His words in every home in the city. He could spread a message to the people of the world. He could do a lot with that time. Stave off his downfall, perhaps. Preempt the Council's forthcoming charge. Push on offense rather than hope for wiggle room after the fact. *If* he could find the right words.

"When is this planned?" Solomon asked, still unsure if it would be the right move.

"In two days."

"*Two days?*" The words exploded from Solomon's lips like a shotgun blast.

"Y–yes… Alanna is adamant. Something about the solstice. Rebirth. Renewal. To be honest, you'll have to ask her."

The solstice? A pagan ritual. *Why would that have any relevance?* It was true Alanna had given up on her Faith learning, but she was nonetheless one of the greatest Faith intellectuals Solomon had ever met. It made no sense that she'd place such weight on the solstice with her knowledge of the truth. Regardless, the news of the timing was encouraging. Although he'd only have a full day to prepare his sermon of sermons, he wouldn't yet have the Council nipping at his heels. They were not to arrive until next week.

"I'd love to, nephew," he said with a smile in his eyes.

Atlas appeared taken by the gesture. His lips quivered, eyes swelling. He stood from his seat and extended his hand.

Solomon figured it could only help to play up the caring uncle angle and stepped around the table for an embrace.

Atlas squeezed as if a hug was all he'd needed in life. And for a brief moment, Solomon felt pity for the boy. Abandoned by both his father and mother. Left to fend for himself in the halls of a corporate orphanage. But before his sympathy could take hold, Solomon remembered that this boy could end it all. His career. His reputation. His legacy.

Solomon placed his hands on Atlas's shoulders and pushed him back with enough force to break free from the embrace—but not so much to let slip his disdain. When the boy was at arm's length, Solomon smiled and gestured him into the nave.

The screams nearly punctured his eardrums. At least a dozen young girls awaited their "savior" among the pews. How they knew he was here, Solomon wasn't sure. But he'd need to put an end to such inappropriate behavior in the house of God.

"SILENCE!" he bellowed. "This is not a concert hall. This is a place of worship. Take your teenage hormones outside."

The girls simmered, their moans of excitement buried beneath their restraint, tears still flowing freely. They slowly made their way to the doors, turning back every few feet to get another glimpse of Atlas standing next to Solomon by the pulpit.

When the doors finally closed behind them, Atlas looked at Solomon. "I will never get used to that," he said, doing his best to restrain a smirk.

Solomon eyed his nephew intently before responding, "You are a Faith leader now. Best not succumb to temptation. It will be your ruin—I promise you that."

Atlas looked to his shoes. "None of that means anything to me beyond flattery. Alanna is all that I want."

"For now," said Solomon.

"The thing is... It's just all new to me. I don't really know how to act. What to say. I just...don't feel like a prophet."

Solomon leaned over to Atlas's ear. "I will let you in on a secret," he whispered, eager to let loose the words dancing on the back of his tongue the entire night. "You're the farthest thing from it."

Solomon patted Atlas on the shoulder before walking back into the sacristy alone.

Climbing the steps to the small room above the nave, Solomon could feel the shame weigh heavily on his footfalls. Each step a thousand pounds of regret. It wasn't the boy's fault. None of this was. It was his. And only his.

After pulling the door closed behind him, Solomon shuttered the window blinds before falling to the floor and prostrating to his Lord, the dust and debris on the rickety floorboards pressing into his forehead. Anger swirled among feelings of self-pity and regret.

"Forgive me, my Lord," he started. "I have sinned. I have felt pride. I have felt envy. I have felt rage. Forgive me my emotions and guide me through the storm ahead.

"All I have done was in your name. For the betterment of the Church. To raise it from the ashes of the flames set by those who knew not what they have done. And now I face a tribulation that I fear I will not survive. I have committed my life only to you. And if that is revoked, what else would I have?

"What I ask of you, Lord, is not without great understanding of its significance. I know the shame of the plea. The threat of its fulfillment. But I do not see how else to proceed. How else to rid the Church of the damnation I have brought upon us. We will all be labeled as charlatans. The Church will lose its might. Something must be done.

"Lord. I ask you for your intercession. I ask for your favor. Please. Rid me of this boy."

Solomon wept.

CHAPTER 26

ARVIN SEES

Arvin would be whipped for this. He could picture Sister Mary Anne with the folded leather belt clutched in her palms. The old bag seemed to enjoy only two things in life: whippings and gossip. Some sister of the Faith she was. But he had no choice. Not after what he'd led Miron into the other night. The poor kid was frightened stiff, barely saying a word on the way home, even after pressed about *The Deaf Detective*. It was a conversation that would usually get him talking for at least twenty minutes as he summarized the happenings in the previous episode. Now, Miron just followed him silently until they arrived at his doorstep. He could barely even get out the word, "Bye."

Poor, sweet Miron. He shouldn't have witnessed any of that. Arvin had been preoccupied with his thoughts, forgetting Miron was tagging along. He should have ushered the little guy home after the pawnshop, not expose him to the deprived underbelly of the Undercity. He had to make it up to him.

A few seconds after he knocked, Miron's mother answered the door. She was a kind woman with curly brown hair and large glasses. She typically wore one knitted sweater or another, hanging down to her knees, concealing the broad poof beneath her midriff. Today, however, she wore a sparkling dress with matching heels and shiny dangling earrings.

"Oh, hello," she said. "I was expecting someone else."

"Is Miron home?"

"Why, yes. Yes, he is." She turned and called out, "Miron! Your friend is here," before turning back to Arvin and welcoming him inside. "I'm so glad to see you. Miron hasn't been himself lately," she said with a whisper. "Maybe you can cheer him up?"

"I think so," said Arvin. "I'm gonna take him to see—"

"Excellent. I'm so happy to hear that."

Another knock at the door, and Miron's mother beamed.

"Ah. I have to go now," she said. "But you two don't be out too late."

"We won't."

When she opened the door, a short man in a suit stood on the other side with a clutch of flowers. Miron's mother greeted him politely and slipped out the door, pulling it closed behind her.

The apartment had a homey feel: beige walls, carpeted floor, and the smell of freshly baked bread. The couch in the main room was a brown sandy color with a woolen texture that looked as if it would keep you warm on the cold winter nights. Directly across from it was a small television set, propped up on a wall unit with a shelf above it, holding pictures of Miron through the years. *He was always small,* Arvin noticed. And always bespectacled.

"What are you doing here?" a voice called out from the

darkened hallway.

"I have a surprise," said Arvin.

Miron stepped out from the shadows. "But it's Tuesday. You always have runs on Tuesday."

"I skipped it. The surprise couldn't wait. It's one night only."

Miron would ordinarily have jumped at the mention of a surprise, always up for anything and eager to tag along. But now, Arvin could see hesitation in his eyes. A look of concern. Of fear.

"Don't worry. It has nothing to do with the big man. You won't ever have to worry about him again."

"Are you sure?"

"Yes. Positive."

Those first few moments had been shaky after Arvin and Miron stepped inside that seedy drug den. He could hear Miron's breathing hasten with each step and felt the tug on his arm when they passed an open side room door, a broken and bloodied man tied to a chair beyond its threshold. The house wasn't usually so ghoulish. But that night, it was as if violence was the theme of its decor.

When the boys stepped into Barrel's office, another hit of terror laid open on his desk. A severed finger sat next to a small box on one side with a stack of bills on the next.

"Hey, kid." A gruff rumble seeped from the large man's lips. "Who's this?"

"J…just…a friend," Arvin stammered. "He was gonna

leave, but…"

"Yeah, he can't leave. That's not how it works, kid." Barrel placed the finger in the box and tossed half the bill stack along with it. "Don't worry, though. We'll find something for him."

Arvin could feel sweat seep through his shirt as the horror of his absentmindedness took hold. Miron would now forever be a part of this life. Another errand boy, forced to serve the man in black and his monstrous goon.

"What's your name?" asked Barrel, eyes still on the package.

Miron froze, standing completely mute.

The large man's eyes shifted from his desk as the silence swelled. "What's your name, kid?" The menacing grumble reverberating throughout the room.

"He's just nervous," said Arvin.

"I don't give a fuck if he's had his tongue ripped from his head. When I speak, I want an answer."

"Mack. His name is Mack."

Mack was dead, of course—at least according to his mother that morning. But Barrel didn't know that. All he would know when he searched for his new errand boy was that Mack had died that day. A terrible accident Arvin would play up if he were ever confronted afterward.

"Grab your coat," Arvin said now to Miron, who appeared to be coming around to the idea of a surprise.

After leaving Miron's flat, they headed down the roadway

toward their junkyard hangout. Although Miron wasn't as talkative as his typical self, he did push out a few details of the Deaf Detective's newest mystery. It was a gripping episode, according to Miron, involving a mysterious overdose of a hotel heiress who'd never been known to do drugs found in her penthouse flat with a syringe in her arm. The detective's heightened sense of sight helped him spot several specks of crushed drugs on her cheek, and he knew instantly it was murder. Killed by a powder that was deadly to inhale. And the prime suspect, her brother, second in line to the fortune.

What a terrible show, Arvin thought. But he was happy Miron was talking again.

They approached the junkyard to a stream of workers in hard hats and clipboards surveying the building across the street. Blocking the fence where they typically entered the yard was a dark green armored SyndiGuard vehicle with two Guardians standing in the flatbed at its rear.

"What's happening?" asked Miron, his eyes large behind his replacement glasses.

Arvin smirked and extended his arm across Miron's chest to prevent him from getting closer. "A demolition," he said.

"WHOA!"

The excitement in Miron's eyes said it all. He was back to his annoying, lovable self, beaming as he took in the goings-on around the abandoned building.

"How'd you know they were doing it?" Miron asked.

"My brother called yesterday. He has a friend on the Fire Team—that's who *they* are." Arvin pointed to the Guardians chatting at the back of the truck.

"Your brother is the coolest," Miron exclaimed.

Arvin couldn't help but feel pride.

"You two can't hang around here," a voice called out from the distance.

Arvin turned his head to see one of the men in hard hats fast approaching.

"It's too dangerous. Go!"

Arvin grabbed Miron's arm and pulled him around the other side of the junkyard fence.

"We can't see it from here," said Miron.

"Don't worry. We're going to watch from inside the yard. But we have to find a different way in."

They crept around the fence, searching for an easy point of entrance. At ten feet high, lined with barbed wire, the fence didn't offer much opportunity to scale. They would need to find an opening. As they rounded the back portion of the yard, a row of posters clinging to the fence caught Arvin's eye. *Rally for Renewal*, the poster read, with a large fist in the center. The date was two days from today and was to be held in Liberty Park.

Miron eyed the poster. "What do you think this is about?"

"I don't know," said Arvin dismissively. "C'mon. We don't have much time."

After finding a small gap in between two fence posts, the

boys squeezed their way in, tearing through the yard until reaching the rusted bus resting steps away from the Guardian vehicle on the other side of the fence. Arvin heaved Miron up first before finding his footing on a flattened wheel and pulling himself to the top of the hood. Miron sat on a patch of rust and leaned back against the bus windshield. Arvin settled in, and they both watched the building across the street suddenly implode. Loud claps rang out across the roadway, vibrating the bus beneath them, and a large huff of dust and debris swirled in the air above. In seconds, the building that had stood empty and crumbling for as long as Arvin could remember was no longer there.

The image of the box resting beneath his bed flashed in his mind. *Are those capable of that?* But before the thought could cure, several more claps rang out, muffled and not as loud, but nonetheless the same. Through the thinning dust cloud now spanning the entire neighborhood, he eyed the workers beyond the fence and saw confusion in their shared looks. The secondary explosions were not part of the demolition.

Arvin's nerves climbed his throat as he looked to where the sounds had come from. The east. Beyond the Under Eastside gates.

CHAPTER 27
SAMI RELIEVED

The television looked weird in her main room. Sami had lived her whole life without one and wasn't used to seeing something so ugly, so utilitarian, take up so much space in her home. Her mother had been adamantly against them. Not for the typical reasons most point to when criticizing television. But rather, it would throw off her decor. She was obsessed with antique, rustic furniture, much preferring it to the plain, uninspired stuff sold today. *If people just wanted something functional, all the large cocks and wet vaginas in the world would have found homes by now,* she would say. So, she refused to allow a plain black box anywhere in her home. And Sami had continued the tradition after her mother's passing. But having run through her collection of books twice over, she was getting restless—and curious about what was happening out in the world.

She'd only had a couple of visitors in recent weeks. The Mastersons' adopted son had come by with a horror-filled tale of how he was going to be responsible for blowing up the entire Under Eastside. It had taken Sami nearly twenty minutes to calm him down and gather the facts. It was troubling that Bass and Stixx had the boy smuggling explosives beyond the military boundary. But after witnessing the demolition of an old library, replaced with one of the Citizenry's brand-new shiny rehab centers, Sami knew a wagon full of explosives was not enough to do any more than destroy a small home. Certainly not enough to cause a level of destruction the boy was concerned about.

There had been a moment last night when reports of explosions in the Under Eastside had Sami on edge, fixing her eyes on her new TV. When the boy had brought her his worries, she didn't have the capacity to deal with another crisis, dismissing the risk as small, with any repercussions landing on Bass and his ilk. But as she waited for more news to emerge about the explosions, the cloud of her dismissal loomed large, and the reality became clear. Explosives had been smuggled in. And even if only a small amount of damage were possible, it would still be enough to harm several people and could cause a full-blown war between undersiders and the SyndiGuard.

Sami was sick at her inaction. Her selfishness. But when reports returned that no damage was uncovered beyond the boundary, she nearly cried with relief. The sounds had been mere shockwaves from the several planned demolitions happening throughout the Undercity.

The only other visitor at her home in recent weeks had been Marcus, returning once to check in after the news spread that Bass had been replaced. Apparently, the Faction had some support leak back to the other side, attracted by rumors of Atlas being a prophet of the Faith. Sami laughed at the absurdity of it all. It went to show how foolish the whole idea of the Faith truly was. She almost wanted to intervene, smack Solomon upside the head with a hit of truth. But the man was so vile, she couldn't stand being in his presence. And besides, it was not her sideshow. Not her bearded woman.

According to the news, there was to be a grand rally tomorrow. Atlas's official coming out, broadcast across the entire city. At first, Sami was shocked that the Syndicate had agreed to air it. But the more she considered it, the more it made sense. The Undercity was torn between the Faction and the Citizenry. And if Atlas was going to restore Jericho's arrangement with the Syndicate, he'd need the full weight of the city behind him, with no more questions about who the true leader was.

Jericho had always preached the power of the stage, its ability to ensnare an audience and warp perceptions. If wielded just so, a stage of only a foot could make a man feel ten feet higher in status than those on the floor. And a broadcast seen citywide could turn a former city Guardian into the underside's long-awaited savior.

The glow of the TV filled the darkness of the main room. Sami just stared at the screen as the news anchor droned on about the growing stray dog population and weak water pressure levels on the Mantle. After the excitement of yesterday's news, it must have been a slow news day, she figured.

She clicked off the TV and sprawled out on her couch.

The velvety touch of the green fabric on her bare arms reminded her of Lenora's coat after a fresh clipping. The smell of her heated frozen dinner coalesced with the lemon scent of the floor cleaner. Her eyes adjusted to the darkness of the room, and she could now make out the bumpy ceiling texture ringed with a smattering of years-old leak stains. *Is this it?* Her new life's purpose. Counting water stains on her ceiling. She missed the smiles of the people she had helped, watching their lives blossom into ones worth living. She missed the joy of being part of something bigger than herself, fighting to serve those who couldn't serve themselves. The idea of returning to the Faction had crossed her mind before Marcus's recent visit. But when she saw him standing on her doorstep, the Citizenry legend who'd done so much to keep the underside free, she felt shame and embarrassment for her past hubris. Who did she think she was? Everything she touched, she ruined. She was not a leader of the people. She was merely a helper. Not the queen bee. Just a drone.

Before Rupert had become the underboss of their Local, Sami had overheard an argument between him and her mother. After their old underboss died, the people were adamant Rupert take his place. The risk of putting someone else in charge less inclined to serve the people was too great. But he was unconvinced, frightened of making things worse. Not knowing how to do the job. The idea of her Uncle Rupert being afraid of anything made Sami smile. Such a big, scary man, afraid of the happy families in the neighborhood. But eventually, her mother had convinced him.

Her words at the time didn't make much sense to Sami. But now, the meaning was as glaring as the Mantle lamps in the day. *Those who seek to lead have everything to lose. Their ego is their sword. Those who are sought have everything to gain. Their humility is their shield.* Sami wished her mother had been around to guide her. She would no doubt have steered her away from the foolishness she had started.

Sami closed her eyes with her mother's words resting in her ears. She hoped for Atlas's success tomorrow. She hoped he could bring everyone back together. Maybe then she could go back to her old job…and have the weight of the Mantle raised from her chest.

CHAPTER 28

ATLAS READS

Atlas had gone over the speech dozens of times. It wasn't bad, crafted by Amelia and Alanna. Easy words. Nothing too complicated to trip up on. And the repetition had calmed his nerves some. Which was good, since he could now hear the crowd growing outside.

They'd found him a spot to prepare right across from the park. The apartment of a Citizenry supporter—and devout Faith believer. Passages from the Testaments were embroidered on throw pillows, and newly minted pictures of Atlas rested on the mantle and hung by the entranceway. Seeing his face in a stranger's home was odd at first. But after a while, it offered him some comfort. A safe place where he was welcome. The owner had popped in a few times, claiming she'd forgotten something or other. But Atlas hadn't seen her leave with anything but a cheeky smile and red face. She was younger, quite attractive, in fact. Someone Atlas might have even considered a go with before Alanna. Blond hair and blue eyes. Modestly dressed—befitting a woman of the Faith. Though Atlas swore he saw some risqué nightwear laid out on the edge of her bed on his initial tour of the place—which only added to her appeal.

Atlas had become restless lately, doing his best to subdue his male urges. But Alanna hadn't been helping the cause. Since the Syndicate agreed to broadcast the rally across the city, she'd been particularly randy. Clutching his arm as they walked the streets. Sinking into his chest as they cozied up on the couch. Pressing her firm body into his while they lay in bed. She had even started dropping subtle hints about the after-rally celebration, alluding to how nobody had ever made her burn with the desire he did. And how, after the rally, he'd be hers completely. The months-long build-up of sexual tension finally to be released. He wondered what about the rally had her so excited. But then again, it was natural for a person to be attracted by power. And Atlas was to be the center of attention when all was said and done. He'd just need to make it through his speech without bumbling it too much.

Atlas scanned the creased and crumpled paper once again, the words of his speech having now lost all meaning. He tried to remind himself that he didn't need to understand what he was saying. He just needed to say the words. Get them out with enthusiasm and vigor. Enough to excite the crowd, at least. And when he was done, he could leave and be with Alanna. But knowing how much the rally meant to her, how much it would mean for their relationship, he wanted to get it right. This wasn't to be his half-assed presentation on Mantle critters. And the audience was to be a little more than a bunch of rowdy kids and a disinterested teacher. The entire city would be watching. Millions with their sights fixed solely on him. The idea had frightened him until this morning. But after realizing what he was about to accomplish, the only worries still tickling his insides involved how he was to push out the words.

Atlas could imagine all the faces of his past watching him on television. His old friends. His rivals. He wondered if even his old housemasters would be watching. Seeing the man he'd become. Someone of importance. *What will they think?* Redefining his image in the eyes of his past was an intoxicating idea. Knowing that everyone would see his success. Shedding all his embarrassments and missteps. Replacing them with strength and authority. A nobody from SyndiCares Home #3, now leader of the Undercity. He was about to have it all.

"You all set?" a perfect voice called out from the entranceway.

Atlas raised his eyes from the desk to see Alanna standing in the doorway. A bright smile washed over her face, a flush of red painting her soft, round cheeks. She wore a slightly modified Citizenry uniform, matching light gray pants and jacket, with the oversized left lapel folded back over her heart. Atlas's uniform was similar, only thicker and more robust. But where he wore a white dress shirt beneath the jacket, Alanna had opted for a black halter She looked incredible. Sexy. Seductive. He couldn't restrain his excitement at the thought of the after-rally celebration.

"Come here," he said confidently.

Alanna closed the door and sauntered over, playfully

reluctant, her face demure and twinkling.

"What?" she said.

Atlas pulled her in by her waist as she stepped closer, wrapping his arm around her while he sat perched on the edge of his seat. He looked up into her eyes and brushed her hair back before resting his hand behind her neck. He led her softly to his lips and kissed her with the intensity of his new authority. She straddled his legs, stretching her arms along his shoulders. He could feel the muscles in her arms tense as she clutched the chair behind him. His hand fell from her neck to her breast, the other from her waist to her seat. He felt the passion rise through his legs to his loins, and he slipped his hand up the back of her jacket and inside her pants.

"Stop," she said with a smirk, face flushed with excitement. "After. We're almost there."

She shot to her feet, and Atlas dropped his head in playful resignation. "Okay. Fine."

Alanna pulled a folded piece of paper from inside her jacket and slapped it to his chest. "Edits," she said.

"Edits?"

"Yes. The final changes to your speech."

"But I basically have the last one memorized," he said.

"It'll be fine," she said dismissively. "Just a couple of minor changes. Amelia didn't like how some parts flowed."

The speech had sounded fine to Atlas, but he wasn't about to question Amelia's ear. She could be frightening when she was mad. Even more so than Bass. And he was nervous enough about speaking in front of millions. He didn't really want an angry Amelia on his heels.

"Did the Syndicate approve this version yet?" he asked.

Alanna stared blankly. "No... Are they the leaders of the Undercity? Or are you?"

"I know. I just—"

"Just nothing. Don't worry about it. They'll be fine with it," she said. "Come on."

Atlas hesitated. "Can I take a look first?"

"No time," she said, grasping his hand and pulling him up from the chair. "We have to go. Solomon will be on any moment."

"But—"

Alanna pushed to her toes and sealed his lips with a quick kiss. "It'll be fine," she whispered, kissing him once more.

The crowd was massive. Fifty square blocks of people were crammed within the boundaries of Liberty Park and the surrounding streets. The breadth of the vibrant green turf was swallowed up by at least a million underside citizens. The rumble from the sea of bodies bounced off the Mantle, intensifying the loud din. Monstrous video screens capped the surrounding buildings, all playing images of the empty stage and podium where Atlas would soon stand to deliver his message.

Escorted by Alanna and Citizenry security, Atlas crossed the roadway through a cordoned-off barrier to the side of the stage. The contrast of the immense crowd on one side and barren Midriff buildings on the other was impossible to ignore. He could see Guardians manning the empty Midriff streets, bordering the park and Grove, clutching their rifles next to large armored vehicles. And the tall Under Eastside gates stretching toward the Mantle, a backdrop for the blocks of vacant buildings and Guardian forces.

Before stepping on stage, Atlas's uncle nodded in his direction. Dressed in his long ceremonial robes and tall golden headpiece, Solomon appeared almost regal, a far cry from the brown housecoat he'd worn during their introduction a couple of days ago. Atlas wasn't sure how he'd felt about his uncle after that encounter. He'd done his best to be respectful, even withholding judgment when Solomon appeared uninterested in their conversation. But the jealousy exuding from his uncle's barbed words was almost too much to overcome. He was a dick. An obvious personality flaw that explained Alanna's hesitance to speak kindly of him. But even so, it was his uncle. His only family. And Atlas hoped that he could eventually make things work between them.

Alanna clutched Atlas's hand as Solomon opened the rally with a prayer. Now, being a prophet of the Faith, Atlas hoped he wasn't expected to speak spiritual insights. Nothing in the speech Alanna had prepared even alluded to the Faith or its teachings—unless Amelia had added a line or two in the revision. But he wouldn't find out until standing on stage.

"This is a historic moment," Solomon started following the prayer, his voice booming over the loudspeakers, cascading across the throng of people. "A unification of the entire Undercity. The Citizenry. The Faction. The agnostic. All under one banner. And for those of you still undecided, I urge you to look around. See the strength we have in numbers. See the camaraderie and friendship. See the future of our city. And come join us. Join us in solidarity. Join us in purpose. Join us in the salvation of your soul.

"It's not often that we unite. That we come together as one. Coalescing around a single source of inspiration. A uniting message. The Faith has undoubtedly seen it in our history. The melding of monotheistic traditions that spanned thousands of years. The integration of different cultures and beliefs, building upon shared histories and differences. Learning to leverage our collective strength. But this was only possible with a unified purpose. A single understanding of God and his messages. If you've read the history books, you know that before the Faith, war defined many relations between existing religions. Millions died believing their death was a death of truth. A death for God. When, in fact, their death was for ego. The belief that their traditions served the one true God. All others be damned. But it was when we finally came together, unifying our beliefs, establishing common ground, understanding that belief in one God was at the core of it all. Only then could we come together and build our great Faith in praise of our Lord.

"And now you all have a similar chance. A chance to build. A chance to unite. A chance to reclaim our souls from the idols of the self. Standing behind a new leader. Under one banner.

Under one purpose. Understanding our collective goal and how we can reach the promised land together. Both on this earth and in the hereafter." The crowd erupted with cheers as Solomon paused and looked over to Atlas.

Atlas's heart thrummed. He could feel it pulsing in his limbs. He pulled Alanna's hand to his lips to distract from the throbbing. Her cold skin chilled his warm lips. He looked into her eyes, the deep greens suddenly darker under the blackened Mantle lights. And the simper above her chin as cold as her touch.

Solomon continued. "But although I come with glad tidings for us all, I also come with a warning. In the history of man, there has never been a time where the evil among us doesn't work to sow distrust. Reap hatred. They are busy, busy bees. Plotting and planning. Pollinating and returning to their hive. Some may come as a trusted emissary. Others under the guise of a needy hand. Plots designed to deceive and bewilder. And although we should always welcome and embrace outsiders with the same respect and love we have for each other, we must also be wary of such plots. Their plans to divide. Their plans to conquer. Their plans to claim everything we've worked so hard to achieve together.

"We shall not let outsiders divide us. We shall not let them tell us what we've experienced—what we've seen—isn't true. The unity here and now is as firm a fact as the ground beneath us. And together…trusting one another, we can make certain our future is secured. In this world and the next."

Another eruption of the crowd boomed. Atlas could sense

his introduction coming. He cleared his throat and shook out the remaining jitters. Alanna tugged on his arm to get his attention, the noise too loud to know if he'd missed her calls. He turned to see her crooked finger beckoning him to lean forward. *A good luck kiss,* he thought. He lowered his head, leading with his lips. But Alanna weaved past his advance and cupped her mouth to his ear.

"Just read the words and you'll be fine!" she yelled but still barely audible.

Atlas mouthed what he'd heard back to her. She nodded and leaned in again.

"It will be over soon! Then we celebrate!"

He nodded to her with a smile as Solomon called him to the stage. Alanna returned the nod and looked to the ground. He wouldn't let her down.

Atlas's foot was pushing off the first step to the stage when he felt a firm hand on his shoulder. Glancing back, he could see a pencil-thin mustache above a wide smile. Greasy Reg. The suit extended his hand, and Atlas shook it firmly. He was mouthing something, but Atlas couldn't make it out above the sea of cheers. He nodded in response and climbed the steps to the stage.

Bedlam. The only word that could describe what Atlas witnessed when he stepped to the podium. He did his best to scan the faces, but there were too many. It was as if the entire crowd was a single entity. A sole spectator crying out with delight at his arrival on stage. He waved as the noise grew. Their excitement, their love, fueling his resolve. A wash of immense joy pimpled his skin as the crowd's energy coursed through his bones. Atlas looked to the side of the stage, eager to see Alanna's reaction. This was her doing. She was as deserving of the praise as anyone else—even more than he was. The bow was hers to take. But beyond the table of audio equipment and the few Citizenry men standing guard at the stage's edge, only empty space remained. She was gone. His eyes searched the surrounding area, the faces in the throng. But nothing, as if the thick underside air had swallowed her up. She was no doubt pulled away for some emergency, he figured. Maybe even a quick trip to the restroom. But before his mind could settle on the innocuity of her disappearance, another thought stormed in. Reg was also nowhere to be seen. *Had they gone somewhere together?* His disbelief tried to usher away his jealousy. Push it beneath the rumble of the crowd. The screams of admiration. But as the cheers died out and the people awaited his words, the green climbed its way free and sank its claws into his throat.

Atlas took a large breath and pulled the speech from his inside pocket, anxiety spreading to every crevice of his body. He unfolded the paper onto the podium before looking back out over the crowd. *Focus*, he told himself. *She's yours.* The affirmation eased his breathing, and he glanced at the first words at the top of the page.

"Welcome, everyone."

A loud screech from the mic cut through the crowd's rumble, followed by a deep, long creak from above. Atlas adjusted the mic and continued. "Thank you all for believing in me." The crowd boomed once again. His nerves, controlling his tongue, refused to wait for calm and pushed on through the cheers. "We are going to do something special, you and I. Something great." His echoing voice smothered out the lingering din, and the sounds above grew more varied, hissing and crackling amid a long, deep groan. "We've done our best over the years. My father did his best." *Father.* The word was still a stranger on his tongue. "But that wasn't good enough. We needed better. We deserve better." The crowd's clamor ebbed and flowed with his words as the sounds from above hurried. "I will do better." Cheers and screams of support carried through the park. "What I have planned will redefine our great city. Under me, under my leadership, we will no longer be separated as a people. No longer undersiders and topsiders. We will be one people. But we will have to stand firm to do this. And understand that our hands cannot stay clean. Not when they've forced us to the dirt for so long." *Where is this going?* It was supposed to talk of reaching past the Mantle. Extending our hands to each other. Not dirtying them. *A couple of minor changes* was not how he'd describe the complete rewrite. "Forget fire and brimstone. Our enemy's creation will be their undoing. Their tomb." Atlas's heart raced, the murmurs of attendees giving him pause. The metaphor was too strong. Too dark. He could see it on the faces in the crowd. Pops and whistles rang out from the sky as Atlas questioned the words on the page. He scanned the lines ahead as quickly and seamlessly as he could. He needed to know what was coming. *Only a few lines left.* Thankfully, none as objectionable as the last. The momentary relief pushing him forward. "For too long, we've stayed quiet. Subdued. Obedient. But no longer. Now is our hour of glory—"

The large rooftop screens blackened as a cavernous moan filled the air, screams of terror scratching atop its surface. Horror masked the faces in the crowd looking to the Mantle behind Atlas. He turned to see the Midriff buildings crumbling in the distance, the surface beneath them warping and curving inward. The platformed sky bending to the will of the sinking ground, folding over its edge like dough without a firm hand beneath. The sounds of glass shattering adding to the medley of falling brick and cries of bending steel. And in an instant, a deafening clap ripped the Mantle's edge from the sky, plunging it into the caving ground beneath, engulfing the entire Undercity in a dense cloud of dust and death.

CHAPTER 29

SOLOMON DECREES

His only words were, "Find Alanna." Like a lost puppy dog searching for their owner. Unable to comprehend a life without a scratch behind the ears. "Find Alanna." As if she could dust him off and cleanse him of his sins. *No, nephew. Only God can save you from the fine mess you find yourself in.*

Solomon knew the boy wasn't smart enough to have concocted such a cataclysmic event himself. His dim-witted nephew, who'd only risen to prominence through the trickery and plotting of others, hadn't even been aware of the puppeteer manipulating the strings hanging from his limbs—let alone being clever enough to have dreamt up something so diabolically brilliant as a sinkhole. But the words on his tongue seconds before would certainly damn him to Hell as its author. He would pay for the sins of others, even if all he'd been was a fool given a mouthpiece and a slap on the ass. *Here boy, come get this peanut butter.* Unaware of the nefarious intent beneath its sticky goodness.

Some still believed the collapse to have been an act of God, devoid of the fingerprints of man and his plotting. But Solomon saw the truth of it. And soon everyone else would too once the dust had settled. In a single act of desperate rebellion, the Syndicate Tower, atop the eastern Mantle edge, surrounded by blocks of its corporate buildings and luxury condos, was brought down upon the head of their military might. The entire Under Eastside, consumed by the earth and buried beneath its once canopied sky for good measure. One act of retribution, wiping the Syndicate clean from the city and changing the landscape of Midian forever.

Even if God hadn't been the sole source of the destruction, there was no doubt that He had aligned the pieces. God, who allowed the water beneath the ground to erode the dirt and weaken the supports restraining the Mantle above. *For all things come from God. That which we love, and that which we despise.* Solomon wasn't certain where his feelings lay on that spectrum. Love or hate. He loathed the Syndicate for their dismissal of the Good Word. They had damned themselves by thumbing their noses at God and his servants, sweeping the Faith beneath millions of tons of steel and concrete. Forcing him to preach in the shadows while they plotted and planned their pursuit of profits under the sun. But such devastation, such death, was just too hard to applaud. The blinding cloud of dust, snatching the sight from the collective eyes of the Undercity, had been too thick. Lasted too long. And when the air thinned and the moonlight shone down through the ruin, the images of people coated in the snow of destruction were as horrific as the destruction itself. Gray. Everything was gray. People screaming for loved ones, unable to see beyond their noses. Others struggling to flee, unsure if more ground was about to open up. Thousands flowing from the park, blanketed in dust like a large body shifting beneath thin bedsheets, finally woken from slumber.

Even with many assuming the Faith's newest poster child was the prime suspect in the attack, Solomon's nave was still full. He scanned over the faces in the pews as he sat in his large ceremonial chair several feet from the pulpit, turning over his prayer beads in his hand. Some parishioners were heartbroken, seeking mercy for the souls of their lost loved ones. Others were frightened with the remembrance of death. And a few were even revelrous, pleased with the Syndicate's removal and praising God and his new messenger for the respite. But despite the hardline extremists, most had yet to connect the attack as a product of the Faith, an inevitability Solomon knew was only days, if not moments away. After emotions had waned and people began considering the reasons with a sober mind, they would understand that as a prophet of the Faith, Atlas's actions could not be solely attributed to the Citizenry. He would have been acting on behalf of God. And then the pitchforks would follow.

Since the collapse yesterday, Solomon had been doing everything he could to distance the Faith from Atlas, even letting slip the passages on the Antiprophet in his words of condolement. He hadn't come right out and labeled Atlas as the promised evil from the Good Book, a conclusion he figured he'd let others draw out of respect for his bloodline. But it was undoubtedly the only way to save the Faith in the long run. And was certainly to be the message out of the High Council on their arrival. They had endorsed Atlas as a prophet even before meeting the boy, relying solely on Solomon's words and miracle as proof. But now they were stuck having labeled an alleged terrorist as a messenger of God and had but one path to redemption.

The Testaments were clear that before the end of time, before the trumpets of Paradise could be heard the world over, an Antiprophet would rise and lead even the most devout astray. It was a convenient prophecy that would exonerate the Council of their support of his nephew. Though it wouldn't do much to save Solomon. It would be obvious Atlas wasn't the promised deceiver once they'd spent two minutes with the boy. And although they might convince the masses of his evil to save the Faith, they would undoubtedly excommunicate Solomon under suspicion of heresy. With his rally speech now buried beneath the pain and sorrow of the attack, Solomon wouldn't have a single soul to act as his shield.

He stared up at the ceiling, the faces in the pews beginning to eat at him. He would mean nothing to them if the Council uncovered the truth. Just another face in the crowd. His world was spiraling, and he was doing everything he could to hold on. But the board was growing ever scarcer of viable moves.

He pressed down on the beads in his hand, sliding them one by one along the string, silently cycling through the prayers of salvation, when the large nave doors creaked open. Solomon's eyes fell to the group of five now heading down the long walk between the pews, shoulders and hands dusted in white.

"This your usual lot? Or did the apocalypse put these asses into the seats?" asked Marcus Bertram, scaling the steps to Solomon's chair.

"It is busier than usual," said Solomon, pushing to his feet. "I suspect we will see even more at this evening's sermon. A lot of confusion right now. People in need of guidance and comfort."

"Well, we won't take up much of your time."

Standing with Marcus was a peculiar group. Men Solomon had known from their status in the Undercity. A woman who may have well been considered a man with her short hair and red flannels. And an average-looking bloke wearing what appeared to be an altered SyndiGuard uniform.

"Jonah. Derick. It's a pleasure to see you once again," said Solomon. "And you are?" He extended his hand to the stout female lumberjack standing next to them.

"Amelia Stintz."

"Ah, yes. I know your brother. How is Randolph?"

"Probably shit-faced with a syringe in his arm."

Solomon pulled back his hand, now coated in the dust of the city. "Hmm. Unfortunate." He turned to the Guardian. "And you, sir?"

"Commander Mathias Lovie—former Commander…Mathias Lovie."

Solomon could see the commander's eyes well as he worked to keep his emotions restrained.

"This here...is an interesting union?" Solomon said to Marcus.

"Well, there ain't no reason for our bickering anymore. We need all the hands we can get while people lie trapped under that shit. But don't you worry. We'll be back at each other's throats soon enough," said Marcus.

"And how can the Faith be of service to your cause?"

"We need everything you can drum up for search-and-rescue," said Marcus. "We have all our people siftin' through the rubble for survivors, but it ain't enough."

Our people. They'd been rivals only days ago, enemies, in fact. Fighting one another for territory and power. And now they worked hand-in-hand for a cause greater than their egos. A commendable effort, but unfortunate that only tragedy could unify their aims.

"Yes, of course," said Solomon. "The Faith is at your beck and call. We will have the Filth assist in bringing you supplies and food, and we will urge the people to come and lend a hand."

"It isn't just topsiders under that rubble," said Amelia. "Thousands of undersiders were buried as well. Kids forced into their Guard placement. Remind your people of that, will ya?"

"Certainly," Solomon obliged before turning back to Marcus. "And what about Samantha? Has she finally reemerged? I haven't heard much of her since Big Town."

"Yeah, she's back. Leading the search. She refused to take even a minute away from digging. Poor girl hasn't stopped cryin' since the sky fell."

Despite their last encounter, Solomon felt sorry for Sami. Her heart was always in the right place. And if she'd been successful in her grasp for power, all this may never have happened. He could only imagine the pain she was harboring, thinking of all the souls she could have saved. Unfortunately, those not guided by the Faith linger on matters out of their control. She could have done nothing to prevent it if God had willed it so.

"At least she's back with the people," said Solomon.

"Yeah, I think her days of hidin' are done," said Marcus. "She blames herself, you know, for all this. Thinks she could've stopped it if she'd been in a better state of mind."

"Well, you remind her for me that our will is no match for the Creator's. Hopefully, she can find solace in that."

Marcus gave a subtle nod before turning to the others. "Okay, you guys get. I need to make a...personal prayer with the Grand Magus here."

Despite the looks of disbelief on the faces of Jonah and Derick, the others turned on their heels and headed for the doors. Marcus stretched his thick, dusty arm across Solomon's shoulders and led him behind the curtain into the sacristy.

It wasn't until the curtain was pulled closed completely and Marcus had stepped inches from Solomon's chin that he whispered, "You gotta keep the boy hidden."

The ginger mane of the old-time Citizenry leader reeked of onions and liquor. Solomon tried stepping back to put air between the scent and his nose, but Marcus held him firm by the arm.

"What boy?" Solomon asked, attempting to free himself from the grip.

"Your nephew."

"I don't know—"

"That's good. Keep doin' that. We know you got him. Just don't let anyone else know. Most of the city wants his head. And those who still think your God responsible will eventually come around to the same conclusion soon enough." Marcus released Solomon's arm. "We know he didn't do it. It was something Bass had in motion way before the kid took over. But try convincing the people of that. The millions that heard him preach the city's destruction. That poor fucking kid. It's over for him. But maybe we can buy him more time."

Solomon nodded to Marcus in agreement, and the pungent scent evaporated with his fiery red locks behind the curtains into the nave.

Solomon pulled a chair from beneath the table and collapsed with the weight of his worries. He placed his elbows on the table and held his face as his mind raced. His final move was exposed.

Solomon hadn't been sure why he'd felt the urge to rescue his nephew from the frenzy, retrieving him from the stage soon after the chaos ensued. Atlas was frozen from shock, only Alanna's name on his lips, covered head-to-toe in a thick layer of pulverized

Mantle. But as Solomon hauled him along the streets by the hand like a small child, avoiding large swaths of people, it became clear his instincts had been two steps ahead. Stowing his nephew away from the Council could prevent the unraveling of his parish. But if the Citizenry, or Faction, or whoever the fuck, knew he'd been concealing his nephew from the world only a day after the collapse, by the time the Council arrived in Midian, it would be as known as his brother's preference for other men. It takes but one to let slip a rumor. One angered and frightened soul seeking justice for the devastation. It would not stay secret for very long.

Solomon gazed up at the clock by his wardrobe through his spread fingers. The time for his sermon was fast approaching, and he had little prepared. Ordinarily, it was a simple message to share after a tragedy. Standing firm in faith. Firm with the Lord, trusting his methods. But with Solomon's impending removal looming, it was a nearly impossible message for him to sell, stitching together words of acceptance for the masses while he worked in the shadow of the pulpit, tirelessly raging against it. The hypocrisy twisted his mind in knots as the proverb of the anchored horse echoed in his ears. *Anchor your horse and trust in God. For allowing it to roam free under God's watchful eye alone is an affront to the Creator's gift of sovereignty.*

Solomon had tried to anchor his horse, sealing his nephew beneath the nave in an abandoned room once used for exorcisms. But now that his red-haired visitor had signaled the anchor's weakness to maintain its hold, only one other anchor was strong enough to withhold the bucking of his wild steed.

It wasn't enough to ship Atlas out to sea. Smuggle him into some far-off state to disappear among the locals of a new land. He'd been on screen, preaching the destruction of one of the world's largest city-states. His face would be known and notorious the world over. He'd be found and extradited. Tried and executed. But not before the Council had their time with their fallen prophet. Not before Solomon was permanently shamed and removed from his post. Labeled among the Faith's darkest embarrassments for generations to come. A fraud. A phony. An enemy of God. It was too great a risk to accept. Too crippling a fear to live beneath for the rest of his life. There was but one way to spare himself this fate.

Solomon's stomach squeaked and groaned at the thought. How could he ever? He wasn't Asher. He wasn't a savage, able to murder on a whim and a prayer—his nephew, no less. But despite how far he pushed the idea from his thoughts, how deep he struggled to bury it beneath the heft of his guiding principles, it somehow kept sailing back as his saving grace. Fluttering atop the solemn words of Marcus Bertram: "That poor fucking kid. It's over for him."

Solomon knew it was true. Not even if the perpetrators themselves announced their guilt and swore to Atlas's innocence would the grieving mothers and fathers, sorrowed sisters and brothers, allow him to go free. His words had damned him, and justice would be done. And if it was inevitable, if his nephew was to be put to death either way, why shouldn't it occur before the

Council arrived? Why shouldn't he lead the posse?

An eye for an eye was as firmly rooted in the ancient Faith texts as the unity of God. If Solomon were to decree Atlas's execution under the law of the Almighty, he would be well within his right. Well within settled Faith jurisprudence. It might even establish the Faith as the arbiter of justice in the post-Syndicate era of Midian. In the end, the execution of his nephew might serve a greater purpose. A means to prove the Faith's innocence in the collapse and plant its flag in the Mantle rubble.

Solomon could feel the burn of his digested lunch climb his throat and sear the back of his mouth. He swallowed hard to stop the vomit from spilling through his lips and rushed to the sink to douse his tongue in the cold water now gushing from the tap. He could feel the heat of his sickness slather his body, reaching for his neck, but halted by the cold sweat at its nape. The room spun fiercely, and Solomon pressed his back to the kitchenette, sliding to the floor against the smooth cabinet doors. With his head between his legs, he clutched his knees and huffed the stale church air as deeply as he could muster.

After finally being embraced by calm, he rose to his feet, peering up at the clock. The time was at hand. His sermon had come due. And so had his nephew's life. He would declare God's judgment tonight.

As he stepped beyond the curtains to condemn his brother's son, the memory of his passionate prayer days ago cycled through his mind like an old film reel, complete with burn marks and dust squiggles, pleading for the riddance of his nephew. It had been years since he'd prayed with such vigor. Years since his plea had been so solemn. And God had been ever watchful. *The servant asks, and the Master provides.*

CHAPTER 30
SAMI HEAVES

Sami might have thought the night beautiful if it hadn't been for the horror beneath her feet. The bright pale moon above rained down its light over the vast ocean at the city's shore, the calmness of the water reflecting its glow. The quiet of the night extending an offer of tranquility. An evening of peace for neighborhoods of the Undercity no longer starved of the night sky. Plainsview, Big Town, and Agriville were still too far beneath the intact portion of the Mantle to experience the gleaming white moon. But now, anyone could make their way to the city's edge for a breath of fresh ocean air and show of the stars. They need only endure a mountainous climb of loose debris, the bitter winter chill, and the mass grave of thousands at their toes.

Sami heaved another large rock from the pile and rested it into a nearby wheelbarrow, her palms raw from the thousands like it she'd lifted before. She watched a volunteer carefully wheel the barrow down the mound toward a waiting truck, half filled with a mixed load of rocks, steel, and wooden remnants. She'd lost count of how many loads the trucks had been through since arriving at the site. Several dozen, she suspected. A long trip from ground zero through the southern pass and out beyond the city limits to the Barrens. They had needed several trucks to maintain the rotation to keep up with the pace of the volunteers. Most were fiercely committed, only slowing efforts for a brief meal and a quick snooze—and when a body was found. The workers in the area would congregate and say a brief prayer before loading the corpse into one of the transport vans, standing silent out of respect as the van pulled away, en route to a meat locker in Agriville. Sami often worked through the informal ceremony, refusing to cease her efforts until her bones and muscles gave way. She had barely even slept since the collapse, closing her eyes for only moments at a time after finding a firm spot of rubble that could support her weight. Time was of the essence, and she couldn't waste a minute with anything that wasn't absolutely necessary.

But as the hours and days slowly slipped away, Sami knew her efforts were nearing their end. Not much hope for survivors anymore. Not after this long. Even with the hundreds of Citizenry, Faction, and Faith volunteers trudging through the debris, they'd been unable to save a single soul. The devastation was too great, the fall too high.

Sami looked up to the Mantle. She still couldn't shake the weight of the sight. Broken roadways overhung the Mantle tear, with thousands of long steel rods and beams poking out from its edge like candles on a birthday cake. She watched smaller pieces of the Mantle rain down with each gust of wind, triggering a horrifying image of the fall in her mind. Thousands of feet in the air amid the crumbling structures, now serving as the victims' tomb.

Sami had heard countless stories of people being pulled from fallen buildings after earthquakes and other catastrophes around the world, fueling her hope when she first arrived at the smoking mounds of the aftermath moments after the dust had settled enough to see. But it being the third night with no survivors, the recovery of any life was becoming ever bleaker. And with each passing minute, each lifeless body pulled from the wreckage, the demons swirling above her head grew ever more emboldened, echoing calls of her guilt that whispered from the rubble beneath her feet, reminding Sami of the selfishness underpinning the collapse. Slowly cranking the knife embedded in her chest.

Sami had tried to explain it to Marcus. How she was responsible. How she had ignored the warning. But he refused to allow her to blame herself. "It's as much your fault as it is Atlas's," he'd said. A sentiment she may have believed if she hadn't climbed the mountains of concrete and steel to survey the damage. The site where the gut-sinking truth had revealed itself.

Cutting the large mounds of debris along where the Mantle pillars had stood was a miles-long trench dipping beneath massive swaths of fallen roads and building remnants, stretching the width of several city blocks and the length of the entire Under Eastside. A sinkhole. The cause of the destruction, now filled with thousands of tons of debris. But to Sami's eye, it was too straight a path to have been formed so naturally. Too far from the ocean for the natural erosion of the earth to have displaced the pillars' footings. Staring out over the valley of the crumbled Mantle, the image of the Bottoms shot to the forefront of her mind. At one time, the city's landfill had rested atop the same spread of land as the rest of the Undercity, eventually reduced to a furrowed plain after a water main burst beneath the ground.

The explosives from the little boy's wagon may not have been enough to have taken down a single building, but it had been more than enough to blow the entire stretch of pipe along the path of Mantle pillars, the water main installed to feed the Uppercity with fresh, clean water, used as Bass's instrument of destruction.

In Sami's haze of self-pity and anger, she'd missed all the signs. Overlooked all the warnings. And now the gaping pit of guilt seated in the depths of her stomach would only be sated by doing all she could for those she had once abandoned.

Sami looked to the bottom of the mound she'd been working through and slowly descended back to the hard ground. Without the hope of survivors feeding her will any longer, she knew with the dead was now where she belonged. Not yet as one of them—she hadn't earned that respite—but rather among their bodies. Caring for their families. Offering condolences and comfort amid all the despair. It was what she deserved after her massive failure. Even with thoughts of flinging herself into the near-frozen waters of the shore, she knew she had to press on, undeserving of escape. She refused to burrow once again into her hole while so many were left grieving. She wouldn't dare make that mistake ever again.

"You done for the night?" said a deep, authoritative voice, accented by the crunching of rubble.

Sami turned to see Mathias Lovie approach with his boyish smirk and long, overhanging blond bangs. His warm breath billowed from his lips, sky-blue eyes twinkling in the pale moonlight.

"Yeah," she said after a brief hesitation. "Do you mind taking lead on the rescue from here on out? I think I'll focus on the families for a while."

"Of course. Whatever you need."

Commander Mathias Lovie was the highest-ranking SyndiGuard official still alive, lucky to have been on the far western Mantle at the time of the collapse. He was one of a couple hundred Guardians still standing and had thrown his hat in with Sami soon after she'd successfully organized the search team. Sami was hesitant to trust him at first, keeping him and the remaining Guardians at arm's length for the first couple of days. The SyndiGuard had lost more than anyone else in the city, and she wasn't sure of their intentions. She had also found it miraculous enough that the Citizenry underbosses were willing to accept her leadership and didn't want to press her luck with another former adversary. But Mathias seemed genuine enough in his willingness to help, never refusing a request, taking orders as commanded. And his ability to still maintain control of the remaining Guardians gave her hope that the city's security wasn't yet a complete write-off.

"Thanks. I—"

"Have you eaten anything yet?" he asked, stepping over to one of the dozens of coolers resting at the foot of the wreckage.

"No, but I don't—"

"You have to eat something, Samantha." Mathias pulled two wrapped sandwiches from the volunteer food reserves and patted a seat on the lid of one of the closed coolers.

Sami had gone days on only small sips of water. Even after the shelter children had wheeled in the food donations to the site, she had refused to take a moment for nourishment, pushing through the dizziness and hunger pains, envisioning someone just beyond the next stone waiting for her to find them. But now, with Mathias waving the sandwiches in the air and offering an even seat for some comfort, Sami could feel the feverish hunger overwhelm her stubbornness.

She took a seat on the broad plastic lid next to him and snatched the sandwich from his hand. The rush of energy coursing through her after that first bite was like nothing she'd felt before. It was like a hit of life rejuvenating her muscles and instantly reviving her mood.

"It's good, huh?" said Mathias, wide-eyed, with a broad smile plastered across his lips. "Don't go too hard there, though. I have a treat for after." He reached down beside the cooler and pulled up two slices of yellow bread. "Lemon loaf. Trust me when I tell you these will knock your socks off."

The vision of her filthy socks flinging in the air made Sami spit out a bite from laughter. It hadn't been all that funny of a remark, but the combination of the food high flooding her body with nutrients and the surprise of joy she felt from the friendly conversation gave it the muster it needed. Not since she'd ushered Jasper away had she had anyone to share a meal with. Or even anyone to offer her a kindness without needing something in return. It was a pleasant feeling to simply sit, eat, and talk for once.

"So, what's your story?" she asked before taking another large bite of her nearly finished meal.

"Oh, nothing too interesting. You know, same old. Rich parents. Top of the class in my senior year. Captain of the driftball team. Rugged good looks—"

"And humble, too," she said in a playful tone.

"The humblest."

They both let out a quiet laugh and returned to their sandwiches. It was as if Sami had been transported away from the sadness and despair of all the death and destruction, until a call in the far-off distance shook her back to reality.

"Another body! Another body!"

The air drained from the site as dozens of volunteers flooded toward the corpse. Sami put down the last bite of her sandwich, about to push off her seat, when Mathias gently clasped her arm.

"Don't," he said in a whisper. "They got it. It's okay."

She could feel tears in her eyes as she relaxed back onto

the hard plastic seat.

Mathias released his grip and folded his hands in his lap. "Sami. Do you know why I follow you?"

She turned to catch his eye, but his sights were set out into the distance, gazing down the line of the wreckage.

"I've been in the Guard since I was eighteen. That's almost twenty years now. And in that time, I've had commanding officers who were smart. Strong. Caring. Committed. Some of the most remarkable men I'd ever known. Most probably somewhere in that pile of shit now. But none of them, not a single one, had it all. You have it all.

"I watched you when I first arrived with the other Guardians. How everyone just gravitated toward you. Carrying out your every command with unflinching commitment. It was incredible to see. No one questioning your authority, despite the dozens of large, burly men who most would have gravitated to in a crisis—at least where I come from. But even those men, scarred and battle-forged, were following you. Hanging on to your every word. It was baffling at first, I have to admit. But after seeing you these past few days—directing the trucks, coordinating the volunteers, making sure everything was running as smoothly as possible to maximize the chance of recovering survivors—all while you continued to dig yourself, proved to me the people weren't wrong. *You* are what the city needs, Samantha. You are what the people need. And I will follow that until the rest of the Mantle comes down on our heads."

Sami could feel her blood warm her cheeks as she stared down at her toes. It was a flattering speech. And if it had been a week earlier, it might have pushed her to get back into the arena. Continue her fight for the Undercity. But now his words meant nothing. He hadn't known what her motivation had been these last few days. What was driving her to lead. What he thought he saw was not the truth of it. All he'd seen in reality was a terrified woman overrun with guilt, doing everything she could to try to fix the mistakes of the past. She wasn't a hero. She was, in fact, the villain.

Mathias leaned forward with his elbows on his knees. "I just still can't believe it, though," he said. "How someone could be so evil? It's one thing to disagree or even revile the system in place. But it's another thing completely to kill so many for an idealistic wet dream. What did the dead ever do to him?"

Sami's anger boiled at the thought, reminded of all the times Bass had promised to take down the Syndicate. All bluster and noise. And each time, she had simply dismissed him.

"He really believed it was in the best interest of the people," she said. "I don't think anyone could do something so despicable if they didn't believe it to be a necessary evil for the greater good." She let out a laugh of disbelief. "He even cleared the homeless from the Midriff before it happened. Making sure only the Syndicate was targeted. He really believed he was doing a good thing."

Sami could see Mathias's face now shade red. His bright eyes darkened.

"Fuck him," he said with a subdued rage. "I'm just glad someone is going to do something about it. Send that fucker to his maker."

"In due time. When we're done here, we can assemble a group to hunt him down."

"Hunt him down? We already know where he is. The Faith has him."

The Faith? Not even if all the magi in the city tried to wrestle Bass to the ground would they be able to hold him.

"They've already announced his upcoming execution," said Mathias. "Judged under 'God's Law.' I don't care which law he was judged under. As long, in the end, he's under the dirt."

This was all news to her. Bass to be executed, by the Faith no less. It wasn't making sense.

"Are you…sure?" she asked.

"Oh yeah. We're all really excited about it too. I'm just hoping the execution is public. Let's see if the girls still swoon for that pretty boy when he's swinging from a stretch of rope."

Pretty boy. The words sent shivers down her spine. He wasn't talking about Bass. They were going to execute Atlas.

CHAPTER 31
ARVIN GRIEVES

"An eighth," said Arvin.

Barrel looked up with his eyes, head still tilted toward the scale on his desk, a fold of skin overhanging his brow. "You sure, kid?"

"Yes. That's what he said."

Arvin watched as the large, hairy paw dipped into the sack on the desk and pulled a thickly packed baggie from inside. Barrel placed it on the scale and then tossed it several feet to Arvin, standing in the middle of the room. He fumbled for it in the air before the baggie slipped through his fingers to the filthy floorboards at his feet. The danger didn't register at first, but as the dust billowed from the floor, Arvin immediately held his breath, quickly raising his shirt over his face.

Barrel's deep, hearty laugh shook the small room. "Relax, kid. A simple drop ain't gonna do it. It needs to be smushed first. And trust me, covering your face wouldn't do shit to stop it from getting into your lungs."

Arvin let out a breath of relief and dropped his shirt before picking up the baggie from the floor.

"I'd be more worried about getting robbed than suffocating," said Barrel, turning back to the count on his desk. "When was the last time your friend had enough money for an eighth? Sounds like a setup to me."

Arvin shrugged and slipped the baggie into his pocket.

"Okay. But no mulligans this time, kid. You get robbed, it's your funeral."

The image of his brother's framed picture, surrounded by flower bouquets and finely dressed attendants, flashed in his mind. Arvin had already come from his funeral and wasn't worried about another. This was to be the reception.

He turned to the door when Barrel's grizzly voice tugged on him to turn back around. "Your friend. Mack," he said. "He hasn't been by. I got work for him."

Hardly shocking, Arvin thought. Especially with Mack long buried in the Filth mound at the cemetery. But it was even less shocking that the friend he'd actually been referring to hadn't been around either.

"I haven't seen him," said Arvin as confidently as someone telling the truth.

"He another Filth?"

"Yes."

"From the shelter on Thirty-Third Street?"

"Yes."

"I'll send someone to go look in on him. Get going. You're gonna be late for your robbery," he said with a grunt of laughter.

Arvin was frozen momentarily as the implication set in, but he forced his feet to shuffle from the room before his concern was made obvious. The thought of Barrel and his goons heading to the shelter wouldn't usually have given Arvin pause. He had expected it when he threw out Mack's name to protect Miron. But with the shelter on his list of stops for the evening, he now had to be careful about slipping in and out without bumping into Barrel's men. It was unlikely he'd simply drop all questions when the sisters revealed Mack's passing. And Arvin would need to make sure he was nowhere in sight when the oversized knuckle came searching. He only had tonight to make everything work and couldn't afford to waste any time on the other end of Barrel's scorn.

The walk to the Marketplace was a blur as Arvin envisioned his victory again and again. He could almost feel the relief with the euphoric thoughts flooding every inch of his body. The joy. The satisfaction. The justice. Even with the oversized lout on his tail about Miron, Arvin's confidence had only grown with the bulge in his pocket and his feet nearing the market, reducing the threat of Barrel's men to a minor hiccup in his plans that should do little more than cause a slight delay. He'd just take a moment or two extra to survey the shelter before sneaking in. What were the odds they'd wait around anyway?

It's going to work, Arvin thought. He could feel it in his bones, an insulating feeling of warmth that seemed to shield his flesh from the harsh winter wind. There had been a moment earlier in the day when he'd been unconvinced, turning to God with a plea for justice. It had been the first time he'd ever asked God for anything, and the response was deafening. The utter silence was telling. But from that silence came the freedom he'd been searching for. The permission he needed to do what he must.

Arvin approached the Marketplace alley where his meet-ups typically played out. It held a far more ominous feeling than before, much darker than usual, blanketed in shadows from the dim streetlamps. A reality for most of the Undercity since the collapse. Large sections of Lower Midian were still without power, and even with the eastern portion of the Mantle razed and the moonlight able to reach farther in, the glow wasn't enough to find its way into some of the darker crevices.

Arvin stood at the edge of the alleyway, some residual light from the market streets kissing the pavement at his feet. He peered into the darkness, squinting, hoping for movement. He would rather not enter a blackened alley carrying a pocket full of skeet without a familiar face to greet him. But he knew he might not have a choice if his regular didn't wave him in soon. He couldn't waste any more time with fear. He was already late after the funeral had run long, and now his customer would likely be searching for another score. Somewhere in the area, for certain. And down the alley would be Arvin's best bet.

He turned to survey the street one last time before heading into the darkness. The once bustling Marketplace core was a skeleton of its former self. People were still flowing from shop to shop. Street performers and preachers still demanded attention.

But where a gushing crowd once roared, a trickling stream was all that remained. The mood was now more anemic than electric, a somberness Arvin could appreciate, especially after the week he'd endured.

Unable to spy the junkie's sores among the faces in the sparse crowd, Arvin slipped into the corridor, hand pressed on the outside of his pocket. His eyes had attuned to the dim lighting, and he could now see the trash and discarded syringes intermingled with the passed-out patrons of the alley. Dumpsters and fire escape ladders delineated building boundaries, with makeshift shelters swallowing up any recessed crevice—prime real estate in the forgotten cuts of the Marketplace.

Unshaken by the ambiance, Arvin pressed deeper into the alleyway, reaching an intersecting street at its end. Still technically part of the market, the street housed lesser-known shops with drab signs and unkempt storefronts. If the core traffic had been reduced to a trickle, the flow of shoppers along the stretch of the back alley stores could only be considered sporadic drips. Unlit and as quiet as a shelter night after a Filth death, the street lay bare for the few passersby he could make out in the distance. His customer was nowhere to be seen.

As he scanned the roadway for his next path, he felt a firm hand clutch his shoulder and tug him back into the mouth of the alley.

"You're late!" said the man. "I almost did some crazy shit to catch a hit. Figured I would check back here first. Thankfully, I did." The man scratched his neck with one hand as he massaged his chest with the other, an addict tic Arvin had seen all too often. "What took you so long? As if you'd leave me hanging like that."

The thought of someone hanging had run through Arvin's mind several times that night. But it wasn't his customer at the end of the rope.

"You got it?" asked the man, pulling a wad of cash from his pocket.

"Yeah," said Arvin. "But no cash."

"Whatcha mean, no cash? Since when?"

"I need information."

Disbelief washed over the man's face, and he shook his head brusquely. "What information?" he asked.

"The big man. Bass. And his lanky friend. I need to know where they are. Where they live."

"For fuck sakes!" the man cried out. "What the fuck? What is this shit?" He paced back and forth, running his hands through his filthy hair as he appeared to argue with a figment of his imagination.

Arvin cut in as the rant grew louder, "I'll make it worth your while!"

The jerking of his head and flailing of his arms slowed as the man ceased his pace, eying Arvin carefully. "How?"

"For an eighth. You tell me what I want to know, and I'll give you an eighth."

The whites of the man's eyes nearly lit up the darkened

alley as Arvin flashed the thick baggie from his pocket.

"Don't screw me, though," said Arvin. "You do, and you'll never get another gram from me again." It was a threat he'd used many times in the past. Cutting off a junkie's supply was akin to threatening death and was the only way to keep them in line. But this time, it was an utter lie. This was his last deal either way.

The man lifted his gaze to Arvin's face. "I don't know where they are. Nobody does. That fuck fell off the face of the earth. He hasn't been seen in weeks."

Arvin's heart sank, but he refused to resign himself to the mere word of a junkie. He was sure the man knew or at least had ways to find the information he needed. He'd spoken as if he'd known Bass personally at their first encounter. As if he'd been part of the Citizenry at one point in his life. He'd even known Arvin had been smuggling for them. How could someone with all that knowledge not know something as insignificant as an address?

"Okay..." Arvin said with a shrug, tucking the swollen baggie into his pocket before heading toward the street.

"Wait! Wait!"

Arvin kept his pace, unwilling to show how much he cared for the information. He needed to keep his cool, despite the raging inferno of fear scorching his insides.

"I'll find out! Don't worry! I will!"

A smile crept to Arvin's lips, extinguishing the blaze within.

"Tonight," he said, turning back around.

"Tonight? That's impos—"

Arvin turned toward the street again, but the man rushed to his back and spun him around, arms firmly on his shoulders.

"Fine. Fine. Tonight. Give me a couple of hours. Okay?"

Two hours was a lot of time to waste when he only had until lamps-on to get everything done. But Arvin didn't have any other choice. He nodded, and the man took off into the shadows.

Arvin headed back through the alley to the market core. Stepping into the light, he looked at the large clock affixed to one of the storefront walls. It was already ten o'clock. He'd need to stay productive while he waited, just in case he encountered more bumps along the way. Time was not on his side tonight. Not with such a monumental task at hand and only a few hours to make it work. By tomorrow morning, he would be back at the shelter, unable to be cared for any longer by the grieving Mastersons. They had sworn it would be temporary, just until they could come to terms with their son's death. But Arvin knew better. He would never see them again. And once back at the shelter, he wouldn't have the freedom to do what needed to be done. This would be his only chance.

He did the rough math in his mind, calculating the distance between the market and the shelter, the shelter and his home, and back to the market again. There might be just enough time while he waited. He could sneak a holey roller from the shelter in under thirty minutes. Arrive at the Mastersons in another forty-five minutes. And make it back to the Marketplace in just under thirty. There was only one lingering question: how long it would take to rig the wagon with the explosives from under his bed?

CHAPTER 32
ATLAS FREED

The dreams had ceased altogether—both the good and the bad. Even Alanna's childhood scream was gone completely from its decade-long home. Just a blank slumber that seemed to end when his body shook him awake for water and nourishment. Atlas wasn't certain whether it was from the utter boredom dulling his thoughts or having the past horror shaken from his mind with the sights of the collapse. But either way, it had provided much-needed sleep. He could barely remember the last time he'd felt so rested. Probably not since summer break back at SyndiCares, when his mornings consisted of little more than comic books and lazing around. And although now there had been nothing as interesting as a SyndiCape Weekly to keep him entertained—just an old copy of the Testaments at his bedside—the hours each day he'd spent sprawled out atop the moth-eaten sheets of his basement refuge rivaled some of the most immobile days of his youth. An indulgence he was learning only children could truly endure.

After so many long days holed up in the bowels of the Central Faith Church, Atlas was ready to leave. The musty stench of the church basement, mixed with the lingering odor of the toilet in the corner of his room, was unsettling his stomach. The brightly painted walls reflected the fluorescent lights buzzing above his head, searing halos into his vision. Everything was now glowing with a heavenly aura. And even with the much-needed rest, his mind was slowly looping from being locked away for too long. His worries of Alanna. His yearning to hold her. The anxiety ripping at his sanity. Did she know he was okay?

Alanna had disappeared during his speech, so he doubted she'd seen Solomon usher him away after the chaos ensued. He'd been adamant with his uncle that she needed to know where he was. Needed to know he hadn't abandoned her. Hadn't been killed. And now, with the time between their last encounter stretching further and further away, she would grow ever more fretful about his return. Too many days had passed without word. It was hard to say for certain, but Atlas guessed at least four days—maybe five. He could picture her face pained and morose, resigning herself to his disappearance. Slowly letting go of all hope. He needed to leave. He needed to find her.

With no windows to the outside world, the passage of time was marked by only the brief moments he shared with the Faith sister who brought him his daily meals, a kind woman with a pointed nose and warm smile. He hadn't yet learned her name, but she'd been nice enough, offering Atlas words of prayer and encouragement as he worked to cope with his life away. "It won't be much longer," she would say on each pull of the door. But with his growing fear for Alanna, the sentiment had grown stale.

On the sister's last trip to his room, Atlas had asked to speak with his uncle—a request she seemed willing enough to relay. But that was nearly a day ago, and she had yet to return with any of the day's meals. Atlas hadn't spoken with Solomon since the night he'd been tucked away, simply placed in a room once used to house the possessed. His new sanctuary from those who sought to do him harm—or so he was told.

"The locks are for your safety," Solomon had said. But as the days inched by and he awaited the all-clear for his release, the line between protected and prisoner grew even more blurred. The toilet in the corner that had at first seemed like a convenience was now giving off vibes of SyndiGuard cells.

They couldn't think I was behind the whole thing, could they? The idea had brushed his thoughts over the last couple of days but was easily dismissed by the enormity of the devastation. There was no way the collapse of the Mantle had been planned. Only nature could force such destruction. And even if his words before the collapse hinted at his involvement, he could simply point to Amelia as its author. That should prove him innocent—at least in the eyes of those that mattered. And no doubt Alanna would come to his defense. But he'd need to find her first.

The footsteps beyond the large metal door grew louder as Atlas sat up on his bed. The clicks and clanks of rustling keys sending nervous jitters through his legs. He leaped to his feet, and the broad metal door swung inward with a gush of stale basement air. Solomon stood at the threshold with a neatly stacked pile of clothes on his arm.

"How are you, Atlas?" he said before heaving the door closed.

Something about the friendly inflection in his voice irked Atlas something fierce. As if he'd been put up in a Mantleside resort, with caterers serving his every need. His utter annoyance wrestled away the lingering jitters, and a flush of rage coated his pale skin.

"How *am I*? How the fuck would you be if I locked you away with nothing but a toilet and your thoughts for days on end?"

Solomon stalled, contempt brewing in his eyes. "Calm yourself," he ordered, resting the clothes on the tousled bed sheets. "Your clothes are filthy. Put these on."

Atlas ripped the sheets off the bed, tumbling the neatly stacked pile to the floor. "Where have you been?" he yelled. "You just lock me away. Don't even visit? Leave me down here to rot!"

Solomon huffed, reaching for Atlas's face with one hand, squeezing his cheeks inward with his fingers. "How dare you speak to me like that?" he said with a tremble of indignation. "You ingrate. The world wants you dead. And I was doing my very best to keep you safe out of loyalty to my brother." He released his grip with a shove of Atlas's face. "Now dress!"

Solomon's words sapped the heat from Atlas's blood, the red anger painting his skin easing to a pink flush of shame. Atlas reached down for the clothes, stacking them neatly on the bed: a plain long-sleeved shirt and blue jeans, with a fresh new pair of underwear and clean socks.

"Thank you…for these," Atlas said meekly before pulling off his sweat-stained shirt.

"Yes, well, if you are going to have a visitor, I can't make it appear as if we aren't treating you well."

Atlas froze, bare-chested, with the clean shirt in his hands. "Visitor?" he asked. "Did you find her?" The words leapt from his mouth.

The question went unanswered as Solomon glared at Atlas's topless body, squinting with curiosity as if examining something remarkable on the exposed flesh. It was an awkward moment that urged Atlas to quickly slip on the clean shirt and repeat the question.

Solomon stammered momentarily before responding. "Ah…yes… Ms. Thistle is here."

Alanna. A feeling of joy overwhelmed him as he rushed to change out the rest of his clothes, tripping over his feet, pulling his legs into his garments.

"Where is she now?" he asked with hastened breath.

Solomon couldn't match Atlas's urgency. As if in a daze, he was slow to respond, stammering over his words. "Uh…just…upstairs."

The shift in Solomon's demeanor made Atlas question whether he should have turned away before switching out his briefs. Something had shaken his uncle, making him wonder whether the rumors about the magi and their sexual proclivities were true. But the rush of excitement from Alanna's visit washed the thought away, and he wrapped his dirty clothes in the holey bedsheets before handing the large wad to Solomon to remove from the room.

"Do you mind?"

His uncle collected the wrapped-up sheet and stepped toward the door. After entering the hall, he turned back to Atlas, his stern glare displacing the confusion from moments earlier. "We will need to talk afterward, nephew. I've done my best…but sometimes it's not in God's plan."

The words failed to register as Atlas's excitement deafened him to their meaning. All that mattered now was that he was going to see Alanna.

He couldn't help his sweaty palms as she entered the room, a smile etched across his face. She wore her full Citizenry getup from the night of the speech, complete with armband and her hair pulled back in a ponytail. Her face appeared flushed, and her eyes were swollen and red as if she'd been crying only moments earlier. Crying from relief, he figured. Atlas's smile brightened toward her, but her sorrowful look ushered the light away. There was something in her expression that stalled his feet, holding him back from snatching her up in his arms. He stared carefully, cautiously, his back against the windowless wall. Something was wrong. He could feel it flood the room. An energy that consumed all the life within.

"I'm so sor—"

"Stop," she snapped. "Don't."

Across the room, Alanna slid to the hard floor against the wall. She pulled up her knees to her chest and glared at him with a pain he could feel in his heart. A spreading ache climbed his throat. His legs weakened, and he eased himself to a seat on his bed. Alanna looked to the ceiling as if watching a memory play out above, holding a moment of silence before she finally spoke.

"I was so good at school," she said. "It just came easy to me. My teachers would even give me extra work because I'd finish so quickly and end up bugging the other kids out of boredom." She let out a breathy laugh. "You know, they even made me take tests—like medical ones. They'd give me a task and scan my brain to see how it worked. I remember seeing all the lights on the screen pop up in the corner of my eye while I flew through anything they gave me. It was all so easy. Even the stuff they said was at a college level.

"I remember my parents being so proud. Telling all their friends. Bragging about me. I didn't know what it all meant. Or even how it could help me in life. But they seemed to think it was amazing—which made me feel special. It wasn't until I got older that I realized how special it was. People just couldn't think the way I thought. Put things together as easily as I could. But I eventually realized it was only one thing that really set me apart from everyone else. Well, that set me apart from the smart ones, at least. The difference between me and them. My little secret." She gazed at Atlas curiously. "Do you want to know what it is? My little secret?"

It was an odd question. A strange greeting after days of being apart. Atlas fumbled for a response, but she spoke before his tongue could gather the sounds.

"It's my memory."

His chest sank at the implication. The sound of the words leaving her lips. "Alanna—"

"NO! It's not your time to speak!" she shrieked. Alanna closed her eyes and took a deep breath before reopening them with a chilling glare. "Do you know what the problem is with a good memory? I can remember everything. Every…little…fucking thing. Even the shit I want to forget. I can remember the color of my mother's shoes the day she died. The cowlick at the back of my father's head as he lay in a pool of his own blood. The number of blood spots that ended up on the purse my nana gave me… And your trembling lip after you killed them out of fear."

Atlas stared vacantly at Alanna from across the room as shame overwhelmed him. He could feel a cold sweat brewing on his forehead. His insides were wrenching. Shoulders weighty. *Did she know the whole time?*

"I have to admit, the shades threw me off a bit—the ones you wore in the parade. I was pretty sure it was you in the bar that first night. And almost certain when you came to meet me at the Hall. But your reaction at my nana's…you basically admitted it. Yes, it was a tragic story about my nana. But only someone with a right filthy soul would have been as shaken as you were."

There was nothing to say. Nothing to defend.

"When I first moved to my nana's, she gave me a dog. Astro was his name. He was super cute. Running up and down the hall. Fetching his leash for me to take him for a walk. We even played this game where I'd pretend something hurt me. A piece of wood. A ball. Anything. And he'd bark so loudly at it. Growling and showing his teeth. It was cute. He was my protector. But after a couple of months, he started to get really sick. We weren't sure from what, so we had a vet come and check him out. Turns out a rat had been sharing his food bowl, dropping little turds inside. And Astro was eating it. The vet had some medicine he said could help, but we didn't have the money to afford it. So, we had to put him to sleep. It crushed me for days. Here was another thing I loved, gone in an instant. But this time, I wasn't just going to let it go.

"At night, I used to lie quietly on the couch under a blanket, staring at Astro's food bowl. Waiting for the rat to come eat. I just watched for a while. A couple of weeks, I think. Just to see what he did. Where he'd go after. He'd usually do the same thing every night. Eat. Sniff around. Go back into his hole. But after enough time, after I figured I learned all I needed to know, I began feeding the rat in its hole instead. He'd defiled the bowl enough. I would toss a few bits of Astro's food inside the opening each night, and they would be gone by morning. I grew kind of attached to the little guy. It wasn't like he knew he'd killed Astro. But still, I couldn't just let bygones be bygones. He did kill my dog.

"One night, I took several bits from Astro's bowl and

soaked them in a jug of old antifreeze I found in the neighbor's yard. Then, when it was time for the rat to feed, I tossed them in his hole like every other night before. I couldn't see too far in, but I could hear him nibble. It was quiet, but I could still hear it. And then I took a small picture of me my nana kept in her wallet—one of those pictures you get from school—and pushed it into the hole while he ate. I don't know exactly why it mattered, but it did. I needed him to see it was me. That I killed him. I wanted him to look into my eyes and know. He needed to know. And that's why I'm here."

Atlas strained to keep his sights on the ceiling, his muscles squirming beneath his flesh. If he could have leaped from his skin, he would have without a second thought. Anything to escape the judgment that was finally coming due.

"I am curious what you were thinking, though. Coming to find me. A chance at redemption, I know, but as if it would be that easy. As if killing your friend would wipe clean my pain. Poor Thomas. He didn't sign up for that."

Atlas's eyes darted down to hers. Her sharp and playful glare only added to his bewilderment. A subtle simper curled her lip, replacing the somber mask she'd worn moments before.

Alanna pushed herself to her feet. "You know, he was pretty easy to find. Bass recognized him almost instantly when I showed him your class yearbook. SyndiCares Home #3, right? Did you know they kept yearbooks? No, I don't think you did. You would have had at least one in your stuff at the motel—the way you used to ramble longingly about your time there. But they do. They don't include the last names, but a face and a first name are more than enough."

Impossible, he thought. *There was no way.* He could feel his slow, defeated heart thump harder in his chest as the reality of her ruse seeped in.

"I learned a lot about the poor after you killed my parents. The time I spent with Logan and the other Filth. Playing in the Bottoms with children who were so poor, they wore shoes made from old shirts. Soles from old jeans. It's an interesting thing. They own nothing, have nothing, except their memories. Their experiences. Their most prized possessions. When I knew for certain you were the one…the one who'd taken everything from me. I so badly wanted to return the favor. Make you feel what I felt. But you had nothing. Literally nothing but the clothes on your back.

"When we left my nana's, you spoke only of your childhood. I think you were trying to relate. Trying to show me you'd had it rough, too. But I could see in your eyes how much that time meant to you. The smile on your cheeks when you bounced from story to story. It gave you joy. And you were so undeserving of joy.

"So, we found Thomas. Just some ruffian running with a crew in Bottoms Edge. Gave him some cash. Told him what he had to do. I knew you'd do the rest. My knight in shining armor. Redemption, as near as a twitch of a finger."

She was sick. Twisted. Atlas began to retch, but he hadn't eaten since the night before. Only bile spilled out as he bent over his mattress. The pain hammering his insides while the shame and guilt swirled in his veins, anger at its heels. He had made this. He had turned her into what she'd become.

"If it was any consolation, I did initially want to kill you once you'd taken care of Thomas. Probably not immediately, but after you'd suffered for a few days. But Bass figured we could use you in his *grand plan*. Pin it all on you. And have him sweep in afterward and pick up all the pieces.

"I refused at first, knowing to keep you around would mean...we'd have to get close. Something I didn't think I could stomach. But then it struck me... If I can give you the world, everything you ever wanted...and then watch it all crumble in front of you, you might finally understand what I've been through. The pain I lived with. My disgust was a small price to pay."

Alanna stepped over to the bed and knelt beside it. Atlas watched her pupils dilate, cheeks flush. He'd seen it on her face a hundred times before, but he'd always taken it as affection. Her love. But now it was as clear as the words spilling from her lips. It had been hatred the whole time.

She whispered, "The night before the speech, I thought I made it as clear as I could. That you made me burn. That you were going to be mine completely. Did I lie?"

Atlas turned away his gaze, unable to look her in the eyes any longer. He could feel her lean into his cheek. Her warm breath on his skin sent shivers down his sweat-soaked spine.

"I hope you're remembered as the monster you are," she said with an airy breath, turning his chin softly toward her with her hand. "I hope that the Faith's promise is true." She brushed the hair gently away from his eyes, staring deep past the surface. "And I hope God roasts your soul among the embers of Hell for all eternity."

Atlas pressed his eyelids closed as a stream of tears slid down his cheek, his chest bubbling for breath, unable to suck in enough air. He felt Alanna's hand release his chin and a gush of perfume replace her presence as she pulled back from his face. Unable to restrain it any longer, his head fell to his hands, and he howled in pain.

"I'm sorry," he muttered. "I'm so sorry!" His cries echoed down the long basement corridor. He struggled to pull himself together, to hold back the tears. But it was as if the demons of the past exorcisms had lingered in the room, awaiting this moment to consume him. His terror would not be subdued. Visions of blood and death, Tommy and Alanna's parents, and now countless others, swelled in his mind. *What have I done?! God, what have I done?!* He wanted to die. Free himself from his burden. *Would she help?* She wanted him dead, after all. The excitement of the thought briefly halted his pain, and he pulled his face from his hands. But Alanna was gone. The door to his room left open. And his uncle was in the doorway, wearing a horrified expression.

"Atlas. Atlas. What is it?" he asked, rushing to his

bedside.

Atlas looked up through his swollen eyes to the face of the only person left that could help him. That could ease his pain. "Kill me…please. Kill me."

The bed bounced beneath him as Solomon took a seat at his side. He extended his arm around Atlas, pulling him in tightly. "My child. You have come to accept your destiny, and I will oblige it."

On the words of his uncle, it was as if all the pain, all the heartache, all the demons were instantly released. His heart calmed and breathing slowed. He felt peace.

"I don't know what she could have said to you that could make you wish for death. Likely a heartbreak, I suspect. But just so your soul is not held to account for the sin of taking your own life, I must tell you, your death had already been decreed under God's law. You will not suffer the penalty for self-murder. It will be a sanctioned act."

Atlas reached for Solomon's hand, squeezing it tightly. "Now. Now, please," he pleaded.

He watched his uncle reach into one of his deep robe pockets and pull a single pill from a leather sleeve inside. Atlas snatched it from his hand and swallowed it with a large gulp of mucus collecting in his mouth. He fell back on the bed and stared up at the ceiling, doing his best to push out any more thoughts of his life. His guilt. Clearing his mind completely of this world. The pain would be over soon. The torment was in its last throes. And as he slowly felt the warmth overtake his body, one final thought lingered while his mind drifted away: *orphans are such notorious liars.*

CHAPTER 33
ARVIN SEIZED

There was only Logan on the steps, stillness overtaking everything but his rocking chair. The light in the sisters' quarters gleamed through the top window into the gloomy underside night like a lighthouse beckoning Arvin to pull ashore. Nothing out of the usual that he could see. Nothing to send up any red flags as he slipped into the shelter's back lot. Not even the hum of a passing car in the distance. How could he have known they'd been waiting?

"It was a pretty good attempt, kid," Barrel said from the passenger seat of the long black sedan, looking back at Arvin in the rear. "But next time, don't use a dead Black kid for your friend's *nom de plume*. You didn't think we'd ask for a description?" His laugh rumbled throughout the car cabin.

Arvin rubbed the nape of his neck, the burn from Barrel's rough grip now fading to a rumor. He'd been so close, his hand on the wagon handle when he felt the thick, cold mitts on his neck.

"What do you want from me?" he asked, contempt undercutting his tone.

The rustle of Barrel's thick coat filled the car as he turned to face the road ahead. "Like I said before, kid, you only get one mistake. One fuck-up. And now, we do what we must."

Arvin slumped in his seat, annoyed but unshaken. His fear was limited to losing the chance at his revenge. And being trapped in the back seat of a locked car with violence incarnate inches away, his opportunity was slipping away.

"Then do it already," he said. "What are you waiting for?"

A symphony of laughs broke out from the front seats. The driver turned his face toward Barrel with a gaping smile. "Would you get a load of this kid?"

"Yeah, he's something special, ain't he?" Barrel jostled in his seat until building enough momentum to swing back around. "It ain't my call, kid. I'd have left you back there in the dirt by the wagons if it was. But now that you're famous and all, it's up to the boss to decide what to do with ya."

Arvin's annoyance washed to confusion. He waited for the punchline, the final word that would have the driver howling with joy at the absurdity of a Filth's fame. But as he scanned the large knuckle's hairless face, his folds of skin cutting shaded channels across his brow, he could only find sincerity in Barrel's beady eyes.

"What do you mean, famous?"

The large man smirked widely, his teeth shimmering in the streetlight spilling into the cabin. "Kid, you're a hero. You didn't know? Right up there with General such-and-such and Commandant who-gives-a-fuck."

The car swerved violently into the adjacent lane as the

driver doubled over with laughter. He quickly regained control, jerking the wheel back to correct course and tossing Arvin across the empty back seats.

SMACK! Barrel's meaty hand rained down on the driver's head. "Eyes on the road, you fuck!"

Arvin pushed himself upright, settling back in his seat and inadvertently glancing past his captors to the road ahead. His interest in Barrel's remarks instantly fled as the mountainous rubble grew in the windshield. They were nearing his brother's tomb. Nearing the site of his ultimate sin. Arvin's heart thrummed as the car sped toward the wreckage, streetlights sporadically popping on and off, engulfing entire city blocks in darkness. Scores of homeless, pushing carts of salvage away from the devastation. The burn from Arvin's stomach climbed higher and higher as the mounds of debris grew closer and closer. He tugged on the door handle to no avail before pulling his knees to his rapidly pumping chest, breathing as deeply as he could to soothe his raging nerves. He had avoided the images on the news, avoided glancing to the east without a blur on his eyes. The sight was too powerful for his heart to endure. But now he was being thrust into the shadows of the collapse, forced to face his shame.

With a few blocks left between them and the rubble, the car jerked abruptly, turning down a quiet, well-lit street. The only roadway for miles still served with constant power and void of scavenging homeless. Arvin's breathing shallowed as he searched the passing street for signs of their final destination. Well-dressed men were scattered down the sidewalk, each stationed at regular intervals along the road. And the pavement was clear of all debris despite the collapse only blocks away.

The car slowed in front of a tall, glowing building, the soft gray brick flecked with metallic shards that twinkled under the bright streetlamps. And outside the front double doors stood a tall doorman with a long black trench coat and hat, waving the car to a halt.

"This is your stop, kid," said Barrel. "He'll take you up from here. Give my regards to the boss."

The doorman tugged the back door open and extended his gloved hand. Arvin ignored the gesture, climbing past to the street. The door clunked shut, and the black sedan zoomed off in a cloud of burnt oil. Arvin watched it turn the corner out of sight before pivoting on his heels to scurry his escape. But as his foot stepped off the curb, the firm hand of the doorman snatched his shirt collar.

"Nope!" he said, pulling Arvin backward through the building's double doors.

He did his best to wiggle free, but the doorman's grip was too firm.

Inside the building, he was handed off to two other men. Unlike Barrel's crew, who often appeared as though recruited from one of the many Bottoms Edge street gangs, these men had the feel of corporate executives. Dressed uniformly in matching suits and clean-shaven with short hair, they were a far cry from the tattooed-riddled half-junkies that filled the halls of Barrel's drug den.

Each grasped one of Arvin's arms and led him through the lobby to the elevator. With the threat of having to confront his disgrace extinguished, rage seeped into the void left by his fleeing anxiety. His anger climbed with the ascension of each floor. Each ding taunting him with its pleasant tone. Every passing moment drifting him further from his chance at justice. Bass needed to pay. They all needed to pay.

The image of his adopted parents hunched over an empty casket was seared into his mind. The dozens of condolences they'd received from neighbors and family friends, all with a somber embrace and bouquet of flowers. But what about him? Nobody had even looked his way. Not a single sympathetic word or even a caring glance. He had suffered too. A loss they could never imagine. His entire world was taken from him. Something he could never get back. And it was by his own hands, at the word of a devil.

Arvin had once overheard a sermon warning the parish of the devils among them. Evil that would seek to lead them astray, pressing on the faithful's wants and desires to control their minds and actions. At the time, he didn't give it much thought. As a Filth, he had wanted nothing but a peaceful existence. Until, that is, the supposed blessing had arrived.

Arvin wished he had read the fine print before accepting his adoption. The adage he'd heard about it being better to have loved and lost than never to have loved at all was undoubtedly authored by one of the devils warned of by the Faith.

After reaching the top floor, the men escorted him down a long hallway to a broad golden door. They pushed inside, the doorway opening into a flat Arvin could have sworn existed only in the Faith's Paradise. Large white marble tiles lined the floor and walls, and ornate golden chandeliers hung from the decoratively painted ceiling, reflecting shards of light across the room. Steps from the door, monstrous plush couches ornamented the sunken living room, with a solid block of crystal between them acting as a table. Beyond the furniture, three divided panes of glass separated the room from the rest of Lower Midian, overlooking the still smoldering rubble of the Midriff and Under Eastside.

Arvin's knees weakened at the sight, his brother beneath it all. The men tugged on him to move, but he pulled back, refusing to get any closer to the site of his brother's grave. They lifted his arms and carried him to the couch, releasing him with a shove and watching him collapse across the flower-etched cushions.

"The prodigal son returns," said a voice from the adjacent hallway.

Arvin's head darted toward the sound and watched as the man in black sauntered into the room. His hair was loosened atop his head, no longer slicked to curls, and his black suit had been traded for a black silk robe with matte black patterns contrasting its sheen.

"My boy, you are a hero," he said, stretching out his arms.

"The savior of our city. Your name will be known by all, echoed through the ages when people talk of your great deeds."

Arvin had seen the man in black only once before, and he'd been far more frightening than Barrel had ever been. A smooth but menacing tone spilled from his curled, thin lips. His leaky, lazy eye gazing off as if keeping his sights fixed on his surroundings. But the man in front of him now was far removed from the creepy funeral director he'd met back when he was held by the Guard. He was downright jovial.

"Come. Come, my boy," he urged, extending his hand.

Arvin sank farther into his seat, unsure of the man's intentions.

"Oh, don't fret. Do you think I give a shit about Barrel's ego? I only had him bring you here to stop him from doing anything stupid. You're done with him now. You've paid your debt."

The reassurance was welcome, but Arvin was still hesitant.

The man offered his hand once again. "Come."

Arvin reluctantly eased from the couch and stepped toward the outstretched hand. The man placed his arm on Arvin's back and gently ushered him toward the window overlooking the devastation. The sight stalled his momentum, and his feet shuffled backward.

"What's with the fear?" said the man in black. "There is nothing there that can hurt you."

He was wrong. It was, in fact, the only thing that could hurt him. The image was like fire to his soul, each glance a kiss of one of its searing tendrils. Arvin worked against the man's urging hand at his back until a reflection in the window caught his eye. Next to the men now standing guard by the entrance, the hour of a large gem-encrusted clock was clear as day. Midnight. Still half the evening remained. Arvin could still make the night work as long as the man's promise was true. He would just need to indulge the man his moment and escape with as much time as he could save.

He stepped toward the middle pane, the man in black standing at the one on his left.

"It's beautiful, isn't it?"

Despite the sea of stars and bright moon on the horizon, Arvin was sure he was referring to the rubble, the jagged steel puncturing the mounds of dirt and concrete like broken bones through flesh. He could feel the muscles in his legs give way as his mind worked without permission to piece together where his brother likely lay.

"This wouldn't have been possible without you. Sure, I could have had my men smuggle the load. Hell, I could have simply walked past the gates carrying a tray of explosives myself, and no one would have said a word. But then too many would know of my involvement. And that would not be good for business." He leaned in toward Arvin's ear. "Especially if I wanted to play the hero and breathe life back into the city after such a cowardly attack." Then, straightening out, he refocused his gaze to the horizon. "No. It was best my involvement was kept to a minimum. And I hope you can oblige me this secret. Not even the architect of it all is aware of my foreknowledge." The lift chime echoed through the flat. "Ah, speak of the devil."

The bright tone could not shake Arvin from his gaze beyond the glass. His anger burned, setting his muscles in place. The man in black had known exactly what he was doing when the Guard apprehended him. And yet still forced Arvin into dealing skeet. Still dared to threaten him with his brother's safety.

"Look what we got here!" A deep grumble vibrated the glass.

Without slipping his gaze, Arvin leaned back slightly, watching as the light from the chandeliers transformed his window to the outside into a mirror of the man's flat. His stomach fell to the floor as Bass's reflection floated across the glass pane.

"Join us, Bass. We are just admiring your handiwork."

"Don't mind if I do."

Arvin's thin legs shook, and his fists clenched into solid stone. His heart thumped on his chest like a mallet on a drum. He stiffened his muscles to tighten the tremors, but even if they weren't visible, his beating heart was telling the tale of his fury—loud and unrelenting.

Bass sidled up to the window on Arvin's right, all three now facing outward.

"Good job, kid," said Bass as his large paw rested on

Arvin's shoulder.

Arvin jerked away, stepping back to distance himself from Bass's long reach. The towering devil smirked, pulling back his hand and exposing his palm in acceptance. Arvin couldn't restrain his glare, the violence in his eyes. He would have ripped out the savage's throat if he could. But as Bass turned back toward the underside view, movement in the window's reflection overtook his focus. The tall, lanky man that had introduced him to Bass, who had welcomed him into the Citizenry that first visit, was now standing by the flat door with the suited guards at his heels.

Arvin darted his head toward the man in black, eager for him to see. Eager for him to act. In the moment, he couldn't understand the urge but knew his support lay with his lazy-eyed employer. But as Arvin's mouth widened with words of warning, the rattle of a gun above his head signaled he was too late.

The man in black raised his hands above his head, his robe lifting off the ground and exposing his slippered feet. "Are you going to kill me, Bass?" he said calmly, a smirk on his lips. "I thought we were partners, no?"

Bass held the handgun firm, bolt straight, and pushed a deep grunt off his tongue. "No, Asher. It was a marriage of convenience. But I think I want a divorce."

"Hmm." The man in black casually lowered his hands. "Should we not undergo a trial separation first?"

"Listen, you fuck. I'm building a utopia. Crushing cockroaches one by one. You're everything wrong with this city now with the Syndicate gone. You think after everything you've done to my people, I was just going to cut you in? Let you run your poison through my streets?"

"I just give the people what they want. A release. A moment of peace."

Bass laughed softly under his breath. "Yeah. But I give them what they need."

A loud clap shook the windows and echoed through the flat. Arvin fell to the floor, curling up on his side, covering his ears with his hands, eyes clenched. Arvin had never heard a gunshot before but thought if it were to sound like anything, it would have sounded like that.

After a moment of calm, he felt a soft foot to his rear and eased open his eyes. Bass stood over him, waving him up with the gun in his hand. Arvin turned to see the lanky man standing over the bloody corpse. The lazy eye swimming in a pool of blood inches from its face.

"Get up, kid," said Bass, glancing around the flat as if awaiting more men to burst in.

Arvin eased to his feet, a dull pain radiating from his thigh. He slowly turned to survey the flat, but beyond the body and blood staining the white marble floor, nothing else was disturbed. Standing feet from where the man in black lay dead, the eeriness of the lifeless body overtook him. Moments earlier, he'd been talking. Happy. And now, gone. Still. Was that what had happened to Arvin's brother? Was that what he looked like beneath the rubble?

Arvin couldn't help but think how different a real corpse looked from what they showed on TV. Not the peaceful body, stained with a few splotches of blood and dark-ringed eyes. It was far more brutal. He found himself thinking of Miron. Thinking of *The Deaf Detective*. Of all the phony deaths portrayed for the sake of amusement.

The pain in Arvin's thigh deepened, shaking him from his violent realization. A pulsing bruise that would ache for days. He reached down to massage it away.

"You okay?" asked Bass, tucking away his gun in the waistband of his pants. "Don't worry, I ain't gonna hurt ya. You probably had a shitty week anyway, with your brother and all. I'm sorry about that, but it was for the greater good. Sometimes collateral damage is necessary to build a more perfect world."

Arvin barely understood a word. Hadn't taken a moment to think. His mind focused only on the baggie of crumbled skeet in his pocket. His held breath inflated his lungs as he tore through the plastic, tossing it in the air. Dust enveloped the room, taking seconds for Bass's heavy body to smack the tile floor. His lanky friend followed half a second later, the man in black's corpse cushioning his fall. Arvin hadn't expected it to happen so quickly. To be so effective.

Caught in the chaos, in the dust now settling on his shoulders, he looked to his escape. The door was only steps away. But as his feet danced over Bass's lifeless body, rushing to get beyond the obstacles to the hallway of untainted air, a bright flash lit up the distant sky, snatching Arvin's attention. He pressed his face to the glass just as the shooting star trailed off into the darkness, resetting the night sky to its peaceful calm. Arvin continued to hold his gaze, hold his breath as long as he could, hoping for the light to reemerge. Another chance at one-in-a-million. But as the seconds ticked by, the breath burning in his lungs urging him to flee, the truth finally descended.

What's left? All his wants were now sated. His purpose fulfilled. What was left for him to run to?

Arvin exhaled his remaining breath, resting his hand on the cold glass pane, wondering, if the Faith's promise was true, would he be so lucky as to see his brother again?

CHAPTER 34

SOLOMON'S SEED

The seed, as Asher referred to it, just so happened to be on him. A pill of condensed death Solomon's friend had procured for the execution. Although the Testaments were chock full of executions involving heretics and enemies of the Faith, there were no real instructions for undertaking the decree. Stonings and beheadings were simple enough, but far too barbarous for enlightened modern peoples. Hangings and drownings were less brutal to watch—especially with the head sack shielding the audience from the agonies of the executed—but nonetheless savage. Even with the bloodthirsty calls for his nephew's head, believed to have been behind the deaths of tens of thousands, Solomon's knowledge of the truth and his stewardship over his brother's son precluded any particularly grisly means to undertake his execution.

So, the seed it was, sprouting death. But it wasn't supposed to have taken place until tomorrow. A planned public display where his nephew was to consume it openly and drift away peacefully to the hereafter. Solomon had been working to get it televised. Another opportunity to plant his flag of leadership and authority. Proving the Faith's commitment to the city's security and its people. But how could he have let slip the opportunity that had presented itself?

He'd been swirling about how to inform his nephew of his pending death, an awkward discussion that was to test his resolve when his brother's son no doubt asserted their familial bond. And then finding the words, or methods, to have Atlas consume the seed willingly—in front of millions, no less. It was to be a monumental undertaking, requiring hours of work and preparation. Coordination with the television broadcaster, event planning, and finding time to craft the words that would seize the hearts of the people. Finalizing and executing it all before the Council's red slippers scraped atop the rubble of Midian's wounds. But then a blessing from above, an angel no less, arrived to carry the heaviest of the load.

Alanna's visit had thrust Atlas into the flames of heartbreak, sidestepping all the pomp and circumstance, igniting his will to die. Solomon had never understood the pain of heartache, especially borne of a woman. Though he'd seen it a thousand times, men choosing death over life without their beloved. So, it hadn't been particularly novel when Atlas yearned for his end. But it had been convenient. And how could Solomon have delayed the mercy his nephew was crying out for? He had no choice but to oblige him that one kindness.

Solomon stood by the open door as he watched Sister Margaret strip his nephew's body and wrap him in the white cloak of passing. As she turned the corpse to the side, Solomon glimpsed the birthmark above Atlas's navel that had shaken him only an hour ago. It was so clear. A stamp of Sands. The eclipsed circle above the navel. Not as faded as Solomon's, still darkened with the pigment of youth. And although not shared by Jericho, certainly a holdover from their mother.

Up until Solomon spied the mousy brown stain, he could have always sought comfort in the slight doubt seated within his gut, the chance that the boy hadn't been his nephew after all. Even with the marked features of his brother and mother, there was not any definitive proof. But after witnessing the truth of Atlas's bloodline, the birthmark proving their relation, the doubt had been laid to rest, leaving fear in its wake. Was he really about to forsake his kinship bonds? A question whispered by the great deceiver, taking hold of his resolve. It wasn't until he reminded himself of the greater good, his necessary intercession to save the Faith from its likely demise, that he could cast aside Satan's whisperings. Refocus his purpose and do what he must. *There is no action but with intention*, he had reminded himself.

"Will we be transporting him from the room now?" asked Sister Margaret.

"No," said Solomon. "We will await the mortician. And tomorrow, his body will lie on an altar behind the pulpit while I deliver my sermon to the masses."

"But Your Worship—"

"I know, Sister. But this is an unprecedented circumstance. We must have a little wiggle room for burial rites in such times. The people will want proof of his death. They must be afforded that peace."

"Yes, Your Worship."

Sister Margaret nodded before slipping past Solomon. He gave one final glance over to the body of his cloaked nephew and whispered a silent prayer before following the sister up the stairs. As he stepped from the stairs into the sacristy, the sister pushed past the curtains from the nave and approached.

"Your Worship. You have a visitor. She claims it's urgent."

"It must be, if she's willing to disturb us this late in the evening."

Solomon parted the curtains and looked out over the empty nave. The dimmed lighting left most of the pews in shadows, and the clanks from the echoing pipes were the only sounds to break the utter silence. Solomon squinted to search for his caller, but it wasn't until a soft voice carried through the gaping space that he could locate her in the front row, steps from the stage where his pulpit sat.

"Good evening," said the voice.

Solomon stepped toward the shadowy figure until her features shone through the filthy mask of dust coating her face.

"Samantha, my dear. How are you?" His voice echoed through the nave. "Come. Let's sit in the sacristy."

"No," she said softly, the empty nave amplifying her words. "Here is fine."

He approached slowly, taking care as he stepped from the stage to the front. It was an odd visit. He hadn't seen or heard from her since Jericho's death all those months ago. But it was even more peculiar that she would visit so late at night, unwashed and unkempt, no doubt arriving from the site of the collapse. Solomon's mind cycled through all the potential reasons for her visit as he eased into the seat next to her. Was it possible she had reconsidered his offer now that the Faith was to overtake all others in the city? Had she figured that after his sermon tomorrow, after he had propelled the Faith into leadership, it might be too late for her to edge her way in? She was, after all, quite bright—even if naive. Despite her proven inexperience at Big Town, the best always learned from their mistakes. And Solomon was certain such an ambitious woman would likely recount all the missteps from her previous match before setting the board anew.

"How can I help you, my dear?"

"You can't kill Atlas," she said bluntly.

Solomon huffed. "My dear—"

"No. You can't."

"I know how you feel," he said. "It seems unfair, but we must hold those to account—"

"He didn't do it. It was Bass." Sami's glazed eyes filled as she protested, a tear slipping down her cheek.

Solomon couldn't help but feel sympathy for her, a woman so focused on justice that it pained her to the point of physical anguish.

"I know," he whispered. "I know." Her eyes grew with his words, his acknowledgment softening her stern glare. "But sometimes what is for the greater good is not what is right or even just. The people have condemned Atlas. Even if he wasn't directly responsible for the collapse, he held the mantle of Citizenry leader at the time. And therefore, he was ultimately responsible for their actions."

Sami let out a groan of anger, huffing her breath as she shook her head. "How can you be so obtuse?" she scolded.

Solomon lowered his gaze, resigned that she would never understand what had to have been done. "I think it's time you leave—"

"Madeline Ramsay is his mother!" she shouted, her large hazel eyes drowning in tears.

The name landed plainly on his ear, seemingly undeserving of the forcefulness behind its utterance.

"Excuse me?" Solomon questioned. "Am I to have known this Madeline Ramsa—" As the name leaped from his lips, a faint recollection tickled his memories. The name felt familiar on his tongue. The disbelief in Sami's eyes urging a more thorough excavation of his past.

Madeline. A name he'd encountered at least a dozen times through the years. A parishioner's wife. A sister long retired… A whore in his youth. Suddenly, an explosion of meaning filled the nave. The impact hurled his mind through a tunnel of confusion. He clenched his eyes and shook his head to recenter his focus. But as his eyelids parted, it was as if he was staring down a long, spiraling tunnel with Sami at the end, screaming for his attention. Solomon reached out, grasping something firmly. It was her wrist or arm. He wasn't certain.

Sami placed her other hand on his, holding it with as much vigor as he was holding her. Her grip brought him back to his senses, or as much he could regain.

"It's not possible," he said as soft as a breath. "You are mistaken."

Sami squeezed his hand to the point of discomfort, her face wet and rigid. "Your brother protected you. She came to see him all those years ago. After you denied her. Rejected her. She had nowhere else to go." He could hear the quiver in her voice as she forced out her buried secrets. "Jericho knew if it were to get out, if it was known that…you had fathered a child with a prostitute, you'd be expelled from the seminary. Your only dream dashed. He refused to let it happen."

The pain in Solomon's chest grew with each passing word as the truth bloomed from her lips. The heat radiated beneath his robes, inviting the cold sweat beading across his brow. *It can't be. It mustn't be.*

"Jericho made a deal with the chairman. He told him that Atlas was his and needed to be taken care of. Placed in SyndiCares. The chairman hung that over his head until he retired, forcing Jericho's hand. Forcing him to agree to things he would have otherwise refused. But in the end, the chairman kept his word, even finding Madeline a job that would take her away from the city. Keeping your secret safe." Sami pulled Solomon's hand from her arm and clenched it between her palms. "You can't kill him," she whispered. "You can't kill your son."

"Impossible! Impossible!" Solomon shouted.

He yanked his hand free and pushed to his feet, but the strength of his legs remained in the pews, frozen with the absolute horror of the truth. His momentum carried him forward with nothing to sturdy his stance. He fumbled toward the stage, striking his head on the steps before catching himself in the fall. His ears deafened from the blow, but he pushed himself back to his feet. The nave spun fiercely as he worked to regain his balance. He stretched out his arms to find something to grasp, but by the time he found Sami's hand, he was already falling. His seat slammed the hard tile before thrusting his head violently back, crashing his skull against the edge of the pew.

Solomon's body spilled to the ground. He struggled to open his eyes, his head swimming from the blows. From the truth. The vision of Atlas's birthmark. He felt someone attempt to shake him awake, struggling to lift him to his feet. But his body refused. His mind had resigned. He felt the warm trickle of blood run down the side of his face, his soul drifting above his now broken body, the question of faith fluttering in his mind. *Why, God? Why have you cursed me…*

CHAPTER 35

SAMI CONCEDES

Sami brushed her hand over the etchings on the boundary wall, its rough skin, sunken and smooth, where the carved images imprinted a memorial to the dead. Hands reaching from below, clasping hands from above in unity. The artwork was magnificent.

"Do we know the artist?" Sami asked Mathias.

"We can find out if you'd like."

"Yes. Please do. I'm thinking we'll have them do more along the Wall. At least in the portions we won't be able to raze."

She continued her walk with Mathias by her side, the tips of her fingers tickling the Wall's wavy surface. Thousands of markings had appeared since the collapse. Thousands of prayers, remembrances of the dead, scrawled across the wide gray blankness. Names, birthdates, loved ones left behind. Hundreds of flower bouquets and candles laid out along the path beneath them. The Wall replacing the headstones of the thousands lost. *The brilliance of the people*, Sami thought. It never would have occurred to her to take something so ugly and make it so purposeful. So beautiful.

"We should get going, Sami," said Mathias. "We don't

have much time before the vigil."

"Right." Sami glanced again at the stretch of names along the Wall before being escorted to a row of vehicles along the roadway.

She didn't like having traffic parted for her, the flashing lights of her convoy urging vehicles out of the way. But Mathias was adamant. The threat to her safety still loomed as long as loose ends remained. The biggest threat was Bass. He had not been seen for weeks before the collapse, and she was certain he'd need to come up for air soon. Especially now, with the city reeling. There was no doubt in her mind that he was behind the collapse, planned so precisely, so perfectly, to have Atlas take the fall. Likely so he could set himself up to reclaim the Citizenry after the dust had settled. It would only be a matter of time. And with Stixx missing as well, they were probably planning their return.

Mathias was far more worried about Asher, claiming that the power vacuum created in the collapse would draw him from the shadows. He had been on the Guard's radar for years, threatening the city's power structure with his vast resources and connections abroad. But his sway with the most senior officials always kept him just out of reach, a luxury he was no longer being afforded. With Mathias now the most senior Guardian official, Asher's impenetrable shield of influence was gone, and Mathias was ready to take him down as soon as he reared his cyclopean head. The excitement—and relief—was hard for Sami to contain when she heard of Asher's pending arrest. She had tossed her arms around

Mathias, bursting with tears of appreciation, a release of the years-long rage that had left her scorched and nearly broken. Even after Mathias warned that someone else would almost certainly replace him once Asher was gone, the weight continued to soar like a balloon released against the wind.

Most other threats had been subdued, including the remaining Syndicate board members who had been far from the eastern Mantle during the collapse. They had attempted to reestablish the Syndicate governing structure days after, but it was a short-lived revival without Mathias and the rest of the Guard backing their plans. Mathias quickly had them ousted, replacing the heads of all Syndicate member corporations with Guardian leaders he trusted to act as stewards of the roles. Sami was hesitant at first, concerned about the possibility of a military coup. But in the end, she had no choice but to agree. Even with the Citizenry and Faction merging back into one union, their leadership was needed in the Undercity, manning the different Locals and operations. Not to mention that none of the underbosses had any experience in Uppercity affairs, and she needed someone loyal to the new Union to make sure corporate operations continued without a hitch.

It was essential to keep the city running. Keep the economy working. Otherwise, they risked being preyed upon by other city-states, pecked at like vultures picking clean the bones of their dead meal. Thankfully, there had been no threat there yet. As the new *de facto* leader of Midian, Sami had received a bevy of offers of aid and condolences from several other heads of state. Sentiments she had appreciated at first until Mathias had warned they were likely calls to assess the damage and size her up as a leader. International affairs. Another specialization she'd have to add to her growing list of learning.

Over the last three weeks, Sami had received a crash course in nearly every aspect of city operations. Transportation infrastructure. Power generation and delivery. Water treatment. Interesting overall, but the minutia was challenging for her to follow. She'd done her best, though, and at least power and water had been restored to most of the city. The tramcars were also still operating relatively well, even with many lines cut to the topside. But overall, people could still get around. A win in her books, and a solid beginning to a new chapter for the city.

The convoy pulled up to the entrance of Liberty Park, still littered with debris and remnants of the massive crowd that had graced the grounds weeks earlier. People were trickling in slowly, congregating around the tables distributing vigil lanterns. It was a far cry from the crowds of the Undercity's previous two gatherings. But Sami could hardly blame the people for staying home, even if it was a vigil for the fallen. How could they feel safe after Big Town? After the collapse? The city's wounds would need to heal first. But progress was not yet Sami's top priority. Stopping the bleeding was the first order of business.

She stepped from the vehicle to Mathias's back, his head darting from side to side as he gestured a signal with his hand above his head to the other Guardians scattered throughout the park. Sami couldn't make out the meaning but assumed it had something to do with their arrival.

Moving along the crowd's edge, she spied a collection of Union underbosses gathered next to the stage. As she approached to greet them, a glint in the air above the stage caught her eye. The light from the Mantle lamps reflected off a transparent surface affixed to the entire stretch of the stage.

She turned to Mathias at her side, his arms held out as if to prevent anyone from approaching. "What's that?" she asked, pointing to the clear paneling reaching upward from the edge of the stage.

"It's for your protection, Sami. We can't risk—"

"No," she interrupted. "We need people to not fear going outside. What kind of message would I send if I'm hiding behind a barrier? At a vigil, no less. I'll take my chances." Despite the risk of Bass or Asher, Sami was unwilling to cower in front of her people. But even more so, she doubted either would make a move like that at a vigil. They had already gotten away with an attack of cataclysmic proportions, and she didn't see them pressing their chances further. Not like this, at least.

The group of underbosses carved outward around her, forming a half circle next to the stage with Sami at the center. The faces of her new Union, tired and somber, all turned toward her, awaiting her address. She did her best to smile when her eyes crossed those that had sided with Bass. The Bartholomew Minsks, the Jonah Turrets. Those who'd rejected her call back at the Mantle's Shade. Those implicitly responsible for the destruction over their shoulders. She needed them now. Needed their knowledge and expertise, and they seemed happy enough to fall in line—at the moment. But beneath her smile was the knowledge that she wouldn't need them beyond her immediate cauterization efforts. Once things were stable again, she would release them from their posts. Release them from all positions of authority underside.

Sami had done her best to convince herself it wasn't personal. After all, these men had been complicit in the deaths of thousands—or at least propped up the man who was. But the longer she considered it, the longer she worked to rationalize the decision, the more she recognized the truth behind it. *Fuck them.* There were too many dicks running things anyway. Might as well find people with a softer touch, a nurturer's instinct.

Sami smiled when she saw Amelia's face among the men. A strong, intelligent woman who could go toe-to-toe with any of the stone-faced louts at her sides. She'd heard Amelia had played a part in placing Atlas at the helm but was convinced that the rough-and-tumble mechanic had no idea of the intent behind it. Besides, if Sami was going to forgive Alanna for her involvement—no doubt another victim of Bass's twisted plot—Amelia should also be forgiven.

Sami looked for Alanna's face among the semicircle. Another strong leader she could rely upon, holding high hopes for her in the long run. Although she was young now, Sami considered her next in line as her replacement when all the politicking had worn thin. The girl had a heart like no other, often fighting her darndest for the poor and vulnerable in the Bottoms. A woman like that would be perfect to run the city. But Sami couldn't spy her in the crowd. Likely off caring for the victim's families, Sami figured.

Marcus's face beamed when Sami's eyes met his. The exposed part of his cheeks flushed red. It may have been from the intense cold, but Sami liked to believe there was more to it. He'd been her most ardent defender, even when she'd given up on herself. And she was convinced his support rallied everyone else behind her after the collapse. She knew he was going to pack it all in soon and was thankful for his willingness to hang around a little while longer.

Sami nodded her thanks to Marcus when Jasper's head peeked out from behind him. She shuttered her gaze, refusing to be drawn in again by his soulful eyes. He was someone she couldn't forgive. Couldn't allow a seat at the table. The others were given a stay of execution until calm in the city was restored. But Jasper did not deserve the time. She would ensure his removal before she reached the steps of her home tonight.

"Thank you for coming, everyone," said Sami, eager to speak her appreciation while her anger at Jasper's presence remained subdued. "For your support. I couldn't have gotten to this point without you all, and I can't thank you enough." She drew her eyes across the faces of the Union leadership. "The people are still scared, and we must do everything we can to reassure them. So,

I'm happy you're all here. It will help prove our unity. Our commitment to them and the city. We still have a long way to go. A long way to heal. But I see a path forward. And I know Midian is in good hands with you all here to carry her forward for years to come."

Smiles and applause broke out as Sami touched her chest in appreciation before stepping away from the circle. She reached for Mathias's arm to get his attention and pointed to a small platform beneath a large speaker next to the stage. Without hesitation or instruction, he understood her meaning, removing the speaker and repositioning the platform in front of the stage.

The idea of a vigil without Faith presence had been an unusual one. Certainly not something Sami had seen in her lifetime. But she wasn't about to wade into the waters of that political cesspool. She'd heard that many of the magi in the city were jockeying for Solomon's post after news of his accident spread, appealing to the High Council to appoint an acting Grand Magus while Solomon "recovered" from his injuries. An unlikely chance, even for the most devout of faith. The doctors had told Sami that the bleeding in his brain had caused permanent damage, and he'd need twenty-four-hour care for the rest of his life. She recalled seeing the once despicable religious leader drooling and gazing vacantly up to the ceiling from his hospital bed. Although for a brief second, Sami had noticed a twinge of something—pain, anger, something—when the Faith sister arrived at the hospital, sharing the news of the High Council's canceled trip to the city.

But it wasn't until she noted the date of the message having been weeks earlier that Sami spied the shift on his face. An involuntary twitch, the doctors dismissed. There was no recovering from his wounds.

Sami still couldn't shake the image of him in that bed, even weeks later. She had never liked Solomon, but very few deserved that existence. Even after the sister had revealed Atlas's death to her, it was hard for her not to feel sorry for him. Losing his son and his mind on the same night was a punishment she wouldn't even wish on Bass. But if there was a silver lining to what happened that night at the Central Faith Church, it would be that at least the people would be given some peace by it. And Solomon's sacrifices wouldn't go to waste. Sami would see to that.

Sami climbed the speaker platform, the transparent stage barrier at her back, and looked out over the sparse crowd. Huddled in their winter gear, clutching the vacant lanterns, the people looked up to her solemnly. The Mantle lamps clunked off, and one by one the lanterns ignited with the flames of the accompanied matches. The fierce, freezing wind whistled through the park, hammering at the barrier behind Sami.

"Good evening," she yelled with no microphone or speaker to aid her. "You are all so brave for coming." She pressed her hand to her chest. "I'm inspired by you all. Despite the horrors of the last two large gatherings, you still chose to come. Still chose to pay your respects. I honor you for that. The families of the dead honor you.

"I want to assure you all that there is no more reason to fear. You and your families are no longer in any danger. Not with me. Not with the Union. And not with our new Guard protecting you all. As you all may already know, the collapse was not a natural occurrence. Not the work of God, or the Earth, or any other normal event. It was a cowardly act undertaken by one man. One man with the desire to tear down everything we've worked so hard to build. And I want you all to know...we got him. Atlas Sands has been executed for his attack on the city, and we can all breathe easier now that justice has been done."

Politics was a dirty game. One that Sami loathed embracing. But the people needed calming. Needed reassurance. And she wasn't going to let Atlas's death be in vain. *Petting a dead horse will do it no service, but sharing its meat with the starving certainly will.* Her mother's voice again rang in her ears.

After Sami's words of comfort and tribute to the dead, the crowd released their lanterns, watching as they floated upward with the flame in their bellies glowing through their translucent skin. The eastern wind dispersed them throughout the city as they soared higher toward the Mantle. And with the moon and stars hidden behind an overcast sky and the city's power cut for a moment of remembrance, the lanterns fluttering above were the only lights left to penetrate the darkness beneath.

Made in the USA
Las Vegas, NV
08 March 2024